PRAISE FOR KANA WU

"…Highly recommended for readers who are tired of the typical chick lit romance, and are ready for something light as air and just as refreshing." — K.C. Finn for Readers' Favorite, on *No Romance Allowed*

"An agreeably warm story that bounces along effortlessly on the genuine chemistry of its lead characters, Rory and Peter, Wu takes the much-loved tropes of the genre and makes them her own." — The BookViral Review, on *No Romance Allowed*

"Readers who enjoy romance novels with a touch of suspense will appreciate this book." — OnlineBookClub.org, 4 stars, on *No Romance Allowed*

"Wu offers a relatable tale of a couple struggling to adapt to a long-distance relationship. Peppered with intriguing dynamics of co-workers who threaten fidelity, and judgmental family members sowing doubt, there is palpable tension sustained throughout this compact novel. The main characters are loveable and endearing, and Wu's handling of past regrets and secrets withheld endow the couple with a blithe honesty and vulnerability that is sure to warm the hearts of readers of this engaging series." — Self-Publishing Review, 4 stars, on *No Secrets Allowed*

"Without saying much I would recommend this book if you want a sweet romance overcoming all the hardships. Definitely looking more from the author." —Kriti, Goodreads Reviewer, 5 stars, on *No Secrets Allowed*

OTHER NOVELS BY KANA WU

No Romance Allowed

No Secrets Allowed

Suddenly A Mom (Kindle Vella)

Dear Debby,

Thank you!

Kana Wu

A WARM RAINY DAY

in Tokyo

KANA WU

For my mom and dad –

BELLA

"**B**ella, Bella," The gorgeous stranger whispered.

I let out a quiet sigh because I loved the way he called my name. His voice was gentle, like rustling leaves on a breezy night. With a smile, I tipped my head toward him. The moon hid behind a thin cloud, but its light was enough for me to see his chiseled jaw, long nose, and full, sexy lips.

"I love your baby blue eyes, Bella Bell," he whispered again, lowering his face to mine. "Do you love me?"

"Yes," I whispered back, my heart thundering in my chest as his hazel eyes looked straight at me. *Oh my, he is going to kiss me? Yes … yes … Wait, maybe I have to be bolder.* Swallowing, I placed my hands on his muscular hips.

"Bella," he said, caressing my red hair before his hand stopped on the back of my neck and pulled me closer.

I closed my eyes, waiting for his warm kiss to touch mine,

but nothing came. Clenching my jaw, I cupped his face with my hands and coaxed it toward me. Oddly, instead of kissing me, he called out, "Bella! Bella! Bella!" At the same moment, I heard loud sounds, like someone banging on the door. *What the ...*

As much as I wanted to ignore the annoying interruption, I opened my eyes to find that the handsome, chiseled-jaw guy had disappeared, and my hands clenched my pillow a few inches in front of my face. It wasn't real ... but who dared to disturb my dream? I couldn't moan for too long because the banging became louder, followed by my mom's irritated voice. "Bella, how many times do I have to wake you up?"

Ugh, couldn't Mom have woken me up a bit later, at least after I got my kiss? I groaned.

Jumping out of my bed, I opened the door to see my mom glaring at me. She was wearing a blue blazer and pencil skirt, ready for work at a local library as the senior librarian. In her late fifties, she looked great. She had fair skin and no wrinkles, and was a bit heavy at almost five feet tall. Her new hairstyle, short with blonde highlights made her look younger. I could see a flicker of jealousy in my dad's eyes whenever a man glanced at her in awe. How I wished I had inherited her fair skin and would look like her when I was older. However, my older sister got our mom's looks and I looked more like our dad. But thanks to the height from my dad, I was three inches taller than my mom.

A whiff of jasmine from her perfume hit my nose like the fresh air of spring. But my mom's eyes and expression were far from gentle: They were more like a brewing storm.

"Bellalina Elizabeth Bell." Her voice was loud and high when she called my full name—which she did whenever she was super upset. "You aren't a kid anymore. You are almost twenty-two, for God's sake. Why can't you wake up on your own? I can't believe that I have to wake you up like this in the morning," she scoffed, and turned her body toward the kitchen. "Wipe your drool and brush your hair before going out."

The corner of my mouth was damp as I wiped it with the back of my hand. As I followed my mom down to the kitchen, I tied my shoulder-length hair back with the hairband that was always around my wrist.

"That's your fault," I grumbled, and sat on the tall chair at the kitchen island where she'd already put a half gallon of orange juice, a box of cereal, breakfast sausages, six boiled eggs, and a pile of toast, jam, and butter. "I found an effective way to wake up without your help, but you complain about that."

My mom almost rolled her bright blue eyes at me, but she restrained herself. "You set five different alarm clocks to wake you up every day. Five alarms, Bella. You refused to use your phone alarms and bought five metal twin-bell alarm clocks instead. And those are loud enough to wake up the whole neighborhood."

"But that's effective," I protested, helping myself to a glass of orange juice. "You know I'm not a morning person. Then when I found a way that works, you don't like it."

"Those damn alarm clocks can wake up the whole neighborhood," she said slowly as if I didn't comprehend her words the first time. I widened my eyes, and my mom sighed.

She opened her mouth to say something but was interrupted by Mel's entrance. Mel was willowy, five-ten with tan skin and freckles on her nose. She was tying up her long caramel brown hair into a messy topknot.

"Good morning, Mrs. B. Good morning, Bella," Mel chirped.

"Good morning, Mel," my mom and I said in unison.

Mel's full name was Melissa Clinton, and she was twenty-five years old, a first-year graduate student, and our renter. Although her last name was Clinton, she wasn't related to the famous Clintons.

3

Adele, my older sister by six years, had been Mel's junior high mentor and had always brought Mel to our house. My parents didn't mind, and felt sorry for Mel after learning her parents divorced when she was ten and she lived with her legally blind grandma after that. When her grandma passed away last year, and Adele married and moved to New York, my parents offered Mel my sister's old bedroom, but she insisted on paying rent. Regardless of her position in our house, I always thought of Mel as a sister.

"Another argument about the alarm clocks, I presume?" Mel grinned wider as she sat down next to me. Pouring cereal into an empty bowl, I smiled back at her while my mom finally rolled her eyes.

"Tell her, Mel," Mom said, feigning exhaustion as she picked up her purse and car keys. "She doesn't listen to me."

"I've always listened to you," I complained, my mouth full of cereal.

"Swallow first, then talk," she scoffed, shaking her head. "Okay, girls. I'm leaving now. See you in the evening."

"I'm going to cook for dinner tonight, Mrs. B," said Mel as my mom tapped her shoulder gently and planted a quick kiss on my head.

"No class today?" my mom asked. Her eyes widened as they shifted to Mel.

"Only homework. I have time to cook."

"And what are you going to cook?" she asked with a curious expression. I looked at Mel too.

"Burgers, steamed veggies, and green salad," she answered with confidence, peeling a hard-boiled egg.

I turned away to hide my grin while a smile spread on my mom's lips as she gave an encouraging nod.

Mel was the worst cook. No matter how hard she tried, everything she cooked turned out to be a disaster. The soup was always watery, the pizza was burned, or the grilled chicken was uncooked in the middle. The best meal she could cook was burgers, steamed veggies, and garden salad. No one knew how she never burned the burgers. So, whenever she offered to cook, we could guess her answer.

"Sounds great," my mom said excitedly. "Well, see you tonight, then."

"See ya, Mrs. B," Mel said.

"Bye, Mom," I said as she walked across the living room to the front door. She waved again before closing the door behind her.

"Will you be busy training today?" Mel asked after swallowing her egg. Her hand reached for a second egg and she finished it in three bites before helping herself to two pieces of toast and four breakfast sausages.

Shaking my head, I said, "Not really, but I need to deliver training materials for our new café in San Clemente and introduce myself to the new owner."

"Another new franchise café?" she said, widening her eyes. "It's good to know that Little Bear Café is expanding. Oh, how's about the one in Japan? You mentioned that this summer your company is opening another café there. Is it still happening?"

"Yes, it is. I think the deal should have been closed by now, but I'm not sure," I answered. "We're excited because this will be our second international franchise—after the one in Singapore."

"Ah, I remember when you went to Singapore for a week. So, how many cafes will be opened in Japan?"

I tilted my head, recalling the information. "Bread Lounge – the Japanese company that holds our franchise—will open one in Tokyo, three in Osaka, and more in Kyoto because its headquarters is in the city. The total will be ten. This summer, I'm going to be busy preparing training materials for them. I'm so excited."

Mel nodded, and her green eyes gazed at me from behind her mug. "How about your school? Are you going to continue?"

I groaned silently. When I graduated from high school, I began to work as a data entry clerk at Little Bear headquarters. Because I was a fast learner, my boss suggested to transfer me to the training and development division as an associate instructor to support the café instructors and ensure training sessions run smoothly.

When I got my associate's degree, I was promoted to a café instructor and my days at the office became busier. Then I decided to postpone getting a bachelor's degree. My mom wasn't happy with my decision because she wanted me to get a bachelor's degree and a master's degree like Adele. I wasn't fond of the way my mom always compared me to her, but for the sake of my dad—who was always on my side—I would transfer into the third year of a bachelor's degree student in the fall of this year.

Actually, my mom's demands didn't upset me because my dad understood my decision. For the time being, I was safe from my mom's nagging. What bothered me the most was after Adele left the house, Mel—who used to be my partner in crime—turned into Adele 2.0.

I clearly remembered the last mischievous thing we did. One morning, Mel and I waited for my mom to get her morning juice—we had mixed it with gelatin the night before. It was priceless to see her face when globs of juice dropped into her mug.

But that sweet moment was gone, leaving me with a still-sweet-but-not-fun-anymore Mel.

"Mom should've been happy because I already got my associate's degree. Besides, school and I aren't compatible." I let out a chuckle at my own joke, but Mel didn't smile. I rolled my eyes and continued. "Okay, I'm going to take online school this fall."

"It's going to be tough juggling school and a full-time job," she stated.

"Well," I stood from my seat slowly, unwilling to continue the discussion. "At the moment, my job makes me happy, and my dad seems to agree with me. If my mom doesn't like it, so be it."

Mel watched in dismay as I collected my dirty bowl and glass and brought them to the sink. "Sorry, Bel, I don't mean to make you upset."

Halfway, I stopped and turned to her. "I know you meant well, but don't you know that you sound like Adele now?"

As I spun on my heel, I caught her staring at me incredulously, but I ignored her and left the kitchen after I put the dirty dishes in the dishwasher.

RYO

His computer's clock showed it was almost eleven in the morning, but Ryo Yamada felt as if he'd been in the office forever. Time seemed to run slowly. Was it because of the bad news he'd gotten last night?

Taking a deep breath to release the tightness in his chest, Ryo gazed up at the bright yellow ribbon tied loosely on one of the AC grids waving like a flag. That ribbon reminded him of Akiko, his sister—older by eleven minutes—who loved ribbons and always wore them in her hair.

If he could be honest, he was sick of looking at her with ribbons because there were so many other hair accessories in the world, but she only wore ribbons. However, Ryo had learned not to say anything to make her upset.

His *oneechan* had a congenital heart defect. Their pediatrician had predicted that his sister wouldn't live past three years old, but somehow she survived. When Ryo and Akiko turned seven, the doctor had said she wouldn't live past ten. But his sister was a fighter and was able to live longer than the doctor's predictions. At the age of fifteen, she got a heart transplant that improved her health. Still, her body didn't grow well, and at the age of twenty-five she looked like a sixteen-year-old girl.

Ryo let out a sigh and rolled his sleeves up, revealing his toned arms. He and Akiko were twins, but unlike his sister, he was born healthy. When he was young, each time he asked the question, people around him said he was stronger because he was a boy. He hadn't liked the answer because boys and girls should be the same.

Then one of his uncles explained it to him. Obviously, they shared the same space, but they had different placentas, and somehow there was an imbalance of blood and nutrients flow that favored him and not Akiko. As a result, Ryo grew bigger and stronger while Akiko didn't.

That explanation had haunted him ever since. He had felt responsible for Akiko's condition and kept that thought deep in his mind. The only person who had sensed his guilt was Akiko.

One night, when they were ten, his sister had called him to her room and invited him to sleep next to her. She shared the life and the dreams that she wished to have. Once she finished, she asked Ryo to swear to live the life that she couldn't enjoy. Whatever he did, he would do for them both. Akiko would support him no matter what, even if it meant arguing with their parents.

Ryo agreed and kept his promise as Akiko kept hers.

When Ryo was accepted at UC Berkeley, Akiko was the one who argued with their parents to let him go because it had been her dream to study at that university. She also pushed Ryo to take a job at a prestigious healthcare company in Southern California. Ryo never forgot how brightly her eyes shone when she congrat-ulated him on the new job during their FaceTime.

He owed his oneechan for the life he had in the US.

But all good things must end.

Last night, his mom had called and urged him to return home because Akiko's kidneys were functioning at less than ten percent—a side effect of the immunosuppressant drugs Akiko needed after her heart transplant. His parents thought his presence might give her some emotional support.

The news struck him like lightning. For the hundredth time in his life, Ryo cursed God for only letting his sister live such a short life.

That phone call also put him between a rock and a hard place. He'd gotten his promotion two months ago and wanted to establish his career in his current company. However, Akiko was an important, irreplaceable person in his life. Ryo had sacrificed his dreams for her and would do it again without hesitation. Unfortunately, no matter how much he wished to have the technology to beam him instantly to Tokyo, he couldn't quit on the spot. He was the team leader of an ongoing project in his department, and it would take time to train his replacement. The fastest Ryo could go was next month.

This morning, he submitted his resignation, but his boss refused it and offered him a three-month sabbatical, which was a rare opportunity. Unfortunately, Ryo couldn't guarantee that everything would be back to normal in three months. If something happened to Akiko, it was Ryo's duty to care for his parents, as the only son in the family, which wasn't easy to understand for some people. Heartbroken, he turned down the offer.

His boss was reluctant to let him go, and gave him her personal phone number so Ryo could contact her immediately if a miracle happened and he could return to the States.

Ryo didn't believe in miracles anymore because he'd prayed for years for his sister's health, but still, nothing improved. Would God care enough to listen to his prayers this time?

Letting out another heavy sigh, Ryo unrolled his sleeves and pulled his chair closer to his desk. Tonight, he had to contact

Takeru Fujikawa, his best friend, who worked at his parents' real estate company. Takeru could help him find a place to live. Although Ryo could stay in his parents' house, he'd rather have a place for himself. His parents, especially his mom, had dedicated their lives to Akiko. His presence at home would be another burden for his mother. She would be busy cooking for him and wouldn't listen even if he asked her to stop. Ryo preferred to draw a clear line between them. It sounded harsh, but it was for everyone's sake.

"Now it's the tough one," he mumbled as he placed his fingers on the keyboard. They were shaking when he typed "one-way ticket to Tokyo" into Google. It never crossed Ryo's mind that leaving this country would be difficult for him. He stopped and scrubbed a hand over his face.

"Don't be selfish. This is for oneechan," he hissed, clenching his jaw.

The scolding worked.

Ryo's mind calmed, and his fingers stopped shaking. In less than twenty minutes, he found an affordable airline ticket.

BELLA

After delivering the training materials to the new franchise store in San Clemente, I drove back to Anaheim, where the Little Bear corporate office was. I smiled, remembering my meeting with the new owners. They were a young married couple, maybe in their midthirties. I wished I were rich so I could open my own café. Having a coffee shop in a little bookstore was my dream. Call me crazy, but fresh brewed coffee and new books created the most comforting smell on earth for me.

It was almost noon when I parked my car in the office lot. It was tough to find an empty spot at this hour. After circling the parking lot twice, I saw a Hyundai Sonata back up and leave the lot. I took the spot gladly.

I was about to climb the wide staircase to the second floor when someone called me.

"Hey, Bel."

I turned around to see Ron Miller, the General Manager of Training and Development for Little Bear.

"Good morning, Ron." I smiled at him politely. Since I didn't want him to assume I was late, I added, "I've just returned from delivering the training materials to the San Clemente store."

A smile broke out on his face. Although I preferred a man around my age, I agreed with the rest of the ladies in the office that Ron was one of the most handsome men there. In his mid-forties, Ron was in great shape.

He was also known for his fairness. When Jill Kyler, my boss and his subordinate, had suggested I get a certificate to be a café instructor, he approved it without asking if I had a college degree—which was one of the requirements.

He nodded. "Yes, Jill told me when I was looking for you earlier."

"Oh, what is it?" I asked carefully while I tried to think if I had done anything wrong.

"Why don't we go to my office so I can explain it to you personally?" he asked.

My heart stopped beating for a second at his serious tone. Ron must have caught the concerned expression on my face.

"Ah, my bad," Ron said, rubbing his neck. "I scared you, didn't I?" The corners of his eyes had clear wrinkles.

I nodded, letting out a nervous laugh.

"I'm sorry," he said. "My wife always warns me to watch it every time I say something serious, because my tone makes people scared. Come, let's go to my office."

When we arrived, Ron pointed at the seat in front of his desk, while settling on his high-back chair. Behind him was a big window overlooking a plot of land owned by Little Bear.

"Well, Bella. What do you think about going to Japan?" he asked.

I blinked, gazing at him. "Um ... what do you mean?"

Crossing his arms and putting them on his desk, Ron smiled at me. "Jill and I admire your diligence. Although you didn't give

13

training in Singapore, you were there and observing, and you also worked hard to prepare things before going. You've worked hard on other new stores too and are always willing to learn or ask questions. There's no doubt that you have more knowledge than your coworkers. For our new franchise in Japan, we want to let you have the experience of doing the training for the new stores."

My jaw dropped to the floor, listening to his words—I was speechless. *Me, going to Japan? Wow!*

"Are you ... interested?" asked Ron, looking at me. "If you aren't, you can say so without hesitating."

"No ... no ... ah, I mean, yes ... of course, I'm interested," I said quickly. My heart raced in my chest.

Ron chuckled. "Great. You'll go to Japan with four other instructors. Later, we will decide who will go to Kyoto, Tokyo, and Osaka. In the meantime, you and the team will get extra education about the culture, manners, and language. Bread Lounge, the owner of the franchise stores, will provide translators while we educate their teams, but I think it's better if our team learns the basics of their language too."

I bit my lower lip harder, feeling excited. What a great opportunity! If Mel heard this, she would be jealous, because we've talked about taking a trip to Japan. Yes, we were suckers for anime and manga, but she was the one who introduced me to Japanese cuisine.

"Wh-when are we flying there?" I asked. My voice trembled with excitement. "And for how long?"

"Our team will be there for two months or less. I understand that staying in another country for two months is long, but we have reasons for that, which you'll learn in two days." Ron smiled broadly. "So, that's about it. You can go back to your desk now."

Pushing the chair back, I stood and thanked him for the opportunity before leaving. I clenched my fingers tightly and heard my heartbeat in my ears while I bounced back to my cubicle. If I didn't know where I was, I would jump and scream. It was surreal that I, Bella Bell, was assigned to fly to Japan. *Wow! Double wow!* I wished the clock were running faster, so I could go home and share this good news with my parents.

At home, I broke the news about my new assignment to my parents and Mel during dinner. To my surprise, no one said "yay!" or "congratulations!", but they did become silent and focused on their meals. Looking at them, I sensed that I had just put myself in hot water. All of a sudden, Mel's burger tasted like cardboard.

After we finished our dinner and cleaned the table, my mom called me to the living room. Mel was already hiding in her room.

My shoulders tensed up as I took a seat on the sofa next to my dad, whose face was hiding behind *Skin in the Game* by Nassim Taleb, a book he'd been reading for a week now. Obviously, my dad preferred to focus his attention on the book rather than face my mom's anger.

Crossing her arms in front of her chest, my mom's eyebrows knitted together and formed a deep wedge. "Bella, I won't allow you to stay in a foreign country by yourself for two months."

"I'm not a baby. I drink alcohol," I protested, turning to my dad for assistance, but he didn't lift his face from the book.

"Bellalina Elizabeth Bell," my mom said firmly. "I know you're an adult now. Everything would be different if you had already finished school. If that happened, I wouldn't say anything about your business trip to a foreign country. But ..." She stopped, exhaling loudly before continuing. "Do you remember why your dad and I allowed you to work full time? Because you've agreed to finish your school. I know that I can't force you if you aren't interested in taking a master's degree like your sister, but at least get a bachelor's degree. Right now, your job isn't your priority. Why is that hard for you to understand?"

My mom took a deep breath, locking her eyes on mine. "You should feel lucky because, unlike other kids, you don't have to take a loan or work a part-time job to pay for your tuition or books. Your dad and I have provided enough money for you and your sister's education."

"Uh—" I opened my mouth to protest, but she was quick.

"Last time, I didn't say a word when you stayed in Singapore because it was only for a week." Her voice was rising. "However, this time, you're going to stay in Japan for two months. It means you'll waste your time for two months. Don't assume that I don't know about gaining good experiences from this assignment, or promotion later. But you should know that without a degree, you won't be promoted into a higher rank, into, uh … what …" She turned to my dad for help. But my dad had become deaf and didn't want to be a mediator in the recurring battle about education between my mom and me.

My mom tsked, knowing that she wouldn't get any help from my dad. "A director or a vice president like Dad," she said. "Although no one says anything, you should know that your degree will support your career. Look at your sister. She got her master's degree when she was twenty-five, and now she is a senior manager at Pfizer."

I scoffed, shaking my head. My sister was brilliant and an A student. I wasn't an all-A student, but I did okay. Can't my mom accept me as I am?

"But Mom, this opportunity is one in a million, especially for me, since I'm still working on getting my bachelor's degree," I managed to stay calm. "Please see from my point of view. I won't have to pay anything for this trip. Everything is provided. My flight, my lodging, my food, my transportation. Everything. Besides …" I stopped for a few seconds. "I can do my homework there, since my school is online," I lied, because I hadn't registered yet.

I widened my eyes when my mom hmm-ed with a squint, trying to see if I told the truth.

When my mom opened her mouth again, my dad chimed in.

"My dearest wife," he called sweetly, and dropped his book down on his lap, offering a smile to my mom. Cringing, I bit my lower lip, trying not to laugh, because he sounded cheesy.-

My dad was awesome and knew how to make my mom happy. As a huge fan of Jane Austen, my mom loved to hear those kinds of words. A big smile would appear on her face, especially if my dad teased her by calling her "Mrs. Bell" in a British accent like Mr. Bennet to his wife in *Pride and Prejudice*. Laughing, my mom would call him "Mr. Bell" in response.

My dad didn't use the accent this time, but he looked at her tenderly. The tension on my mom's face softened a bit. I felt a gentle but jealous thud in my heart at seeing them. After more than twenty-nine years of marriage, they still loved each other. My mind wandered: Would I be lucky and find a man I could love and who loved me like my parents loved each other?

"Let Bella go to Japan, my dear. I agree that it's a rare opportunity for her, and if she is chosen, it means her company values her for more than her level of education." His brown eyes looked at her warmly. "Even in my current position as a vice president, I haven't been sent to my company's headquarters in Germany for longer than a week. And Bella? She has a chance to provide training for Japanese franchises and even stay in Tokyo for two months. Isn't that wonderful? You can't put a price on that, dear. To be honest with you, I would be upset if Bella refused the assignment, because I know she won't get another opportunity like this.

"Bella is still young and needs to get more life experience—something she can learn outside of school. I think if she gets her degree later than her peers, so what? It won't hurt anyone. But this opportunity is hard to get. Besides, you always said that Bella is too spoiled, and at her age, she doesn't even know how to clean her bedroom. Now she has the chance to take care of not only a bedroom, but her place in Tokyo. Don't you agree, my dear?"

Still pouting, my mom lowered her eyes and gazed at her hands. She didn't say anything, and seemed to ponder what my dad had said.

I exchanged a glance with Dad, who gave a slight wink. Usually, when he coaxed my mom, her heart would melt, and she would agree.

"No."

Dad's and my smiles ceased as anger flashed in her eyes. Panic raised in my stomach as I looked briefly to my dad, who knotted his eyebrows together.

"I won't let her go," her voice was like thunder during the day. *What?*

"Pardon?" My dad looked at her.

My mom's jaw hardened. "I said no." Then her eyes shifted to me. "And you, young lady. Continue your school, or I won't pay for your tuition anymore."

My muscles quivered as a bubble of anger rose in my chest. For once, I didn't know what caused my mom to be so adamant about preventing me from going.

"That's unfair. I've worked hard, and my boss acknowledged it by giving me a chance to go to Japan," I said, louder than I intended. Mom's face turned red, and her lips became one line when my dad tried to catch my eyes, but I didn't bother to look at him.

"We've been letting you do whatever you want. But now, it's time for you to listen to us," she said stubbornly.

The heat of tears stung my eyes. We'd had many arguments, but her tone made me sad this time.

"I don't care whether you allow me to or not." I stomped my foot on the carpet. "I'm going to Japan."

Curling my fingers, I rose to my feet abruptly and stormed upstairs to my room.

Inside, I threw myself on the bed and pulled a pillow to muffle my scream. Instantly, the pillow sheet became moist. My nails dug into my palms as I clenched my fingers. It was unfair. I got this golden opportunity, and my mom ruined it. *How could she!*

I sniffed and wiped my tears with the back of my hand. *This is* my *life.* I gritted my teeth. *No matter what, I'll go there. If she doesn't want to pay for my tuition, so be it. I'll find a way anyway.*

That thought calmed me down a bit. Rolling to my back, I stared at the ceiling fan and followed the blades as they swirled slowly. A few minutes later, my eyelids became heavy, and the blades grew blurry as I closed my eyes and fell asleep.

BELLA

I glanced at my mom, who silently cut her barbecue chicken with her knife. Since the night she'd refused to let me go to Japan, she hadn't talked to me or even woken me up in the mornings. I was upset with her too and gave her the same silent treatment. My dad didn't want to be a mediator in our quarrel this time. Obviously, Adele felt the same because she didn't want to bring up the topic when she called me two nights ago. Mel had tried unsuccessfully, but she didn't give up easily and made another attempt last night.

"How long until you speak to your mom again, Bel? It's been a week now," Mel had commented while applying black nail polish to my toes as I sat on the floor in her room, leaning back against the bedframe. Since we wanted to save money, we had bought some nail kits to paint our nails at home. "Talk to her tomorrow during our Thursday night dinner. I think that's a perfect time to start a conversation."

Thursday night dinner was the most important and sacred time in my family. Ever since my sister and I had been active in school and church activities, it was hard for us to dine together, so my parents decided that we had to sit down and have a meal as a family every Thursday night.

"Nope." I shook my head. "There're no rules saying a daughter has to apologize first if she doesn't make a mistake."

Pouting, Mel had looked at me. Her hand stopped in the air. "Gosh, you're stubborn. Good thing I'm not Adele. If I were, I'd spank your butt, girl."

I wrinkled my nose but didn't say anything. If I was honest, though, I felt guilty for not speaking to my mom. She was a great mom but also a very stubborn woman.

"Mel, dear," called my mom sweetly as she passed a bowl of mashed potatoes to my dad. "Tell Bella to pick up Adele's favorite bread from PB bakery tomorrow. While she and her husband stay here, I want them to have the bread for breakfast."

I grunted because I was sitting across from my dad at the dinner table. Then, with the same tone as my mom's, I turned to Mel, who was sitting next to me. "Mel, please tell my mom that I can't pick it up, because I'll be home late tomorrow and ..."

I shut my mouth because Mel nudged my leg hard with her toes.

"Yes, Mrs. B. I'll make sure Bella will ..."

A fork clunking hard on a plate stopped her. Almost in unison, my mom, Mel, and I turned our heads to my dad.

"Thank you for your attention, ladies," he said calmly, glancing at us. He didn't raise his voice or tense his face. A little smile formed on his lips when he picked up his fork and scooped the mashed potatoes on his plate. "It's our precious dinnertime, and please behave well and eat like civilized people. If you want to continue your fight, do it later in the yard, and Mel will tell me who the winner is."

Then he brought the potatoes to his mouth and chewed slowly. His other hand pushed up his glasses, which were slipping down his nose.

Pouting, I looked down at the barbecue chicken and steamed string beans on my plate. No matter how hard I tried to get my dad to be on my side, he didn't budge. Neither had he sided with Mom.

Then I heard a light chuckle next to me. It was Mel.

We turned to her, and she was grinning from ear to ear.

"Mr. B, could you guess who the winner would be if Bella and Mrs. B had a fight outside?" she asked.

The brown eyes behind the glasses sparkled at the question. Tilting his head, my dad considered this. "Maybe no one," he said slowly.

"Why?" Mel looked curious.

My eyebrows met on my forehead as I shifted my eyes to Mel and Dad in disbelief. *What?* They were talking as if we weren't here.

My mom raised one of her eyebrows and pressed her lips thinly as she gazed at my dad.

"Well." My dad put his fork next to his plate and took a napkin to wipe his mouth. "Bella is young, strong, and hotheaded. Mrs. B is wiser, but her energy isn't like it was twenty years ago. So, in my opinion, no one wins." Looking at Mel, he asked, "What do you think?"

My jaw dropped while Mel bit her thumbnail like she always did whenever she was deep in thought.

"It doesn't make sense," she mumbled. "I don't understand why you said no one wins, Mr. B."

My dad chuckled. "Well, think again. Carefully. Then, you'll understand why."

Frowning, Mel sucked in a breath while pressing her lips together. She bit her thumbnail again. The crease on my mom's forehead became deeper, her eyes glued to Mel. She shifted her eyes, and they met mine for a few seconds, then I felt my chest tingle when a smile broke out on her face. Then, almost in unison, we cackled.

The discussion stopped instantly as Mel and Dad turned to look at us.

"Oh my God, how childish we've been." My mom laughed.

I nodded and stretched my hand to take hers. My mom squeezed mine gently. "Sorry, Mom. I'm so childish. But I really want to have the experience of living in another country. Besides, it's only for two months."

She sighed and looked at our hands. "Well … I've thought about it, and yes, I think you need to go there and get some more experiences in life."

Heat of anticipation radiated in my chest as I heard her words. "Really?" I widened my eyes.

She nodded. "But." Her eyes turned solemn. "You have to finish your education no matter what."

I groaned and pulled my hand away from her. "Mel, tell my mom that education is not important anymore in this century."

"Oh, Mel," my mom sang, her eyes twinkling. "Tell my youngest one if she doesn't finish her school, she has to pay rent while living here."

"Here we go again," my dad whined, covering his face.

Mel giggled and punched my shoulder hard enough to make me wince.

Then we continued our dinner with laughs and jokes all around. When my mom once again pressured my dad to finish explaining why no one would win if she and I were to fight, he pretended not to hear the question.

I was helping Mel dry some plates and put them back in the cabinet when my mom came to me. "Bella, I've heard summer in Japan will be humid. It's better if you bring some light and comfortable clothes, so you won't suffer there." She leaned back on the kitchen island, holding a folded paper in her hand.

Wiping a plate, I looked at her. "How did you know?"

A pinkish flush spread on her cheeks. "Well." She cleared her throat. "I guess I should know about the country where my daughter is assigned."

"So ... you did research Japan." I turned around and continued my chore.

"And ..." She unfolded the paper in her hand. "I have a list of things you should bring."

I put the drying towel on the kitchen counter. "Mel, tell my mom to stop bothering me with her findings."

"No ..." Mel groaned and wiped her wet hands with a paper towel, then put her fingers on her ears. "La ... la ... la ... la ... I don't hear a thing." In a split second, she rushed up to her room.

My mom and I looked at the half-done dishes in the sink.

"' Night, Mom." I followed Mel upstairs.

"Hey, come back here. One of you should help me," my mom yelled.

"Dad!" I called louder as I entered my room and locked the door from inside.

Snickering, I cupped my face, relieved that the feud between my mom and me was resolved. Although I didn't want to back down to her will, I didn't like arguing with her.

RYO

The half-moon was surrounded by clouds, its faint glow passing through them. The stars were blinking in the sky. The apartment complex was quiet as Ryo parked his car in the lot. The clock on his dashboard showed 10:09 p.m. It was late, but he didn't mind. Staying in the office was better than being at home, because he couldn't shake off the heavy feeling in his heart that his time to go back to Tokyo drew near.

As he took off his shoes inside, his phone buzzed. Akiko's name was on the screen. Running a hand over his hair, he let out a long sigh. Pulling up the corners of his lips, he accepted it.

"Oneechan," he greeted as the screen revealed the sweet but thin face of his twin. Her hair was in fishtail style with a light blue ribbon. His stomach wrenched when he saw how pale his sister was. "How are you?" He put his backpack on his bedroom floor, walked back to the living room, and settled on the sofa.

"Ryo-*kun*," she called, pouting. "*Okaasan* said you'll come to visit us this summer. Don't you usually come in December for our birthday?"

"I miss summer festivals and want to enjoy them again. Do you still want some Goldfish, Twizzlers, and Cool Ranch Doritos? Or do you need any other snacks?" He lifted his feet up to the coffee table.

Goldfish, Twizzlers, and Cool Ranch Doritos were his sister's favorite snacks because they weren't available in Japan.

Akiko huffed. "Don't switch the subject. Why are you coming back? Did you get laid off? Or did you quit?"

Ryo rubbed a hand over his face and then pinched his nose for a few seconds, considering her question. Should he tell her the truth? Maybe. After all, they were twins. Twins could read each other's minds, right?

But … maybe not.

"I didn't quit or get laid off," he lied, looking straight into his sister's dark brown eyes. "My boss gave me a sabbatical for three months."

She stopped and narrowed her eyes. "Really? Or is it because of my health?"

"Can't I be concerned about your health?" he asked.

Akiko took a deep breath and lowered her gaze. "Ryo-kun." Her voice sounded gentle. "No matter what, don't ever quit your job because of me. It's hard to find a job in a company that gives a working visa." She lifted her eyes and looked straight at him. "I hope you've still remembered your promise."

Her words were like a jab to his stomach. "I remember." His voice trembled.

"Good." His twin nodded firmly.

"Ryo-kun," she called again after a few moments.

"Yes?"

"Sara called me two days ago and said she is opening an American café here."

Sara Ito was their childhood friend from Osaka. Although she was born with a silver spoon in her mouth, she wasn't a snob. She was friends with other kids from all different socioeconomic backgrounds. In the seventh grade, Sara had moved to Kyoto because of her dad's business.

When Ryo was accepted as an undergraduate student at UC Berkeley, he met her again. Soon enough, they rekindled their friendship and helped each other navigate the foreign country. After they graduated from the MBA program, Ryo stayed in the States to work, and Sara returned to Tokyo to manage one of her dad's companies. Since then, she had become Akiko's good friend too.

Ryo's eyebrows met in the middle. "What's the café name?"

"She mentioned it, but I forget," she said. "Didn't she tell you? I thought she's always contacted you for everything."

Ryo shrugged. "That's okay. I'll meet her eventually."

"If she heard that, she'd be over the moon." His sister grinned. Sara's feeling for him wasn't a secret in his family.

"Hmm."

His sister clicked her tongue, shaking her head. "She's been chasing you for more than a decade, and your heart hasn't moved yet. Isn't that cruel?"

Ryo let out a small laugh. "I don't know which one is crueler: ignoring her feelings or pretending to like her."

Akiko rolled her eyes. "You're really something, my dear brother. But yeah, I understand your reasoning. I'd like Sara to be my sister-in-law. Even *Otousan* and Okaasan, well, mostly Okaasan, wish you liked her, Ryo-kun. But I prefer your happiness over hers."

"Thanks for always choosing my side, Oneechan. I like that," he said casually, although deep down, he was surprised to hear that his parents wished he liked Sara.

His sister smiled.

"Oneechan, do you have anything else to say? If not, I want to sleep now because I have a meeting early in the morning." Ryo glanced at the clock on his phone.

"Okay. I'll call you again sometime this week."

"Okay. Send my regards to Kento." Kento Ikusa was his sister's boyfriend.

"I will when he comes tomorrow. Bye, Ryo-kun."

"Bye, now."

Ryo stared at the dark screen once his sister hung up. The conversation about Sara rewound in his mind.

It was true that Sara had been chasing him for years and hadn't given up, although he'd given her a signal by dating a few women. Some of his Japanese friends who were jealous of him had called him a "*gaijin* hunter" because he'd always dated non-Japanese women. Ryo *had* dated Japanese women twice, but he didn't care to tell his friends.

For Ryo, his family's opinion was the most important thing. His parents had never intervened in his romantic life. For them, as long as he was happy, they were too.

But now, everything seemed different. It was new to him that his parents wished to see him with Sara. It scared him that they might begin to play matchmaker after discovering he broke up with his last girlfriend. His life would be doomed if his parents shared the idea with Sara's parents, who were their good friends for decades.

Now he dreaded going back to Tokyo. Exhaling loudly, Ryo rose to his feet and went to his bedroom.

BELLA

"**B**el, you should remember to not use your midsole to climb up. Use your toes. Each time you need to adjust your position, you have to do it with your toes. And use your leg to push yourself up, not your arms," Mel instructed, holding my rope.

Heaving a breath out, I pulled my body up. We were in an indoor rock-climbing gym on Saturday morning, three weeks after I broke the news to my parents about going to Japan. I wasn't into this kind of exercise, but I didn't mind learning something new, especially since an expert climber, Mel, was watching me.

I looked up and stretched my hand to grip a boulder above my head, but as I pushed myself up, my fingers slipped, and ...

"Arrgh!" I yelped, feeling my body descend to the ground.

Mel held the rope tightly to slow my fall to the crash pads.

"I don't want to do this anymore," I pouted, sitting on the mattress with my legs spread out like a child. "That girl"—I pointed out with my chin to the left—"started on the same level as me, but now she's on the medium level while I'm stuck. For now, I'm going to stick to my stationary bike, read my novels, and play video games.

"Besides, I shouldn't have come here with you. What would have happened if I broke my arm and couldn't go to Tokyo?" I added.

Chuckling, she sat next to me. "You did well, Bel. You just need to believe that you can do it. Remember, falling is a good thing; it means you haven't surrendered."

"Next time, ask Andrew to go with you," I said, rubbing the chalk from my hands. Andrew Maxwell had been her boyfriend since college and went on frequent business trips for his job as an auditor. He'd returned home this morning and was trying to catch up on his sleep, so Mel had asked me to come instead.

"Okay, Miss Grumpy." She removed her harness, and I followed suit. "Next time, don't complain when you feel bored at home."

"I didn't say I won't come here anymore," I corrected quickly, and tilted my head to the sandy-haired man around my age at the customer service desk. "Thanks to him—he's cute, and I hope when I return, he's still working here."

Mel followed my gesture and then rolled her eyes. I flashed a big smile at her and walked eagerly to customer service, returning our harnesses while Mel followed behind me.

The sun was bright, and the weather was warm, with not a single cloud in the sky as we stepped outside. We were at the end of spring, but the temperature was already hot. I constantly whined that it was wrong to say that California had four seasons. It only had two seasons: cold and hot, winter and summer.

"What time is your flight again?" Mel asked as we walked toward her car. "Andrew and I can take you to the airport."

"Next Friday at ten thirty in the morning from LAX, and I'll stop over at San Francisco before flying to Tokyo," I said, putting on my sunglasses. "It would be nice if my company paid for a direct flight, but no complaints here, because I didn't pay a penny for the ticket."

Mel flashed a smile. A soft beep sounded as she walked near her car. Her keyless car had been a blessing and a curse for an absentminded person like herself. "It would be great if Mr. and Mrs. B could join us."

I flapped a hand. "Yeah, sure they would. Their younger daughter is about to stay in a foreign country for two months."

Mel chuckled. "They'll miss you badly, especially your mom. No sparring partner in the morning for a while."

I laughed as I slid into the passenger seat. "Yes, I'm going to miss it too."

"Will you do training for the whole two months?" Mel asked, sliding into her seat after throwing her bag in the back seat.

"No," I shook my head. "The training from Little Bear will take two weeks. Then Bread Lounge has its own training that the staff need to learn. After that, the staff will practice what they've learned, because we expect them to master the skills before the official opening." I twisted to hook up my phone to her car and then selected the new BTS album that my sister bought for me. In a few seconds, the beats of "Butter" were on, and I swayed my body, following the rhythms.

"That's nice," Mel said. "You can use your weekends for sight-seeing, then."

I rubbed the bridge of my nose. "Hmm... not every weekend for sure, because I have to follow Bread Lounge's working schedule. It means I have to work on the weekend as needed. But my schedule is more flexible than their employees, though.

"The tough part will be in the first two weeks. Other than that, it should be manageable because I'll be there as an observer and a problem solver for any problems that might emerge before the soft opening." I added.

"I see." Mel peered through the windshield. "Hey, tell me. Why is Bread Lounge interested in having Little Bear in its portfolio? I remember you'd mentioned that the owner has many restaurants and cafés too, although mostly for domestic dishes and bakeries."

I stopped dancing and shifted my body toward Mel. "Based on what my boss told me, Sara Ito, the owner's daughter, fell in love with Little Bear Café when she was a student at UC Berkeley. Then she begged her daddy to have the franchisee certificate. You know how stingy my company is when letting people outside America hold its certificate. No matter how much money you have, when the board of directors says no, it means no. In this case, Little Bear may see more opportunities by working together with Bread Lounge." I shrugged.

"What a damn lucky girl!" Mel bobbed her head. "Just begged her daddy, and she got what she wanted."

"Yup, like buying a candy, right?" I commented. "But Sara is a smart woman and still young too. Maybe twenty-five. My boss showed me the article from the Japan *Time* magazine that mentioned Sara as a successful young entrepreneur in Japan. I guess, although her daddy is rich, if she wasn't smart, no one would acknowledge her, right?" I clasped my hands in front of my chest. "I'm so jealous, and admire her at the same time, though. I just hope she isn't snooty."

"I hope so too," Mel agreed. "If you could learn from her that would be better because learning from someone like her is a thousand times better than sitting in the classes."

I dipped my head.

"Why is only one café in Tokyo?" Mel asked, pressing the brake at the red light.

"Bread Lounge wants to focus on cafés in Osaka and Kyoto, which is why all trainers will be there, and only I will be in Tokyo. Also, some big American cafés are already in Tokyo, so they don't want to compete head-to-head with them. Maybe if everything is smooth, they could do some expansion," I explained.

"That's a smart move," Mel commented.

"It is."

"By the way, do you know where you'll stay?"

"A furnished apartment." I grinned widely. "I'm glad when I found out, because I can't imagine staying in the hotel for two months."

"Lucky you," she sighed. "Living in a furnished apartment for sixty days for free. I hope I can go there next year in spring or fall, because my friends suggested I shouldn't go there in the summer."

"Ugh, don't remind me." My shoulders slumped. "Remember our trip to Bali last summer?" I looked at Mel. She slanted her head, then nodded. "The weather will be the same because Japan is also surrounded by ocean. So the humidity will be ... whew!" My hand moved across my forehead as if to wipe off invisible sweat.

"Aw, poor you. Bring comfortable clothes made from cotton, and wear spaghetti-strap tank tops and shorts like you're wearing right now," Mel suggested, gesturing with her head.

"I can't." I looked at my clothes. "Japanese people are more conservative in terms of clothing. HR already warned us not to wear a tank top without a cardigan or a light jacket, especially when visiting temples. I don't want to get banned like when we were in Bali."

Mel's mouth dropped as she covered it with a hand. "Oh my, that's right. I forgot that." Her eyes squinted as a big grin spread across her face. "We'd been offended because the locals forbade us from entering the temple. That wasn't their fault, though. I admit my clothes were skimpy, and we didn't consider the local traditions."

"We felt better after one of the locals explained it to us." I giggled.

Mel put a hand on my shoulder, winking. "Now I'm not jealous of you anymore."

I scoffed and pushed her hand away. "I bet Tokyo won't be that bad, considering it's a big city with tourists coming from different countries. You're bad, Mel. Did you say that because you *are* jealous?"

Mel snickered. Then in a serious tone, she said, "You should enjoy your time while you are there and promise me that you'll take time to FaceTime with me."

I held my hands up in a Scout's honor and said, "I've promised Mom I'll call once a week, and so I'll call you after her. Or I'll call you first, then Mom."

"Whatever you want. But let me know when you're going to call me so I can make sure I'm at home." Mel turned the steering wheel as her car entered the mall's massive parking lot. "Hey, do you want to check out the new bikinis from Victoria's Secret?"

I grinned widely. "Do you want to buy one and show it to Andrew?"

Mel's cheeks heated, and she slapped my arm.

"Oh my, I'm right." I chortled, covering my mouth, and opened the door quickly when Mel's hand rose, ready to slap me again.

"Andrew," I mimicked Mel's voice while swinging my arms and hips like a model. "Do you like my bikini?" I turned around and pretended to unbutton my top while puckering my lips and fluttering my eyelashes.

"Hey, I never do that," Mel protested, then got out of her car and started chasing me.

"Aaaahh," I squealed, and turned, running toward the mall.

BELLA

San Francisco International Airport wasn't as crowded as LAX. People seemed to take their time walking through the long corridor, stopping at the bars or restaurants before continuing to their gates. I liked the airport and had been there a few times. Most of the time, I checked out the gift shops, but not this time.

I was rushing through the terminal. My legs worked hard to get me to the boarding gate on time, and my lungs almost exploded from frantically running. Whoever booked my ticket was either ignorant or had simply never traveled anywhere by plane, so they didn't understand that I needed enough time to walk to the gate for my next flight. Walk. Not run. Good thing my layover wasn't in a large airport.

Damn. I should file a complaint.

"Excuse me … excuse me …" I half said, half screamed while running in a zigzag, avoiding people.

In the critical moment, my phone buzzed in my jacket.

Noooo ... I almost screamed, but I stopped running anyway and fished my phone out just to almost drop it when I saw Tristan's name pop up on the screen.

Tristan Fox was a senior marketing manager whom I'd had a crush on. He also broke my heart into pieces when he engaged with his long-term girlfriend two months ago.

Yes, it was one-sided love. He wouldn't fall for a woman who was six years younger. Besides, it was my fault for misunderstanding his kindness and attention as love since he was also nice to others.

Most people in the office liked Tristan. Except those who were jealous of his bright career. It was understandable because he'd become a senior manager at the age of twenty-eight, one of the youngest managers in the Little Bear corporate office.

"Why is he calling me?" I bit my lower lip, feeling a soft prick in my heart. Taking a few deep breaths to calm myself, I answered. "Hi, Tristan."

"Bel, thank God, I caught you. Are you already at the gate now?" he asked.

"Umm ... almost." I glanced at my watch. It was twelve forty-five, and I only had ten minutes before departure. "What's up?"

"I updated the marketing materials, because the one you have isn't compatible with the Japanese market. But I sent them late," he explained. "I tried to reach the other team members, but Jill told me they're already on the plane, except for you. So do me a favor: Once you arrive in Tokyo, please tell the others about the latest material so when they get Wi-Fi, they can download the correct one."

"Sure, not a problem." I took another deep breath. "Anything else?"

"That's it; see you in Tokyo in five more weeks," he said.

My heart leaped into my throat. "Y-you are going to Tokyo? I thought it was Jill and your boss?"

"My boss has a meeting with the owner in Kyoto and told me to take over the meeting with Sara," he answered.

"I see." I glanced at my watch again. "Oops ... Hey, I have to go. See you then."

"Bye, now."

I pressed the phone to my chest once we hung up. Tristan ... He was going to Tokyo. Although I knew exactly how he felt about me, still, my heart pounded hard and hurt my chest. If he were still single ...

I slapped my forehead. "Stop dreaming and catch your flight."

Shoving the phone back into my pocket, I sped again and wished people could walk faster instead of ambling while chatting and laughing.

I groaned. *Move faster, people!*

Then I caught an empty golf cart coming from the opposite direction. As I swerved away, I tripped over my own foot. While trying to keep my balance, I stumbled a few feet forward and bumped into a man who was wearing a snug gray long-sleeved shirt and khaki cargo pants. Something dropped from his hand as he yelled, "Hey!"

The word sorry was on the tip of my tongue, but I was out of breath, and talking was the last thing I wanted to do. I waved and kept running.

My heart pumped hard as I reached the gate, and I felt warm. Wiping my sweat, I blinked in surprise to see some people were still lining up. The time on my watch showed that boarding should be over.

"Why are we still boarding?" I asked an airline staff member, a short-haired woman wearing a dark blue dress with a long scarf around her neck.

"It has been delayed for fifteen minutes," she smiled. "Please get in line so we can leave as soon as possible."

Thanking her, I walked to the end of the line and stood behind a big man in a checkered shirt and jeans. My legs were shaking, and my breath was sharp and shallow. I forced a wincing smile to the man who glanced over his shoulder as I bent my body forward, catching my breath.

"Are you okay?" he asked.

I nodded. "I didn't have enough time between flights."

He shook his head in sympathy. "I hear you. After this, you can have a nice long rest."

"Yes."

Slowly, more people came to stand behind me as we inched toward the gate agents to scan boarding passes.

RYO

The flight was packed. Ryo groaned silently at his seat. When he'd bought the ticket, he'd already chosen the seat. However, a week before his flight, something happened in the San Francisco office related to his project that caused him to fly to Tokyo from San Francisco Airport instead of LAX. After switching the flight, he forgot to change the seat until the last minute. All the seats were taken except a few in the middle. He didn't like sitting in the middle because his knees would touch the seat in front of him. He wasn't a very tall man, but still, at five foot nine, he had an issue every time he sat in the middle, which was why he preferred to sit on the aisle or in an exit row.

Good thing the passengers on his right and left were petite, so at least he had enough elbow room. The one sitting on the aisle was a middle-aged Asian man who was busy reading a newspaper in Chinese. He might be around Ryo's dad's age or older.

On his right, the passenger was a redheaded woman with baby blue eyes. Her hair was tied into a messy bun. She was wearing a red-and-white striped button-down shirt with comfortable blue pants. At a glance, it seemed like she wanted to be part of the puzzle book *Where's Waldo?* his uncle had introduced to him when he was young. And she looked familiar.

Secretly, he looked closer, and something clicked in his mind. She was the one who bumped him on the way to the gate and caused his mocha to fall on the ground. With no concern or apology, she'd only waved her hand. Lucky his drink was already empty. If not, his pants would smell like milk and chocolate.

Oh man. He let out a sigh. *Among all the passengers, why her?*

He bent down to get the Kindle from his backpack that he'd stowed under the seat in front of him when he heard a sudden high-pitched yelp from his right. Startled, he dropped the e-book device on the floor and turned his head to see Waldo, or Female Waldo, to be exact, rubbing her arm. She gave him a sheepish smile and mouthed, "Sorry."

Did she just pinch herself? How childish. Ryo puckered his eyebrows and looked away, picking up his Kindle.

Wishing to have a quiet and peaceful flight, he began to read a novel his coworker had suggested to him. It was a rom-com novel about a woman who lived with a male roommate without telling her orthodox aunt. He preferred sci-fi, mystery, or thrillers, but he found the novel was a nice story to read.

Unfortunately, his wish didn't come true because Female Waldo couldn't remain seated. First, she shook out her hair before slipping a rubber band off and retying it loosely. His right cheek and eye got hit by the ends of her hair without her realizing it.

Second, she took a few things from her backpack and stashed them in the seat's pocket in front of her before stowing the backpack under the seat. In less than five minutes, she retrieved it to take a bottle of peppermint oil and a bag of candy from it, stashed them in the pocket, and stowed her backpack again. The smell of peppermint candy whiffed to his nose when Female Waldo dropped the oil on her wrists.

Maybe I'll read later then, Ryo decided, and put the Kindle into the pocket sleeve. Exhaling, he let his eyelids drop. He was tired and wanted to sleep, but his mind was active and thinking about the last update on Akiko's health. Last week, she started receiving renal replacement therapy to assist her kidney in removing excess water and toxins from her blood. His mom sent a picture of Akiko during the treatment, and oddly, he felt a sting on his arm when he saw it.

As he was about to doze off, something or someone nudged his right elbow hard. He opened his eyes to see Female Waldo running one hand over the shared armrest while her other hand was holding the cord of her headset.

Her eyes shifted to him as she realized Ryo was watching her. "Oops, sorry, I woke you up." A slight pink color washed over her face. "I'm trying to locate the socket for this." Her hand waved the cord. "I thought it would be there." She pointed at his armrest.

Stirring, Ryo looked at the armrest and shook his head. "Not here." He was surprised to find his voice came out like a growl, which he didn't mean to do. Without saying anything, he scanned the seatback screen in front of him and noticed the socket underneath.

"There," he pointed at it.

She flashed a small smile and inserted the jack in it. "Thanks. Sorry again for interrupting you. I didn't realize the socket is in a different spot than the plane from LAX."

"Maybe because it's a new plane," he blurted out.

A split second later, he regretted making a comment because he wasn't in the mood for talking and now the redheaded woman looked at him and asked, "How do you know?"

"I've taken the same airline each time I visit my family. And two years ago, the socket was located in a different place," he said quickly.

Her mouth made an "O" while she nodded.

"No wonder you know the difference." She scanned around. Her finger pressed the dimmer button under the window. Slowly, the window dimmed and stopped as it reached the standard level of darkness. "So, your family is in Tokyo?"

He nodded curtly, observing her face gleaming as her finger pressed the button again to make the window brighter, and back to dim. She mustn't have seen the technology before, and played with it with utter joy on her face. Strangely, Ryo found it refreshing.

"It's my first time going to Tokyo. I'm so excited." Her voice was cheerful as she finally stopped playing with the button for the shadeless window.

In the meantime, the interior panels and fascia began vibrating with a clear rattling sound, signaling the aircraft was rolling down the runway. Usually, Ryo liked to close his eyes during the takeoff. But Female Waldo didn't let him. As he leaned on the headrest, she asked again, "So, do you live in San Francisco?"

Ryo almost rolled his eyes, but shook his head. "I live in Tustin, Orange County. I was here for work."

"Lake Forest." Female Waldo flashed a smile.

"Huh?" He didn't understand what Female Waldo was talking about.

"That's where I live."

I didn't ask. He grumbled internally. He knew the city because his last ex-girlfriend used to rent an apartment there.

Ryo slumped with relief when Female Waldo looked out the window, and her finger was on the dimmer button again.

What an oddball. He shook slightly and closed his eyes. In a second, he felt a sinking sensation in his stomach as the flaps were extracted, allowing the aircraft to accelerate for takeoff. Bitter tears stung his eyes and congested his chest. As much as he wanted to forget, he felt the ache in his heart become more profound as the plane climbed up to the sky, leaving the airport behind.

Goodbye, California.

Ryo snoozed off and woke up when the smell of food entered his nose. Glancing at his Garmin watch, he found that he'd been sleeping like a baby for an hour. It was amazing because he'd thought he couldn't sleep at all on a plane.

If he could be honest, he wanted to sleep more. However, when the flight attendant offered him a tray of food, he accepted it anyway. But the food wasn't appealing to him. The man on his left side didn't seem interested in the food either but ate the matcha roll, finished his water, and went back to sleep.

On the contrary, Female Waldo was eyeing the plane food with a different approach. She smacked her lips while munching a spoonful of vegetable curry with rice and squealed over the rolled cake as if she'd never seen one in her life.

It was entertaining to see the childlike enthusiasm on her face, especially after she cleaned the whole tray. Most of his female friends or ex-girlfriends ate small portions, and in the end, food was wasted, or he was the one who helped clean their plates. It wasn't fun to go out with people like that. It wasted money to bring them to all-you-can-eat places or Korean barbecue restaurants.

Secretly, Ryo kept his eyes on her. Her pinkish cheeks were soft. She had long eyelashes and a turned-up nose that looked perfect on her round face. She couldn't be older than twenty-five, but she might be even younger. She wasn't pretty exactly, but she had a sweet smile, and her body language brought a grin to his heart.

But his admiration for her soon depleted. After dinner, she became his nightmare.

Once the flight attendants brought back all the trays, she politely asked to go to the restroom, and he and the man on the aisle let her pass.

When she returned, Ryo could smell fresh mint coming from her.

Then, in less than twenty minutes, she asked again.

And another time.

And once more, even after the cabin lights were dimmed to let the passengers rest.

The middle-aged man on the aisle didn't mind. He even threw a light joke to Female Waldo, who gave a witty response.

It sounded selfish, but Ryo minded because he wanted to sleep undisturbed.

As he was about to close his eyes, Female Waldo turned on the light above her and took out a coloring book and pencils from her backpack. "Coloring books make me calm before going to sleep." She glanced at him as she picked a green colored pencil and began to color the grasses on a page.

Ten minutes later, she looked bored, closed the book, gathered her colored pencils, and put them all in her backpack. Yawning, she adjusted the headrest wings before closing her eyes but left the reading light on.

Did she forget? Ryo wondered, slanting his head to her to see if she was asleep.

Taking a few deep breaths, he poked the woman's shoulder. "Excuse me." Startled, she straightened her back and looked at him. "Would you mind turning off the light?" asked Ryo politely.

"Oh yes. Sorry." She pressed the light button, and instantly, their row was dark.

"Thanks," Ryo said, relieved, and closed his eyes.

He didn't know how long he'd been dozing when something woke him up. Blinking his sleepy eyes, he straightened his back and wondered what it was. As he was about to lean his head on his seat, he felt his leg kick from the right side.

What in the ...!

Did she kick me? Narrowing his eyes, he turned to her, but she seemed asleep. Scratching his head, he shook it but eyed Female Waldo. In less than a few seconds, her leg moved toward him again.

"Hey!" He blocked it in time, and then pushed it away.

Female Waldo startled and looked at him with her sleepy eyes. "Wh-why did you kick me?" she whined.

"I didn't," Ryo whisper-shouted. "You kicked me. I just pushed your leg away from me."

"I did? Oh ... sorry," she said sleepily, and leaned back to the window. Soon enough, Ryo heard a gentle snore coming from her.

As his eyes were already adjusted to the dimmed light, he saw Female Waldo sleeping with her lips slightly opened, and a lock of red hair fell on her cheek from sleeping sideways. She looked innocent, vulnerable, and ... cute.

Letting out a soft chuckle, he massaged his neck, and his sleepiness was gone completely. Maybe soft music could soothe him. The bright light from his personal TV glowed when he turned it on. After swapping his finger on the screen, he found a perfect list of soft songs for sleeping. Putting on his headphones, he turned off the screen, let songs play, and moved back into his slumber.

BELLA

I quietly blew a sigh as I dragged my carry-on to the baggage claim. If Tokyo wasn't on the top of my bucket list or if I wasn't interested in the city at all, I'd prefer to sleep off the jet lag of my eleven-hour flight once I arrived at my apartment.

My head hurt because I couldn't sleep. The flight to Tokyo was more brutal than I could imagine, because of turbulence. The seatbelt sign had been on almost seventy-five percent of the time. The plane shook even during mealtime and caused my water to spill on my pants. Good thing they were made of quick-drying fabric.

Walking down the aisle to the bathroom had been tough. Not to mention being inside. My fingers hurt from clenching the armrest, and I felt a deep ache settle in my jaw as I gritted my teeth when the ride was bumpy, followed by a sinking feeling each time it bounced. I wished I had someone to talk to me, to distract me.

I should have brought Tylenol PM, but Mel reminded me that the medicine made me groggy on our last trip to Bali. Which was true.

I did my best to make myself sleep faster: putting peppermint oil on my wrist and listening to soft music. My last resort was doing my coloring book, and it helped. What annoyed me the most was when I finally fell asleep, my seatmate pushed my leg away and accused me of kicking his foot. That was rubbish! No one would kick someone's foot while sleeping, right?

Speaking of my seatmate, he was a grumpy man who never smiled, and he disliked me for whatever reason.

When I looked for a headphone socket, his eyes threw me a laser beam because I accidentally bumped his arm hard. He helped me find it, but from his expression, I knew he wasn't happy about it. Despite the fact that he wasn't friendly, I did my best to be nice to him by starting a conversation, but he brushed me off.

Things got worse. My bladder acted up after the first meal and caused me to go back and forth to the bathroom. The Frowner—I named him that— didn't seem happy and looked at me with a deep crease between his eyebrows as I walked past him. How I wished to put the pencil in that crease.

If he didn't want people to walk past him, he should have chosen a window seat or an exit row seat.

The middle-aged man sitting on the aisle was better and didn't seem to mind each time I asked to pass him. We even traded a few jokes. How I wished the Frowner wasn't my seatmate.

Although the Frowner was so annoying, he was a good-looking guy. Well, *only* if he smiled and didn't frown. His nose was straight, his jaw was chiseled, and his spiked Ivy League haircut looked perfect on his oval face. His tucked-in long-sleeved T-shirt revealed his lean body. He was probably a taller guy because his knees almost touched the seat in front of him. It must have been uncomfortable for him to sit in the middle. I was petite, and any seat in economy class would feel like a business class for me.

When all passengers stepped out of the cabin, unlike the middle-aged man, the Frowner didn't say anything or acknowledge when he strode past me on the jet bridge toward the exit.

Ugh, he is rude!

Trust me, if we were stranded on a deserted island, he would be the last person I would want to be acquainted with.

The baggage claim was packed with people. It took me thirty minutes to get my luggage. After piling my bags on the cart, I pushed the cart to the long corridor toward the arrival exit. In a few beats, I felt tightness in my chest when my senses were overloaded by the hubbub of people flocked in front of currency exchange, restrooms, an information desk, and the bus ticket counter. Loud announcements from the speakers on the ceilings and live billboards from the huge screens seemed to compete with the noise.

I pushed my cart near the cosmetic and perfume store and began to take a few deep breaths to control my senses. That was a good trick my dad taught me. As a professional traveler—that was what I called him—because of his work, my dad knew how to manage the overloaded senses that could lead to frustration and confusion by taking a few deep breaths before moving forward. And his trick worked.

The tension in my chest lessened, and I could think clearly about what I should do next. I pulled out my phone to find the information from HR in my email. Once I saw it, I opened it up and read the information.

Passenger: Bellalina E. Bell

Pick-up by: Mr. Isami Sato

Where: Lobby A, International Arrival.

Time: 2:25 local time.

The clock on my phone showed 2:30 p.m.
Oops!

With all my might, I pushed my cart on the long and busy corridor with travelers. I passed many booths for money exchange, car rentals, luggage storages, and vending machines for buying train or bus tickets, and I maneuvered carefully around travelers who were walking or standing in the middle of the corridors.

As I reached Lobby A, some people stood outside the temporary barrier and held boards written in kanji or English. My eyes caught a middle-aged man dressed in a suit holding a big sign written in English, "Miss Bella Bell from Little Bear," and a crossbody bag hanging in front of his large body. His hair was almost gray and thinned on the forehead. His eyes behind round eyeglasses were scanning the crowd. And he looked severely boring.

I cringed because I wished my translator would be a funny and easygoing person. But I couldn't get everything I wanted, right?

Lifting up the corner of my mouth, I walked toward him. At the same time, his dark brown angular eyes widened as our eyes met.

"Miss Bella Bell?" His voice sounded hesitant.

"Yes, that's me," I answered. "Mr. Sato?"

The wrinkle on the corner of his mouth became more profound as a slow smile appeared on his face when he nodded and gave a slight bow. While I wondered if I should bow back, he held out his hand, and I shook it happily. "I'm Isami Sato, the translator from Bread Lounge," he said in an accent, but I could understand him clearly. "Welcome to Tokyo, Bella Bell-san."

I couldn't prevent a sudden big smile on my face when he called my name. It sounded funny in my ears. However, that's how the Japanese spoke when referring to others in conversation. *San* was similar to "Mr.," "Mrs.," or "Miss" in English. Unless the person was a close friend, you could drop the honorific. Maybe at my next meeting, I'd ask him to call me by my name. "Nice to meet you, Mr. Sa ... uh, Sato-san."

His eyes sparkled as he looked at me. "I parked my car on the third floor. Not far from here. Let's go there." Then he gestured to take my cart. Thanking him, I gave it to him.

"How's your flight, Bell-san? I hope it was pleasant," he asked as we sauntered to the parking lot.

"It was just okay because of a lot of turbulence," I said.

"Ah, yes, the Pacific route can be bumpy all year round. I don't like it either." A thoughtful expression was clearly on his face. "Summer isn't too bad, but winter is the worst."

"Really? Because of the storms?" I asked, my eyes going wide.

He nodded. "Winter storms are harsh in here."

While walking along the row of cars, I made a mental note to not visit Japan in winter. Then Sato-san stopped in front of a silver Toyota Prius and opened its trunk to load my luggage in while I walked around to open the door on the right side of the car.

"The passenger seat is on the left, Bell-san." Sato-san stopped me as he closed the trunk.

"Oops." I grinned bashfully and walked to the other side.

"How tired and hungry are you, Bell-san?" my translator asked as he buckled up.

I raised my eyebrows for an explanation as I looked at him.

"If you're hungry and tired, I'm going to take you for lunch first, then straight to your apartment so you can take a rest." Sato-san smiled. "If you're hungry but aren't tired, I'm going to take you for lunch, then will drive you for a short city tour, then we are going to your apartment. Which one—"

"The second one." I cut him off because I didn't want to let the opportunity for free sightseeing slip away. Before coming here, I'd checked for a local tour guide, and it was expensive. "I'm not tired at all." If necessary, I would take double espresso to stay awake.

He chuckled. "I'd guessed you would choose the second one, Bell-san. That's the best part of being young. No matter how tired you are, you seem to have extra energy for another six to seven hours." He pumped his left arm, smiling. Although he smiled widely, his eyes showed a similar longing that I saw in my parents' every time they looked at my sister and me as we shared stories about our activities. They must have felt nostalgic for the enthusiasm of their younger selves.

"So tell me, do you have anything you want to eat, Bell-san?" he asked, turning his wheel toward the exit.

I tilted my head while I thought, then looked at him. "Do you know any good ramen?"

"I do." He nodded. "I'll bring you to my favorite ramen place. It has only three locations, and one of them is near your apartment. Maybe fifteen minutes' walk from it."

"Awesome. Let's try that." I grinned.

The scenery on the freeway was pretty much the same as in California. Trees on the roadside, low bushes on the slope, road steel dividers, cars, trucks, and road signs. But the sky seemed bluer; the trees and grasses were greener. I must be biased because everything I looked at astounded and confounded me.

And my heartbeat elevated when we passed the blue sign with the words "Welcome to Tokyo" hung on the overpass railing.

I. Was. In. Tokyo.

The words echoed in my ears. It felt too surreal to be in the car that was taking me to the largest metropolitan area in the world.

On the way to downtown Tokyo, my impression of Sato-san changed. He wasn't a boring person as I'd thought. He pointed to the right and left to explain the local landmarks. Sato-san was also a thoughtful tour guide: He knew when to talk or stop because he often let me enjoy and absorb the sceneries in silence.

Forty-five minutes later, we arrived at the ramen place that wasn't packed because it was after the lunch hour. Outside the restaurant, the vending machine for ordering our food greeted us. Although the menu was in Japanese, it was self-explanatory with pictures. I'd eaten ramen in California, so I was quite familiar with it, but I let Sato-san explain it. After choosing our food, Sato-san inserted the money, pressed the button, and dispensed our order ticket before sitting on one of the long tables we shared with other customers.

My stomach growled as the whiff of the broth hit my nose when I got my order: a bowl of ramen in clear brown broth with sliced pork belly, soft boiled egg, fish cake, corn, and sliced scallion on the top.

"*Itadakimasu*," said Sato-san, then wrapped his hands over his chest before picking up the chopsticks.

I imitated him immediately because that was what the Japanese did before eating, and then I picked up my spoon to taste the broth. The warm liquid was smooth and delicious. It soothed my jet-lagged stomach and made me feel whole again. I picked up the ramen with the chopsticks and then put the pork on top of it before eating them together. The al dente ramen and the pork blended perfectly in my mouth and created the best burst of flavor. I had to bestow it as the perfect ramen in the world.

I drained the last drops of the broth and let out a sigh of satisfaction as I put the chopsticks on the stand I'd created from the chopsticks cover. My body warmed and my muscles relaxed. My eyelids became heavy.

"You dislike the ramen." he joked. He pointed at the empty bowl with his eyes.

The tips of my ears warmed at his comment. "Yes, I don't like it so much. I couldn't even stand looking at the broth."

He let out a chuckle. "So, Bell-san, are you too sleepy for sightseeing?"

Automatically, I widened my eyes and rose to my feet. "Of course not. I'm so ready for it."

The corners of his eyes wrinkled as he smiled widely and signaled me to leave the restaurant. We didn't go straight to the car but stopped at a convenience store next door where Sato-san bought me a prepaid card called a *Suica* card. He explained that I could use it to pay for trains or buses or even food, and he also got me a local SIM card to call anyone in Tokyo without paying more for the international fee.

"You need to keep checking the balance of your funds, though. Having enough funds is helpful, especially for transfer tickets when you take trains," he suggested as I carefully put the cards in my purse sleeve.

"Okay."

"Ah, before I forget." He opened his crossbody bag to pull out a turquoise card and gave it to me with two hands. "Bread Lounge had prepared this JR card for you. You can use the card for any train with the JR symbol and also Shinkansen."

My jaw dropped. "Sh-shinkansen? You mean that f-famous bullet train?"

"Yes."

"Oh my God, *me* in Shinkansen?" I let out a shriek and slapped a hand over my mouth to stifle it. If I hadn't remembered where I was and who he was, I'd have hugged him. His eyes sparkled at my reaction, and he tilted his head toward his car. My feet bounced as I followed him from behind.

Our car crawled on the major street as the traffic backed up. I didn't mind because I could indulge my eyes with the hustle and bustle of the city. The words "wow" and "awesome" often escaped from my lips as I saw the grandiose skyscrapers, the enormous sidewalks, the fusion of traditional and modern architecture, and the colorful billboards on the buildings. Instantly, a mixed feeling of joy, overwhelm, and a bit of intimidation rose from the pit of my stomach.

This is the city where I'll live for two months!

"There is a tour for the Imperial Palace, Bell-san." Sato-san's words pulled me back. He pointed to the humongous white building with a single-eave hip roof surrounded by massive stone walls as we drove along the moats outside the borders. "You can't enter the palace, though, but you can still enjoy the palace's inner garden. If you're interested, I can give you the link so you can book it yourself."

"Yes, please. I'd love to see it."

Our car rolled onto the continuous stretch of building after building with bright colors and countless billboards and then stopped at the traffic light.

"Behold the famous Shibuya crossing." Sato-san waved his hand.

"No way!" My mouth hung widely seeing the large group of pedestrians, from five different directions, stride on the largest intersection on the basin of high-rise buildings. That famous crossing was already on my bucket list, but I couldn't believe that I was seeing it on my first day in Tokyo. Automatically, I fished out my phone to record the spectacular moment where hundreds of people sprawled across the intersection. "Are there any collisions among the pedestrians?"

"Not that I'm aware of." Sato-san chuckled at my comment and pointed to the left. "Now, look up there, Bell-san."

I followed his direction and gasped. At one of the top buildings, a giant calico cat was looking down at us, wagging its tail and yawning.

"W-what is that? Is it real?" My voice stuttered.

"That's a new high-tech 3D billboard that spans over three floors of that building. Because of its curved LED screen, it allows for more depth and is perfect for making the ads seem to jump off the screen, like the cat you just saw." I detected a hint of pride in his voice.

"Wow." Placing a hand over my heart, I stared at the screen that was off. "I almost had a heart attack from the cat. It looks so real."

"I was surprised too for the first time I came here and saw it. My wife is a cat lover and always asks me to take her here." His eyes turned gentle as he mentioned his wife. "Let's go to your apartment. Ono-san, your building manager, is waiting for you."

As we left the intersection, I couldn't forget that 3D billboard. Too bad I didn't have a chance to record it. If I had, I could've shared it with my family and Mel, and they wouldn't believe it either.

"By the way, where's the apartment located?" I asked as we passed a white and reddish-orange tower that I recognized from my tourist guidebook as Tokyo Tower. In a swift movement, I took a picture of it.

"Your apartment is in a city called Minato City, Bell-san," Sato-san explained. "Tokyo is one of the forty-seven prefectures. Each prefecture has many cities in it. So, Minato is in Tokyo."

Pressing my lips, I nodded. "I see. Maybe that's similar to a county in the US. Los Angeles County has many cities in it, including the city of Los Angeles."

"Maybe." He smiled at me. "By the way, if you don't mind, my wife and I would be happy to take you out for another city tour tomorrow."

"You would?" I couldn't believe my ears. "Oh, thank you so much, Sato-san. I'm looking forward to it."

"Great. Be ready at nine thirty in the morning," he said.

"Sure."

RYO

Ryo took a deep breath and pushed his cart to the arrival waiting area. His fingers became white as he clenched the handle tightly, and a lump formed in his throat.

He'd moved back for good.

For good.

The words were like a knife slicing his heart into pieces. A thousand times, he'd told himself that he was back this time for his family because if something happened to Akiko, he wanted to be with his parents. He'd known for sure that his parents wouldn't want to move with him to the States. It made sense because they had everything here: their friends and siblings. His dad was still actively working too.

Still, his heart hurt.

As Ryo pushed his cart toward the arrival, he caught a familiar face among the people standing behind the temporary barrier, and the man belonging to it waved at him. He was of medium height, with his hair tied back and a scar on the top of his lip from the cleft lip he had when he was a baby. He smiled wide as Ryo waved back.

"Hey, welcome back," said Takeru as they clasped hands and tapped each other's shoulders.

"Thanks for picking me up, man," said Ryo.

"Nah, don't mention it." His friend flapped his hand, then eyed his cart. "You only brought two bags?"

Ryo lifted his shoulder. "I sold and donated most of my stuff and brought what I need here."

Takeru bobbed his head, looking at him with sympathy. "Got it. Hey, let's go. I bet you're hungry. Any idea what you want to eat?"

"Anything," Ryo answered, although he wasn't hungry.

"Okay, I'll think about it once we're in the car."

Nodding his head, Ryo walked beside Takeru to the parking lot. It didn't take long for them to leave the airport. A knot in Ryo's stomach tightened as he caught the words "Welcome to Tokyo" on the overpass on Highway 295. The tightness sprawled up to his chest and closed his throat as he looked out the window; he had the surreal sense that everything had changed drastically in a month. The happiness from his promotion went south. It was a total one hundred eighty–degree difference.

"I've bought you a local SIM card, Ryo." Takeru's voice brought him back to reality. "It's in my glove box if you want to switch it now."

"Thanks." Ryo opened the compartment and found the SIM card in a small envelope.

"I already gave your new number to Akiko and Kento," said Takeru as he turned his wheel to the left. "I had to tell Akiko because I won't let her worry. I love her, too, just so you know."

"Thanks. You know me well." Ryo took his phone out and switched his American SIM card with the local one. He didn't have the heart to throw the old card away. Carefully, he put it inside his wallet.

"Yeah, you wouldn't tell them until they begged you," Takeru smirked. "Hey, I found a few places for you. Maybe three or four.

It isn't easy to find vacant places lately, especially if you want to be near your parents' house. So, I suggest checking the places tomorrow."

"We can check them today before I go to my parents' place," Ryo said, rubbing his tired eyes.

"Are you sure? Don't you feel jet lagged?" He glanced at his watch. "It's already two thirty, though."

"That's okay." Ryo forced a smile. "I just don't want to ...." His voice trailed off as he clenched his jaw and turned to the window.

In a beat, he felt the weight of Takeru's hand on his shoulder. "I understand how you feel. It's going to be hard for you to see Akiko in her current condition. But you should be proud of her, Ryo. She's a real trooper."

"Yes, she is," Ryo's voice quivered. "She's even stronger than you and me."

"She has a tigress's heart," Takeru commented, shifting on his seat. "Remember when Sara's dog charged you, and your sister jumped in front of you, growling back at the dog?"

Ryo nodded. "I won't forget that. Once the dog was running loose in the garden and all the kids screamed and ran toward the main house, Oneechan didn't follow the kids but ran to me. Good thing Sara's dad heard the commotion and was able to control the dog. If not, the dog would've chewed her into pieces. That Doberman was a beast!"

"Kento is a lucky man for winning your sister's heart," commented Takeru. "I've tried to win a girl's heart, but until now, she hasn't even been moved by it." His voice became flat as his fingers clenched on the steering wheel.

Ryo kept his eyes on the road, watching building after building pass. He knew the girl Takeru was talking about. It was Sara. Takeru loved Sara, but she loved Ryo. Takeru became bolder in chasing her after learning that Ryo wasn't interested.

Unfortunately, Sara was a stubborn and ambitious woman and never gave up until she got what she wanted. Everything was a challenge for her, including getting someone's love.

He knew it, and that scared him the most.

It was also the main reason Ryo hadn't told her about him coming back for good. Sara was his headache. Maybe he had to find a new strategy to make Sara give up on him.

"Ryo?"

"Yes?"

"Focus on cheering Akiko up with your presence, Ryo. She must be sad, scared, and feeling hopeless too. Be there for her. However, when you feel overwhelmed and need a friend, call me anytime." Takeru glanced sideways at him.

"Thanks. I really appreciate it."

"By the way, I know where I can take you to eat. CoCo Ichibanya. There's one near the apartments I want to show you," said Takeru.

"Let's go there. In California, the price is double, so I want to enjoy its fifty-percent discount."

Takeru cackled at his comment and pressed the brake to stop at a traffic light. "Yeah, I was shocked when I visited you in California last time."

Although it was past lunchtime, the curry restaurant was always packed with people, mostly white-collar employees, or salarymen. Ryo cringed to see how fast they ate their food; it was as if they swallowed instead of chewing, and they looked tense and in a hurry. It was totally different from his coworkers in California, who seemed relaxed whenever they had a meal together.

As the curry settled well in his stomach, Ryo was surprised to find how the food affected his mood. His posture wasn't saggy anymore, and he could throw jokes at Takeru during their apartment hunting.

It was almost four o'clock when they arrived at the first apartment. It was affordable but old and far from his parents' house.

The second one—twenty minutes from the first—was affordable, and Ryo liked the location because it was near his parents' house and the train station, which was important since he didn't have a car like most people in Tokyo and depended heavily on the public transportation, especially the trains.

Unfortunately, there wasn't a vacant room available until next year. The third apartment was the same.

"Do you want to continue?" asked Takeru when they were back on the road.

"Yes, let's go to the last one," said Ryo. "Where is it again?"

Takeru swiped his phone's screen with his finger. "Hmm, I'm not sure if you're interested, though."

"Try me."

"It's near a giant cemetery, and mostly foreigners live there," Takeru said hesitantly. "My aunt is the building manager there."

Ryo slanted his head. "If it's near the cemetery, the rent is cheap, then?"

His friend nodded.

"Let's check out the place."

"No one likes living near the cemetery but *foreigners*," Takeru emphasized the last word.

Ryo shrugged. "I don't believe in ghosts or that the place will bring bad luck to me."

"You've been living in the States for too long. Now you think like a gaijin," Takeru teased, shaking his head. "Although you don't believe in ghosts or bad luck from living next to the cemetery, think about your parents or your future girlfriend. They do mind."

Ryo scoffed. "I have no girlfriend, and my parents won't visit me anyway because I'll be the one who visits them. Let's see the place. Are we far from it?"

"No."

"That's great. Let's go."

Takeru looked at him and shrugged. "If your mom or Akiko finds out, I'll tell them that you forced me."

"Don't worry, they won't scold you," assured Ryo.

When Ryo looked determined, Takeru knew for sure nothing would sway him.

"Let me call my aunt, then," said Takeru, tapping a voice control button on his steering wheel and giving a command to call his aunt.

"*Hai*, this is SunRise Home." A cheerful woman's voice came through the speaker.

"*Moshi, moshi*. Auntie, it's Takeru. How are you?" Takeru's finger drummed absentmindedly on the wheel.

"I'm busy as always. And you?"

"I'm well too. By the way, do you remember Ryo, my childhood friend?" He paused, glancing at Ryo.

"Yes, from the cute twins."

"Only the sister is cute, though." He grinned as Ryo glared at him.

His auntie chuckled. "So, why do you call me?"

"I'm helping the ugly twin find a place because he's back for good. By any chance, do you have an available room in the apartment near the cemetery—"

"That's only for foreigners." His auntie cut him off.

Takeru rubbed his eyebrow. "Yes, I know, but Ryo wants to check the place out. And don't ask me why. He's simply a weirdo." Then he winced as Ryo punched his shoulder hard.

His auntie paused for a few seconds before continuing. "I have one available." Her voice hesitated. "Are you sure?"

"Yes." Takeru gave a thumbs-up to Ryo. "Can I see you now?"

"I need to show a room to my new tenant shortly," she answered. "Can you wait until I'm done?"

Ryo nodded his head as Takeru shifted his eyes to him. "Okay, I'll wait outside the building. See you later, Auntie."

Takeru tapped off and grinned widely. "You lucky dog, you."

Ryo grinned back and sunk in his seat as his eyes caught Tokyo Tower in the distance. The afternoon sun was leaning toward the horizon behind them as their car rolled toward the tower.

BELLA

It was a quarter past four in the afternoon when our car stopped at a parking spot in front of a silver six-story building with dark gray trim.

I got out of the car and looked around. It was a quiet neighborhood with many residential buildings that were compact and neat. I liked it instantly.

"What do you think?" asked Sato-san, standing with my luggage next to him.

"Nice neighborhood," I praised.

He looked pleased. "I like this area too. It's close to the pedestrian mall we passed earlier. Also, there're a few *konbini* around here for buying anything you need."

"Kon ... bi ... ni?" I sounded it out. "What's that?"

"Oh, that's what we call a convenience store," he explained.

I nodded and wrote a mental note of the new Japanese word.

"Let's go inside. Ono-san is already here," he said, dragging my luggage as we walked toward the building. "By the way, this apartment isn't too far from a train station."

"That's great."

"It's only twenty minutes' walk from here."

I halted my steps. My mouth gaped in shock. Twenty minutes' walk?

I grew up in a suburb called Lake Forest. In my whole life, the longest walks I'd had were when I hiked with my family, which was not even once a month. Most of the time it was less than three miles because if it was more than that, I'd whine, and my dad couldn't stand it. So, walking twenty minutes every day from the place I lived to the train station sounded unbelievably far.

"Wait." I finally spoke. "You said it's a twenty-minute walk from here to the train station?"

"Yes, because from *that* train station, you don't need to change the line. If you think that station is too far, there is a closer station, but you need to change the line from ... ah, now I forget, and change to Asakusa Line. Changing trains is confusing if you aren't familiar," he explained. "But don't worry, I'll pick you up and drop you off for the time being, until you feel comfortable."

I was about to ask something, but he had already greeted Ono-san, a petite, gray-haired lady in a white blazer and pants who came out from the silver and clear double glass doors.

The building manager was a polite woman and looked a bit older than my mom. After introducing us, we followed her to the main entrance. My eyes caught a metallic brown plate on the wall with the building's name printed on it in katakana.

"Ap ... pu ... ru ... hai ... tsu ..." I read it slowly. *Huh?*

I almost burst into a giggle. In my ears, the name sounded perfect for an apple orchard. Who named this beautiful building Apple Heights?

But I sped up since Ono-san was already punching in numbers on the security system's keypad and pushed the door to let us in. A soft click was heard behind us as the door closed gently.

"This is your code." Sato-san gave me a piece of paper as we stepped onto glossy gray tiles. "Memorize the numbers or put it in your phone so it'll be handy when you need it. If you don't remember, the door"—Sato-san pointed over his shoulder—"can't be opened. I'll give you Ono-san's phone number later just in case you need it."

"Thanks," I put the paper in my backpack.

As we continued walking behind Ono-san, her hands fluttered and gestured to the rooms we passed while Sato-san patiently translated the words to me.

The elevator doors were wide-open when we arrived. Ono-san pressed the fifth-floor button while telling me my apartment number was 520.

Once we got out of the elevator, we were welcomed by a short corridor with white tiles. Ono-san turned to the right and then to the left for another long corridor. There were two other apartment buildings next to this one, but between them, I could see the city skyline in the distance, bathing in the afternoon sunlight. Farther down, I saw single houses and a school.

In the opposite direction from where we were heading, there was a park with arrays of tall stones under trees. It didn't seem like a regular park, but maybe I should check it out later once I settled down.

Finally, we stopped at my unit at the end of the corridor.

"You're lucky, Bell-san," commented Sato-san, turning to me.

"Why?"

"Do you see that wall?" Sato-san pointed at the end of the wall. I nodded. "You don't have a neighbor on that side."

"Does it matter if I have a neighbor or not?"

Ono-san said something and mentioned "wall," but I couldn't catch it since she spoke broken English.

"Ono-san said since you don't have any shared walls with a neighbor, you don't hear any noise from it," Sato-san explained.

"Oh. Is the wall thin?"

He nodded. "Some studio apartments, especially in the city, have thin walls, but some don't. The walls in this building aren't thick. So the only noise you may hear is from your next-door neighbor." He pointed at unit 522.

I nodded and looked inside once Ono-san opened the door and signaled for me to go in. Standing in the doorway, I went into a daze as I caught sight of a narrow hallway with wooden floors. Along the right wall, there was the washer, the kitchen, and the refrigerator in sequence and separated like office cubicles. Then a frosted door at the end of the hallway.

Feeling beyond confused, I stepped farther inside to find myself standing on the recessed white floor, the same color as the outside floor but with smaller tiles. My hand opened the door of a tall gray, narrow cabinet on my right side to find it was perfect for shoe storage or shopping bags, or even jackets and hats.

Closing the cabinet's door, I stepped up to the wooden floor creaking under my shoes and stood still to measure the hallway's width by spreading my arms from side to side. I gave a bitter smile as my fingers touched the walls. *So narrow!*

"Be grateful, Bella," I mumbled to myself.

Pressing my lips tight, I checked the washer and moved to the tiny kitchen next to it. The kitchen came with a sink, a cutting area, top and bottom cabinets, a stove with two burners, and a drawer with an oven grid—like my mom's oven. I peered into it and wondered what it was for. Then I opened the cabinets to find mugs, plates, and cooking utensils.

The wall stopped after the kitchen, revealing a nook with another wooden door that I couldn't see from the entrance. Feeling curious, I opened the door to find a bathroom with a toilet separated from the shower area. The shower had a small bath and a sink.

66

Shaking my head, I closed the bathroom door and looked at the chest-high fridge with a microwave on top of it standing against a wall. Then I checked the last door.

As I'd suspected, behind the frosted door was a single room with the bedroom and living room combined. The living room had a large beige rug under a low coffee table and two floor cushions. A split air conditioner unit below a thirty-two-inch TV on the right wall and a closet with sliding doors were along the left wall. Across from me was a single bed that sat behind a large bookshelf that functioned as a divider for the living room and bedroom. Next to the bed was a sliding door to the balcony.

Overall, my unit was very small, even smaller than my friend's studio apartment in LA. I could feel the bubble of excitement in my chest depleting. Thank God I wasn't a claustrophobic person.

As I was about to turn around, I heard a sharp shriek coming from the front door.

Standing on the recessed floor, Ono-san looked at me with her eyes wide and covered her mouth with one hand while the other pointed at me frantically. I felt my eyebrows touch as I followed her finger that was pointing at my shoes. Sato-san stepped in to see what happened, and then his mouth hung open as he placed a hand over his chest.

My stomach clenched to see their reactions. Rubbing my neck, I walked toward the front door where Ono-san talked to Sato-san faster like an auctioneer, with her hands waving like she was being attacked by invisible flies and occasionally one hand pointing at me.

Sato-san gave the nod here and there with his palms up in front of him as if to try to calm her. Then he grimaced when he bowed twice and said *gomen nasai* to Ono-san, who walked out of the room after giving me a sharp glance.

Why did he say sorry to Ono-san? I wondered, feeling uncomfortable at his expression. Clearing the thickness in my throat, I stopped in front of Sato-san. "What happened?"

Dropping his shoulders, he pointed at my shoes. "Ah, Bell-san, you forgot to take off your shoes."

Huh?

"Why?"

He exhaled and pointed at the recessed floor where he was standing. "This area is a *genkan*, where you take off your shoes before entering your room because, in our culture, no shoes are allowed in the house. You can wear indoor slippers or be barefoot." His hand pointed at a pair of slippers on the floor.

"Oh." I took off my shoes quickly and dropped them on the genkan. "Is that the reason why Ono-san was upset?"

He didn't answer but bent down to set my shoes next to the slippers, with the toes pointing toward the front door. "If you set your shoes this way, you just slip your feet in them when you need to go out," he added, straightening his back. His voice was calm and flat like my dad's when he taught me something.

"And yes, she's upset because you were wearing shoes inside the house. We believe that outdoor shoes bring germs into the house. By changing them to indoor slippers, you prevent germs from spreading to the house."

I bit my lip, lowering my gaze. I'd thought I had enough knowledge about Japanese manners. Obviously, I was wrong and already made a simple blunder in just a few hours in Tokyo. "Sorry."

A gentle smile on his face told me he understood. "It isn't common in the US to take off the shoes before entering your home. But here, it's something that you have to do. I suggest you follow it whenever you enter someone's house."

"Let me apologize to her." Without waiting for Sato-san, I stepped outside and gave a slight bow in front of Ono-san, who was still standing close by. "Gomen nasai, Ono-san. I won't do it again."

Ono-san didn't understand the rest of the words, but she caught the Japanese. The tense expression on her face melted, and she gave me a tight smile, returning my bow, and spoke in long sentences to Sato-san, who was already standing next to me.

"Bell-san, Ono-san accepted your apology," he smiled. "She hopes you remember that."

"Thank you," I said in Japanese to Ono-san, and turned to Sato-san. "Could you tell her that I'm going to clean the floor now so she won't feel upset anymore?"

Sato-san shook. "No need. Keep in mind that you should take off your shoes before going into any house in Japan. If not, people will be upset with you."

"I promise."

After everything was resolved, Ono-san gave me an official apartment tour. It didn't take her a long time to show the rooms. Still, it took some time when she explained how to operate the kitchen appliances, including the drawer oven, which turned out to be a grill for fish or pizza, and then the panels for AC, water, a built-in security camera, an emergency system, and a panic button. Yeah, there was a panic button that would automatically alert security. Just by looking at the button, I felt secure living here.

When we were on the balcony, I fell in love right away because it provided the best view ever. The balcony was narrow and enclosed by a waist-high wall but spacious enough for an outdoor table and two chairs. Ono-san said that since my balcony had an unobstructed view, it would be nice to enjoy my lunch or dinner there.

"Why is that here?" I pointed at the aluminum folding drying rack leaning on the wall next to the sliding door.

"Oh, you can use it for drying your clothes," Sato-san said.

"Uh, don't you guys use a dryer for that?"

Sato-san translated to Japanese to Ono-san, who raised one of her eyebrows. Then they shook their heads almost in unison. "Some people do, but most of us don't use a dryer to dry our clothes, Bell-san. We hang our clothes using drying racks or poles.

During the overcast or rainy season, we dry our clothes in the bathroom," said Sato-san patiently.

What?

It was hard to believe. Tokyo was a metropolitan city, but people used the drying rack for their clothes?

"Um, w-what happens if the wind blows my clothes?" I asked, trying to think of an excuse for not using the rack.

His lips twitched as Sato-san tried hard to hide his smile. Clearing his throat, he picked up a mesh bag hanging on the hook on the wall and pulled out a wood clothespin to show me. The pin was similar to what I played with at my grandma's house when I was young. "We use this to hold our clothes."

My cheeks must have been crimson like steamed lobsters as heat crept up from my neck. It was embarrassing because I didn't know how to dry my clothes without a dryer.

"Don't worry much. You'll get used to it," Sato-san comforted me before going back to the room.

As they were about to leave, Ono-san gave me a blue folder with information that I might need. Once they left, I unpacked my stuff.

It didn't take me long to fill the small apartment with things I brought from home: bedsheets, a hanging closet organizer from IKEA, two framed pictures of my family, a few novels that I wanted to read, my favorite mug, coasters, and then Snoopy and Tigger plushies on my bed. Then I piled my luggage on the floor next to my bed.

I looked around, and all of a sudden, a twinge of homesickness hit my chest. It wasn't my first time traveling in a different country, but it was my first time staying in a foreign country by myself. I wiped the wetness from my nose as the thought of not seeing my parents every day crept into my mind. If Adele had seen me crying, she would have called me a baby. When she was my age, she'd lived alone in Australia for six months before getting her master's degree.

Outside, the sky was still bright and covered by fluffy clouds, mixed with the shade of light gray. Sunbeams were scattered behind the clouds. It was the perfect time to familiarize myself with my surroundings before going to bed. I might need to stop by the convenience store for some milk, bread, toiletries, cereal, or paper towels.

Settled with the plan, I slung my bag over my shoulder, took the house key, changed my slippers with my shoes, and went out to embrace my first adventure in the city of Tokyo.

As I locked my door, the door for unit 522 opened. Ono-san came out with two Japanese men. One was wearing a Ralph Lauren white mesh polo shirt and dark blue pants, and the other was wearing a snug gray long-sleeved shirt and khaki pants. He was talking to Ono-san while she locked the door.

I raised an eyebrow as I noticed that his face looked familiar. *Where did I meet him?* I wondered, and unaware, stared at him. Then ... I felt my eyes widen. *Isn't he the Frowner? Oh God, don't let him live next to me.*

As I considered looking away, it was too late because he caught me. His jaw dropped, and his angular eyes rounded like quarters.

"Y-you." His voice caught in his throat.

"What are you doing here?" we asked almost in unison.

"I live here." I shifted my eyes to unit 522. "Do you l—"

"No," the Frowner cut in quickly, glancing at Ono-san.

The white-polo-shirt man standing next to him nudged his arm and asked in English, "Who is she?"

The Frowner turned to him and spoke in Japanese, and I assumed he might have said something bad about me because he pointed at me with his eyes and shook his head. Ono-san glanced at me and said something to him.

I scoffed and decided to leave them while they were talking. I blamed myself for not learning enough Japanese. If I had, I'd have known what they said about me.

But they left first. Ono-san gave a nod of acknowledgment as she walked down the hallway toward the elevator. The white-polo-shirt man threw a small smile at me while the Frowner walked behind Ono-san without acknowledging me... again.

Grr ... he's so arrogant!

Since I didn't want to be in the same elevator with them, I waited for a few minutes while taking long and deep breaths to calm me down. Being upset wasn't good for me anyway. If the Frowner decided to live next to me, so be it. I wouldn't deal with him, and besides, I wouldn't live here for a long time regardless.

With that decision, I felt much better and started off toward the elevator.

RYO

"**A**fter dragging my aunt to let us check the place today, what changed your mind so suddenly?" asked Takeru as they walked back to his car. "Why?"

Ryo let out a sigh without saying anything. This place was perfect in terms of distance and price. Two factors that he was looking for. It came furnished too, which was better, so he didn't have to buy furniture for the time being. But ... there was no way he would live next to Female Waldo. He knew she was in Tokyo because she'd filled out the embarkation card for foreigners, but it never had crossed his mind they would meet again in this perfect place.

Damn. Tokyo is huge, even bigger than New York. Why is she living there?

"Don't tell me it's because of that redheaded woman," Takeru said again, narrowing his eyes as he opened the door.

He wanted to lie, but Takeru knew better. "She's a pain in the neck," Ryo said shortly, buckling his seatbelt.

"Really?" Takeru's eyes narrowed, and he pressed the ignition before turning the wheel. The gravel crunched under his tires as they left the parking lot. "My aunt is a person who could read someone's personality, and she didn't say anything about that woman."

"Trust me, she is annoying, spoiled, and selfish."

"My … my … my." Takeru shook his head in bemusement. "You just arrived, and you already have a cute redheaded woman as your enemy?"

"She isn't my enemy." Ryo almost rolled his eyes. "A cute woman can be a pain in the neck too, you know."

"So you admit that she is cute?"

"I don't say she's ugly."

Takeru chuckled. "What did she do to turn you, a thoughtful and kind man, into an insensible, grumpy person?"

Ryo gave a dismissive wave. "You don't want to know."

"Try me."

He rubbed the back of his neck, considering it. "We sat next to each other on the way here," he finally answered.

"Okay." Takeru lifted a shoulder. "Did she harm you?"

"Of course not." Ryo exhaled loudly, feeling reluctant to bad-mouth the woman because that wasn't his character. However, Takeru might think he was the jerk if he didn't explaint it. "Okay, here's what happened. She was sitting on the window seat, and I was in the middle."

Takeru nodded, encouraging him to go on.

"She couldn't sit still. For more than eleven hours of flight, she constantly moved around in her seat. She asked to go back and forth to the restroom. When she slept, she kicked my foot. Could you imagine how annoyed I was? I had enough of her. To be honest, I don't know if she could be a quiet neighbor. What would happen if she liked making noise at home, like listening to loud music or TV? Remember, the walls here are thinner than my apartment's walls in California. You can hear any noise from a next-door neighbor." He paused, exhaling out.

"I can't stand her. She is too annoying," he added.

"So, that's the reason," Takeru said slowly.

"Yes."

Takeru's lips quirked up a little, but Ryo could see annoyance on his friend's face. "Sorry for being an ass. I was surprised to see her again. There are many apartments for foreigners, so why does she stay in Apple Heights?"

"That's okay. Don't get worked up. I'll find you another place," said Takeru. "I'd rather search for more apartments for you than receive a phone call from a police officer about you killing her or vice versa."

"You watch too many dramas, like Oneechan." Ryo chuckled.

It took them thirty minutes to go to Ryo's parents' house. The sun was leaning toward the horizon, and a flock of birds squawked loudly while flying west as Takeru's car stopped in front of a two-story house surrounded by high, dark brown walls. Green and lush Japanese maple trees popped up above the walls.

"Thanks, man," said Ryo, holding the door.

"No problem. Say hi to your mom, Akiko, and Kento," said Takeru.

"Are you sure you don't want to go in?" Ryo offered.

"I need to beat the traffic. Today is my mom's birthday. I want to buy her some fruit and flowers before going to her house."

"Okay. Please send my regards and happy birthday to her."

"I will. Thanks."

Ryo waited until Takeru's car disappeared around the corner that led to the main street. Spinning on his heel toward the gate, his nose caught the subtle smell of roses and lavender from his mom's garden. When he was in the States, the scent of those flowers blooming in his apartment's garden had always made him homesick.

For a few minutes, Ryo didn't budge. Then he heaved a long sigh and pushed open the gate. Everything looked the same. The garden looked beautiful and cozy because his mom took good care of it. The roses, the lavender, the magnolia tree near the porch. His eyebrows curled to see a middle-aged lady wearing a light blue garden hat pruning a small plant in a pot.

"Okaasan," he called her.

The lady turned her head, blinked a few times, and then gave a slight yelp. In a quick movement, she dropped the shears on the ground and scurried toward him.

"Ryo-kun," she called as Ryo bowed slightly to her.

A faint smile curled his lips from the way she called him as if he was still a little boy. His dad had stopped using "kun" after Ryo was in junior high.

"I thought you would be here tonight. If you told us you were here early, we could've picked you up," she said, stretching her hands to cup his face and kiss his forehead. His parents were more expressive in showing their affection than other parents he'd known, something that he'd felt thankful for.

"Takeru picked me up," he said gently. It was his intention not to tell his parents the exact time of his arrival. They, especially his mom, had been working hard taking care of Akiko.

"Where is he?" His mom turned to the gate.

"He was in a hurry to buy fruits and flowers for his mom's birthday," Ryo explained.

"I'll call his mom later then," his mom said and looked into his eyes. "Sometimes I want to pick you up from the airport too, you know." Her eyes were misty. And he didn't like it. He knew that deep down, his mom felt sorry for not taking care of him properly.

"Well, maybe next time," he said in a low voice. His arm swung around his mom, and he hugged her. After a few beats, he pushed her shoulder away gently. "Let's go inside."

She nodded and tried to take his luggage.

"It's heavy," said Ryo.

"Do you think I'm not strong enough?" His mom scowled.

Ryo gave a small smile and let her carry his backpack.

"How was your flight? Was it crowded? Are you hungry?" His mom threw the questions all at once.

Patiently, Ryo answered them one by one as they sauntered to the front door, but he didn't mention looking for an apartment. His mom might be upset, although she would understand his reasoning.

"Ryo-kun." A light, cheerful voice called his name as they entered the room.

In the living room, Akiko, in her wheelchair, waved. Next to her was a tall man wearing glasses—Kento— his childhood friend and Akiko's boyfriend. Ryo admired him for his love for and devotion to his sister.

While taking his shoes off and changing into slippers, Ryo blinked fast to clear his blurred vision as Kento pushed his sister's wheelchair slowly to him. Although she was twenty-five years old, she seemed like a fifteen-year-old girl. She looked paler than the last time he saw her. But her eyes were still sparkling like stars in the sky, and her smile was still brighter and warmer than the summer sun.

Forcing a smile, he walked to Akiko and bent down to give her a hug. Ryo felt his throat close to feeling her scrawny body nearly disappear in his arms.

"You didn't respond to my last text," she pouted, gazing at him as they pulled away. "And don't tell me that you were busy," she continued as if she could guess his response.

Kento flashed a wide grin at his girlfriend's comment while Ryo chuckled and shook his head.

"Still witty, isn't she?" Ryo said to Kento.

"Yes." His hand tapped Akiko's shoulder gently.

His mom tsked. "Akiko-*chan*, you should let your brother change his clothes first."

Akiko wrinkled her nose. "I won't let him until I make sure he brought snacks."

"I have them here." Ryo tapped on one of his suitcases.

His sister squealed and clapped her hands. "Great, go change your clothes and come back here with my presents."

Ryo turned to Kento. "I should blame you because she's become bolder since she's dated you."

Kento gave a sheepish smile as he ran a hand over his hair. "Let me bring your luggage upstairs, so can you change your clothes. If not, she'll blame me for not being on her side."

"Yup, we are the victims." Ryo let out a laugh as his sister gawked at him.

Together, they carried the luggage up to Ryo's bedroom and brought down the snacks for Akiko. The delicious scent of grilled fish from the kitchen hit Ryo's nose as he watched his sister squeal happily. He always said each time he came back that nothing beat Mom's cooking, even a simple meal like miso soup. And it was true. In the States, each time he was unwell, he missed his mom's food.

While waiting for dinner to be ready, Ryo went to the house's side yard. The sun lightly touched the horizon, turning the sky into a bright orange. Taking a seat on the lower bench in front of the pond, he gazed at the red and orange koi fish swimming near him with their mouths on the surface, hoping for some food. That spot was his favorite, especially during summer, because when the summer breeze blew, that area was colder than the rest of the yard.

Then, Ryo sensed he was being watched. Turning around, he saw Akiko in her wheelchair, gazing at him.

"Oneechan," he said and got up to his feet to walk closer to his sister. "I didn't know you were here."

Akiko smiled and gestured for him to push her to the pond. Ryo did and sat back on the bench next to her. Holding hands, they cast their eyes on the pond.

The pond was valuable for them because it had been their first project together when they moved to Tokyo more than a decade ago, and it also became their secret place whenever they needed time to calm down or think. If one of them wasn't around, the koi pond was first place to search.

No one said a word until Ryo felt his sister squeeze his hand gently. His head whipped to her. "Yes?"

"Are you happy to be back here, Ryo-kun?" she asked.

Ryo smiled. "Yes."

A deep crease showed on her pale forehead. "You aren't."

"I am."

She shook her head stubbornly. "You aren't. I know it."

"I am," he said again, looking back to the pond.

"I'm your twin, and I know your mind," she said in a low voice, trying to pull her hand away, but Ryo held it.

"I have no regrets, Oneechan," he said patiently.

"But I do!" Akiko hissed, glaring at him. "Why did you quit your job? I'd told you don't come back here no matter what happens." She slapped Ryo's head.

"Hey!" he cried, covering his head. The slap wasn't hard but surprised him.

"I can't fulfill my dreams, which is why I asked you to do it for me. I know I'm selfish by asking you do to that. But I know you like living in the States too, Ryo-kun. If not, you would have come back here once you graduated." Her voice rose as she abruptly brushed away the tears dripping on her cheeks. "Promise me to go back to the States once I …" her voice trailed off. Akiko's shoulders shook hard as a big sob came from her mouth, which she muffled with her hands.

"Oneechan." Ryo rose to his feet and wrapped an arm around her shoulder, but Akiko pushed his hand away.

Sitting back on the bench, Ryo looked down at his hands. A tear rolled down his cheeks, and more appeared on his sister's. The summer breeze stopped. The sky darkened. No stars or moon to be seen as if they refused to witness the twins cry in silence.

BELLA

A gentle alarm came from my phone. I sighed and slapped around the nightstand until I found it. With one eye open, I squinted to see the time. It was eight in the morning.

Groaning, I pulled the blanket over my head. My body ached, and I wanted to sleep in. Unfortunately, my mind acted oppositely and began to replay the things that had happened in the last twenty-four hours.

The airport. The flight. The turbulence. The giant cat was on the top of the building. The gigantic crossing Shibu—

In a jolt, I sat up straight on my bed. I was in Tokyo!

Throwing my blanket aside, I jumped out of my bed and stepped outside to the balcony. The sky was partly cloudy, with the sun hiding. The air was balmy and muggy, but it was a beautiful day to me. The birds chirped from the trees nearby and the sound of a scooter came from the narrow street. Stretching my arms, I inhaled the balmy air a few times and picked up the whiff of incense from the temple nearby, mixed with the smell of delicious food from neighboring houses. The morning bustle and hustle had already begun earlier than back home because in neighborhood around my parents' house would still be quiet at this hour on Sunday morning.

For a few minutes, I looked at the cloudy sky and felt grateful to have the chance to live here. Last night, I had walked around the neighborhood. I was surprised to find that my apartment was located in mixed-use zoning, where you could find many different buildings—multistory apartments, schools, parks, residential areas. Along the way, I saw a laundromat, post office, beauty salon, greenhouse, light brown two-story office building, park, warehouse, daycare, and a shrine. It was an interesting neighborhood.

When I walked farther to the main street, I found the pedestrian mall with many stores, including clothing stores, a cellphone store, a hair salon, a children's pottery store, a doctor's office, and restaurants. I bought my dinner—*yakisoba* and *takoyaki*—from one of the standing bars, and on the way back, I stopped at Family Mart—the convenience store—to buy some essentials.

As I got out of the elevator, I bumped into some of my neighbors, who I learned were Harper Moore and her sister, Avery. They had been in Tokyo for a few years and lived in unit 512, closer to the elevator and in the opposite direction from my unit. They were Canadian but moved to Chicago when they were young. Harper was an English teacher, and Avery was a college student. I liked them instantly because they were so friendly and helpful and had already asked me to come to their apartment for lunch or dinner when I was available. Before leaving, we exchanged phone numbers to keep in touch.

My reverie was interrupted by the rumble from my stomach.

I tapped my stomach gently. "Don't you know it is four o'clock in the afternoon in California, for God's sake?"

I went back inside to have a light breakfast and take a shower because Sato-san and his wife would pick me up in an hour for sightseeing.

Facing the door mirror, I twirled around to see my reflection. The khaki Bermuda pants and the loose white cotton shirt were perfect for fighting the warm and humid weather. I was fine with the heat. California could be super hot too in summer. Sometimes, it would reach a hundred degrees. But the humidity bothered me the most. I smoothed and twisted my hair into a bun to prevent it from clinging to my neck.

Feeling satisfied, I sat on the floor and checked my sling bag to ensure I brought my other armor for the heat: a checkered bucket hat, a water bottle, and a face towel. Feeling satisfied, I pumped my fist. *Yeah, I'm ready for your humid weather, Tokyo!*

I glanced at my watch. It was still twenty minutes before Sato-san and his wife would arrive.

"Hmm, what should I do?" I drummed my fingers on the table. "Oh yeah, postcards."

I stood up and took the postcards that I'd bought at the airport yesterday. My dad traveled a lot for his job and always sent a post-card to us from wherever he was, and as we grew up, my sister and I picked up the habit and sent a postcard to our family and close friends whenever we traveled. After I finished, I put them in my sling bag to mail them out when I passed the post office.

When the clock showed 9:15 a.m., I didn't hear a doorbell ring.

Did he forget? I wondered, biting the side of my lower lip. *Should I call him?*

But I refrained from calling him. Sato-san had volunteered for a city tour out of kindness, and I didn't feel it was right to call him. Maybe the traffic was terrible this morning. After giving more consideration, I decided to wait another ten minutes.

I was in the bathroom when he called and left me a message. He apologized for breaking his promise because his wife fell and broke her wrist. Right as he was leaving me a message, his wife was with a doctor in the hospital.

My enthusiasm fled because I had been looking forward to seeing Asakusa, Harajuku, Akihabara, or any part of the city he wanted to bring me to. I'd also promised to send more pictures and videos to my family.

The wave of regret flooded my chest. Sato-san was in distress because of his wife, and I should call and comfort him.

"Be kind, Bel." I slapped my head.

Gazing outside through the sliding door, I dialed his number. At the third ring, Sato-san picked up.

"Moshi, moshi," he said.

"Uh, good morning, Sato-san, it's me, Bella Bell from Little Bear."

"Ah … Bell-san, good morning," he greeted back. "You must have received my message."

"Yes, I did, and I'm so sorry about your wife."

"Thank you, but I'm sorry for not being able to take you sightseeing."

"Don't worry about that. We can do at another time," I comforted him.

"*Arigatou-gozaimasu*, Bell-san." From his tone, I felt as if he were bowing to me.

"Do you know whether it is a clean break or not?"

"She hasn't come out from X-ray yet, but the doctor was sure that it's a clean break."

"I'm glad to hear that."

"By the way, Bella," Sato-san said. "If you want to go sightseeing by yourself, don't forget to use your Suica card for the train or the bus and turn on Google maps to guide you. Have you ever used it outside America?"

"Hmm, not yet. I never travel outside the States without a tour guide," I admitted.

"It is easy. Let's say you want to go to the Imperial Palace. Type "Imperial Palace," choose the train, and the app will give you information about which train and station. Then follow the instructions on how to get to the train station.

"If you get lost, find a train guard or policeman. They speak English. If you can't find them around, find a big store. But please call me if you have any problems. I'll find a way to help you," he said.

A lump formed behind my throat while listening to Sato-san. Amid his trouble, he had time to comfort and guide me. I felt as if I were talking to my dad for a few seconds, and it made me miss him even more.

"I ..." I cleared my throat. "I'll be fine, Sato-san. Don't worry about me at all."

"All right, Bell-san. Please take care, and see you Monday at nine a.m."

"Great. See you Monday." Then I hung up, letting my hand drop to my side. I didn't feel great about going outside without a friend.

My mind flew to Harper. *Should I call Harper?*

No. It was too sudden. She must have other plans.

Then I snapped my finger. "Stupid, Bella," I chided myself. "You've dreamed of having your solo adventure. So this is your chance."

My heart drummed in my chest at the thought. Feeling giddy, I hugged myself and stretched my hands out, pretending I was waltzing with an invisible person around the room and singing, "Bella is in Tokyo and going to ..." I stopped, giving it thought. The name of Akihabara popped up in my mind. Continuing to dance, I chanted again, "Bella is in Tokyo and going to Akihabara."

I dropped the invisible person to the floor and flopped down on the carpet to figure out if I could go to Akihabara from the train station near me. And yes, I could!

My cheeks hurt from smiling widely. I slung the backpack over my shoulder and marched out of my apartment.

The sky was still cloudy, but the sun was not hiding anymore. The air was balmy and muggy as I ambled toward the train station, following the directions from Google until I reached the station entrance.

Going down three flights of stairs, I found myself in a small-scale shopping area with many attractive stores. I was tempted but had to refrain from shopping, and continued to the ticket gate, tapped my Suica card on it, looked for the right platform, and got in line behind the rest of the passengers.

It didn't take long for the train to come. I boarded the car and chose the empty spot next to a brunette Caucasian woman in a light-yellow blouse on one of the long benches. She glanced at me and gave the nod as I sat.

A big grin crept onto my lips. What would my mom, Adele, and Mel say if they knew I was on the train by myself in a foreign country? Would they be surprised?

For evidence, I took selfies and shared them with my family. Then I sat with my hands on my lap, scanning the car. The car was mostly empty, with only a few passengers on the benches. Most of them were busy with their phones or just had their eyes closed.

I took a deep breath and held my knee with a hand to stop it from bouncing up and down, disturbing other passengers sitting around me.

"Exciting, isn't it?" the woman in the yellow blouse asked me in English.

I whipped my head to her.

"Yes." I grinned and nodded. "My first time going around Tokyo by myself. How about you?" I used the chance to look at her carefully. She might be the same age as Mel. Her hair was tied into a loose ponytail. She was pretty.

"I've been here for five days." She smiled, then extended her hand. "I'm Rory, by the way."

"Bella." I shook it.

"America?"

I nodded. "California."

Her beautiful eyebrows flared up. "Me too. Which part?"

"Lake Forest."

"Irvine, not far from you." Her brown eyes gazed at me. "What brought you here?"

"Work. I'm a trainer for Little Bear Café and will train the new franchisee here for two months. And you?"

"Oh, you work for Little Bear? I like that café," she commented. "I'm here to visit my mom's homeland."

"Your mom is Japanese?"

She nodded. "Half, because my grandma was Australian."

"So, where are you going?" I asked, hoping she would be going in the same direction as me.

"Tokyo National Museum." She chuckled. "Sounds boring, doesn't it?"

"Not really. I like going to the museums. When my sister and I were little, my parents loved taking us to museums," I said.

She smiled. For a few moments, we spoke in lowered voices, then exchanged our business cards. I almost smiled to read her full name, Aurorette Arrington Williams. What a cute name.

From the speaker above me, lovely chimes and jingles with female voices announcing in Japanese and English that the Akihabara station was next.

"My station," I pointed out. "Nice to meet you, Rory. Enjoy the museum."

"Nice to meet you, Bella. Good luck with your training, and contact me when you're back in the States," she said.

"I will."

I stepped out of the car with some passengers. When I turned to wave at Rory, someone already stood in front of her, and I had to continue because I didn't want to block people.

RYO

The sun was already high but hiding behind the gray clouds as Ryo and Kento walked out from the Akihabara station. It was early summer. The weather wasn't too hot, with some bursts of rainfall. To Ryo, the air was already muggy with a slightly tangy smell. Ryo's shirt was already damp from sweat that rolled down his spine. His backpack made his back hotter and caused the shirt to stick on his skin. It was uncomfortable. He couldn't imagine how awful it would be in the middle of summer.

Ryo missed California's dry weather. After living in the States for years, he never returned to Tokyo in the summer because as a student he always took summer classes so he could graduate faster. Once he got his job, he loved summer gatherings with his friends. Ryo only went home in the fall for his and Akiko's birthday and his parent's wedding anniversary.

Wake up, he rebuked himself. *You're no longer in California.* Exhaling softly, he forced a smile and turned to Kento. "Thanks for accompanying me to look for a new laptop. My Chromebook finally gave up two weeks before I flew here."

"I'm happy to do that." Kento smiled back. "Have you decided what brand you want to buy?"

"Not yet."

"Okay. We can still come back here or look at the other places if you can't find what you want today."

Ryo glanced at Kento, who pushed his glasses up on the bridge of his nose. "I'm surprised that you would leave my oneechan's side for me," Ryo teased.

"She's been bored, seeing me every day because she doesn't know how to get rid of me. Now she found a chance to," Kento answered.

Ryo chuckled at his joke. Kento's love for his sister was unquestionable. He'd fallen in love with Akiko in junior high in Osaka. He'd had a broken heart when the Yamada family moved to Tokyo. It didn't surprise Ryo when Kento finally declared his love to Akiko, after he was accepted at the University of Tokyo, and he lived in an apartment near his parents' house so he could see Akiko every day. Kento's dedication to his sister touched Ryo's heart. No one knew how long she would live, but Kento's love was stronger every day, even at the most difficult times in Akiko's health.

"Akiko said you're looking for a new apartment," Kento said as they arrived at one of the computer stores. A young man greeted them as they entered the store, and then Kento continued the conversation with Ryo. "Why don't you stay in the house? Your parents and your sister love to have you."

Ryo looked at him. "You've dated my sister for so long and know my mom well. She would force herself to cook a meal every day or stay up late if I came home late. No, I don't want that. Besides, I got used to living alone."

"Any thoughts about where you want to live?"

"Takeru showed me three places yesterday, but they aren't available right away, and he promised to get back to me today with more."

"Yeah, I think there is a shortage of living space now. Well, I hope you get it settled soon. And if you don't mind, I'd suggest you find a place near your parents' house. So you could come over whenever they need," said Kento.

"Yes, that's what I planned," said Ryo.

They didn't talk more because Ryo was busy checking and trying the laptops on display shelves. Many choices made it hard for Ryo to decide.

As they moved to the next store, Kento tapped a hand on Ryo's shoulder. "It might be a little bit late to say it, but thanks for coming back home. It meant a lot to Akiko and me."

A lump formed in Ryo's throat after hearing those words. "That..." His voice croaked. Clearing his throat, he continued, "That's nothing."

Pursing his lips, Kento looked skyward. "Don't say that. I know your career was good there. You were promoted after working there for a year, which meant your company valued you above others. It even sponsored a visa for you, which isn't easy to get. My friend who graduated in the same year as you had to come back here because the company where he worked didn't offer to sponsor his visa." He pressed hands into his pockets as he lowered his gaze to Ryo. "I'm sorry, and thanks for your sacrifice."

Ryo turned to him. "Thanks for being with her for these years. I won't forget that. And I hope my presence can strengthen her."

"I hope so too ..." Kento's voice trailed off, and he looked away.

Ryo's stomach clenched to see Kento's lips tremble, and Kento brushed a tear that rolled down his cheek. "We'll face everything together, Kento," Ryo said, trying to keep his voice from shaking. "Please remember, you're more than oneechan's boyfriend to us. You're my brother."

Kento sniffed and forced a smile. "Likewise." Then he pointed at a white-and-green building that sold souvenirs and gifts, with a massive billboard of *Dragon Ball Z* on top. "Do you mind checking out this store? I'm looking for something."

"Sure."

As they entered the store, they split up. Ryo didn't have any intention of buying anything. The last time he'd come here was to get souvenirs for his friends in the States. But he didn't mind browsing the manga and anime keepsakes and books because he liked them, and they helped him cope with his current stresses.

BELLA

A kihabara was amazing. I wanted to jump up and down like a child when I came out of the train station. The city lived up to its name as the center of modern Japanese culture and the main shopping area for video games, anime, manga, and hobby stores. All buildings, some street walls, were painted and covered by manga or anime icons.

As I walked down to the white-and-green building, my mouth dropped to see Pikachu's face on the hood of a Subaru Impreza parked on the curbside under cherry trees. The car was adorable. Obviously, the Japanese had found ways to show their obsession with anime or manga, not just on their T-shirts and hats but also on their cars. I took a few pictures of it and entered the store.

Going in and out of stores in Akihabara was so tempting. My eyes must have been as big as saucers when I saw the extensive merchandise collections from *Naruto*, *Dragon Ball Z*, and *Pokémon*. Most of them were affordable, except for special collection items which could be very pricey. If my sister or Mel were here, they would freak out to see the accessories, figurines, and toys of *Sailor Moon*. I wasn't into that anime, but I could buy some for them.

I was browsing near the keychain racks, my eyes caught a keychain of Monster Hunter's Airou on one of its pegs. Amazon didn't sell it often, and when it did it was outrageously expensive. As I was about to reach out, a hand took it first. A Japanese man with glasses and a bouffant gazed at the keychain with a smile on his lips. His head whipped toward me, surprised to find me staring at him.

"I saw it first," I blurted.

That man blinked, and as he was about to turn around, I stretched my hand to stop him and repeated my words again. Looking at his squished eyebrows, I realized he didn't understand what I was saying.

Extending my left arm out to prevent him from moving, I pulled out my phone with my other hand, recorded my words in Google Translate, and let him listen in Japanese.

He bit his lower lip, then, to my surprise, pressed the record button while talking, then let me hear them in English. "You stared at it but didn't take it. Now I took it, then you're complaining about it."

My mouth dropped to hear the answer. Then I said, "I didn't complain, I told you that I saw it first. Can I have it? I'm collecting Airou," and let him hear the words.

He looked at me and said something in Japanese. I signaled him to stop and thrust my phone toward him to record his words.

"I'm collecting it too," he said. Shaking his head, he walked to the cashier.

"Not my lucky day." I sighed, gazing at him, wishing my Japanese was good enough to give some explanation to him about how difficult it is to find in the States. Rubbing the corners of my eyes, I turned and bumped my forehead into someone's chest.

Holding my forehead, I looked up and realized the person I bumped into was the Frowner. As our eyes met, he raised his eyebrows briefly and furrowed them. Ignoring him, I passed him by and walked toward the exit. From my peripheral vision, I saw the bouffant man approach him, and they talked.

Any person related to the Frowner pisses me off. I scowled and left the store.

Pushing him from my mind, I focused on my time in Akihabara. If my stomach hadn't growled and demanded food, I wouldn't have realized that I'd been in the city for more than three hours. I had so much fun in the VR Ninja Dojo, where I got lessons about *ninjutsu*—ninja techniques—and swordplay before heading to the virtual ninja training.

Where can I go for lunch before going to Ginza?

I looked around and remembered about a Maid Café near the train station. A Maid Café was a café where all their employees wore maid uniforms and treated the customers as their masters. The travel guidebook said it was fun to experience, which is what I wanted.

It was easy to find the café because the entryway—a white plaster gate with a big pink bow on top—reminded me of an old Disney movie. I entered the gate, which led me to a tunnel covered with posters of young women in maid costumes smiling widely and rode an elevator up to the seventh floor. As the door opened, I found myself in a narrow corridor which was the café's entrance. Two young maids greeted me and called me "princess" and "mistress." One of them brought me to a large room painted in bright pink and settled me at one of the long tables facing a narrow stage.

The café was too raucous for my taste, but it was also entertaining. Something that I couldn't find in the States. As the maid—her name was Keiko—provided me with a pink, heart-shaped menu. In broken English, she suggested to try their omelet fried rice called *Pipiyopiyopiyo* Chickpea Rice. She smiled when I agreed to order it.

When my food came, Keiko used a ketchup bottle to draw my face—in manga style, complete with my checkered bucket hat—on the omelet because I didn't have any specific request. Her white teeth showed fully as she grinned, accepting my praise for her skill. But she forbade me to eat.

"Why?"

"Need a spell," she chirped.

"Spell?"

"Me first." She pointed at her nose. "Then you." She pointed at me.

I nodded and watched her.

Still smiling, Keiko used her fingers to make a heart sign and began swinging her body while saying "*moe, moe,*" and thrusting her heart fingers toward the food while saying "*kyun.*"

I didn't know the meaning of the spell, but it sounded cute.

"Remember?"

She gave me two thumbs-up as I repeated the words and the movement perfectly and said, "Together."

In unison, we did the spell's words and the movements, and then she let me eat and took the tray back with her.

In the meantime, four maids came out on the small stage and began singing and dancing while the visitors clasped their hands, smiling. No wonder the Maid Café was one of the tourist destinations because this place was fun, and the staff was amusingly cheerful.

I had a good time in the café. Before I left, a different maid came to me. "Mistress, you paid for a meal and picture." She spoke in good English. "Let's take one before you go."

Then she called Keiko, and we took our picture together with a Polaroid camera.

While walking to the station for my next stop in Ginza, I couldn't stop smiling. If I went back to Tokyo with my family, I'd bring them to the café and let them experience the fun.

RYO

"Ryo, look what I found for Akiko." Kento lifted his finger with a keychain of Airou dangling from it. "She'll be excited because I finally found the one she likes."

Ryo eyed the keychain. "I didn't know she liked *Monster Hunter*."

"She started playing the game a year ago and loves it so much," Kento explained. "Although she doesn't really collect Airou keychain plush toys, I thought it'd be nice if she had it too."

"What happens if she doesn't want it?" Ryo asked curiously as they left the store.

"We'll see."

Ryo watched him put the keychain into a brown bag before putting it in his backpack. "I saw you had a conversation with a redheaded woman earlier. She showed her phone to you. What did she want?" he asked casually.

"Oh, that one," Kento shrugged, adjusting his backpack's straps. "That gaijin couldn't speak Japanese and used Google Translate to ask me to give the keychain to her because she claimed she looked at it first when I took it from the display. When I refused, she said she has collected the keychains and doesn't have the one I bought. So she asked me to give it to her." He shook his head. "That lady was so demanding. But to be honest, if it wasn't for Akiko, I'd have given it to her."

"Why?"

"She almost cried when she begged."

"Really?" Ryo pursed his lips, considering why the Female Waldo was desperate for the keychain. "Well, good thing you didn't give it to her. She is selfish."

Kento raised his eyebrows. "How do you know that woman is selfish? Do you know her?"

"Not really." Ryo wiped his damp forehead with his palm. "I ..."

His words were interrupted by a buzzing coming from his phone in the back pocket of his pants.

"It's Takeru." He looked at the display. "Sorry, I should take this. He might have found more apartments for me."

Kento nodded, and Ryo brought the phone to his ear.

"Hey, Takeru."

"Hey, Ryo. How are you?" A cheerful voice came through from the other end.

"Great. Still jet lagged, but I couldn't sleep, so I went to Akihabara with Kento to look for computers," said Ryo.

"You chose the right person for computers." Takeru chuckled. "Hey, were your mom and Akiko upset that they had to wait so long for you yesterday?"

"Nah, they understood." Ryo looked at his shoes and kicked a tiny pebble on the sidewalk. "Did you call me because you have good news?"

Ryo felt his stomach drop to the floor as Takeru let out a long sigh. "Sorry, I checked all the apartments I know of, but no one is available right away. Unless you want to wait a month or two...."

"No," Ryo interrupted, massaging his temple. "I won't wait for next month. It isn't good for me to stay in my mom's house." He glanced at Kento pretending not to listen to the conversation and looked at the Demon Slayer billboard on one of the buildings. "You know what my mom did this morning?"

"What?"

"She woke up very early to prepare a complete breakfast with grilled fish, miso soup, rolled omelet, and pickle. Don't think that I don't appreciate her effort. I do appreciate it." Ryo rubbed the back of his neck. "I know she did out of love, but this is too much. For twenty-five years, she's been busy with Akiko, and I don't want her to have extra work because of me."

"I think you're overreacting. First, moms always love spoiling their kids. Second, your mom loves cooking, so it's normal for her to cook a lot," Takeru said. "Besides, the only available room is the one near the cemetery."

Exhaling, Ryo closed his eyes.

"Can you wait for another month?" asked his best friend.

"No."

There was a silence on the other end, and Ryo only heard Takeru's breath.

"So ... what do you want to do?" Takeru finally asked.

"Well." Ryo pressed his lips together hard, giving an immediate consideration. "Let's try the one near the cemetery." He shrugged as Kento's curious eyes locked on him as he heard "cemetery."

"Are you sure?" Takeru sounded hesitant. "Remember, my aunt is the manager there, and I don't want to make her upset if you cancel because of the redheaded woman."

"Don't worry, I won't."

"Okay. If you can guarantee that, I'll call my aunt," said Takeru.

"Thanks." Then they hung up.

Ryo felt Kento's eyes on him as he put the phone in his back pocket. Forcing a crooked smile, he met Kento's eyes. "My new apartment will be near a cemetery."

"You're crazy!" Kento's voice raised. His eyebrows met in the middle of his forehead. "Your mom and sister expect you to stay with them, but since they respect your privacy, they'll let you have your space. But you ..." Kento stopped and shook his head. "Did you forget that living near the cemetery is taboo? That's bad luck, Ryo. Besides, if they knew, they'd be very, very, very upset."

Somehow, Ryo could have guessed Kento's response. "I know. But this is the only one available within my budget."

"Can't you wait another month?"

"Considering how much my mom cooked for my breakfast, no," Ryo said stubbornly. "I'd rather live with instant ramen than see her like that. Look, that place is cheap, with a semi-furnished option so I don't have to worry about buying new furniture. Yes, the drawback is the apartment is near the cemetery. But I don't believe ghosts. Once someone dies, their spirit will go somewhere else, not roam around teasing people. Further, there is no such thing as having a stroke of bad luck just because you live near the cemetery."

The corners of Kento's lips turned down as he looked at Ryo solemnly. "You think like a gaijin."

Ryo's lips twitched. That was the second time someone had told him that. His friends and family never knew that he didn't believe in ghosts or myths, even before he went to the States, because he'd never openly shared his opinion about that.

Pressing his eyes shut briefly, he said, "I've already made up my mind."

Kento seemed about to say something, but no words came out of his mouth. Ryo took it to mean he was disappointed with Ryo's decision but didn't want to argue more. He watched Kento, who shrugged his shoulders and crossed the street. Ryo dragged his feet, following him. Not even a Subaru Impreza with Pikachu's face on its hood parked on the curbside sparked any comments. Their conversation became boring and focused on laptops and their specs. Beyond that, they didn't seem to have interesting topics to discuss.

BELLA

I had a blast in Ginza once I left Maid Café. The main street was closed to cars for weekend pedestrians. People took pictures in the middle of the road or simply walked around without worrying about cars or buses.

On Monday morning, as we'd planned, Sato-san picked me up at 9:00 a.m. As the car rolled through the rush hour traffic, I'd noticed that Sato-san was not meeting my eyes. He must have felt bad for not being able to take me out yesterday.

"Sato-san," I said. "How's your wife? I hope she feels much better today."

His face beamed. "Yes, she feels much better this morning. Yesterday after coming back from the hospital, she was still in pain, and the medicine didn't help much until we doubled the dosage—as directed by the doctor. She slept well last night. Thank you for asking, Bell-san."

He sighed, rubbing his eyebrows with a finger. "It isn't easy to get old. Once we are injured, it will take a longer time to heal."

I understood his remark. A couple of years ago, my mom fell and twisted her ankle. It took her two months to be able to walk normally again. My parents were a few years younger than Sato-san, but still, it took them longer to heal.

"I'm glad she is getting better." I gave Sato-san a sympathetic look. "And about yesterday, don't worry too much. I had a blast."

"Where did you go?" he asked.

"Akihabara and Ginza," I answered. "They are so amazing. I had lunch in a Maid Café." With a wide grin, I showed him the picture of Keiko and me.

Sato-san glanced at the picture. "I'm glad you had a wonderful day yesterday, Bell-san."

"Since you know I had fun yesterday, please don't feel bad for not being able to take me on the city tour. I still have fifty-eight more days to explore Tokyo."

"Thank you. My wife was so excited to meet you, Bell-san. Once she feels better, we can plan to go sightseeing again. Tell me where you want to go, and I'll take you there."

"I'm looking forward to it."

Sato-san looked please as he slowed down before a traffic light.

"Sato-san?" I asked.

He glanced at me.

"Is it … possible for you not to call me Bell-san but Bella?"

His eyebrows flared up. "Why?"

"I mean …" I pursed my lips. "I'm younger than you. I think it's better if you call me Bella."

"Ah." He nodded. His forehead smoothed, and wrinkles appeared at the corners of his eyes as he smiled. "I understand. But, since you're Bread Lounge's guest, I should call you Bell-san when people from Bread Lounge are present. That's how we show respect, Bella. If not, I'd be seen as a brazen person."

"I understand."

It had been twenty minutes—the rush hours were as bad as in Los Angeles. My eyes narrowed at the large golden sculpture on a black building as we stopped at another traffic light. I recognized the tall white tower as a Tokyo Skytree, but I didn't know what the sculpture was.

"What is that sculpture?" I pointed.

Sato-san followed my finger. "Oh, that is a golden flame from Asahi Beer, a well-known beer company in Japan."

I stared at it, but it didn't look like a flame to me.

"It looks like poop to me," I commented, then covered my mouth. "Sorry, I said something disrespectful."

"No need to worry, Bella." He chuckled. "That's what people say too."

"Really?"

He nodded.

I chuckled. "So, where are we now?" I put the dark-colored hat over my head. I wished the cap had a hole for my ponytail, so my hair didn't stick on my neck because right now, I had to hide it under the hat.

"Asakusa near Sumida River," he answered. "Ito-san managed to find a perfect location in the tourism area. If everything goes well, the café will be successful."

Then we passed a green bridge with three arches. "That bridge is called Umaya Bridge," said Sato-san, pointing at it.

"Umaya Bridge?" I pronounced it slowly. "What does 'Umaya' mean?"

He nodded. "It means 'horse stable.' In the shogunate era, they used this bridge to transport rice to the government with horses. If you cross the bridge, you can see some horse ornaments featured on the base of some lampposts."

"Interesting."

"It is. My wife and I like strolling the bridge and admiring the ornaments. If you walk to the northwest, you can find Sumida Park. It has many cherry trees, so people come here to enjoy the cherry blossoms when the flowers bloom around March and April. Too bad you came in summer. But keep it in mind. One day if you revisit the city, make sure to come then," he said.

"I hope I can come back again," I said. "So, are there any activities I can enjoy in summer?"

"Summer festivals and fireworks," he answered. "I'll give you the English-language link so you can check it out and find them. I believe you can have good memories while staying here."

"Awesome." My voice raised in excitement. I couldn't wait for the weekend. "Thanks for letting me know, Sato-san."

"Don't mention it, Bell-san, uh, Bella," he corrected. "Look, that's the café." I followed his direction and saw the green-roofed café on the corner of two streets as we passed in front of it.

Sato-san turned to the aisle between the café and office and parked behind the café. Soon we were standing on the patio where outdoor chairs and tables were tied on the ground with thick chains. There were no cream-colored umbrellas for each table with a bear hugging a red mug yet.

"Welcome to Little Bear Café in Tokyo, Bell-san." Sato-san grinned widely; his shoulders fell back while gesturing for me to enter the café. Pride gleamed in his dark brown eyes.

As we entered the café, a lady greeted us. She wore a white shirt and black pants with a light brown apron around her waist. Her short hair hid under Little Bear's dark brown cap. Her silver tag read "Naomi." She must be the manager because her hat was darker than the other staff's. Behind her were a dozen staff members, male and female. Most of them were young, maybe college age. Only a few looked older, possibly close to thirty. Most of the employees looked tense and lowered their eyes when they greeted us. That gesture made me uncomfortable.

Sato-san must have sensed my unease because he leaned forward and spoke to me in a low voice. "If they seem tense, it's because they aren't confident speaking in English, Bell-san."

"Oh."

Pulling up the corners of my lips, I stepped forward and bowed slightly. *"Hajimemashite, douzo yoroshiku."* In English, it meant roughly "Nice to meet you."

They all—including Sato-san—gasped, and their eyes widened like I had cast a spell that made things fly in the air.

What I did brought smiles to their faces, and their shoulders relaxed. That was what I expected to see.

"Bell-san, that's a wonderful surprise," said the manager. "My name is Naomi Mori. I'm a manager for this café. You can call me Nao, and you speak Japanese well." She smiled and gazed at the staff behind her, who nodded their heads, and some of them grinned widely, giving me a thumbs-up.

"Thank you," I said. If only they'd known how many times I'd practiced those words. "I'm still learning, and I hope you can help me with my Japanese."

"Yes, of course," said Nao. Then she turned to speak with her staff. Almost in unison, they turned and walked toward the chairs lined up around the projector screen for our teleconference with Bread Lounge headquarters later, and Sato-san signaled me to follow him for the café tour.

The café was terrific. The walls were painted cream with four big windows facing the streets, which could be cracked for air circulation and covered with shades on bright days. There were contemporary modular black sofas near the windows, softened with pastel pillows facing a few white square tables for a clean and modern look.

There were light-gray tables with metal legs for two and four people piled next to each other at the corner. Once the café was open, the tables would be placed in the middle with the chairs that we were using for the teleconference.

A cashier counter was facing toward the glass door to welcome visitors. Behind it was an oval counter with low shelves and cabinets. There were barstools around the counter where customers could enjoy their coffee while watching baristas make the coffee.

The café was perfect for everyone because it had a modern and youthful vibe but was also cozy with a soft touch of Japanese tradition with small cream paper lanterns on the ceiling and some *ensō* paintings—circular brush strokes—and simple Japanese calligraphy on the walls.

It was beautiful, and I fell in love with it.

After the tour was done and I was about to sit on the empty chair next to Sato-san, my ears picked up the sound of skinny high heels clicking on the floor. Everyone else must have heard, too, because, almost in unison, we turned to the entrance where a thin, tall, and pretty woman in a slim gray business suit elegantly entered the café. Her brown, curved-out bob made her angular dark eyes pop. And I recognized her.

That twenty-five-year-old woman was Sara Ito, the daughter of Bread Lounge's owner. Instantly, her credentials flashed in my mind: bachelor's degree and master's degree with honors from UC Berkeley, and the Japan *Time* magazine named her as one of the most successful young entrepreneurs in Japan.

Standing up from my seat, I approached her while the rest of the people in the room rose to their feet, bowing slightly to her.

"Welcome to Tokyo, Bella Bell-san." She stopped in front of me and extended her hand. "It's nice to meet you."

"Thank you, Ito-san." I accepted her hand. "Likewise."

We smiled as our eyes met, and she turned to give a nod of acknowledgment to Sato-san and the staff.

"When did you arrive, Bell-san?" she asked as we walked to the seat. She spoke in perfect American English.

"Saturday morning."

"I hope you had a chance to take a glimpse of this city."

"Yes, I did. In fact, I visited Akihabara and Ginza yesterday, and those are amazing," I answered.

"It sounds like you had a blast," she smiled, and I caught a gleam in her eyes as they scanned the café. "So, what do you think about this café?"

"It's so wonderful, Ito-san. Kudos to the interior designer."

"I'm glad you like my design," she said, her cheeks going slightly pink.

My mouth fell open. "You ... did this? Wow! You're so talented, Ito-san."

"Thank you, but when it's only the two of us, please call me Sara, as my American friends do." She offered me a smile.

"Ah, you should call me Bella, then."

Her smile became bigger. "Sure." Then she turned to Sato-san. "What's the agenda for today?"

"You'll give a short speech to us here, then at ten o'clock, our teleconference will start, and Ito-*sama* will give his speech; after that, Bell-san can start her training," said Sato-san respectfully. He called Sara's father Ito-sama, to show more respect because he was the owner of Bread Lounge.

Nodding, Sara rose to her feet and stood in front of a podium with her shoulders back and chin high, giving her short speech eloquently. She welcomed everybody to be part of the café's journey, introduced me as the trainer, and wished us luck with the training sessions.

While listening to Sato-san's translation, I couldn't take my eyes off her and wished I could give a speech like she did. At ten sharp, the teleconference began. When her father gave his speech, I knew where Sara got the skill.

Sara rose from her seat as the conference was done, and I followed suit.

"Thank you for arranging everything," she said to Sato-san. Then she turned to shake my hand. "Bell-san, I have to leave now, and good luck with the training. It's nice to meet you, and I hope to see you soon."

"Thanks, Ito-san," I said as we shook hands. "It's nice to meet you too."

"When you aren't too busy, let's have lunch together. I'm happy to show you many good foods that you can't find in the States," she offered.

"I'd love to."

After saying a few words to Nao and her staff, Sara turned and left the café. I took a seat next to Sato-san while Nao was already standing in front of the white screen, ready to teach.

RYO

Ryo stood on the patio in front of Little Bear Café and glanced at his watch to find that he was five minutes early for his appointment with Sara.

Last night, he'd finally contacted her for the first time since he came back home and told her about him moving back for good. She sounded happy with the news and invited him to check out her new café and then have lunch with her. Although he was reluctant, he agreed to meet at eleven on Monday morning.

From the big window, he saw Sara inside the café, talking to her staff. While waiting, he decided to check the café's façade and its surroundings.

Sara was a brilliant businesswoman because she found the best location for the café. It was near tourist attractions like Oshinari Park—a canal with greenery and flowers by Sumida River—Tokyo Skytree, Sensoji Temple, and Sumida Park. The café would be packed with people who came to Sumida Park during the cherry blossom season in spring.

The café would benefit from international tourists who were not familiar with Japanese cafés. Although Little Bear had limited cafés outside the States, the brand had become famous among the millennials, TikTokers, and Instagrammers.

A warm fuzzy feeling of joy for Sara's achievements rose to his chest. If Little Bear agreed to trust her to carry its flag for Japanese markets, the company valued her more than others.

He was taking a picture of Tower Skytree from the patio when Sara called his name. Turning around, he felt his heart jolt to see Sara sway toward him. She looked more beautiful, mature, and confident than he'd remembered. Her dark eyes sparkled under long eyelashes, and her cheeks were pink and vibrant under her thin layer of makeup.

"Finally." Sara extended her hand to shake his hand. "Good to see you again, Ryo."

"Likewise." Ryo felt her soft hand firmly shake his. His nose caught a whiff of pleasant and clean perfume that he recalled as Sara's favorite.

"You look great." Sara gazed at him.

"Getting old here compared to you," Ryo smiled, catching the admiration in her eyes. Instinctively, when a pretty woman looked at him like that, he wanted to puff his chest proudly like a peacock spreading its beautiful feathers. However, his feelings toward Sara were purely friendship, and he wasn't interested in crossing the line.

"I hope you haven't waited too long," she said, glancing at her watch. "The teleconference took a bit longer than I'd anticipated."

"No," he answered. "I chose an early train so I could see the surroundings."

"I'm glad." Her eyebrows smoothed. "Come, I'll show you my café." Pride was noticeable in her voice.

"Are they in training now?" asked Ryo as they walked closer to the café. Inside, the staff was sitting in a semicircle. Each of them had a folder of training materials where they wrote notes while listening to a woman in a dark brown cap pointing at the projector screen.

Sara nodded. "Today is their first day."

"If we go in, are you sure we won't interrupt them? I think it's better to look from the entrance. Only if you agree," he added quickly.

Sara tilted her head, considering, and nodded. "Okay. We can see the whole café from here anyway." She smiled.

Ryo smiled back at her.

Listening to her explanation, Ryo admired the café's interior. It looked modern and youthful but cozy at the same time. It didn't look like the Little Bear Café near their university. Still, it was enough to wake up some memories where he and Sara had spent time in the café during group studies or discussions.

"Those are my staff in Tokyo." She pointed. "Since I don't want to compete head-to-head with other American cafés, I've only opened one right now, but we plan to open more next year."

"I think that's a good move," Ryo agreed.

Sara beamed. "The lady who's giving a lecture is my café manager. She's been working with us for years, and I trust her to manage my café here. And do you see the middle-aged man in the front seat?" Ryo nodded. "That's my translator, and next to him is the trainer from Little Bear corporate."

"It's nice of you to provide the trainer with a translator." Ryo looked at her sideways.

"I wish I didn't have to. But that's okay. It's easier to find a translator who can speak English than to find a trainer who can speak Japanese," Sara said.

"That's right." Ryo nodded in agreement.

"So, what do you think about my café?" Sara asked as they stood facing each other on the patio. Her eyes looked straight into his.

"Well." Ryo smiled, shifting his eyes to the café. "It's a beautiful café. I love it. You chose the right color and decoration. The furniture looks comfortable too. I believe many people will enjoy the café as much as we did when we were students." His eyes shifted back to catch her cheeks becoming redder.

"I'd thought you didn't remember our time together in the café," she whispered, lowering her eyes.

"Of course, I remember." Ryo chuckled. "Our friendship is beautiful, and I'm glad to have you, Takeru, and Kento as my best friends. You guys have always been there for Akiko and me. Especially you, Sara. I know you're busy, but you've always made time to accompany my sister to her doctor's appointments. That means a lot to Akiko and me, Sara."

All of a sudden, the pinkish color on her cheeks was gone. A numb pain pricked his heart to see her confidence shaken as Sara wrenched her fingers, shifting from one foot to another. He didn't want to hurt her, but he wanted her to realize that he never wanted to change the fact that she was one of his best friends.

An awkward silence fell between them for a few moments until Ryo remembered something. "Sara, you told me yesterday that you're going to show me your office in Tokyo. I want to see it before lunch," he said casually.

The words pulled Sara back. A small smile spread on her lips but didn't meet her eyes. "That's right. Let's go now, so we still have enough time to catch up before your meeting with Takeru." She looked at him carefully.

"Takeru can wait for me if I'm late." Ryo smiled.

Her eyes sparkled at the answer, and they walked to Sara's car parked behind the café.

"Is Jinbei still your favorite place to go?" asked Sara as their car was rolling to the main street. "I remember you like its *okonomiyaki*."

"I'm surprised you remember," Ryo commented.

Sara glanced sideways. "That place is my favorite too. So it isn't difficult to remember."

Ryo nodded and peeked through the windshield. No wonder Takeru stopped pursuing Sara because her feelings for Ryo were strong.

"That's Takeru's favorite too," he said casually, pulling the sun visor down and opening the mirror. He fixed his hair with his fingers.

Sara looked at him across the car before turning her eyes to the traffic. "Really?"

"Yup." Ryo closed the cover and pulled the visor up. "He introduced me to it. You might have forgotten how much of a picky eater I was when I was young. I didn't like much food, including okonomiyaki. When I met him for the first time after we moved to Tokyo, he brought me to Jinbei and forced me to eat that dish."

Sara wrinkled her nose. "Takeru is always a brute among us."

"That's because you don't know him as well as I do," Ryo commented. "Takeru seems to be rough, but his heart is gentle. I owe him a lot for everything, including learning to love Akiko better."

Sara squeezed her eyebrows. "You're always gentle to her."

Ryo shook. "Nope."

"I don't understand."

With a sigh, Ryo shifted his body on the seat. "I never shared this story with anyone. But it happened. I'd known about my sister's condition once I realized she was different than any girl our age. My parents had told me to be kind to Oneechan, and I obeyed, so they didn't need to repeat that. But they didn't know that I was jealous of all the attention they gave Akiko.

"One time, when I was eight, I stole her favorite Barbie doll and cut its hair before putting it back in her basket. That doll was her favorite, and I destroyed it." A short noise of surprise slipped out of Sara's throat as Ryo paused.

"You might want to defend me by saying 'you were little at that time,' which was true. But I was mean." Ryo continued. "Oneechan cried once she found out and had a high fever after that. As you know, she isn't supposed to be too emotional. I was scared, but I didn't tell anyone about that. But Takeru knew."

"How?"

Ryo gave a bitter smile. "He happened to be there because he was about to invite me to play with his new Legos."

"Did he tell your parents?" Ryo detected curiosity in Sara's voice.

He shook. "He didn't corner me or tell my parents. He pointed out about Akiko's condition and why I shouldn't hurt her feelings. The way he explained it to me was different than my parents or other adults did." He turned to Sara. "Can you imagine that, at the age of eight, Takeru gave me the best advice I've gotten in my life?"

Sara glanced at him but didn't say a word.

"Yeah, I've become a good man because of Takeru," said Ryo. "And I've liked eating much more food because of him too." He let out a low chuckle and tapped his stomach. "Good thing I exercise a lot."

"Since then ... you changed?" asked Sara.

Ryo nodded, shifting his eyes skyward. "Takeru made me realize how short her time is, and I want to make my sister happy. Since we are twins and I believe she can feel me, I always imagined her next to me in anything I did." With a small smile, he looked at Sara. "That will answer your questions about why I always did my studies and exercises with full speed and energy."

For a few moments, no one said a word. Sara clenched her fingers on the wheels.

"And ... w-why did you tell me that story?" Sara broke the silence and sucked her lower lip.

Ryo shrugged. "I defended my best friend because you called him a 'brute.'"

Sara mumbled something under her breath, and Ryo didn't hear what she said but didn't want to know either. Deep down, he wished she would stop loving him and begin to see Takeru with fresh eyes because his best friend was a kind man.

The sun was at its peak when they passed Tokyo Tower in silence.

BELLA

The digital clock on the bedroom wall showed five thirty when I entered my apartment. Carelessly, I threw my purse on the sofa and then crawled onto the floor before flopping down on my back with a huge sigh. I felt tired, and my jet lag hadn't been worn off yet, even though I'd been in Tokyo for eleven days. The idea of going to bed was so tempting, but I refrained since my stomach growled, demanding food.

I stared at the white ceiling. My days in the café were productive, and my training sessions were fine. It was not as smooth as I'd expected, mostly because of the language barrier, but Sato-san and Nao were a great help. They worked simultaneously to translate words from and to the staff.

But I dreaded the training because Sara had moved the soft opening date up from the fifth week to the fourth. It meant the grand opening would move up too. It didn't surprise me because it happened with any franchisee anyway. It was manageable most of the time, especially if the café staff had experience making drinks.

But moving up the date for Tokyo's café was too ambitious for my taste. Not only did I have to speed up my training, but I also had to make sure the other staff had the same skill sets as the baristas.

"Please reconsider your plan, Sara," I had commented during my meeting with her earlier today in the café's back room. "Look at this calendar." I pointed at a big calendar on the wall. "This week, I'll spend half of my time training Nao and her assistants using Little Bear's software system for accounting and ordering. It won't be a big deal because the software is user-friendly, and our programmer has already added the Japanese alphabet underneath the English words.

"However, I am concerned about the staff's skills. All recipes and instructions are in English. The staff will be busy writing them down in Japanese and won't watch me make the drinks. They need to observe me more than they write." I turned to her. Her lips became thinner, listening to my explanation. "If you agree, we could ask Sato-san to translate the recipes and the instructions in Japanese, but it would mean he has to juggle assisting me and working on the project. I suggest keeping our original timeline."

Sara gnawed her lower lip. My stomach clenched, anxious for her decision.

"Well, they can learn while doing their job," she said. "Let's give it a try first. If we find the staff hasn't mastered the skills by the third week, you should tell me."

My shoulders dropped. "Okay."

From my conversation with Sara this morning, I knew she was an ambitious woman and wouldn't change her mind about something until it hit a wall. But she was a smart woman too. It was just too bad she forgot that not all people were as bright as her.

Rubbing my eyes, I decided to pacify my stomach first and then think of a way to make the staff learn quickly. I might need to seek advice from my manager.

Pushing myself up, I went to the kitchen, took out a rice curry from the freezer, and popped it into a microwave for five minutes. I wanted to cook, but I was too tired each night I got back home from work.

While waiting, I pulled the drawer open for a spoon when my nose smelled something rotten coming from the sink.

Huh, something must have stuck there. My nose wrinkled. *I'll flush it down.* My eyes searched for a garbage disposal switch, but I didn't see it anywhere.

Maybe in the main panel near the bathroom? I wondered.

In front of the panel, all the buttons were in Japanese.

"Yeah, great!" I huffed in exasperation.

I went back to my bedroom for my phone and brought it to the panel. Using Google Translate, I couldn't find any word for "garbage disposal."

Let me call Harper. Maybe she could help. I dialed her number. Since we'd exchanged our numbers, we'd texted back and forth because I asked many things, and the Moore sisters were always happy to help me.

"Hi, Bel," she said. "What's up?"

"Are you at home?"

"Nope. My Thursday class is always short, so I'm at Mike's apartment now. Why?"

Mike was her boyfriend whom I'd never met.

"Um, I think I have a problem with the kitchen sink."

"What problem?"

"My sink smells like sewage. Something's stuck in there. Could you tell me where to find the garbage disposal switch?" I asked.

For a few seconds, there was silence on her end. Then I heard her chuckle.

"Are you laughing?" I felt offended.

"Bella, there's no garbage disposal here."

"What?"

"Shocking, huh?" she commented. "But don't worry. Since last year, the management building has added disposals in each apartment. However, the progress is slow. I just got mine a month ago, so your apartment might have one ... once you return to the States."

Great.

"So, how do I get rid of the sink smell?" I scratched my temple.

"Just clean the sink," she answered cheerfully. "Are you in your kitchen?"

"Yes."

"I'll guide you. Now, look at the drain. You should see a basket with a filter or a net. Do you see it?"

Holding my breath, I looked down at it. "Yes."

"Great, take it out and toss the filter away. Clean the basket with soap, then cover it again with a new net," she instructed.

"W-wait. Why should I clean the basket? Isn't it a barrier to prevent cockroaches or bugs creeping up through the pipes into the house?" I asked. And her response confused me.

She laughed hard, and I could hear Mike laughing too in the background. I groaned and closed my eyes, imagining they were rolling on the floor, laughing while hugging their stomachs.

"Stop it. That's not funny."

And she did. "Well." She cleared her throat. "Sorry. I shouldn't have, but you're funny."

I pouted as if she were in front of me.

"Don't be mad. That is a common misconception. But trust me, no bugs would crawl up to the fifth floor," she said lightly. "So just take the net out, clean the basket, and put the new net over it. And no more sewer smell."

"Any other solution?" I asked.

"Nope. That's what you have to do."

"Okay. Thanks." I sighed and hung up. Reluctantly, I looked down at the sink again and backed away as the sewer smell entered my nose. "Eww ... that's gross!"

I bit my lower lip, considering Harper's advice, but I didn't want to touch the basket with my hands.

I grabbed my bag and the house key and went down to the Family Mart to buy gloves. It was about a thirty-minute walk. The sky was darker when I reached the store. I took one of the shopping baskets and began picking up cleaning items.

After paying, I carried the bags and pushed the glass door with my elbow. The smell of rain embraced me when I was halfway out. It was pouring!

My jaw dropped. How could it be? Wasn't it summer?

Groaning, I went back into the store for an umbrella. I vaguely remembered there was one umbrella left on the shelf near the magazine rack. But I was too late; a man with his back toward me walked closer and picked it up.

Oh no!

Feeling dismayed, I looked at the man as he paid and left with the last umbrella. Hoping the store had more stock in the backroom, I came forward to the cashier and asked in broken Japanese. *"Kasa arimasu ka?"*

"No more," he shook his head. Then he said something in long sentences that I didn't understand, but he must have explained why there weren't more umbrellas.

My stomach sunk. There was no way I could walk four blocks in the heavy rain. I missed my car.

After thanking him, I walked out to the patio and gazed up at the dark sky. The heavy drops were drumming down to the asphalt and creating puddles that splashed each time people stepped in them. I stretched my hand to feel the rain. It was slightly warm.

Letting out a sigh, I dried my hand on my pants. *Great. I'm hungry, my sink smells, no more umbrella in the store, and it's pouring! God, why is it raining in summer?*

As I wondered how long until the rain would stop, I felt a tap on my left shoulder. I jumped and turned around to see a man standing in front of me. Under the fuzzy white light coming from the fluorescent lamp above me, I found he looked familiar. In a split second, I recognized him.

The Frowner.

My mouth opened but clamped down quickly as he handed me the clear umbrella with a sticker that said "500 *yen*" stuck on it. He was the man who bought the umbrella.

Composing myself, I glanced at the umbrella and shook my head. "No, thank you." My voice was flat. I didn't want to accept the offer from a stuck-up man.

"It's pouring. You'll be drenched if you walk into the rain without an umbrella," he said.

Like you care! But I said, "No, thank you. I'll wait for the rain to stop."

He looked skyward, then stretched his hand to feel the rain. "I don't think the rain will stop soon, though."

"Are you a weatherman now?" The words just came out of my mouth.

The Frowner chuckled. "I grew up here, so I know better about the weather than you." He waved the umbrella again in front of my nose like a windshield wiper. "Take this. You need it."

I didn't budge and looked away.

"Are you ... too proud to take this?" he asked, tilting his head.

My head whirled to him. "Me, proud?"

He nodded.

I scoffed. "Look who's talking."

A crease appeared between his eyebrows. "It's okay if you don't want it." He shrugged but didn't walk away. Instead, he crossed his arms, hugging the umbrella in front of his chest.

Why won't he leave? I thought with an exaggerated sigh.

As I lifted my eyes to the sky, a single stroke of lightning flashed, illuminating the buildings and trees around us, followed by thunder booming loudly.

Gasping, I covered my eyes with my hands. My shopping bags fell on my feet, and a can of cleaning powder rolled out from the bag and dunked into the flood around the curbside. My heart was pounding so hard I could feel it in my fingertips around my eyes. That lightning was scary; it was as if the sky was angry.

"Are you okay?" the Frowner asked me as I opened my eyes.

I nodded, swallowing. "That was a scary one."

"It was."

Holding the umbrella under his arm, he picked up the can, gathered the plastic bags, and gave them to me.

"Thank you." My fingers touched his as I took the bags from him.

"My pleasure to help my neighbors." He flashed a smile.

"So you already moved in?"

He didn't answer.

Gazing at him, I adjusted my hands on the shopping bags. "I remembered you said you were here to visit your family. Why do you live in the apartment then?"

"You have a good memory." He tapped his forehead. "My reason to live in an apartment is my business."

I scowled.

Another lightning strike, but this time wasn't as scary as the first one because it happened in the distance. The rain tapered off a bit but didn't stop.

The Frowner thrust his umbrella forward again. "Take this."

"How about you?" I asked, looking at him without taking the umbrella.

"I'm a man."

"What's that supposed to mean?" I pressed my lips tighter.

Looking at me, he pointed to the sky. "It's pouring. If you walked in the rain, your thin blouse and pants would stick on your body." His eyes moved up and down my body in a practical manner. "And would reveal everything. Under the neon lights from the stores and the streetlights, it would be the best view along the way for men ... or women."

Automatically, I lifted one hand across my chest.

He chuckled and waved the umbrella in front of me.

Something swirled in my chest to see him gazing down warmly at me. He was starting to act human and not haughty and cold like he had on the plane. He'd helped pick up my shopping bags without me asking. Maybe he wasn't a bad man after all.

"Thanks." I took the umbrella.

He didn't say anything but lifted his shirt collar, ready to step into the rain.

"Hey, wait, if you've already moved to Apple Heights, we can share this umbrella," I offered.

The Frowner turned around. His lips twitched. "Will you feel disappointed if I say I'll move in soon, and now I need to go somewhere else?"

I felt the heat rush into my cheeks. It must have been noticeable because his lips quirked up, and his eyes sparkled with mischief for a moment.

With a huff, I opened my umbrella and stepped out into the rain. The rain hit my umbrella like pebbles pelting me from above.

"Bye, neighbor, try to avoid open space, okay?" the Frowner said loudly as he stood next to me. He hunched his shoulders, holding his collar as the rain poured over his head and dripped down his face, his neck, and his body.

Before I said anything, he flashed a smile, turned around, and jogged toward the main road.

What a weird man!

Stunned by his act, I followed his figure for a few seconds. But the thunder growled in the distance and forced me to walk faster.

Forty minutes later, I arrived at my apartment, and my body was wet from my knees down. The rain slowed me down. But the Frowner was right. Without the umbrella, I would have been drenched and revealed my curves.

I shook the excess water off the umbrella before entering and leaned it against the wall. If I met him again sometime, I'd return it to him.

The rain here wasn't as cold as the rain in California, but still, a warm shower felt good on my skin. After changing into my pajamas, I went to the kitchen and cleaned the sink. It was easier than I'd imagined. After that, I heated up my curry rice again.

Chewing my food slowly, my mind went to the Frowner and his weird act. He had to go somewhere but gave up his umbrella for me and let himself get drenched. It was enough to erase his haughtiness from my mind.

Still, thinking of him as my next-door neighbor was too much.

"Well, don't worry about it, then," I muttered. "If, in the end, we still can't get along, I won't be here too long anyway."

I got up to put my dirty plate in the sink and went to the bathroom to brush my teeth. A redheaded woman with soft baby blue eyes looked back at me. "Too bad, this Saturday, I have to work. If not, I could explore Tokyo." I spoke to myself in the mirror with my mouth full of toothpaste foam. "I can't wait to see it all." I looked directly at my eyes and sighed. "Hang in there, Bella."

I spat the foam in the sink and rinsed my mouth with water. The warmth of my bed called me as I dried my face with a towel. Turning off the light in the hallway, I entered my bedroom and jumped on the bed. It was nice lying on it, but it would be nicer if I were on my bed in California.

"Well, life is good, and I should be thankful," I reminded myself.

Outside, the rain continued falling, and there was a soft rumble in the distance, and I let the sounds soothe me to sleep.

RYO

Ryo stood on the balcony of his new apartment, looking at the afternoon sky. The Tuesday weather was less humid, with a soft evening breeze. The sun was almost to the horizon, creating a glorious dark orange sky, and a flock of blackbirds flew toward the cemetery.

Yesterday, when he moved in, it didn't take Ryo long to arrange everything because he didn't have a lot. His clothes were already in the wardrobe, his shoes in the tall gray cabinet near the genkan, and his books were on the bookshelf. The semi-furnished apartment came with more furniture than he needed. He only bought a bed and pillow covers, a blanket, towels, and personal toiletries.

His mom lent him a few *zabuton*—cushions for sitting on the floor—and a *kotatsu*, a low wooden table with an electric heater underneath. They were already in his living room, an area practically shared with his bedroom. The kotatsu would be great for winter, but for now, it was a regular table until the weather became unbearably cold.

Ryo didn't have to worry about food either, because his mom had packed almost a dozen containers of food that were in his fridge.

Earlier in the morning, he'd had an interview with a popular American online marketplace based in Japan. The interview was challenging but went well. Ryo expected to get a second interview sometime next week.

Massaging his neck, Ryo closed his eyes as the soft breeze picked up and touched his face. As his mind was preoccupied, his eyes snapped open when the gentle wind brought savory wafts of sizzling meat with molasses. At once, his olfactory senses exploded in delight and stimulated his saliva.

That delicious smell also brought him back to the summers he and his friends had spent barbecuing in parks or on beaches. A year ago, Ryo was playing beach volleyball in Corona del Mar with his friends.

"Stop it!" he rebuked himself, slapping his forehead. "You're in Tokyo now."

Yet he lifted his nose up to find out where the smell came from. It must have come from the other side of the building.

His stomach rumbled.

"What do I want for dinner?" he muttered, not feeling like eating his mom's food. "I want something grilled." Then Ryo remembered the *yakitori*—chicken skewers—at one of the standing bars in the strip mall. "Maybe I should go there," he decided.

He locked the door and glanced at the unit where Female Waldo lived. The last meeting with her almost a week ago flashed in his mind. Initially, he hadn't recognized her because the neon light outside the store wasn't very bright. Then, as his eyes adjusted, he recognized the turned-up nose and red hair.

Ryo didn't want to deal with her. However, something on her face that night stopped him from leaving. Maybe the sorrow on her face or her whining about the rain, the smelly sink, and the umbrella. As a person who had lived in California for years, he'd known there was almost zero rain in summer.

However, Tokyo's weather was different. The rainy season was in the early summer, and Female Waldo came right before the end of the season when bursts of rainfall happened unpredictably.

She'd also trembled after the lightning struck. Ryo had felt her fingers shaking when he gave the shopping bag to her.

Deep down, he felt sorry because no one told her about the weather.

Although he didn't like her much, he found bantering with her was refreshing. Oddly, he might want to look for more of that.

But maybe she thought of him as a nuisance.

Letting out a chuckle, he put the key in his back pocket and tapped his other pocket to check for his wallet. Spinning on his heel, he heard a high-pitched voice come from somewhere near the elevator. "Here, kitty, kitty, kitty. Here, Shiro, Shiro. Come here, boy."

The voice belonged to a woman with long blonde hair, and she was wearing a light orange button-down blouse with white wide-leg pants. At first, she didn't see him because she was scanning the hallway searching for her cat. After a few steps, she realized she wasn't alone. A deep crease appeared on her forehead, but it disappeared quickly and was replaced by a smile.

"Hello there." She waved. "You must be our new neighbor. I saw you move in yesterday, but I didn't get to say hello."

"Hi." He waved back.

"I'm Harper Moore. Unit five twelve. Nice to meet you ..." She stuck out her hand.

"Ryo Yamada." He accepted her hand. "Call me Ryo. Nice to meet you, Harper."

Her eyebrows flew up. "You're Japanese? I haven't seen any Japanese people in this building."

To his surprise, Harper switched from English to Japanese, and her Japanese was excellent. Rubbing his cheek lightly, he offered a smile and replied in Japanese, "I know. Mostly foreigners live here."

"Aren't you afraid of the cemetery?" Her eyes narrowed. Then she covered her mouth. "Oops, sorry, I didn't mean to offend you."

Ryo chuckled at her straightforward manner. "Don't worry. I'm not offended at all. And no, I don't feel afraid. Even before I lived in the States, I didn't believe in ghosts."

"I see." Harper nodded and spoke in English again. "No wonder your English is good."

"Your Japanese is better than my English," Ryo commented and took the chance to look at Harper closely. She must be around his age. It would be nice if he could get along with her.

Harper chuckled, tossing her hair. "I'm an English teacher in Akasaka International School."

"No wonder." He nodded. "By the way, are you looking for your cat?"

Harper placed her hands on her waist. "Well, I didn't really lose him. My cat must have slipped out when I brought my groceries in. I didn't realize it until I couldn't find him. Umm, it's happened a few times, though," she added quickly as if she could read his mind. "But Shiro always comes home quickly. Today is the longest he's been outside, and I'm getting worried. If my sister knew I lost her cat, I'd be doomed." She looked around the hallway again.

"I see. Let me help you," he offered. "What's its name again?"

"Shiro."

In a few minutes, they were busy calling the cat's name.

"Are you American?" he asked between callings.

"Canadian, but I moved to Chicago when I was ten," Harper explained.

"Ah, Chicago." He placed a hand over his heart. "I've fallen in love with Lou Malnati's."

"Really? That's my favorite pizza."

"No kidding." Ryo widened his eyes. "It's going to be difficult for me now if I crave it."

Harper tilted her head. "You're moving back for good?"

He nodded.

She must have detected the wave of sadness in his face because she offered a genuine look of sympathy. For a few beats, they didn't say a word.

Ryo almost jumped when Harper gave a happy squeal as a big, fat white cat with beige on the tips of its ears appeared from the corner and sauntered toward them with its tail high in the air.

"Shiro!" Harper darted to the cat, picked it up, and cradled it as if it were a baby. The cat let out a gentle mew. "Bad, bad boy! I was worried about you."

"So, this is Shiro." Ryo looked at the cat, who pressed his head on Harper's arm and purred when she tickled his chin.

Before Harper could respond, a female voice called her name. He turned around to see another tall woman with honey-blonde hair in a ponytail coming out of the elevator. He could see the relation in their features. The woman had Harper's face but with different colored eyes and a smaller nose. She carried a heavy backpack on her shoulders and two thick books in her hands.

"That's my sister, Avery," said Harper, pointing with her chin. "She is a student at—" But Avery interrupted her.

"Shiro." She stopped in front of her sister. "What happened? Did you let him out again?" She squinted at Harper.

Harper rolled her eyes. "No, he just slipped out when I got back from the grocery store. Ask Mike."

"He'd defend you." Avery gave her books to her sister, took the cat, and cooed at it in a low, gentle voice. Then she turned to Ryo. "Hi. I'm Avery. Nice to meet you."

Ryo waved. "Ryo. Nice to meet you too."

"Ryo is the new tenant in unit five twenty-two. The only Japanese person here, and he isn't afraid of ghosts." Harper grinned widely.

Ryo grinned back at her. Somehow, he already liked these sisters.

"Five twenty-two," Avery muttered, then her eyes lit up. "Oh, you live next to Bella, then."

Harper clicked her finger. "That's right. Have you met her yet?"

"Um, who?" Ryo arched one of his eyebrows. And a face flashed into his mind. *Oh, she must be talking about Female Waldo.*

"Maybe you haven't because she's been busy lately," remarked Harper before allowing him to answer.

"Will she join us this evening?" asked Avery.

"I don't know."

"Too bad." Avery caressed the cat's head. Then she turned to her sister. "Why don't we invite him?" She gestured toward Ryo. "Mike and Joe would be happy to have another man to help them."

"Ah." Harper glanced at her sister and then Ryo doubtfully. "Maybe it's too sudden …."

"I'll be happy to help," Ryo blurted out. Heat rushed to his cheeks after that. "If it's okay."

"Of course. We always have plenty of food," said Harper cheerfully. "Come. The more, the merrier." Gesturing Ryo for following, the sisters turned around and sauntered to their unit.

With a smile on his lips, Ryo followed them. As he entered their apartment, he caught a familiar smell.

"So, this is where the smell is coming from," he muttered.

Inside, Harper introduced him to Joe, Elena, Cameron, and Mike—Harper's boyfriend. All of them were English teachers in Tokyo, except for Mike and Cameron. They were programmers.

A happy smile flashed on Mike's face as he gave Ryo a floral kitchen apron. Together with Joe, the three men went to the balcony.

While flipping the burger patties and sausages on the grill, Ryo had a good conversation with Mike and Joe about the Los Angeles Lakers and New York Knicks. Ryo chuckled to see Cameron banter with Joe over the sausage she stole as she came out of the balcony.

For the first time since he'd arrived in Tokyo, Ryo's heart felt lighter, and everything looked brighter.

BELLA

My watch showed 6:45 p.m. Harper had invited me to dinner at six, but something had happened in the café that Nao and I had to fix before I could leave.

After checking my reflection in the mirror, I went to the fridge and took out a box of cheesecake that Nao had introduced me to. I fell in love with the tangy, moist, and cotton-soft cake. Yesterday, I went to the bakery to buy one, hoping that Harper and her friends might like it too.

Locking the door, I looked at the unit next to me.

Has he moved here? I wondered. Since the day we met last time—almost a week ago, I hadn't heard any sound from it. The walls were thin, and I should have heard something. *Maybe he changed his mind. Huh. Good then.*

Carrying the box carefully, I walked to Harper's. The comforting smell of sweet, smoky grilled meat teased my nose as I got closer.

I brushed the bangs on my forehead and looked at my clothes before pressing the doorbell. After two rings, Harper opened the door.

"Yay, you made it. Come on in." She grinned widely.

"I'm sorry I'm late." I took off my shoes. A burst of loud and hearty laughter came from behind the door at the end of the hallway.

"No worries. We haven't even eaten yet." She closed the door and bolted it. "Come, I'll introduce you to my friends." Harper's head pointed to the room.

"I brought this cheesecake. Hope you like it." I gave her the cake.

She accepted and read the name of the box. "Aw, I know this bakery. Yes, that's my favorite. Thanks! Come, let's go inside."

Avery was sitting on the floor in the living room with three people around a low square table, with food containers and plates covering the surface. Their heads turned in our direction as we entered.

"Hi, Bella." Avery waved to me and tapped an empty cushion next to her.

"Hi, Avery." I waved back and nodded to the others, who smiled and nodded back.

"This is Bella from California." Harper pointed at me as I sat on a cushion. "She's a trainer for the Little Bear Café and will be here for two months, right?" she looked at me for confirmation.

"That's correct."

Sitting on her heel, Harper pointed at an olive-skinned woman with wavy brunette hair. "This is Elena from Spain. She's an English teacher and lives on the third floor, in unit three ten." Harper motioned to a woman with a blonde bob who had a freckle on her nose. "Cameron from America. A programmer." Harper pointed to a Black man with a petite goatee. "And this is Joe, also from America, and he's an English teacher as well."

Smiling, I scanned them. "Nice to meet you guys."

"Nice to meet you, Bella," they said almost in unison.

"We still have two men on the balcony doing the holy grill." Harper chuckled. "So please enjoy all the appetizers while I'm going to check on our dinner."

She went to the balcony, and everyone else continued talking, so I used the chance to scan the apartment. Unlike my apartment, Harper's was a 2LDK—two bedrooms, dining, and kitchen areas equivalent to a two-bedroom apartment in the States. It was bigger than mine, and the sliding door was in the living room instead of the bedroom.

"Bella, don't be shy. Take anything you want," said Elena. Her voice brought me back to the moment, and I remembered the appetizers in front of us. "Yes." I nodded and took three pieces of a smoky bacon-wrapped hot dog. Munching the hot dog, I watched Avery pour sake into the paper cups in front of us.

"You aren't allowed to drink sake, Avery," commented Joe as Avery took one of the cups. His eyes twinkled. "You aren't twenty-one yet."

"Hey, I just turned twenty last week, and I'm allowed to drink alcohol here," Avery protested, sitting back on her cushion. "Only in America is the drinking age twenty-one." She turned to me and then back to Joe. "Why don't you say the same to Bella? She looks no more than twenty."

"I'll be twenty-two in November." I grinned to see a pout on her lips.

"See, only you—the baby here," teased Joe.

Cameron put a hand over her forehead, and Elena shook her head in bemusement, listening to Joe and Avery's banter.

I chuckled, liking them instantly.

Harper came through the sliding door with a man who had wavy dark hair right as I finished my second bacon-wrapped hot dog and began to chew the third one. He carefully carried a plate piled with burgers. Behind him was another man, and I caught a floral kitchen apron wrapped around his waist. But I didn't look closer at his face because Harper introduced me to the first man.

"Bella, this is Mike, my handsome British boyfriend." Harper tapped his shoulder lovingly. "Mike, that's my new friend, Bella."

"Hi, Bella. Nice to finally see you. Harper has mentioned you." Mike smiled at me, thrusting his hand.

"Nice to meet you too." My mouth was full of food, I shook his hand.

"And this is our new neighbor." Harper pointed to the second man. "I just met him earlier but already forced him to give Mike a hand grilling." She snickered.

"My pleasure." The familiar voice caught my attention. Tilting my head, I looked at the man, and half of a bacon-wrapped hot dog fell from my mouth.

The Frowner's eyes lit up, and he grinned widely as he put a plate of sausage—kielbasa, and bratwurst—in front of me.

"Ryo, this is Bella." Harper turned to me as she sat in front of me. "Bella, Ryo Yamada, and he is your next-door neighbor."

"Hi, Bella. Nice to meet you." He casually reached out his hand.

"Hi ... R-Ryo," I stuttered. His hand was warm, and he didn't let go. I caught Harper's raised eyebrow as she looked at me. Clearing my throat, I forced a smile. "Nice to meet you too, Ryo."

He nodded and took a cushion next to mine.

"Have ... you guys met before?" Harper looked at Ryo and me.

Stiffening at her curious eyes, I scratched my chin. "Uh ... kind of."

"We sat next to each other on the flight here from San Francisco," answered Ryo quickly.

"No kidding!" Cameron exclaimed. "What a small world."

I bobbed my head and put my plate on the table. Suddenly, I didn't feel hungry anymore.

"But ..." Avery tilted her head sideways in confusion. "You guys seemed not to know each other's names."

"Well, we—"

"We hadn't asked. But now we know." Ryo answered again and popped a bacon-wrapped hot dog in his mouth.

"What a weird coincidence," Joe commented. "And now you guys even live next to each other."

I glanced at Ryo, who happened to look at me. He quirked a smile as I looked away. Then Avery's claps saved me from more awkward moments.

"Okay. The introduction session is done. I'm hungry." Half sitting, Avery took two burger patties for her plate.

Harper shook her head then put two pieces of kielbasa and a burger patty on my plate. "The bun, lettuce, and tomatoes are over there, Bel." She pointed to a tray on the other small table.

"Thanks." I began eating slowly. Ryo's presence affected my appetite. The juicy kielbasa suddenly tasted dry in my mouth. I hadn't even touched the burger yet.

"You aren't hungry?" Ryo asked in a low voice, looking at the untouched burger patty.

"When I'm tired, I'm not hungry," I answered shortly.

"Really?" he said, taking a big bite of his burger. "I've never heard that."

I started to glare at him when Cameron, who had heard our conversation, chimed in. "Me too, Bel. And that's not good for our health. My doctor suggested that I eat in small portions every two hours so my stomach is never empty. So, if I'm tired, it won't really matter. Maybe you should try."

"Stop talking about such a boring subject," Avery protested.

"Talking about health isn't a boring subject," Cameron argued.

"Let's talk about *ghosts*." Avery nudged Cameron as her eyes shifted to Ryo and me.

Cameron's eyes lit up. Joe groaned. "Ah, don't do that." He signaled Avery to switch seats with him. Although she grumbled, she did. "I like Bella." Turning to me, he said sweetly, "Don't worry, Bella. If you're scared, you can hug me."

I grinned widely at him. "I don't believe in ghosts."

"Me either," Ryo said.

"No one asked you," I muttered.

Harper heard me but didn't say anything because Mike let out a loud chuckle.

"All right, then. Did you know"—Avery lowered her voice—"that our apartment is next to a cemetery?"

Ryo nodded while I widened my eyes. "W-we live n-next to a cemetery?" Unaware, my voice dropped, and I felt my heart pounding hard.

Ryo raised his eyebrows. "You didn't know that?"

I shook my head, feeling my stomach twist. "Did you know?"

"Of course." He gave a smug smile.

Ignoring him, I looked at Harper and pressed my fingers over my lips. "Where is it?"

"You can see it from the balcony." Mike turned to Harper. "Do you want to do the honors?"

"Absolutely." Grinning, she rose to her feet and signaled me to follow.

Someone made a sound like "whoo-oo-oo-oo ..." as we stepped out to the balcony. A breeze touched my face and hair as I stepped outside. The leftover smell of flame-grilled meats was still strong.

"Do you see that?" she said, pointing down at the array of black and gray columns. I nodded, feeling my heartbeat increase. "That's the cemetery."

"Oh, that's the one? I thought it was some kind of park with weird, tall stones." I shuddered.

Harper shook and wrapped a hand over my shoulder.

"Don't you worry. So far, I haven't seen any ghosts," said Harper as if she could read my mind. "I don't care at all because I don't believe in any ghost. What I do care about the most is this apartment is cheaper than other apartments."

"Really?"

Harper nodded, releasing her hand from my shoulder. "Ono-san told me that living next to the cemetery is considered bad luck by locals. So, the management shifted to focus on foreigners because most of them don't care about ghosts. For me, this building is a blessing in disguise. It's cheap, quiet, and peaceful. No tall buildings nearby, so I can enjoy the view. At night when the sky is clear, you can see the city lights sparkling in the distance. I think from your balcony, you don't have any building blocking your view either, right?"

"Yes."

She nodded and gazed down at the graveyard. "Plus, my neighbors and I respect each other's privacy. So, I'm good."

I chuckled shakily at her joke and felt relieved when we went back inside to the bright room. The whole dinnertime, I felt unease, but I hid it.

When the gathering ended, Ryo and I walked back to our units. The light in the middle of the hallway had died two days ago, and it hadn't bothered me, but it did now. The moon was high in the sky, and its light shone against us, creating shifting shadows on the wall to our left. The temperature was a bit cool, and each time a soft breeze blew, I felt goosebumps on my arms. My eyes focused on the dark corner and walls.

Then Ryo stopped abruptly. My nose and forehead hit his shoulder.

"Ouch!" I yelled, rubbing my nose. "Why did you stop suddenly?"

"Why were you walking too close to me? I could even feel your breath on my neck," he said.

"I'm shorter than you; how could my breath reach your neck?' I snapped, rubbing my forehead.

"Does that hurt?" He leaned forward, looking at me.

"You think?" I tsked and looked away.

"If you didn't walk so close to me, you wouldn't have bumped my shoulder." He studied me. "Are you *scared* of ghosts? I thought you said you weren't afraid."

I pouted. "I'm not."

"Then why did you walk so close to me? Is it because now you know where the cemetery is?"

Placing my hands on my hips, I glared at him for bringing up the topic that I wanted to forget. "Then, do you expect me to be afraid?"

He shrugged, pressed his hands into his pockets, and continued walking. I followed him immediately.

As we reached our units, he offered his hand, palm up. "Give me your phone."

"What for?" I puckered my brows.

"Just do it, but unlock it for me." He ignored my question.

Reluctantly, I took out my phone, pressed my thumb on the fingerprint reader to unlock it, and then gave it to him.

Ryo typed something before returning it to me. "My phone number. Call me if you see something tonight. Harper's unit is at the other end of the building, so if you cry for help, it'll take time for her to come here."

I scoffed. "I told you I'm not afraid."

"Even of the one without a face?" His palm made a circle around his face.

"There's no such thing." I wrinkled my nose.

He shrugged, unlocking his front door. "By the way, I kind of saw a shadow behind me last night over there." He pointed behind me.

My stomach clenched as I glanced over my shoulder.

"Well." His lips curved as he stood in the doorway. "Good night, Bella." He winked and closed the door without waiting for my response.

What a gentleman he is, going straight to his unit without waiting for me.

Although I didn't believe what he said, my heart raced when another breeze blew. I felt something cold touch my neck. The key jingled because my hand shook as I inserted it into the hole. It seemed to take forever for me to open the door. Once the door cracked open, I rushed in and closed it with a *bam*. In a jiffy, my ears caught a cackle from the next door.

Damn Ryo!

That night, I slept with the lights on and a blanket over my head, the window curtain shut tight because I didn't want to see any shifting shadows from the moonlight. Hairs on my neck rose for any slight noise, but I didn't bother to get up and investigate.

I shouldn't have gone to the gathering.

BELLA

The following day, my body ached when I woke up. I couldn't sleep the whole night and lay on one side because I was afraid to turn on my bed. The Frowner had to pay for the scary story he'd told me. There was no faceless ghost, right?

Groggy, I dragged my feet to the bathroom and splashed cold water on my face. There were dark circles under my eyes as I looked at myself in the mirror.

"Good thing I'm off today. If not, they might have mistaken me for a ghost," I grumbled and dried my face with a towel. *Damn, Ryo.*

My phone buzzed as I entered my bedroom. Picking my phone up from the bed, I looked at the message from Mel.

I hope you have a good day off, Bel. You deserve it.

I texted back, *Thanks. Yes, I need that.*

Another buzzed. *And don't check your work email.*

Mel had known about my crazy work schedule and kept reminding me to eat and sleep well. I didn't tell my parents or Adele because I didn't want them to worry about me.

I smiled and responded. *I won't.*

Letting out a sigh, I laid down the phone and rubbed my neck. I'd worked nonstop since last week to teach some English phrases to the staff. Since the café was located in the touristy area, it was important for the staff to learn phrases to accommodate foreign customers.

"Yes, Hiroshi-san, you used the correct pronunciation for 'our coffee of the day is Sumatra coffee'," I'd said during our role play with me as the customer yesterday. His cheeks flushed as he sat down. "Who wants to try next?"

"Me!" a girl named Chizuko raised her hand.

"Sure, Chizuko-san, go ahead."

Chizuko stood tall with her shoulders back, and began to pronounce it slowly. She stopped herself and repeated the words until she felt comfortable.

Something expanded in my heart to see how hard the employees strived for perfection. No matter how difficult the words were, they practiced them and didn't shy away from asking me to correct them.

Today I was off because the staff would learn and practice various phrases in Japanese to greet customers. Someone from Bread Lounge corporate would come and teach them how to speak to customers appropriately, with the right tone and expression. So, they didn't need me until Monday. I was also looking forward to working from home tomorrow because I needed to create progress reports for Little Bear.

Speaking of my day off, my sluggish body perked up a little, and I began to think about what I should do today. Running would be the best choice to start my day.

Wearing black shorts and a slim-fit T-shirt, I was ready. Standing in the lobby, I chose my jogging playlist on my phone from Spotify. As I was about to insert my phone in the armband sleeve, an elevator opened with a soft ding, and three people stepped out. One of them was Ryo, who I didn't want to forgive for making me scared last night. From the way he was dressed, he might have been coming back from exercising. His lips quirked up a little as our eyes met briefly.

"Morning," he greeted as he stood with one of his hands holding the elevator door.

"Morning."

"Jogging?"

I nodded curtly and stepped inside the elevator.

"Did you sleep well last night?" His eyes were on me.

"Of course. Why wouldn't I?" I forced a cheerful tone while pressing the ground floor button and signaled him to move his hand from the door.

"Glad to know," he said and pointed at my face. "Although the dark circles under your eyes say otherwise."

"I was born with those circles," I said flatly and pressed the close button.

Slowly, the right and the left door slid to meet in the middle, and when it was about to close, a hand stuck in, and the doors slid back open while Ryo stepped back into the elevator.

I raised an eyebrow when he stood next to me.

"What you said is interesting," he said, pressing the close button. "I've never heard of someone who was born with dark circles under their eyes, except pandas."

The doors closed with a soft jerk as the elevator went down to the ground floor. I scoffed as his reflection grinned at me.

"Now you've heard, Yamada-san." I pouted and used the honorific to tell him indirectly that I didn't want to act friendly to him.

"You can call me Ryo like the others do," he said quickly.

"I'll stick to Yamada-san."

The elevator doors opened on the ground floor. I stepped out with Ryo on my heels. I let out a heavy sigh when he followed me to the hallway entrance.

"I'm not following you. I'm going to run," he said as if he could read my mind.

I looked him up and down. "Didn't you just come back from exercising?"

"From the gym, and now I need to run."

I shrugged but didn't say a word.

On the sidewalk, outside the building, he waved and ran toward the main street. I sighed in relief and began to stretch my legs and arms. Bringing the Garmin watch around my wrist closer to my eyes, I chose the "RUN" option and then "START" to activate my jogging timer. Although I wasn't a fast runner, it was nice to run again as I hadn't been able to since I got here.

The weather felt the same as yesterday: muggy and hot. Yesterday, Nao had said the rainy season was over, and the weather would now become unbearable. The killer during summer wasn't the temperature but the humidity. On the worst day, it could reach up to 85 percent humidity. And I couldn't imagine how much worse it could get because, on my first day, my lungs had already worked hard to take in the air.

My lungs contracted in and out following the pace of my breaths. I felt my heart rate elevate, pumping blood throughout my body. I was glad I decided to run.

While jogging, I enjoyed the uniqueness of the neighborhood. The roads were narrow, clean, and quiet. On each side of the streets stood utility poles or crisscrossing power lines.

Ten minutes later, I reached an area with no houses or offices but a stretch of high walls on both sides. My eyes caught on two vending machines next to the pole on the roadside as I passed them. Chuckling, I shifted my eyes and saw a small truck coming toward me. I moved to the other side only to hear a loud horn behind me. Startled, I jumped and looked over my shoulder to see a taxi around thirty feet behind me.

Wait! Is it a two-way road? My chest tightened as I realized there were no sidewalks to wait for the cars to pass me.

My foot slipped when I turned around, and I lost my balance. Before I touched the asphalt, a hand grabbed my waist to hoist me up and drag me away from the road.

"Are you okay? Are you hurt somewhere?" a familiar voice asked me.

I blinked a few times and fixated on two concerned eyes.

Ryo!

In the meantime, in front of us, the truck and the taxi were well-behaved. The drivers slowed down and gave each other enough space to pass, and once they left, the road became quiet again as if nothing had happened.

"I'm okay." I swallowed, calming my heart. Then I felt his hand on my waist.

Ryo caught my eyes on his hand and removed it from my waist. He gazed at me with concern. "Don't you know this is a two-way road?" he asked gently.

His gentle voice surprised me. I'd expected he would roll his eyes or speak in a condescending tone.

"No." I shook my head, rubbing my collarbone. "This road is too narrow for two cars. Besides, every time I walk here, the road is always quiet, and I've never seen two cars at the same time." I checked my left foot and winced as I touched the ankle.

He gazed at me before lowering his eyes to my ankle. "Did you hurt your ankle? Let me see." He crouched down in front of me.

"Don't worry, I'm okay." I waved my hand. "My ankle is weak, so it happens all the time."

Still, in the same position, Ryo looked up at me. "Take off your sock, so I can see it."

"I've told you I'm fine, Yamada-san. Besides, I don't want people to give us weird looks."

A crease appeared on his forehead while he maintained eye contact. "Don't be stubborn." His voice was stern. "And call me Ryo."

I didn't know whether his voice or his eyes made me obey him. I leaned against the pole and took off my sock, revealing a slightly pinkish color around it. I winced as Ryo's fingers lightly touched my ankle.

"As I thought, it needs to be bandaged."

I raised my eyebrows. "Where can we get a bandage? There's no convenience store around here."

"I can use this." He untied a dark blue bandanna that had been around his neck. "It's clean but slightly wet because, you know ... I was running. If it's okay, I can use it for a temporary bandage."

I thought about it. If I used my ankle without a bandage, it would be more painful when I arrived at my apartment.

"Okay."

In silence, he knelt and placed my ankle on his thigh, and he folded the bandanna diagonally a few times. "Are you sure?"

I nodded.

With the assurance, he began to wrap my ankle snugly. I felt the dampness as it touched my skin.

"Wiggle your foot, then try to walk." He placed my foot lightly on the ground before rising to his feet. "I want to see if you can walk comfortably with it wrapped."

I wiggled my foot and took a few steps. "It isn't as painful as earlier. Thanks."

"Don't mention it." He waited as I carefully placed my foot into my shoe and adjusted the shoelace.

"Were you a Boy Scout when you were young?"

The corner of his lips lifted slightly, but he didn't answer me.

"Well." I offered a smile. "If you want to continue jogging, go ahead. I'm okay," I said, rising to my feet.

"Nah, I'm done." He moved his arms up, down, left, and right. "I need to stretch."

Gazing at his expression, somehow, I had a feeling that he wouldn't leave me alone. It was useless, anyway, to tell him to go, so I let him walk with me.

"By the way, how did you know I was here?" I looked at him sideways. "Did ... you follow me?"

"If that's a joke, you're the worst joker," he said.

"Do I look like I'm joking?" I frowned.

He flashed a grin, and then his face became solemn. "No, I didn't follow you. Since I'm not familiar with this neighborhood, I didn't want to go farther. You must notice that most streets are nameless and only have block numbers. I don't want to get lost here. So I decided to turn back. On the way back, I saw a redheaded gaijin who looked stunned when two vehicles moved toward her from different directions." Then he pointed to my ankle with his eyes. "Is it better?"

I nodded. "It's better because of the wrap."

A satisfied smile appeared on his lips.

"Hey, do you think that's an unusual place for vending machines?" I pointed as we passed the vending machines.

"That's a common practice here." He stretched his arms upward.

"Oh. Why?"

"Many reasons. Mostly for convenience and a good side business," he answered. "The vending machines must belong to the laundromat." He pointed. "That's a perfect idea because while waiting for their clothes, people can buy something from the machine."

"But don't you think the machine can become an eyesore, though?"

"Not for the Japanese. It's a matter of convenience in terms of money and time." He turned his head to me. "Let's say you are thirsty. Vending machines for cold drinks or hot drinks are everywhere, so you don't need to go to a convenience store to buy them. Besides, people can buy anything from vending machines now, including cell phones," he added.

My mouth opened slightly before I spoke. "That's amazing. I never knew about that."

He nodded. "At night, the colorful lights on the machine can be beautiful and help to illuminate the roads too." He grinned.

I titled my head. "That's smart."

It took us longer to get back to the apartment, but I didn't feel bored or upset because Ryo was good company. He was relaxed, easygoing, and thoughtful. It was a different Ryo than I'd met on the plane. I wondered why he changed.

"Are you sure you don't want to go to a doctor?" Ryo asked as we reached our units.

"Nope. I've had worse, so this one is nothing. I just need to keep my ankle up and ice it, and I'll be fine tomorrow," I said, unlocking my door. "Thanks for everything. I'll return the bandanna after I wash it."

"Don't worry about that." He smiled. "If you need anything, let me know. You have my number, but I don't have yours."

"Ah. Let me give it to you." I took out my phone and typed *hi from your next-door neighbor.*

A buzz came from his phone.

"That's from me," I said.

He looked at the screen. "Got it. Well, take a rest, and hope you feel better tomorrow." He turned to his unit.

I nodded and went into my apartment. I heard a faint sound coming from his unit when he closed the front door and another when he opened his bedroom door.

I was glad that Ryo was turning out to be a nice person. Weird, but nice. That made it hard for me to fight off a smile, but I did. As I'd said, living alone in Tokyo wasn't too bad if we had good people around us.

I took my regular ankle brace from the closet and brought it to the living room. Sitting on the cushion, I swapped the bandanna with the brace. When I was about to toss the bandanna into my dirty clothes hamper, my fingers felt embroidered initials in light yellow on the corner of them. I looked closer but couldn't tell what they were. Maybe his initials. Shrugging, I threw it in and would wash it sometime this week.

Before noon, I called my mom from my bed. She looked worried when I told her what had happened earlier.

"Do you need to go to a doctor?" She wrung her eyebrows.

"No, I'm okay. It isn't my first time. Besides, I brought my ankle brace and a boot, so don't worry about that. If it gets worse, I'll go to a doctor," I assured her.

"How do you explain if your Japanese isn't good?" my dad chimed in.

"I've met some friends who can speak Japanese better than me."

"Harper and her sister?" my mom asked. "What would happen if they were busy and couldn't help you?"

That was what I admired about my mom. She remembered all the friends I'd had since kindergarten. Many of them she never met, but she would connect the name with their faces once she did.

"I have five more now. Harper introduced them to me. Two of them are living in the same building." I smiled proudly.

My mom and dad exchanged a glance as small smiles crept onto their lips. "It's good you have more friends," my mom commented. "Is it almost lunch time? Do you have food to eat? Or do you need to order it?"

"I have something in my fridge. And tons of instant noodles for an emergency." I grinned to see her nose wrinkle. "If it's necessary, I can order online. And I'll ask my friends to help me," I added quickly. "My next-door neighbor is Japanese but speaks English well because he has been in America for some time. He was also the one who helped me when I fell earlier."

"He?" The corner of my dad's lips went up. "Is he handsome?" His eyebrows rose playfully.

I let out a chuckle. "Well, Dad, no time for dating now. I'm busy with my work."

"Okay, pumpkin. You should rest more." My mom nudged my dad; her medium brown eyes signaled him to stop teasing me.

"Okay, bye, Mom, Dad."

"Bye Bel-bel," my dad called, using my nickname before the screen turned dark. Something that he hadn't done since I complained about it when I was in fifth grade. Now, listening to him call me by that name made me miss them even more.

A buzz for an incoming message interrupted me. Pushing my homesickness away, I looked at the screen and frowned because Ryo had sent me a short message. *Call me.*

I pressed the call icon next to his number.

"Hey, Bel."

"Hey, Ryo. What's up?" I asked, sliding a pillow under my injured ankle.

"I'm going out to buy lunch. Do you want something?"

Huh?

"Uh, that's okay. I think I have something to eat in the fridge," I said.

"Are you sure? Because my offer is only available for today."

I chuckled and considered his offer. "Hmm, what do you want to eat? I'll follow you."

"If I eat stinky tofu, do you want that too?" he said.

"I bet you won't eat that one either," I laughed. "To be honest, I want a burger."

"And french fries and ketchup?"

"Yes!" I almost clapped my hands.

"Got it," said Ryo. "McDonald's or Carl's Jr?"

"Anything that won't make you take a long trip," I said.

"Okay. I'll let you know once I'm outside your door," he said.

"Thanks, Ryo. Do you have Zelle or Venmo?"

"Zelle. But don't worry. You can pay me back anytime."

"Okay. Thanks."

"Sure." And he hung up.

I stared at the phone in disbelief that Ryo offered to buy me lunch since I couldn't walk.

Is he the same person as the one who sat next to me on the plane? I scratched my hair. Something must have happened that caused him to be so irritable then.

I shrugged. The current Ryo was a hundredfold better than Ryo the Frowner.

RYO

"**Y**ou look tired, man," Takeru commented, lifting his glass of beer and sipping the contents. It was nine in the evening. They were in an *izakaya* near Ryo's apartment for dinner.

Ryo let out a sigh and rolled his long white sleeves up. He tried to ignore his throat itching from the smell of cigarettes. The government had already banned indoor smoking, except for small bars like the one he was in. But still, it wasn't California, where no indoor smoking was allowed, so he had to learn to ignore the smell. "It's been a long day. Last night, I stayed at my parent's house, taking care of Akiko because my mom had a headache, and my dad has been on a business trip and will be back tomorrow. So this morning, I left the house at six thirty because I had two interviews, and both were in opposite directions."

"Is Akiko okay, though?"

"Same old, same old."

"And how about your interviews?"

"We'll see. I don't think I did as good on the last interview with an IT company." Ryo shrugged, running a hand over his face. "I miss my old office."

Takeru gave a sympathetic look. "I understand. It isn't an easy adjustment." Leaning forward, he said in a low voice, "I do hope there is a miracle for your sister."

Ryo looked down. "I won't bet on it. No matter what, my parents need me now."

"I know. But you have to take care of yourself too, man. It'll be tough from now on." Takeru picked up a chicken skewer and brought it to his mouth. "But anytime you need help, I'm here for you."

"Thanks." Ryo took a swig of his beer to push the itchiness from his throat. Then he shifted his eyes to Takeru. "I have to tell you something."

"Sure."

"Sara offered me a job at her dad's company." Ryo examined Takeru's face.

Takeru's chewing slowed; his eyes focused on Ryo.

"I refused it."

Takeru jerked his head back. "Why? That's your opportunity to settle down here."

Ryo shook his head. "I have reasons." He picked up his chopsticks and began to eat his okonomiyaki. It was slightly cold in his mouth.

"Was I one of the reasons?"

Ryo put the chopsticks on their stand and wiped his mouth with a napkin. "You and I know that she hasn't forgotten her feelings for me. Although I need a job to settle down and help my parents with Akiko's hospital bills, I can't cross over the line I've drawn between Sara and me. I was afraid I'd be in her debt if I accepted the job. Besides, yes, I don't want to hurt you. You aren't just my friend, but my brother. I can't hurt my brother."

Takeru sighed. "Thanks, man. But I'm okay even if you finally fall in love with her. I'm happy if she is happy."

Ryo nearly rolled his eyes and itched to smack the back of his head to wake him up. Deep down, he blamed Sara for changing Takeru's personality from goofy to serious. It was suitable for his profession but not good for him as Ryo's close friend. Takeru used to make him laugh, and he missed it. Good thing his sense of humor was still there.

"I can't love her, and she has to know and accept that," he said rather coldly.

Takeru didn't respond but finished his beer in one gulp.

"Let's talk about something else," Ryo decided. "This morning, I was almost accused of being a *chikan*."

Takeru's mouth hung open. "How come?"

Heat rushed into Ryo's cheeks as he remembered. "Because I stayed at my parent's house last night, this morning for my interview I had to take Asakusa line. The train was more packed than usual. Trust me, somehow, it was worse this morning. I don't know why. No matter how small I squeezed my body, still, people's bags or arms touched mine. I wanted to tell them to wait for another train."

"You must have forgotten how grueling the rush hour is, huh? Especially since today is Monday, that's the worst." A small smile formed on Takeru's lips. "Why don't you borrow your dad's car? You said he's been on his business trip."

"I need time to adjust to driving with the driver's seat on the right." Ryo let out a sigh. "Last time, I almost caused an accident because I turned in the wrong direction."

"Next time, call me. My job is flexible," said Takeru. "Okay, tell me more about getting accused of being a chikan."

"In the hectic and packed car, someone hit my back pretty hard. Initially, I thought she did—"

"She?" Takeru interrupted.

Ryo nodded. "So I thought she did it on purpose, but then I realized she was pushed from behind. I guess she might not be used to the packed train. She kept murmuring, 'excuse me,' each time she inched deeper. I felt—"

"Is she a foreigner?"

Ryo glared at him for the interruption.

Takeru grinned.

"When the train began to accelerate, it was apparent that she wasn't ready and fell forward, toward a grandma sitting on the long bench in front of her. Trust me, the grandma shut her eyes tightly as if she was waiting for disaster.

"Without thinking, I stretched an arm around her waist to stop her from falling. And then I felt excruciating pain in my foot. I believe she wanted to break every bone in my foot when she stepped on it. On top of that, she screamed at the top of her lungs, 'Chikan!' And everybody in the car turned to me. Can you believe how shocked I was?" Ryo put his head in his hands. "I never touch any woman without their consent. And I think I have a hairline fracture on my foot."

Takeru's eyes widened. "That's crazy! And what happened next?"

"I screamed back, 'I'm not a chikan; I'm keeping you from falling.' And she turned around. Can you guess who she was?"

Takeru shook his head.

"My next-door neighbor."

Takeru blinked. "Wait ... you mean the redheaded lady? The one that you dislike?"

He scoffed. "I don't dislike her. I said she was annoying."

Takeru smirked but waved his hand, signaling him to continue.

"The annoying part was once she knew who I was, she grinned and hung on to my suit and asked why she didn't see me on the way to the station. Her voice sounded so cheerful and innocent for a woman who had been screaming and stepping on my foot. I don't understand at all why she hung on to my suit. Couldn't she find a pole or a strap or whatever to balance?" He shook his head. "But I answered her anyway."

"Did she still hang on to you after that?"

"Of course not. I told her to hold on to the pole near her."

"Did she say sorry to you for the misunderstanding?"

"Yes, and later she texted me asking about my foot," said Ryo.

"You exchanged phone numbers with her—an annoying woman that you don't like?" Takeru's snicker slipped because Ryo glared at him.

"By the way, how did she know about chikan?" asked Takeru solemnly, scratching his chin.

"Maybe someone has told her to be careful in the train during rush hour because some crazy men are out there and like touching women's bodies," Ryo answered.

"Clever woman! I bet all the passengers were shocked, not because you held her but because she was screaming. Most of the women here keep their mouths if a similar thing happens to them," Takeru took a deep sigh, grieving. "All chikans should be thrown in jail. They make our city unsafe."

"Agreed."

"So, tell me, how's your life living next to the redheaded woman? Any issues?"

Ryo shook his head. "No, we get along well now."

"Really? Have you fallen for her?" Takeru raised an eyebrow.

"Shut up." Ryo laughed. "One neighbor invited me to her weekly gathering last Tuesday and happened to be Bella's friend, and Bella was also at that gathering. So we introduced ourselves properly, and yes, we've become friends now."

"Her name is Bella. That's a cute name."

Ryo nodded. "I think so too."

Takeru narrowed his eyes.

"Come on, don't give me that look." Ryo waved his hand like he was slamming something.

"What look?"

Ryo scoffed. "I won't fall for her. I've been nice to her because she is my next-door neighbor now. There is no way to avoid her, so I think it's better if I'm friendly."

Takeru lifted his second beer. "Whatever happens, I'm glad the old Ryo is back."

Ryo chuckled and tipped his glass to Takeru, and they finished the beer before asking for more.

"Hey, are you interested in going to the Mitama Matsuri, the one in the Yasukuni shrine?" asked Takeru as they left the izakaya and walked toward his car. "Since you haven't ever come home for summer in the last seven years, I was thinking of going to the festival with you and our other friends."

"Who's going?" Ryo asked.

"You, me, my cousins Keiko and Kimi, Keiko's boyfriend, and Sara."

His eyebrows arched on the last name.

"You really invited her to join you?" Ryo turned to Takeru as they stopped in front of the car.

Takeru pursed his lips, nodded, and slid into the driver's seat.

"I don't understand you," Ryo mumbled, then opened the passenger door and sat down. He felt Takeru looking at him across the car, smiling.

"Sometimes, love is a mystery, Ryo," Takeru pressed his finger on the ignition. "Just looking at her makes me happy."

"You're hopeless," Ryo grunted and closed his eyes. He was sleepy and didn't refuse when Takeru offered to drive him back to the apartment. "Wake me up when we arrive."

A hard punch landed on his arm. "Your apartment is less than five minutes away. You're the hopeless one."

BELLA

I glanced at my watch. It already showed 7:41 a.m.

"Damn!" I finger-combed my hair quickly, glancing in the mirror, and grabbed my bag before scurrying into the hall to get my shoes and apartment key from the gray cabinet. Because of my movement, the bag's strap caught on the door handle and pulled me back. "Ugh!" I released it and sped up to catch the next elevator.

Since I decided to start taking a train, Sato-san had reminded me to leave my apartment between seven and seven twenty because the rush hour in Tokyo was terrible.

I'd followed his advice.

But this morning, I woke up late.

It took me fifteen minutes to run to the train station from my apartment. I was sweating and breathless when I reached the right platform for the Asakusa line. Good thing, I didn't have to wait longer because a minute later, my train came and I jumped on it with other passengers.

I didn't surprise to find myself wedged between people on the crowded train. Planting my feet to the car floor, I firmly clenched the pole to keep my balance as the train picked up speed.

The train swayed, and I felt someone's bag nudge my back. Instead of feeling upset and uncomfortable, I felt a smile spread across my lips because I remembered my unexpected meeting with Ryo yesterday.

That day, the train was cramped and horrible. My hand couldn't reach the strap on the ceiling. Going farther down the train was more challenging because I was petite, and my head was sandwiched between people's shoulders and backpacks.

When the train accelerated, I stumbled forward, almost hitting a grandma on the bench, until a hand caught my waist to stop me. My heart stopped beating in a second as I remembered what Nao had told me a few days ago about chikan or men groping women in public—mainly on commuter trains during rush hours. With all my might, I stepped on his foot hard as Andrew—Mel's boyfriend—had taught me and screamed 'chikan.' The man screamed in pain and released me. In a high voice, he said in Japanese and English that he wasn't a chikan. Because his voice was familiar, I turned to see that the man was Ryo.

I wouldn't forget the mixed expression of pain, amusement, and anger on his face as I clung to his jacket suit. I didn't feel bothered by his expression because I was happy to see a familiar face in the crammed car.

"Fancy seeing you here," I said after he told me to hold the pole near me. "My first time on the cramped train."

"I figured," he said curtly with a grimace of pain as he shifted his foot.

I bit my lower lip, glancing down. "Sorry."

He let out a grunt but didn't say anything.

"By the way," I said again in a low voice. "I still have your bandana. I'll give it back to you tonight after work. Will you be at home?"

"Um… I won't be home until late. But, don't worry about that, though. I have many," he half-whispered.

I nodded and tightened my fingers around the pole.

For at least a half hour, we stood side by side in silence. I wanted to talk but decided to shut up and learn to stand firmly on the moving train. To my surprise, whenever the car wobbled around the curves or the corners and threw off my balance, Ryo placed his hand briefly on my shoulder to steady me. Oddly, it didn't annoy me.

At almost 9:00 a.m., I entered the café and went straight to the back room.

"How was your train this morning, Bella-chan?" asked Nao as I put my bag and clothes in the locker after changing into my Little Bear uniform. On the table, in front of her, there were stacks of colorful laminated drink recipes for our training today.

Since the day we met, Nao and I had become good friends. I liked her and talked to her a lot because she was the only one who dared to speak with me in English. Although the rest of the staff had become comfortable around me, they were still reluctant, and most of the time, if Sato-san wasn't around, we did sign language while grinning at each other. But they were nice enough to teach me some Japanese words, slang, and curses. Nao forbade me to use the curses. In certain ways, she reminded me of Adele. Plus, once she learned I was almost eight years younger than her, she began to call me Bella-chan if no one was around, and I didn't mind.

"It was crowded. My shoulders hurt because they were bumped by people's backpacks." I whined and rubbed my shoulders. "How do you survive every day on the train? It's my second time, and I can't stand it."

"I understand. It isn't easy, but you'll get used to it later, though." Nao offered me sympathy. "By the way, why have you never taken any public transportation in California?"

I tilted my head, trying to find an easy way to explain. "California is huge, and I live in a suburb. Unfortunately, the public transportation in the suburbs isn't as good as here. The train doesn't come every five minutes. Weekdays are better because more trains are available for commuters but never expect that on the weekend. So going from one place to another is not convenient if you take public transportation. Unless you live in big cities like San Francisco or Los Angeles."

"I see. That's why people who live in your city should have private transportation." She nodded her head, picking up the recipes. "Do you need more time to take a deep breath, or are you ready to work?"

"I'm okay." I smiled. "Let's go to work." I pushed the office door open and held it for her. "Nao-san, this morning, in one of the stations, I saw a few men in uniform with white gloves who pushed the passengers in. Who are they?"

Her eyebrows met in the middle. "Pushing like this?" She imitated a pushing movement.

"Yes."

"Oh, they must be train station staff or the train conductor. That happens during rush hour when the cars are packed. The staff and the conductor want to make sure passengers won't get caught in the doors," she answered.

My mouth shaped into a large "O" listening to her explanation.

"Why didn't the passengers complain? Or wait for another train?" I commented, taking two laminated recipes and putting them near the counter where I would show everyone how to make the drinks.

"We have no choice, Bella-chan." She shrugged. "Like most people in Tokyo, we don't have cars, but our public transportation is affordable and reliable. For us, the trains will bring us from one place to another. So during rush hour, we have to accept our fate, which means being pushed into the cars. The worst part is some men take advantage by groping women in cramped trains like I told you. But we have a solution, though." I looked at her, waiting for the answer.

"Women's trains." She smiled. "Next time, if you don't feel comfortable in the packed train, try those trains. They will have pink labels, or the whole car is painted pink."

"Oh, that's awesome. Thanks. I'll keep it in mind."

My day was similar to riding in a crammed train. Regardless of how many times I repeated the steps for making foam milk, only one staff member could make it correctly. The other nine couldn't. My face was hot as I blinked back tears of sheer frustration that threatened to fall. My hair and the front of my shirt were slightly wet because whenever the staff didn't put the pitcher properly under the steam wand, the milk sprayed on me.

"Don't put the pitcher too low for the steam wand, Chizuko-san. Move it a little bit." I put my hand on her elbow and gave a small push to make it higher while Sato-san translated my instructions. "There, yes, that's better. Yes, keep it until you see the foam begin to form." I pointed. "Then lower the pitcher slowly from the wand." But the foam didn't form well.

I ran a hand over my hair and wanted to pull it out in frustration. My expression must have been grim because Chizuko's hands started shaking. Closing my eyes briefly, I took the pitcher from her hand and dumped the milk into the sink. Chizuko took a step back, tightening her shoulders. The rest of the staff lowered their eyes.

"I'll show you one more time. Please observe." I turned to Sato-san, who gave me a concerned look. "Please don't translate it, Sato-san. I want them to focus on watching me."

He nodded and instructed them in Japanese to observe me.

I poured a good amount of milk into the pitcher and cleaned the steamed wand with a rag. By not letting Sato-san translate, I was taking a gamble. But I had no choice. I'd lost my wits on making the training move forward in the right direction. My reputation was at stake if they couldn't make the drinks properly before the soft opening. I would be seen as a failure, and never would I be chosen again for another international business trip or even a domestic one. My chest became tighter at that thought. Taking a few deep breaths, I signaled the staff to focus on the pitcher.

"*Ichi.*" I spoke in Japanese the number "one." I submerged the tip of the wand just below the milk's surface.

"*Ni.*" I positioned the pitcher straight up.

"*San.*" I angled the pitcher slightly.

"*Shi.*" I pressed the button on the steamer and held it until the milk became hot, bubbly, and the foam began to form.

"Go." I slowly lowered the pitcher and turned off the steamer.

I took a spoon to scoop the foam from the pitcher and showed it to the staff. "You have to make the foam this thickness."

A soft hand touched my elbow when I signaled Sato-san to translate my words. It was Nao.

"Why don't you take a break, Bella-san? Let me and my assistants take over." She spoke gently. "You've worked hard since yesterday. If you want, you can leave early and rest. So tomorrow, you can come fresh."

Heat swelled behind my eyes. I turned away and blinked hard, fighting off tears. "I can't." I forced a smile. "I want to make sure everything is perfect. The training session in this café is my responsibility."

"I know, but you're stressed now."

"It's okay, Bell-san," Sato-san chimed in. "Come, let me take you home."

"Yes, better you take rest now," said Yukari, one of Nao's assistant managers, in broken English.

Warmed by their concern, I nodded. Then I turned around, facing the staff, and bowed slightly. "I'm sorry I can't finish training you today. See you tomorrow."

The faces of Chizuko and the staff turned pallid, and they bowed deeply and said in Japanese, "We're sorry, we made you angry."

"No, please don't be like that. I'm just tired," I said after Sato-san translated it for me, and they straightened their backs. "All right. See you tomorrow."

They murmured as I walked to the backroom to get my bag and changed out of the uniform into my own clothes. The smell of milk became sour and lingered on my skin. As I stepped outside the room, I found Sato-san waiting for me, and together we padded toward the front door, not wanting to interrupt the training.

Outside, I glanced over my shoulder at the café and started to feel guilty. The staff were hardworking people. Whenever they didn't understand, they would practice it over and over again. For some reason, it felt that I failed them.

"Don't feel bad, Bella," said Sato-san once we were on the road. "It happens all the time, especially with the language barrier. So take it easy—is that what Americans always say?"

I forced a smile. "Yes."

"When you are at home, don't do anything but relax. Okay?"

I nodded again.

"Sato-san," I called after a few beats. "What I did at the café was childish, wasn't it?"

Sato-san whipped his head to me. "No. That can happen to anyone. Why do you say that?"

I let out a sigh, looking down at my hands. "I came here because my company trusted me. But now I feel I can't do my job properly."

Sato-san gave a fatherly smile. "You've handled many things well without any supervision. Ito-san admires you and says you're the best trainer Little Bear has sent here. You don't complain about the sticky weather, the tiny apartment, the long working hours. You're patient with the café staff and have tried hard to communicate with them. You're better than any other expat, if I could say that."

His words were a firm hand that lifted the heavy burden from my shoulders. "Did you say that to make me happy?" I asked.

He chuckled. "To make you feel better about yourself."

"Thank you."

The afternoon sun warmed my face as I leaned my head near the window, watching the pedestrians milling about the never-quiet streets and sidewalks.

BELLA

The breakdown I had at the café a few days ago forced me to change how I trained them. Instead of teaching the whole team, I trained Nao and the assistants. Then they trained the staff while I supervised and stepped in whenever they needed help. The method worked. I was less stressed and could see their progress objectively. The team looked happier, and laughter was heard every day now.

And I finally had my free weekend. No more conference calls on Saturday morning with other Little Bear trainers in Osaka and Kyoto. No more preparing reports on Sunday.

It was also perfect timing because Harper had invited me to enjoy the summer lantern festival called Mitama Matsuri in the Yasukuni shrine.

"You should come with us, Bel. If you can't go now, you have to wait until next year," Harper had said.

Initially, I wasn't interested, especially after she said the festival honored ancestors' spirits. I didn't want to deal with anything related to spirits or ghosts. But I was intrigued after I learned that people from around the world come to see the light of walls made from thousands of yellow lanterns in the shrine.

Adjusting my backpack, I rang the bell on Harper's apartment door. Mike would drive us to Ida, one of Harper's friends I'd never met, who lived near the shrine. In her place, we would change into yukata, a traditional Japanese dress, and then walk to the shrine.

"Hi, Bella." Avery opened the door and held it with her arm.

"Hi, Avery." I waved to her and to Mike and Harper behind her, changing from their indoor slippers to shoes. They waved back at me.

"Hey, I like your skirt. It looks comfy," Avery commented as she looked at my plaid overall skirt.

"It is." I nodded. "Perfect for this sticky weather."

"Yeah, it gets stickier and stickier," Harper commented as she stepped outside. "I've been here for a few years, but still, I haven't become accustomed to summer in Tokyo."

"Okay, guys. Let's go," Mike said as he stood next to Avery.

"You look great in your blue yukata, Mike," I exclaimed as we began to walk toward the elevator.

"He does look handsome in it, right?" Harper sounded proud.

"Thanks," Mike said. "Ida doesn't have any yukata for men, so I have to wear mine. But I don't mind because I prefer to wear it now than later. You ladies need to doll up anyway." He grinned.

"Ida has many beautiful yukatas. You'll like it," chimed in Avery. "I'm always looking forward to wearing yukata in summer. Even my hair is ready." She pointed at the braid on top of her hair.

"I'm so excited because I've never worn a yukata." I admired her hair.

"You'll like it. It's a perfect dress for summer," Harper commented.

We went down to the parking lot outside the building, jumped into Mike's old Prius, and drove to Ida's place.

As we passed the Imperial Palace, I recalled on the first day I arrived. It was hard to believe that I'd been in Tokyo for a month. Time flew.

We arrived at Ida's apartment around 4:15 p.m., and Harper introduced me to her. She was a petite lady around twenty-five. Her hair was shoulder-length, and her eyes were big with beautiful eyelashes. She was a teacher and worked with Harper.

Inside Ida's apartment, my mouth hung open because her apartment was four times larger than mine.

Harper tapped my dropped chin playfully. "Careful, you might catch a fly."

"Is this *her* apartment?" I whispered as we walked to a room where colorful yukatas were laid out on a queen bed.

She nodded. "Her dad bought it for her once he knew Ida would stay in Tokyo. That's good because if her mom or her sister visits her, they can stay with her."

"Wow, she must be loaded."

"Yup. If she chose not to work, she could." Harper picked up a light-blue yukata with cherry blossom flowers. "Hey, is this good for me?" She pressed the yukata to her chest.

I gazed for a moment and nodded.

"Great." Then she disappeared behind a thick curtain that Ida hung to create privacy for changing.

"Have you chosen yours, Bella?" Ida asked as she entered the room carrying a makeup bag.

"Not yet. I don't know which one is perfect for me."

Ida gazed at me and then at the yukatas. "The light yellow is good for you." She pointed with her chin.

I picked it up, pressed the yukata to my chest, and looked at my reflection in the mirror. She was right; that color was good on me.

"Okay, I'll take it," I said.

At the same time, Harper came out with her yukata.

"Let me help you," said Ida, who took a red cord and sash and began to wrap the cord around Harper's waist while I stepped behind the curtain.

It was almost five o'clock by the time we were ready. Mike nearly fell asleep on the sofa waiting for us. He grinned when he saw we had dolled ourselves up and offered to take our picture, which no one refused.

"I look weird wearing these sneakers with a yukata," I said, eyeing the sandals on my friends' feet as we ambled the roads leading to the shrine.

"I wish I had your size, Bel," said Ida.

"It's okay, Bella. Nowadays, people aren't too strict." Harper comforted me.

The humidity was unforgiving. The back of my yukata was already wet, even though I'd been fanning myself with a rechargeable pocket fan. Feeling jealous, I glanced at my friends, who didn't seemed bothered by the weather and missed wearing my spaghetti top and shorts.

The sun didn't seem ready to dive into the horizon yet and was still bright. For a while, I put a hand over my eyes to block the blinding sunlight. I'd forgotten my sunglasses—but maybe it was better to not wear them because I barely saw Japanese people with sunglasses and my friends didn't wear them either. Perhaps that was part of the culture here; I had to learn to adopt it too.

Still, my poor eyes!

As we came closer to the shrine, we bumped into women and children in colorful yukata and men primarily in dark blue or gray yukata. Enthusiasm beamed from their eyes as they bounced from foot to foot as if there were coils in their shoes.

Then we were welcomed by Daiichi Torii, the first gate at the shrine's entrance. Others were attracted by long walls of glowing yellow lanterns, but I stopped and looked up at the two cylindrical posts topped by a crosswise beam extending beyond them, with a second beam below. I felt small in front of the giant *torii*.

"Bella, we're going inside," called Harper.

I nodded without turning to her. Carefully, I walked closer and touched the pillar. If they could speak, these beams could tell many stories of what they witnessed during the festivals.

Letting out a sigh, I continued. After a few steps, I stopped again and gazed at the walls of lanterns stretching on both sides of the street toward the entrance.

"That's amazing," I whispered.

"There are more inside," commented Ida, who was standing next to me.

"More?" My head twirled to her.

"The lanterns won't stop until they reach the inner shrine." She signaled me to continue.

As Ida and I walked toward a tall bronze statue, my nose caught the delicious smell of food. I scanned and spotted the street food vendors lined up outside the shrine's grounds. The scent of a combination of foods wafted toward us. It was mouthwatering, though I wasn't interested in the food, but the shrine grounds.

"Can we eat first?" Avery asked her sister.

Harper exchanged a glance with Mike, who smirked and shrugged. "Okay," she said and turned to me. "Since this is your first time, why don't you walk around? She"—Harper pointed to her sister, who was already in line for some fried noodles—"won't do anything if she is hungry."

"I'll go with you," offered Ida.

"Really?" My expression must have been hopeful because Ida grinned widely.

She nodded.

Almost squealing, I grabbed her wrist and dragged her behind me.

"Watch your behavior there, Bella," I heard Mike tease me.

"Do you want me to buy you something?" Harper asked loudly.

"Anything," I answered loudly over my shoulder.

The shrine ground was crowded with people who milled around. I almost bumped into a group of teens who tried to take their pictures with a selfie stick.

"Crazy, right?" Ida raised her voice over the hubbub and the buzzing of cicadas in the background.

I nodded. "It would be perfect if no mosquitos were trying to suck in my blood." I waved a hand to get rid of the whining sound of the bugs around my face and ears.

Ida snickered. "It'd be perfect if we met handsome men here."

I grinned and swatted a mosquito on my hand.

"Bella." Ida tapped my shoulder and pointed to her left. "Let's go this way. You need to see this event."

I followed Ida toward the crowd watching some men carry a beautiful red and gold-colored palanquin.

"What is that?" I asked.

"It's called a *Mikoshi*. It's a sacred palanquin for Shinto believers," she explained. "It serves as transportation for a deity from one shrine to another."

"Wow, interesting." I pulled out my phone to take pictures.

Ida nodded. "Japanese culture is so rich. You'll be amazed if you learn more about it."

We watched the parade for some time and decided to go to the other side of the shrine. As I turned, someone bumped my shoulder, and my phone slipped out of my fingers.

"Oh no!" I crouched down to pick it up before it was trampled under people's shoes. But a hand had already picked it up.

I looked up at the hand's owner, and it was Ryo. His eyes widened to see me too, but the surprised look was wiped by a gentle, warm smile.

Something fluttered in my stomach to see his smile, and under the lanterns, he looked incredibly handsome in his dark blue yukata with embroidery on the sleeves.

"It's a surprise to see you here, Bella," he gave me my phone, and looked at my clothes. "That yukata is perfect on you."

"Thanks." I smiled, looking at it proudly. "My first time wearing it. I think you look great in your yukata too."

He smiled and glanced at Ida, who looked at him with her mouth slightly open. Holding in my laugh, I gave a nudge on her arm. She almost jumped. "Who is this, Bel?" she asked, without taking her eyes from him.

"My next-door neighbor, Ryo," I said and turned to Ryo. "Ryo, this is Ida, one of Harper's friends."

They shook hands. "Your English is good," said Ida, without dropping her eyes from Ryo.

"Thanks. I've lived in the US for more than seven years," Ryo answered.

Ida nodded, and I bit my lower lip at seeing how Ida was mesmerized by Ryo.

"Are you alone?" I looked behind him.

"I'm here with my friends." He turned around and pointed in the direction of colorful giant streamers.

"Those streamers are huge. I've never seen anything like that." I focused on the streamers.

"That spot is famous for pictures. Let's go there. I can help you both take some pictures and introduce you to my friends," invited Ryo.

Ida instantly dragged me and followed him.

"Is he single?" Ida whispered, looping her hand around my arm.

"How do I know? Ask him yourself," I whispered back, jerking my arm free.

"You're his next-door neighbor; please help me." Ida gave me puppy eyes.

"No," I said, half laughing, half feeling annoyed.

She pouted but flashed a smile as Ryo slowed his pace. "Where's your friends?" she asked.

"Over there, under the green streamer," Ryo said.

I felt my eyes round as I walked closer to the colorful streamers. They were so beautiful, and when the wind blew, they waved gently. I raised my fingers to touch one when a female voice called my name.

"Bella?"

I turned to find the voice's source was a thin, tall lady with a bob in a light turquoise yukata with peonies on it.

"Sara?" I recognized her.

A smile broke out on her lips. "What a surprise to see you here. And look at you. You're beautiful. The yukata's color is perfect for your hair."

"Thank you." Smiling sheepishly, I touched my messy bun.

Ryo approached us and raised his eyebrows as his eyes shifted between Sara and me. "You know each other?"

I nodded. Before I said anything, Sara intervened.

"She is a café trainer from Little Bear corporate," Sara said, looking at Ryo. "I thought when you went to the café a few weeks ago, you'd seen her."

Ryo shook. "I know there's a trainer, but I didn't see her face."

Taking my hand, Sara smiled at me. "She is my favorite trainer because she has more patience with my employees."

"I just do my best," I answered politely. "And I'm surprised that you and Ryo know each other."

"He's my childhood friend," said Sara, beaming at Ryo.

"Yes, that's right," Ryo nodded.

A soft jerk pulled in my heart at the way Sara looked at Ryo. It was similar to how my sister, Adele, looked at her husband or Mel at Andrew. I touched the base of my neck when I realized that I didn't like it.

"What's your problem anyway, Bel?" I murmured to myself, tapping the side of my head.

"Are you okay?" Ryo asked.

My cheeks warmed, and I was glad that the sky was dark, so the only illumination was from the lanterns and lamps around the shrine.

"Mosquito," I lied. "It's whining around my head. See that?" My finger pointed at the air, and I swatted twice.

One side of his mouth kicked up in a smile as he nodded, accepting my reason. "Come, let me introduce you to my other friends." He waved his hand to the other four standing near us. "This is Takeru, Kimi—Takeru's cousin, her sister, Keiko, and Albert—Keiko's boyfriend."

Ida and I shook their hands. I recognized Takeru as the man who was with Ryo the first time we met in Apple Heights. He seemed to remember me too because he smiled knowingly. Kimi and Keiko were pretty, and they each wore their hair in a side braid. Albert was a head taller than Keiko, and from his accent, he must have been Australian.

"So, how do you guys know each other?" asked Sara, gazing at Ryo and me once the introductions were done.

"Ah." I scratched the back of my neck. "That's a long …"

"She is my next-door neighbor in Apple Heights," Ryo answered quickly.

"Really?" A smile disappeared from her lips as Sara straightened her body. Her brows wrinkled as she turned to Ryo. "I didn't know you live in Apple Heights. It's near the cemetery."

He nodded. "It's cheaper, and I could choose the option for semi-furnished. Fit my budget," he said breezily.

"If you'd asked me, I could have found you the affordable apartment," she remarked. Her brows were still wrinkling as she glanced at me.

"Thanks. Apple Heights is okay." Ryo seemed uncomfortable and gave a short exhale mixed with relief when Albert engaged him in conversation.

I pressed a smile as I avoided Sara's cold gaze by pretending to admire Kimi's yukata. Kimi took my bait, and Ida chimed in. For a quick second, the three of us talked about the difference between yukata and kimono.

Our conversation was interrupted by the loud songs and drums coming from the speakers.

"The Obon dance begins," commented Ida, tilting her head toward the sound. "Bella, you should join in the traditional dance. It's fun." Then she turned to Ryo and his friends. "Do you guys want to join?"

"I'll join." Kimi raised her hand.

Sara shook her head. "It's too muggy for dancing. Let's go watch the small lanterns in the shrine's courtyard." She looked at Ryo. I detected hopefulness in her eyes.

Ryo flashed a small smile. "I'll join them. It's been so long since the last time I participated in the dance."

Ida's face shone as she moved closer to him. Somehow, I, too was happy for his answer, although I managed a placid expression.

"How about you guys?" He looked at Takeru, Keiko, and Albert.

They shook their heads almost in unison.

"I don't want to sweat," added Keiko.

"Okay, let's meet again in thirty minutes near Daiichi Torii?" Ryo turned to Takeru.

Takeru glanced at his watch and nodded. "Yes. See you there."

We split. Ryo, Kimi, and I followed Ida while Takeru, Sara, Keiko, and her boyfriend entered the shrine's courtyard to see the small lanterns.

"This dance is fun, Bella," commented Ryo.

"Yes, I like it too," Ida chimed in.

"I can't wait." I smiled.

By the time we arrived, multiple layers of people were already dancing, imitating the women in light purple yukata on the stage built around the bronze statue near Daiichi Torii.

"Let's join. Just follow the women on the stage." Ida scurried and sneaked between a ponytailed lady in a green yukata and a short-haired white man in a gray yukata. I followed her. Ryo was standing behind me, and Kimi followed him.

The dance's movements seemed simple and straightforward, but it wasn't as easy as it appeared. When the masses turned to the left, I turned to the right. When they clapped three times, I clapped two.

As we danced, Ryo let out a loud chortle each time I made a blunder. But he was nice enough to tell me the next movement in advance. That way, I danced a bit more smoothly.

"Fun, isn't it?" he remarked, standing next to me as we applauded the dancers on the stage. Our shoulders brushed.

"It is, although I made a lot of mistakes," I said, scanning the happy faces of the participants.

"You did a good job. Just need more practice."

I chuckled. "Yeah, I should check it out on YouTube and practice so when I come again next year, I can dance gracefully."

"Wait." He touched my shoulder to get my attention. His eyebrows furrowed. "What do you mean by coming bac ..."

His voice was drowned out by the racket of people as they dispersed in different directions. My eyes caught Mike approaching us.

"Ryo!" Mike called. "What a surprise to see you here. Are you alone?"

"No, with my friends, but they are on the other side of the shrine," he answered. "This is my friend, Kimi."

"Bella, Ida." Avery waved as she and her sister joined in a minute later. Harper's eyebrows rose slightly as she shifted her eyes between Ryo and me before shaking Kimi's hand to introduce herself.

"Did you dance too?" Harper asked me.

I nodded, grinning broadly. "It is fun. I like it."

"Good. I'm glad you like it. Hey, are you guys hungry?" asked Harper, taking Mike's hand.

"I am," said Ida.

"Me too," I said.

"Bella, you should try the food here." Avery pointed at the food stalls.

"What should I try?" I craned my neck toward the stalls.

"Lots of things," Avery giggled. "*Kakigori*—the shaved ice—*wataame*, which is the cotton candy, and the choco-banana."

"Those are snacks." Harper chuckled. "If you're hungry, you can order fried noodles, yakitori, takoyaki. Ryo, Kimi, come and join us." Harper turned to them.

"Please," Ida begged Ryo.

He smiled and nodded. "Sure."

I grinned as Ida bounced on her toes next to Ryo as we joined the crowd walking toward the stalls.

RYO

Ryo's face was etched with guilt and sadness. He swallowed a few times, glancing at the phone on the kotatsu.

A few hours ago, he had fun celebrating the summer festival with his friends. In the bright illumination of the lanterns, they joked around, danced, savored delicious street food, and enjoyed traditional ceremonies in the shrine.

Initially, he didn't want to join when Takeru had invited him because he knew that Takeru had also asked Sara. Ryo needed time before facing Sara again after he refused to take the job that she'd offered him.

Ryo was thankful for Sara and her offer. If he hadn't felt like taking the job would have encouraged Sara's feelings for him, he would have had almost no objection to working in her dad's office. But what upset him the most was he that was offered the IT senior manager position on the spot as if the job was a gift: without any effort to compete against other applicants. He wasn't a charity case; he had a sense of pride and integrity.

The highlight of his day was the unexpected meeting with Bella at the festival. Was it fate that they kept bumping into each other?

Ryo wouldn't forget how adorable Bella was in her light-yellow yukata that made her red hair pop. Typically, while wearing yukata, women would wear flip flops, sandals, or, preferably *geta*, traditional Japanese sandals. But Bella wore sneakers, and Ryo found it unique and imaginative.

His heart twirled and floated at seeing her serious expression while dancing during the Obon or her lively smile over the giant cotton candy that she'd shared with Avery.

When they were about to leave the shrine, Ryo was happy as Mike asked if he wanted a ride home, considering he lived in the same building as Harper.

"So, you're going back with them?" Takeru asked as they walked together on the dirt road to the parking lot.

"Yes. That way, you can go back to your place after dropping your cousins and Sara off," Ryo reasoned. "My apartment is far from your house."

"It doesn't matter, but okay." Takeru shrugged, then nudged his elbow. "Is there any other reason?" he asked in a low voice. "I won't tell anyone."

Ryo chuckled. "Just for a practical reason."

Takeru had winked and clicked his tongue before turning away without saying anything.

It was almost midnight when Mike's car arrived in the parking lot. When they had reached the fifth floor and split up with Avery, Harper, and Mike at the fork, Ryo wished the hallway would turn into a labyrinth so he could spend more time walking with Bella alone and cherish the excited smile on her face.

"Bella."

"Hmm?"

"I didn't know you work in Sara's café," Ryo said as they ambled toward their units.

"I don't work for her. I work for Little Bear," she answered.

"Ah, that's right." He nodded.

When he was about to ask something, Bella cut him off with a question: "By the way, how far is Harajuku from here?"

"Not far. It's between Shinjuku and Shibuya if you take the Yamanote line. Why?" he asked.

"One of my friends told me that city is popular for fashion trends and bizarre food. I want to see what it looks like, but Harper and Ida have to work next Saturday. Avery is busy with her summer classes. Going to a fun place like that isn't as fun without friends." She shrugged.

"I can take you there if you want." The words blurted out of his mouth. He bit his lower lip, waiting for her reaction.

Her baby blue eyes widened as she turned to him. "Really? You want to take me there?"

"Yes."

Ryo couldn't take his eyes off Bella, who was practically bouncing on her feet.

"So next Saturday, then?" Her face shone.

"Sure. But I'll warn you, it'll be super crowded unless you want to be there in the morning."

"Yes. Let's go there in the morning."

However, the happiness had been taken away by the phone call from Kento. Akiko fell—at the same time Ryo was dancing—and was rushed to the hospital. There were no broken bones from the X-ray, but she had a hairline fracture and needed to wear a sling on her wrist for a month so it would heal.

Everything was fine. His sister was already sleeping at home by the time Kento called him. However, Ryo couldn't shake off the tightness in his chest. He felt guilty because when his family, especially Akiko, was in distress, he hadn't been available. He should have been the one who helped them, not Kento.

Ryo rubbed his face with both hands and ran them through his hair. Inhaling wearily, he rose to his feet and dragged his body to the bed. He took off his yukata and long pants, letting them drop on the floor.

Wearing only his underwear, Ryo climbed into the bed, lay on his side in the fetal position, and pulled the blanket over his head. His pillow was wet with silent tears that rolled down his cheeks. He wished he could enjoy time with his friends without feeling guilty about not being there for Akiko. All he wanted was for them all to have happy lives and for things to be easier for his twin.

BELLA

Bread Lounge had a special training session with the staff in the morning for a whole week. Since they didn't need me during that time, I started work after lunch, and I loved it because I didn't have to deal with a rush hour or cramped train.

And this morning, when I woke up, I craved American food. I longed for pancakes, French toast, sausages, hash browns, a bacon-and-mushroom omelet, and cheeseburgers. I even missed my mom's fresh orange juice.

Too bad there was no McDonald's or Denny's restaurant nearby.

To satisfy my craving, I walked to a small café named Ohayo that served American food. Harper had mentioned it, but she didn't say whether the café served breakfast.

There were three people inside the café when I arrived. My heart jolted to read the sign in the window that said: "Breakfast Only."

Rubbing my hands together, I climbed the café's front steps and pushed the glass door open. The bell above the door sounded, and a middle-aged woman serving food to a male customer looked up and smiled at me.

"Good morning." She greeted me cheerfully in English. "Please choose any seat. I'll be right with you."

"Thanks."

I chose a beige table near the window and took the chair facing the entrance. While waiting for the lady to come back, I picked up the laminated menu on the table and looked it over. My mouth watered at the pictures because everything looked good.

The woman came again with a glass of water and put it on my table. "Are you ready to order?" she asked.

"Yes," I said. "I'd like the number three, but can I add two sausages?"

"Sure." She wrote carefully on her small note. "For the egg, do you want it sunny side up, over easy, or scrambled?" She looked at me.

"Scrambled would be great," I answered.

"How about the toast? Whole wheat or white?"

"White."

She nodded. "Would you like a free glass of orange juice? It's our Tuesday special."

"Yes, please."

The woman smiled and then picked up the menu. She stopped at the customer two tables from me before walking to an adjacent room behind the counter and disappearing behind a thin curtain with birds and bamboo printed on it.

I leaned back in my seat and gazed out the window, enjoying the quiet morning. An elderly woman ambled with her cane on the empty sidewalk. A salaryman in a gray suit strode past her in a hurry. Two teenagers talked while they strolled. Everything would be all hustle and bustle again when all the stores opened in an hour.

My moment was interrupted by a buzz from my bag hanging on the chair. I took it out and saw a message from Harper asking to have breakfast together.

I typed a message to her. *I'm in the Ohayo Café.*

A split second later, she texted back. *Miss American breakfast?*

I smiled and sent a smile emoji to her.

Care if I join? She texted me.

Sure. But I ordered my food. Want me to order some for you?

No. Eat your food. Don't wait.

Okay, I responded.

I was about to put my phone in my bag when a soft ding from the bell indicated a new guest had come in.

I looked up, and my eyes widened to see Ryo enter the café with a backpack on his shoulders. Although we lived next to each other, I didn't bump into him often, and the last time we met was at the festival last Saturday, which was only a few days ago but it seemed too long, and somehow running into him again made my heart sputter joyfully. Ryo saw me too and his eyes beamed.

"Good morning." The middle-aged woman came out from the kitchen and greeted him in Japanese. "Please choose any seat."

"Thank you." He walked toward my table. "Morning, Bella. I'm surprised to see you here. May I?" He pointed at the empty seat in front of me.

"Sure. Harper will join too, though," I said.

"Will I interrupt you guys?"

"Of course not. She texted me after I came here." I smiled. "Please take a seat. I'm happy to have breakfast with you." Instantly, I felt heat creep up my neck. *Why did I say that? He might think I'm interested in him.*

My eyes must have tricked me because I saw color on his cheeks that was gone in a split second.

185

Thanking me, Ryo took the seat in front of me and put his backpack on the floor. Once he settled, I gave him the menu. His hand was a bit shaky as he held it.

"Any good food in here?" he asked without looking.

"It's my first time too, but I ordered the number three."

He looked at the menu. "Hmm, looks good. But number four looks delicious too."

While he was busy browsing, I secretly took him in. He looked extremely striking in his dark khakis and a light blue T-shirt this morning. The bangs on his forehead were a bit messy, and I had to fight my urge to smooth the few errant strands.

My order came. Everything looked appealing and neatly arranged: something that I'd admired at Japanese restaurants. The pancake took up half the plate with scrambled eggs, bacon, and sausage above it. There was a mini pitcher with maple syrup and a few single-serve butter on another plate. My orange juice looked fresh.

My ungrateful stomach growled loudly as the delicious smell of bacon and sausage hit my nose. When Ryo and the woman smiled at me, I wished to bury my head in the ground.

"The sausage and bacon smell so good," he said.

"Yes," I said casually.

"Well, bon appétit," the woman said to me and turned to Ryo taking her small notepad and a pen from her apron pocket. "Ready to order?" She spoke in Japanese.

Ryo placed his order and held up a hand while turning to me. "By the way, is the sausage added? Because I don't see them in number three."

"Yes."

He requested it to the woman, who nodded and wrote everything down. Then she returned to the kitchen.

"I had to order the sausages too. The smell is so tempting," Ryo said.

"Yes." I picked up the fork. "Itadakimasu."

He nodded and looked out the window. After a few beats, he turned to me. "About this Saturday, our plan hasn't changed, right?" he asked. I caught a hesitance in his eyes.

"Why? Do you want to cancel?" I put my fork on my plate, feeling my stomach clench because I had been looking forward to exploring Harajuku with him.

"No, I just want to make sure you haven't changed your mind," Ryo reasoned.

"I'm so looking forward to it," I said.

Ryo let out a shaky chuckle. "Great. Me too."

My heart hammered at his answer. *Is he really eager to go out with me?*

But I pushed the thought away from my mind.

"By the way," I said after some time. "On my first day here, I was encouraged to enjoy all the summer activities while I'm here. But there are many things to see in my short time here. Any suggestion which one that I have to see first?"

"W-what do you mean by many things to see in your short time here?" Ryo shifted in his seat.

His question was interrupted because the woman came with his order and put everything in front of him. "Anything else I can bring for you both?" she asked, hugging the tray to her chest.

"No, thank you," Ryo and I said in unison.

"Bon appétit." Then she turned back to the kitchen.

A second later, another soft ding came from the bell above the door, revealing Harper in her summer dress. Her eyes scanned around and stopped as I waved at her. In the meantime, the woman peeked out of the curtain. "Good morning, please find any seat."

"Thank you." Harper walked toward us.

"Fancy seeing you here, Ryo." She flashed a smile at him, but her eyes were on me as she sat next to Ryo.

"I was craving American food and bumped into Bella here."
Ryo smiled and clasped his hands. "Itadakimasu."

"What do you want to eat?" I asked Harper, who was looking
at the menu.

"Just something light." Her eyes fell on my juice. "How is it?"

"It's tasty and free for today."

"Nice. I'll take that and a matcha muffin." She put the menu
back. "I have a class at eleven. If I ate heavy breakfast, I'd starve
in the class later."

"Makes sense." I nodded.

As the woman came to us, Harper placed her order. In a short
time, she returned with the juice and the muffin.

"I thought you always worked early in the morning?" She
looked at me, sipping her juice

"Not this week because Bread Lounge has special training for the
staff in the morning. So my shift has been around noon," I answered.

She nodded and turned to Ryo. "How about you?"

Her serious tone tickled my stomach. I exchanged a glance with
Ryo and grinned broadly.

"What?" Harper narrowed her eyes at us.

"You sounded like a mom checking on her children's schedules,"
I teased her.

Color crept on Harper's face as she scoffed. "Sorry. I guess
taking care of Avery made me act older than my age."

I looked at her questioningly.

Harper sucked her lower lip as she glanced at Ryo and me. "My
mom passed away two years ago. My dad married a woman my
age. Avery wasn't even eighteen at the time. Since I didn't want
Avery to stay with them, I told her to come here," she said. "Well,
Avery hasn't been a docile girl, but that's okay. I'm her only sister.
We only have each other now." She took a gulp of orange juice as
her eyes became red and sparkled with tears.

I put my fork on the table and squeezed her hand gently. It must be tough to change her role from sister to mom. If I were her, I might not be able to do that.

"I'm sorry for the pain you've been through," Ryo said in a low voice.

Harper forced a smile and shook her head. "Ah, silly me. Why did I tell you this sad story?" Then she tapped her cheeks with both hands.

"That's okay, Harper. That's what friends are for. Anytime you need to dump your feelings, we're your ears." I glanced at Ryo, who nodded in agreement. "As foreigners here, we need to help each other."

"She's right," Ryo chimed in. "When I was in the States, my close friends were my family, and I got plenty of help from my American friends. Just call me whenever you need my help, okay?"

Harper blinked her eyes a few times. "Thanks." Her voice croaked.

For some time, we didn't say anything, just ate our food.

Around nine, we left the café. Ryo headed to a train station while Harper and I walked back to our apartment.

"He's cute." Harper nudged me.

"You have Mike," I reminded her.

She clicked her tongue impatiently. "Not for me, silly. He's for my single friend."

"Ida?"

Harper roared, doubling over. "Oh my God, you're so innocent."

My cheeks warmed. "Is it obvious?"

She nodded and wrapped her hand around my shoulder. "Yes, Bella. It is. But you have good taste. Ryo is a good guy, and I've liked him since the first time I met him."

I chuckled.

"And I think he likes you."

I raised an eyebrow at her comment. "How do you know?"

"His eyes light up when he sees you." She grinned widely. "At the festival, I caught he stole a glance at you a few times."

Her words brought a smile to my face.

"You should keep him," she added.

I didn't say a word, but I was practically bouncing with pleasure while walking beside her.

I arrived at the café ten minutes before eleven. The staff was role-playing: one team without an apron became customers and ordered drinks from the team with an apron. The assistant managers observed the team with an apron to ensure they used various phrases in Japanese and English with proper intonation, body language, and facial expressions. Little Bear didn't require them to get the training, but Bread Lounge did. Since the café would be managed under that company, all staff had to follow the rules. Tiptoeing, I went straight to the back room.

I was typing a report on my laptop when Nao entered the back room during recess time.

"Bella-chan," she called cheerfully.

"Nao." I looked up and smiled at her.

Nao took a seat in front of me and laid her head on the table. "I'm tired," she mumbled.

"Go eat your lunch. You need a sharp mind to attend my training, and I don't like students slacking off," I teased her.

She chuckled. "Hey, thanks for the role-playing idea. It helps my staff explore their weaknesses and gain more knowledge through the process. I guess they've become foam art experts now."

"I'm so glad the role-playing works well for the staff because coffee foam art is an important skill in Little Bear." I smiled.

Nao stretched her arms and rose from her seat. "Okay, then, I'm going to take lunch now. See you a bit."

"Okay." I nodded, closed my laptop, and went to sit at the office computer in the corner.

Thirty minutes later, Nao and her assistants were sitting around me. They took notes while listening to my explanation of the Little Bear report system. Since the system was user-friendly, even for those whose second language was English, it didn't take long for Nao and her assistants to learn it.

By four thirty, they had an adequate understanding of the system. I gave them some homework to practice while I wrote a progress report.

I was about to leave the café when I noticed Sara talking to Sato-san.

"Bella." She waved to me before turning back to Sato-san, who bowed slightly and left her.

I waved back. "I didn't know you were here today," I said.

Her eyes sparkled. "I'm here to invite you for dinner. I'd thought to do it last week, but I've been busy. Could you join me?"

My dad always said that the Japanese valued gathering after work because it was a moment for the bosses and the subordinates to get to know each other. Although I wasn't her subordinate, I was her business partner.

After giving it thought, I nodded. "Yes."

"Do you like sashimi?"

"I love it."

She smiled. "Great, let's go now."

Sara took me to a fancy sushi restaurant twenty minutes' drive from the café. Once we sat in our private room, two food servers brought a tray of different sushi and sashimi and a tray of assorted tempura with a special dipping sauce on the side.

Everything looked delicious. While eating, we talked about many things, and Sara was a pleasant person to be with. She shared her experiences living in the States and mentioned that she and Ryo had attended the same university and that she had returned to Tokyo for good, while Ryo stayed for work.

In return, I briefly talked about my family. Sara nodded here and there while listening and throwing in a few questions.

"What do you think about the food?" she asked as we finished.

"Fresh and tasty." I smiled, then poured sake into her empty cup with both hands. "The *otoro* melts in my mouth. I *love* it. Thanks for introducing me to the exquisite food."

"My pleasure." She looked pleased. "So, have you had a chance to visit different places in Tokyo?"

I nodded. "I went to a few places like Sensoji Temple, Meiji Shrine, and then with friends who you met during the summer festival, we went to Tsukiji Fish Market for sashimi bowl."

"The sashimi there is tasty and fresh too," Sara commented and poured sake into my cup. "By the way, speaking of your friends, can I ask you a question about Ida?"

I raised an eyebrow. "Ida?"

"Yes. Do you know how close she is with Ryo?"

I blinked. "Um ... why do you ask?"

"She seems to like him." Her hand flicked a speck of invisible dust from her sleeve.

I blinked again. Her direct manner surprised me. She must have seen Ida going gaga over Ryo at the festival. I almost said something when another memory flashed in my mind: the adoration in Sara's eyes when she looked at Ryo that night. Sara loved Ryo, and she didn't hide her feeling.

And all of a sudden, my stomach heaved, and I wondered if Ryo liked Sara too. Harper believed he liked me, but she could be wrong.

Clearing my throat, I looked at her. "Well, I don't know Ida well because I just met her that night too. If I can be fair, I think everyone in Harper's group likes Ryo because, you know, he's an easygoing person, considerate and helpful. He even offered his help to grill meat when Harper invited him to join her party the other week. He is nice to us all."

Sara didn't respond. Her eyebrows touched together while her fingernails tapped against the sake cup lightly. A few seconds later, a slow smile appeared on her lips. "You may be right. Ryo is always nice to everyone." I let out a sigh of relief as Sara seemed satisfied with the answer. She raised her cup. "Cheers."

I followed suit. Instead of sipping the sake, I gulped and let the clean, slightly sweet drink flow down my throat and into my stomach. After that, I felt the time ticked slowly like an eternity, and I couldn't wait to leave the restaurant.

BELLA

The light, coming through the sliding door, fell on me and woke me up. I moaned and buried my face into the pillow. I forgot to draw the curtain shut last night: Something that I never had done because I liked sleeping in the dark.

"That's your fault!" I chided myself loudly. "You shouldn't have let your mind wander."

Groaning, I forced myself into a sitting position.

Since I had dinner with Sara yesterday, the unbidden memory of how she looked at Ryo at the festival flashed into my mind before I could stop it. It became vivid as if they were standing in front of me: Sara's eyes were full of compassion, and Ryo smiled at her.

Wait, did Ryo smile at her? Or didn't he?

A long sigh escaped my lips as I rubbed a hand across my forehead and moved slowly into the bathroom. Leaning over the sink, I splashed my face with cold water a few times and looked in the mirror.

"You should focus more on your work, Bella," I muttered to myself and grabbed a towel to dry my face.

I was in my room, tying up my hair in a ponytail, when my phone buzzed. Avery's name showed on the screen.

"Hi, Avery," I greeted her through the speakerphone. "What's ...? I stopped because I heard a groan on the other end.

"Avery?" I called. I felt acidity rising to my throat. "Are you okay?"

"Bella, my stomach hurts," she groaned. "Harper has already left for work."

"What happened? Did you eat something that didn't agree with your stomach?"

"I don't know ... aagh." This time, the groan was longer, and she sounded pained.

"I'll be there," I said quickly.

I grabbed my house key, locked the door, and darted to her apartment.

"Avery, it's me, Bella." I pressed the doorbell and knocked on the door hard. "Open the door, please." I leaned my ear to the door, but I heard nothing.

"Avery," I called louder.

I heard a soft click, and the door swung ajar. Leaning on the wall, Avery was half-bent with a hand on her stomach. Her face was pale and crumpled.

"Avery!" I rushed in and helped her sit on the floor. Sweat pooled on her forehead. Her skin was damp and cold as I touched her forehead. "You need a doctor. Can you walk?"

Although she nodded, I doubted it.

"Let me get my bag, and then we'll go to the doctor." My breath came fast.

"Grab my insurance card and ID." She pointed at a tall gray, narrow cabinet. "My wallet is in the brown bag."

My hand shook slightly as I took her wallet from the cabinet then placed it next to her. "I'll be back," I said.

Without waiting for her response, I returned to my unit and called Harper, but it went to voice mail. I left her a short message and grabbed my bag. When I was about to lock my door, Ryo stepped outside his unit.

"Hey, Bel. What happened? You look tense." He widened his eyes in alarm.

Something inflated in my chest as I looked at him. "I'm glad you're here. Please come with me." I grabbed his hand without thinking, but a deep crease appeared on his forehead stopped me.

"Can you tell me what happened?" He looked puzzled.

"Avery—she's in pain. I think we need to take her to a doctor," I sputtered. "My Japanese is elementary, so I don't know how to explain her condition." My voice was shaking.

Solemnly, Ryo put his hands on my shoulders. "Bella, calm down. Don't panic. Now, take a few deep breaths." Looking into my eyes, he took a deep breath and encouraged me to do the same.

I obeyed him. Slowly my breath became deep, and my heartbeat slowed. As he noticed me becoming calmer, he squeezed my shoulders gently. "Now, go back to her place. I'll meet you there."

I closed my eyes briefly and nodded. "Okay." Then I scurried down to Avery's apartment and told her that Ryo would go with us to a doctor.

It took Ryo longer than I expected. I paced in and out of the doorway to check on him.

"Is Ryo coming?" Avery wondered.

I forced a smile and crouched next to her. "He'll be here." Then I heard footsteps running in the hallway.

"Sorry." Ryo panted slightly. "I called my friend who is a doctor in a hospital nearby, and he is waiting for us."

"We need a taxi," I commented.

"I already parked my car near the entrance." Ryo slipped his arm over Avery's other shoulder. "Bel, take her shoulder."

I imitated him and locked her apartment with my free hand before we half dragged her to the elevator and down to the sidewalk where Ryo had parked his car.

"Tell me again what happened to her?" asked Ryo when we were on the way to the hospital.

"She only said her stomach hurt." I glanced over at the back seat.

"I see. My friend can check her out thoroughly once we're in the hospital. I'm glad he's working today because he's usually off on Wednesday. " He looked across the car. "Has Harper contacted you yet?"

I shook my head. "Where's the hospital again? I can give her the address."

"I'll share it with you." With his free hand, Ryo shared the location and I forwarded it to Harper.

"Thanks for coming with us." I looked at him. "Avery's Japanese is good, but in her condition, she won't help much."

"If I were you, I wouldn't worry. In hospitals, most nurses and doctors have adequate English skills." Ryo comforted me.

My phone buzzed. I looked down to see Harper's name. "It's Harper." I brought the phone to my ear. "Harper, thank God you called me back."

"Bel, how's my sister?" Her voice was concerned. "Are you on the way to the hospital?"

"Yes, we're on our way to the hospital. Where are you?" I asked.

"I'm waiting for a taxi. The school principal permitted me to take the day off," said Harper. I heard her breathing speed up. "How did you get to the hospital? Is my sister strong enough to give an explanation in Japanese?"

"Ryo is with us now." I glanced at Ryo. "Just meet us there."

"Yes, I'll be there shortly."

"Great."

"Bella," she called to me once I was about to hang up. "Thanks for your help."

"That's what a friend is for."

I felt her smile at me before we hung up.

"Your sister is on the way to the hospital too," I said to Avery.

"Thanks, Bell," she said weakly, without opening her eyes.

Letting out a sigh, I sat back in my seat and felt a gentle nudge on my arm. "Don't worry, everything will be fine." He smiled gently.

I nodded and glanced at my watch. "Oh no!" I jumped in my seat, covering my mouth. Ryo whipped his head back to me. "I have to be at work at ten thirty. It's nine forty-five now."

"I can take her to the hospital," Ryo offered.

"Let me contact Nao." I dialed her number, and she picked up on the third ring.

"Good morning, Bella-chan," she greeted cheerfully.

"Nao, I'm taking my friend to the hospital because she is very sick," I informed her.

"Oh, no. What happened?"

"I don't know. She only said her stomach hurt," I shifted, looking at Avery.

"I see. Well, don't worry about us. Today is just rehearsing, anyway. Just focus on helping your friend. See you tomorrow, and I hope your friend is okay," she said.

"Thanks, Nao."

I breathed out a sigh as I rubbed my forehead with one hand.

The traffic was light with only a couple of choke points. Twenty minutes later, we arrived at the hospital. Ryo stopped the car on the entrance curve and together we took Avery in. One nurse—her name tag read "Maiko"—saw and rushed to help us. She nodded, glancing at Avery when Ryo gave a short explanation to her.

"She instructs us to wait in the waiting room while she goes to call my friend," Ryo told me.

"Great."

Sitting next to Avery, I watched Ryo talk to a different nurse at the front desk. He gave the nod and answered the questions from the nurse. He looked calm and poised. When the nurse typed something on the computer, Ryo must have sensed he was being watched because he turned to me and smiled.

Looking down, I felt a gentle flutter in my belly, and my face heated up.

"Your face is red."

I turned to see Avery, who had made a comment. Although she was in pain, her eyes studied me.

"It is?" I cupped my cheeks and felt warmth on my palms.

From the corner of my eyes, I saw Ryo approach us with Maiko pushing a wheelchair behind him. I rose to my feet instantly as though stung by a bee. "My friend will check on her once he's done with his patient. Right now, she's going to take Avery to the exam room." He glanced at the nurse.

I nodded and watched him help Maiko move Avery to the wheelchair.

"You'll be fine." I took Avery's hand.

She nodded.

Ryo and I stood watching while Maiko and Avery disappeared behind the double swinging doors. I settled back in my seat with a sigh and Ryo followed suit. For some time, people's voices and activities in the waiting room became background noise.

Ryo shifted in his seat to take his phone out from his back pocket, and his shoulder brushed mine. The touch was subtle, but I could feel his shoulder was strong and taut. Again, I felt butterflies in my stomach. Silently, I clenched my phone tightly to calm myself down.

"She'll be all right," Ryo comforted me. He must have misunderstood my silence.

I nodded. "I believe sh—" I stopped because I saw Harper enter the waiting room. She looked pale, and her hand clenched her Tory Burch bag. Relieved, I stood up and waved at her.

"Bella, Ryo," she called, speeding up to reach us. "How's Avery?"

"The nurse already brought her into the exam room. I believe she's with a doctor now." I glanced at Ryo for confirmation.

"The doctor is my friend, so don't worry; Avery is in capable hands," said Ryo.

"Sit here." I tapped an empty seat next to mine.

She did and let out a sigh. Her fingers wrenched each other.

"She'll be fine." I comforted Harper. "Maybe she ate something that didn't agree with her stomach."

Harper tucked a strand of hair behind an ear. "I don't know. Since the day after the festival, she's been unwell. Maybe it's the weather. Last year, she was sick too."

A tall man with glasses and a long white coat came through the double swinging doors and walked toward us. Ryo stood up to greet him, and they shook hands and spoke in Japanese while they glanced at us.

My heart stopped beating for a second when Ryo's expression changed, and his hand signaled Harper to come closer. I furrowed my eyebrows since Harper gasped and covered her mouth with her fingers.

For a few moments, she didn't say anything. But I could see tears in her eyes threatening to spill over. Blinking her eyes faster, Harper turned to the doctor and said something in Japanese. Her voice cracked. The doctor nodded and signaled her to follow him. They disappeared behind the swinging doors.

"W-what happened?" I turned to Ryo, who was sitting back in his seat.

Ryo took a deep breath before answering. "At first, my friend assumed Avery had severe cramps until the blood tests confirmed that she is pregnant."

"Oh my." I flopped down in my seat, covering a hand over my mouth.

Avery was two years younger than me, and she was … pregnant. It surprised me because I didn't know Avery had a boyfriend.

For a few moments, I sat in silence until a gentle nudge on my shoulder brought me back to the room.

"Are you okay?" Concern showed in Ryo's eyes.

I nodded, still in shock. "I-I'm just surprised because I never—"

My words were cut off because Harper burst through the swinging doors with Avery walking behind her. Harper's face was red, and her eyes protruded. She brushed her tears abruptly as she walked past us out of the room toward the entrance. Avery's eyes were teary too, and when they locked to mine, they were begging for help, but I looked down.

"Bella," she whimpered.

I stood from my seat and said weakly, "Go, follow your sister."

Sniffing, she dragged her feet.

Ryo held my elbow as I was about to follow them. "Can I give you advice?" His palm was warm and pulsed electricity onto my skin.

"Yes."

Dropping his hand to his side, he said, "I don't know how long you've known them, but if it's possible, stay away from their problems. You can comfort them, but let the sisters solve it themselves."

"You're right. They should solve their own problems."

"Unless later Harper or Avery want to talk about their feelings," he added.

"Okay."

Outside, the sisters stood apart on the boulevard in front of the hospital. Harper stood with her back to Avery, while Avery, no longer crying, stood with her head hanging down, staring at the ground. I patted her shoulder gently before moving to Harper. She turned and gave a sad smile to Ryo and me.

"Thanks for your help," she said.

"Don't mention it," said Ryo, gazing at Avery, Harper, and me. "Come, I parked my car in the parking ramp over there." He pointed at the gray three-story building.

On the way to the parking lot, I walked next to Avery behind Harper and Ryo.

"Are you okay?" I whispered.

"I don't know what to do." She cried softly and held my elbow to stop me. "Now, Harper is angry and demands me to call Kevin."

"Kevin? The father?"

She nodded. "My sister hates me." Her lips quivered.

I sighed and rubbed her arm to give her some comfort. "Your sister doesn't hate you. She is just shocked. But I think she is right: you should tell Kevin about your pregnancy."

Avery sniffed. Then we ambled to Ryo's car in silence.

RYO

Ryo glanced across the car at Harper, who was sitting stonily with her hands clamped on her lap. Her eyes were blinking hard. It looked like the pregnancy news was shaking Harper to her core. Sighing, Ryo reached out to hold Harper's hand.

A tear rolled on her cheek as she turned to him. "I'll be fine." She swallowed hard. "I just hope Kevin doesn't run away."

"The father?"

Harper nodded. "They've been dating for three weeks and …" Her voice trailed off.

"Let's hope he's a responsible man," Ryo gave a gentle squeeze on her hand before releasing it.

Harper dropped her head for a moment and turned to stare out the window.

Ryo shifted his eyes to look at Bella in the rearview mirror. As if Bella sensed that he was looking at her, she lifted her eyes to him and flashed a weak smile.

It was already one o'clock when Ryo's car stopped in the parking lot. Once they were outside the car, Avery positioned her willowy body behind Bella as if Bella were big and tall. Without wearing heels, the top of Bella's head was under her earlobe.

His heart warmed to see Bella take Avery's hand and give a comforting smile to the tall woman. She signaled her to go to her sister before she stood next to Ryo.

"Thanks for your help, Ryo and Bella." Harper looked at them.

"Don't mention it," Bella and Ryo said, almost in unison.

A slight smile appeared on Harper's lips as she turned around and walked toward the entrance. Her shoulders dropped. Avery followed her from behind like a sad puppy.

Bella took a deep breath and wrapped her arms around herself. "Poor them." Her eyes followed the sisters until they disappeared behind the glass double doors.

"Yes." he agreed.

Biting her lip, Bella turned to him. "I wish I could be like my sister, Adele, who would know how to respond in this kind of situation. I'm a useless friend, while they've helped me a lot since I came here."

"Don't underestimate yourself. You brought her to the hospital and waited until Harper came. You did well."

"That's because you were there."

Ryo shook his head. "Even if I weren't at home, you'd have brought Avery to the hospital anyway, right?"

She nodded slowly, shifting from one foot to the other. Her fingers played with the strap of her bag.

Unbeknownst to Bella, Ryo took her in. She looked cute in her white puffed-shoulder dress and white sneakers. Her hair was up in a slightly messy ponytail, with tendrils of hair falling around her ears and nose. He pressed his lips tight as she blew a strand away from her nose, but it fell back.

"Since you're off, let's go to Harajuku now instead of Saturday," he blurted out.

Her baby blue eyes widened in a combination of surprise and excitement. "Really?" Her voice sounded disbelieving. "But don't you have something to do?"

Ryo shook his head, and his heart smiled as she bit her lower lip to stifle a squeal of happiness. "Let's go." He turned back to his car with Bella following him.

Their hands touched as they both reached to open the driver's door. He felt tingles at the brief contact point as if touched by a small shock of electricity. This was the third time it had happened today, the first when their arms brushed as they held up Avery, and the second when he held her elbow.

Bella tsked and tapped her forehead. "I always forget that the passenger seat is on the left." Chuckling, she walked around the car and lowered herself to the seat.

As Ryo buckled up, he glanced at Bella. She looked calm as if nothing had happened. Was he the only one who'd felt the tingling sensation?

He pushed the thought away and pointed at the compartment in front of her. "Bella, would you mind getting my sunglasses from the glove box?"

She nodded and gave him the case. "You're wearing sunglasses, but why have I barely seen other Japanese people wear them?"

"It isn't common here because people will stare at you as if you're a gang member or a famous artist," he answered, then put on his glasses and slid the case into the side pocket.

"Are you joking?"

"No." He shook.

"So, are you a gangster or a famous artist?" she teased after looking at him for a few beats.

"Hmm, what do you think?"

A line appeared between her eyebrows as she tilted her head. Her pinkish lips pouted slightly, and Ryo's heart pounded hard as he felt his lips tingling. Clearing his throat, he looked away.

"Gangster."

Her answer forced him to turn back to her. "Why?" he chuckled lightly. "Do I look scary?"

"No, you're a good-looking man," she answered. Instantly, a shade of pink appeared on her neck and crept up to her cheeks as she covered her mouth with hands.

"I—I mean," she stuttered, waving her hand. "If I said 'famous artist,' it would sound boring. Ninety-nine percent of men would choose that. Since the options are a gangster or a famous artist, the gangster sounds more intriguing and sexier."

Ryo couldn't help but laugh hard. "Hmm, gangster, intriguing, sexy. Should I take it as a compliment?"

The corner of Ryo's mouth turned up as the flush on her face deepened from pink to red while she looked out the window.

Not willing to tease her any longer, Ryo shifted his eyes to the road but stole a glance at Bella. Without her knowing, Bella's existence wrapped around his heart and soul.

As he'd expected, Takeshita Street was packed; the crowd swarmed on the pedestrian shopping street lined with trendy stores, boutiques, cute cafés, and fast food in Harajuku.

"Is it always like this?" Bella asked loudly as they waded through the crowd.

Ryo nodded. "This street is famous and is also the center of fashion trends in Japan. We're lucky that we came on Thursday because weekends are the worst." He placed his hand a few inches behind her back to protect her from people who didn't look where they were going.

"Oh, look! Sailor Moon," she pointed at two young women in Sailor Moon costumes who stopped and gave a free *uchiwa*—traditional Japanese fan—to each of them. "Could you take a picture of them and me?" She gave her phone to him. "My sister and my friend Mel love Sailor Moon. I want to give the picture to them."

"Okay." He took the phone then spoke to them. The Sailor Moons nodded happily, and Bella bounced closer to them.

Through the screen, Ryo watched Bella's face come alive with pure joy as she posed between the Sailor Moons. It had been so long since he'd witnessed someone so filled with joy.

"Okay, ready." He waved his hand to get their attention. "One ... two ... three ..." He took their picture three times.

"Arigatou-gozaimasu." She bowed slightly to the Sailor Moons once they broke away. Her eyes sparkled as she walked toward him. "Thanks, Ryo."

With a smile lingering on her lips, she scanned around, fanning her neck. The weather was unforgiving today. The humidity level was more than 70 percent. Some visitors were staying under the shade of buildings or fanning their faces frantically with the uchiwa. Still, here and there, Ryo heard laughter and squeals of joy from visitors.

Twenty feet away from them, two men in costume, Vegeta and Goku, two characters from *Dragon Ball Z*, approached them. They laughed and shouted while pushing each other's shoulders. As the men passed them, Vegeta lost his balance and stumbled into Bella.

"Hey, watch out!" Ryo protested, instinctively wrapping his arm around her shoulder, and pulled her closer. Vegeta and Goku didn't hear his protest. Whether they ignored him or the hubbub of laughter and chatters drowned out Ryo's voice, they didn't say sorry but kept walking.

As Ryo looked down, he realized that Bella stared back at him with eyes bigger than saucers. He might have pulled her a little harder because her arms rested on his chest, and her nose was a half-inch from it. They were so close, the subtle, fresh smell from her shampoo filled his nostrils.

"Are you okay?" His voice came out just above a whisper.

"Yes." She swallowed. Her cheeks turned pink. Lowering her gaze, she broke herself free. Her hand tucked a strand of her hair behind her ear. She looked adorable.

"Thanks." She forced a smile.

"Don't mention it." Ryo dropped his eyes and cleared his throat awkwardly.

"I think we should continue," she suggested after a few beats. Her cheeks were no longer pinkish.

"Ah yes." Ryo nodded.

As they continued, Bella's kept checking her phone. Ryo didn't dare to ask what she was looking at but kept matching her pace.

Suddenly, her eyes lit up as she pointed at a pink bear sitting outside a colorful little shack. "Let's try that."

To his surprise, she grabbed his hand and dragged him toward the shack. For a petite woman, Bella was strong. He wished her fingers were always holding his hand.

"This shack sells anything in rainbow colors. Its rainbow sandwich has been all over Instagram. I want to buy one," she explained as they joined the long line.

It took them fifteen minutes of waiting in line and another five to get the sandwich. Many people in front of them bought ice cream or slushies that looked tempting in the hot and humid weather.

"You look disappointed," commented Ryo after Bella got her order and pulled her sandwich out of its wrap.

"It looks like a regular grilled cheese." She brought the sandwich to her nose. "Smells like ordinary cheese and bread too."

"Look can be deceiving." He shrugged, playing with his phone. "Why don't you break the sandwich apart to see the inside?"

She nodded. Her fingers began to pull the sandwich apart, right on the cut in the middle, and then ...

"Oh my God," she squealed, her eyes popping at the vibrant rainbow colors coming out from the gooey, stringy cheese. Tilting her head, Bella lifted half of the sandwich high and sucked the stringy cheese until her lips touched the edge of the toast.

Smiling, she licked the lips that were now smeared with rainbow cheese. Then her eyes widened as she realized what Ryo was doing. In a grunt, she covered her face with both hands, still holding the sandwich. "Ryo, you're bad! Stop recording me."

Ryo chortled and dodged her hand, continuing to record her.

"You knew about this since the beginning." She pouted, looking away. Red spread up to her ears.

"Yes, and your expression when you tore that sandwich apart was priceless. Your lower lip was hanging down, and your eyes were so round, like coins," Ryo laughed hard.

"You're bad!" She kept trying to avoid the camera. "Stop it."

Ryo obeyed and stopped the video. His lips curved up as he put the phone in his pocket. "I'll keep it for me," he said calmly.

"My face must have looked ugly." She turned to him.

"No, you looked cute."

As he expected, Bella reached for his phone, but he easily dodged her. Grinning, he caught her hand before it went near his pocket, but Bella tripped on her foot. The toast slipped from her hands, falling to the asphalt at the same time as she landed in his arms.

Startling, he pushed her away gently. "I'm sorry, Bella, I didn't me ..." his voice trailed off as he felt Bella's other hand around his waist, preventing him from breaking away.

For a few beats, they looked in each other's eyes, motionless. He felt his heartbeat in his throat as he gazed down to find Bella looking at him unblinking. Absentmindedly, he lifted his fingers to tuck her hair behind her ear. Bella's eyes closed briefly.

"People are watching us," he whispered above her ears. "We have to move."

"Okay." She nodded as she broke away and took a step back.

With a small smile spreading on his lips, he took her hand and laced his fingers in hers. Her hand was soft and small.

Bella's eyes were on him as they left the spot and ducked down to a side street that was quieter than the main street.

BELLA

He liked me.

Ryo liked me.

Standing face-to-face in the quiet corner, my heart almost burst in my chest as our eyes met. With a slight smile on his lips, he brushed my jaw lightly with his thumb. His touch made electricity course in my veins.

"You should send me the video," I blurted out, shifting my attention away from the touch.

"Sure."

"Next time, you should've asked for my permission. It not polite to record someone without her consent," I said again.

"Bella, can I record you?" he leaned in, grinning.

"Too late." I nudged his shoes with mine.

Tilting his head, he said, "So, I should ask you every time?"

"I think so. Promise?" He didn't answer. His eyes sparkled with mischief. "Hey!" I lifted my hand to slap his shoulder.

"Okay." He caught my hand to pull me closer. "I promise."

Butterflies fluttered hard in my stomach as he looked at me.

"So, where do you want to go next?" He scanned around. "There are many exciting things in here. If you tell me where you want to go, I'll take you."

I titled my head, recollecting the information I'd gathered from the internet. "I want to try the cookie bar. People said that is one of the must-visit places."

"Um... I think the bar name is Cookie Time?" he asked.

"Yes."

"All right, let's go there."

Hand in hand, we walked toward the bar and avoided people who congregated in the middle of the street.

"Is it okay to hold hands in public?" I glanced at him and to our hands. "I've read online that PDA isn't allowed."

"Yes, that's true. But it isn't as strict as it was for the older generations, though, especially in Tokyo," he said. "Some people observe the rules, but holding hands isn't something that is frowned upon anymore."

"That's good," I swung our hands. "I like holding hands."

"You can hold my hand anytime you want." He winked.

And I liked the idea.

The cookie bar was also crowded when we arrived. It took us twenty minutes to get our order. I bought a cookie shake with a floating cookie on top, and Ryo bought cookie dough in a cone that looked like ice cream.

"How's your shake?" he asked as I sucked it down.

"It's tasty, like eating liquid chocolate chip cookies."

His nose wrinkled. "Hmm, that doesn't sound appealing to me. I prefer the baked ones."

"It isn't disgusting, though," I convinced him. "It's more like chocolate milk but thicker and creamier."

"So that's a fake chocolate chip cookie."

"And that's a fake ice cream." I pointed at his cookie dough.

"Yup, you're so right." He bit into his cone.

"Hey, let's take a picture of us with our fake cookies and ice cream." I pulled out my phone and gave it to him. "Your arm is longer than mine."

Ryo took the phone and lifted it up, aiming at us. "Lean closer so I can get the store in the picture."

I did and positioned my milkshake next to his cookie dough. Our heads almost touched.

"Ready, one ... two ... three!"

Ryo took a few pictures before giving my phone back. "Send them to me too," he said.

"Okay."

Ten minutes later, we continued walking on the street lined with everything from large-scale stores to gift shops to quirky inexpensive clothing boutiques. "I'm full." I touched my stomach. "I shouldn't have finished that shake."

Ryo nudged my arm gently with his. "Is that my cue to take you back home?"

I slapped his shoulder lightly. "You're kidding me! I've been dreaming of going to this place. There's no way I'll leave so soon."

He grinned. "You're a firecracker. Just a soft touch on the fuse, and you'll explode."

I pouted. "Is that bad?"

"No, I find that cute!"

I wrinkled my nose but smiled at him.

"Hey, let's try that." I pointed at a store called Santa Monica Crepes.

"Didn't you say you're full?" Ryo raised an eyebrow.

"I want to see if this one tastes better than the one in Santa Monica," I responded solemnly.

"Is there one in Santa Monica?"

I grinned widely at his remark, then he rolled his eyes as he realized I was joking.

Around 4:15 p.m., we decided to leave. When Ryo's car rolled out from the parking lot onto the vibrant street, the sun was a giant orange ball suspended above the skyscrapers. The colorful neon signs became brighter and alive as though they didn't want the day to be over and let the night reign.

"I wish the day could be longer than twenty-four hours." Ryo glanced at me, took my hand, and cradled it in his palm.

"I wish that too. So many things to do in such little time."

For some time, we didn't say a word.

"Thanks, Bella."

"For what?" I asked, glancing at him.

"For liking me."

I smiled and squeezed his hand. "Thanks for liking me too."

His eyes looked at me gently.

Once more, we drove in silence. We kept our fingers laced as we walked toward the apartment entrance, up to the elevator, and down the hallway.

"I should complain about the light." I looked up to the ceiling. "It's dark around here."

"I disagree," Ryo said calmly.

I scoffed. "It's dark, Ryo."

"I know. But I like it because you'll walk closer to me, like right now." He flashed a mischievous smile and wrapped an arm around me when I rolled my eyes.

"Thanks for taking me to Harajuku today, Ryo," I said as we stood in front of my unit. "It was awesome."

"I'm glad you liked it," he said. "By the way, are you free this Saturday evening?"

"Um… yes. Why?"

"Let's go watching fireworks in Sumida Park."

I covered my mouth. "Are you kidding?"

He shook his head.

Half shrieking, I jumped and wrapped my arms around his neck. Ryo was taken aback but seemed to like the surprise and circled his arms around my waist to support my body as my feet lifted ten inches off the ground. "Thank you. I really want to watch those fireworks." I released my hands when my feet were back on the ground.

A wide beam spread over his face as he looked at me.

"So, this Saturday ... is our first date then?" I asked, biting my lower lip.

Sliding his hands into his pockets, he suppressed a smile and said, "Yes."

I almost squealed happily, but I pushed the excitement down, trying to maintain my feminine mystique. But I flashed a small smile at him and turned to unlock my door.

"Good night, Bel," he said near my ear.

I spun on my heel only to find his face a few inches from mine. To my surprise, Ryo leaned in to give me a quick kiss on the cheek.

I was stunned for a second but stood on tiptoe to kiss his cheek too. "Good night, Ryo."

For a few beats, we looked into each other's eyes until he signaled me to go in.

Peeking out from behind my door, I smiled and waved to him. He smiled and waved back. Still looking at him, I shut my door slowly. My ears picked up his movement next door. Leaning my back on my door, I sighed, putting a hand over my pounding heart.

Then I heard a knock on the wall on my left side.

Jumping, I stared at the wall and took a step back. Another knock on the wall, and my phone rang. Ryo was calling me.

"Did you just knock?" I blurted out as I put my phone on my ear.

"Yes," he answered, then I heard a chuckle. "Did I scare you?"

"Yes! I almost had a heart attack."

"Sorry, I thought you knew."

Oh, man!

"Not after you told me about the faceless ghost the other night." I rolled my eyes, walking toward my bedroom.

"Ghosts can't knock, Bella. Besides, you said you don't believe in ghosts."

"I don't, but still."

He chuckled. "What are you planning to do later?"

"Hmm, I was thinking of taking a shower, reading my book, then going to sleep. But … since you called me, I'd prefer to talk to you," I said, sitting on the floor cushion.

"I interrupted your plan."

"You did."

"I feel bad."

"You should." I chuckled and listened to the clicking sound briefly on his end. "Are you cooking something?"

"I'm heating water for tea."

"Tea?"

"Chamomile tea. I like something warm before going to bed."

"Even in the summer?"

"Even in the summer." I heard a smile in his voice. "My mom said when I was a toddler, I liked warm milk. But as I grew up, I preferred to have warm tea," he explained. "Hey, why don't you take a shower, and then I can call you again if you don't feel sleepy."

"Okay, but you should call me in twenty minutes."

"Promise."

I hung up and took the fastest shower I'd ever had in my life, and brushed my teeth just as quickly. After changing into my pajamas, I jumped on the bed and waited for Ryo's call. That night, we talked, watched the news while Ryo translated for me, and spoke again until we fell asleep.

The following day around seven thirty, Ryo surprised me by bringing me a Japanese breakfast that he'd prepared in his apartment. The surface of the outdoor table on my balcony was covered with rice, miso soup, two grilled fish, pickled vegetables, a vegetable side dish, and cooked soybeans.

"Do you eat like this every morning?" I looked at the food, taking a seat in front of him.

"No, I eat oatmeal and fruit or boiled eggs and sandwiches. Sometimes leftovers from the night before," he said, placing chopsticks next to my bowl. "My mom used to prepare breakfast like this when I was young, but not anymore. It takes time to prepare this. But I want to share it with you so you'll have a chance to taste my childhood Japanese breakfast."

Something expanded in my chest. "Aww, thank you. It's a real experience for me." Then I clasped my hands. "Itadakimasu."

"Itadakimasu."

"What time did you wake up this morning to cook?" I asked as I chewed my rice.

"It didn't take me too long to prepare these because I only cooked the rice and the grilled fish. The rest were from instant packages. Next time I'll cook all of these for you from scratch." The corners of his mouth lifted.

"Promise?"

He nodded.

The miso soup was light and quite tasty for an instant one. When I took the small bowl of cooked soybeans, Ryo watched me with a spark of amusement clear in his eyes as if he was waiting for something. I flashed a smile and scooped up the beans with the chopsticks. My jaw dropped to see how slimy and gooey they were. "Th-this is already spoiled."

"No. It isn't. That's fermented beans. We call it *natto*," he answered matter-of-factly. "Normally, I don't eat them, but since my purpose this morning is to give you a taste of a traditional breakfast, I included them."

My eyes narrowed, and my nose wrinkled as I sniffed the food. "Smelly." I pushed the bowl toward him.

"It's nutritious and healthy, though. At least, that's what people claim. I don't really like it, but my parents and sister love it."

"Sister?" My eyes lit up. "I didn't know you have a sister. Do you have her picture?"

He nodded, pulled out his phone, picked something on it, and gave it to me. "Akiko, my sister."

On the screen, I saw a tiny woman wearing a green dress sitting on a bench, smiling. "She is pretty. How old is she?" I gave his phone back.

"Twenty-five."

"Twenty ..." I turned to him. "She is your age? Are you guys twins?"

He nodded again.

"Really? I don't believe you." I lifted an eyebrow. "You say that because she took all the good looks from you."

I gave a squeal and covered my cheeks as he leaned forward, pretending to squeeze my cheeks with his hands.

"You almost knocked my glass over." I held my glass, laughing.

Half laughing, he sat back in his seat and pointed at the food. "Let's finish our food. If not, it will get cold, and you'll be late to work."

I nodded, and we ate our breakfast while listening to the birds chirping from the trees nearby.

At a quarter to ten, I arrived at the café. Standing on the patio, I dialed Avery's phone. I was worried because neither Harper nor Avery had returned my text from last night. They were my first friends in Tokyo, and I cared about them.

I exhaled as the phone was sent directly to voice mail. I hung up and sent a short message to them.

How are you? Please call me.

Taking a few deep breaths, I stepped into the café. Sato-san and the staff were cleaning the counter for my session. Lifting the corners of my mouth, I greeted them happily.

"Good morning, everyone."

"Good morning, Bell-san," they responded. Sato-san raised his eyebrows but smiled at me.

Waving my hand, I went straight to the backroom to find Nao, who was busy folding clean aprons.

"Good morning, Nao."

"Good morning, Bella-chan," she replied. "How's your friend? Is she okay?"

I took a deep breath. "Yes, she's okay now. The doctor had assumed she had severe cramps until the blood tests came out and confirmed she is pregnant."

Nao gave a sympathetic smile. "I hope everything will be fine in the end."

"I hope so too."

"So, did anyone help you while you're there?"

"My next-door neighbor happened to be at home, so he helped us."

"I'm glad because I was worried," Nao said. "Living in a foreign country is sometimes challenging and stressful, especially when you're in an urgent situation and can't speak the language well.

"And I hope you didn't spend the whole day in the hospital," she added.

"No, we came back around one in the afternoon. Since I was stressed out, I decided to go to Harajuku after that."

"You did?" She turned to me, widening her angular eyes. "How was it?"

"It was so crowded, chaotic, and unexpected, but wonderful and amazing at the same time," I laughed.

The corners of her eyes wrinkled as she laughed, covering her mouth. "Did you try the food I told you about?" she asked.

"Yes, I like all but the rainbow sandwich."

"Why?"

"It tastes the same as a regular grilled cheese sandwich. The difference is the filling color," I said.

"Yes, I've heard that from my foreign friends too." She nodded. "The owner may not care enough about returning customers but focuses on getting lots of tourists who go there once. Nothing wrong with that. Just different kind of motivation, I guess."

Then she squinted her eyes, scanning my face, trying to detect something. "Did you go there by yourself or with someone else?"

"What the difference?" I shrugged, took an apron, and wrapped it around my waist. Today I wanted to test the employees' skills for the last time before the soft opening next week.

"Your face reveals everything."

"How so?"

She clicked her tongue, placing her finger on her cheek. "You were blushing. That's exactly the same behavior my sixteen-year-old sister had when she went out for the first time with her boyfriend, but she didn't want me to know."

A smile broke out on her face as I covered mine. "Is it too obvious?" I looked at her between my fingers.

Grinning, she nodded. "Who's the lucky guy?"

"He is … my next-door neighbor. His name is Ryo Yamada."

"The same guy who helped you go to the hospital? How did you guys meet?" She looked curious.

"I met him in the plane on the way here. He came here to visit his family. Initially, I didn't like him because he seemed arrogant. But I found out he isn't. He's kind and thoughtful," I said. "Oh, he's also a childhood friend of Sara-san."

Nao nodded, but her eyebrows puckered.

"You know what, Ryo promised to take me to watch fireworks in Sumida River this Saturday. I can't wait." I clasped my hands in front of my chest.

"Will it be you guys' first date?"

I nodded and stopped smiling as Nao looked at me solemnly. "Why do you look at me like that?"

"Bella-chan, do you like him?"

Her question surprised me, but I nodded. "I think I like him *very much.*"

"That means you're ready to have a long-distance relationship once you return to America, right?"

"But he'll go back to the States too, though," I answered.

"Did he tell you that?"

I bit my lip. "No, we haven't talked about that yet."

"I bet he doesn't know that you're here for a short time too, then?"

I blinked. "I guess so," I said slowly.

Nao took a deep breath. "I'm not the right person to say this. But I suggest you have that conversation with him. At least to give you peace of mind. If he's back like you said, you don't have to worry."

I nodded. "I guess … you're right. I should. Thanks."

She smiled and stood up from her seat. "Let's go outside. They are ready for you."

I nodded, and followed her out.

RYO

The sky over Sumida River lit up with colorful and fantastic explosions. Oohs and aahs were heard each time fireworks shot up to the sky.

"It's wonderful." Bella gazed skyward as the bright balls of blue, green, yellow, and red flew through the sky and burned themselves out. "I've never seen anything like this." She turned to Ryo, who was sitting with his back against a cherry blossom tree.

They were lucky to get a nice spot under the tree in Sumida Park because Ryo had reserved it after Bella agreed to go with him. The reservation wasn't necessary, but it gave them a better view because thousands of people went to Asakusa for the fireworks.

"Have you watched the fireworks at Disneyland?" Bella asked, hugging her knees to her chest.

He nodded.

"Disney's fireworks are spectacular. *Amazing*." She let the word hang in the air. "But this one." She clicked her tongue. "This isn't fireworks, but the art of fireworks."

"That's why we called this *Hanabi*." Ryo wrapped his arms around his bent knees, looking sideways at Bella.

"Ha ... na ... bi ... Hanabi." She repeated the word. "What does it mean?"

"That's a word for fireworks. If you translate it, it means 'flower fire.' "

"Flower fire." She nodded, repeating the words slowly as she looked up. "I think that's the perfect word to describe these fireworks because they are like flowers." She nudged his shoulder with hers. "Thanks for taking me here."

"You're welcome." Ryo smiled, leaning back on the tree. A slight smile played on his lips as he gazed up at the fireworks in the dark sky.

All eyes fixed heavenward while hands stretched up, holding phones and recording the fireworks. The screeching, whistling, and banging sounds roared continuously in the sky. Ryo felt the ground shake as a few giant fireworks were shot into the dark sky, producing a shock wave and tremendous booms.

Amid the awe, Ryo caught a slight movement from the corner of his left eye. Just as he turned his head in the direction, Bella leaned in closer and touched her lips to his. For a few seconds, he froze because it never crossed his mind that Bella would kiss him in the park. The softness and the warmth of Bella's lips had awakened the adrenaline in his veins. He gazed at her long eyelashes as her eyes closed. Her soft breath on his cheeks gave a tingling sensation that ran throughout his body.

Then Bella opened her eyes and pulled away abruptly, shaking her head in shock.

"I-I'm sorry," she stuttered. "I shouldn't have."

When she scooted back to her spot on the blanket, Ryo reached out, slipped his arm around her waist, and pulled her closer. She let one palm rest on his chest, and he hoped she didn't feel the thundering of his heart.

Letting out a soft sigh, he gazed at her beautiful face and caressed her cheek gently.

"I'm sorry," she said again in a low voice.

"What for?"

"For kissing you because … you looked adorable." She bit her lip, smiling sheepishly.

He chuckled, then leaned in to nuzzle her nose with his and brushed her cheek with his lips. "Don't say sorry because I'd hoped to do the same," he whispered.

"You did?" She looked straight into his eyes.

He nodded and lowered his lips to kiss hers. Her lips tensed as if she wasn't sure, but then she kissed him back.

The beautiful flower fires became dull and unattractive compared to the kiss they shared. And he had to admit that Bella was a good kisser. She kissed gently at first, then added slight pressure before returning to a gentle touch. His stomach clenched, and his heartbeat pounded in his ears. Dizzy and euphoric, he felt his body respond to the kiss.

And … he had to stop.

Gently, he pulled away and looked at her glowing eyes. "Sit next to me." Ryo tapped a spot on his left.

Bella nodded. Their arms touched as she sat next to him. She smiled when Ryo took her hand and enclosed it between his hands. He wished time would stop.

In the meantime, the fireworks continued. This time, long-burning silver and gold stars shot to the sky, and then they fell like a weeping willow.

But his attention wasn't on the fireworks.

"Bella," Ryo whispered.

"Hmm."

"Tsuki ga kirei desune."

Bella nudged his arm. "My Japanese level is still elementary."

Ryo chuckled and pointed to the pale half-moon behind a thin cloud over the city skyline. "Do you see the moon over there?"

Bella slanted her head skyward and turned to him. "So what you just said relates to the moon?"

He nodded. "The moon is beautiful, isn't it?"

"I don't know." She shrugged. "What is beautiful about it if the moon is hiding behind a cloud? If you said the fireworks were beautiful, I would say yes."

Ryo let out a laugh softly and gazed at her for a few beats before looking back to the moon. "That would work too."

He yelped when Bella playfully pinched his arm. "So, were you talking about the moon or the fireworks? Don't lie to me."

"I didn't." He rubbed his arm.

Bella wrinkled her nose. "Ryo Yamada-san," she said jokingly. "You can lie to me now, but wait until my Japanese is advanced. Then I'll know if you're lying to me or not."

"I'm waiting patiently." Ryo smiled, and they sat with their hands intertwined for the rest of the fireworks.

Around nine, they sauntered back to where Ryo had parked his car. Since the main roads were blocked in anticipation of many people, all visitors had to walk at least twenty minutes from the fireworks. Ryo didn't mind because he had Bella next to him.

As they got closer to the parking lot, his phone buzzed. He took it out and frowned. "My dad. He's called me three times." He looked at her. "Sorry, Bella. I should call him right away."

"Sure." She adjusted her backpack as Ryo put his phone to his ear.

"Moshi moshi? Otousan?" He spoke in Japanese.

"Ryo-kun, where are you?" his dad asked.

"Just left Sumida Park's fireworks. Dad, what happened?"

"Can you come to the hospital now? Akiko has a breathing problem. Right now, her doctor is checking on her."

The news was like a sudden storm on a sunny day. Ryo felt a sudden coldness hit his core. Everything moved in slow motion. The sounds around him became incoherent.

Ryo had always understood his sister's condition. The doctor had reminded them to be ready. Yet, he had never been ready. She was part of him, and he was part of her. They had shared their mom's womb for more than nine months, and they had shared a strong bond their whole lives.

Ryo looked up as tears welled in his eyes. He wanted to scream at the unfairness to his sister.

A soft touch on his arm startled him. Bella looked at him with concern all over her face.

Clearing his throat, Ryo said, "Okay ... I'll be there." He hung up, and his arms drooped at his sides.

"Ryo, are you okay?" Bella asked.

Forcing a smile, Ryo looked at her. "I ..." He paused, swallowing the big lump that formed in his throat. "I have to go to the hospital."

"What happened?" she whispered.

"My sister ..." Ryo paused again, clenching his fingers to control his emotions. He was afraid if he talked more, he would bawl.

Bella stepped forward, took his hand, and smoothed out his fingers. "Let's go there."

Ryo stared at her in surprise. "Are you sure?"

Bella nodded. "Your sister needs you."

The evening sky was bright from the neon signs, the flickering light from the gigantic screens on buildings, and glowing skyscraper windows. The crowds were still walking around from one place to another. It was a lively night. However, inside the car, the silence was deafening. Ryo glanced at Bella, who looked outside and felt he shouldn't have brought her with him.

"Sorry, our date ended like this," he said in a low voice.

She shook her head. "Do you want to tell me what happened to your sister?" she asked.

Ryo chewed the inside of his lips. "Since we were born, she's had a weak body because of a congenital heart defect. She's always sick. Her condition prevented her from going to school, so she was homeschooled. My parents, especially my mom, have taken care of her since then.

"When we turned fifteen, she got a heart transplant and had to take immunosuppressant medicine. That drug affected her kidney function. Her doctor had told us about the side effects. Now she's in the hospital because she is having trouble breathing, but I don't know if that is also a side effect." He looked away, blinking his eyes furiously as tears threatened to fall.

A soft hand took his hand and cradled it. Bella looked at him gently. "I hope she'll be all right."

Ryo sniffed. He wanted to tell Bella the whole truth about Akiko's prognosis, but maybe later once he could control his emotions.

"Thank you for coming with me," he said.

"Don't mention it."

Ryo let Bella hold his hand because her touch was comforting and calmed his nerves.

BELLA

Ryo ran from the parking lot to the hospital's main entrance. My short legs couldn't catch up with him. Once he realized I was left behind, he slowed his pace. "Sorry."

I shook my head, panting. "That's okay. You should go."

But he walked slower anyway.

As we rushed through the automatic doors into the lobby, an antiseptic smell filled my nostrils, and I felt the air conditioning on my face and arms. It felt good because the outside was muggy even at this late hour.

We stopped in front of the admissions desk and Ryo spoke to the nurse on duty. She looked down at the computer, then looked up to tell him something.

Thanking the nurse, Ryo turned to me when a man's voice called his name.

Almost in unison, we pivoted to see a tall, serious-looking man with glasses walking toward us. He lifted an eyebrow at me before he shifted his eyes to Ryo and said something in Japanese. I took him in because I thought I'd seen him somewhere.

Ryo nodded and responded in Japanese, too, glancing at me.

"Bella, this is Kento, my sister's boyfriend," Ryo said in English and turned to the man. "This is Bella, my friend from America. We happened to be at Sumida Park when Dad called and told me what happened."

"Nice to meet you." We shook hands.

As our eyes met briefly, Kento's mouth opened and shut, then he said something to Ryo. Ryo's eyes widened, and he slapped his forehead.

"Yes, Akihabara. That's right, she was the one who wanted to buy the Airou keychain." Ryo gazed at me. "He said he met you in Akihabara. Airou keychain, remember?"

I looked at Kento again, and slowly, I remembered the bouffant and the glasses. "Oh, you're that guy."

"He bought the keychain for my sister," Ryo said.

"I see."

Kento talked to Ryo, who listened to him carefully and nodded a few times as his lips pressed into a thin line.

"I'm going up with him. Are you okay to wait in here?" Ryo spoke to me.

"Sure, I'll wait."

To my surprise, Ryo took two long steps forward and hugged me tightly as if he wanted to borrow my strength before he went upstairs. In a beat, he broke away, then nodded to Kento.

They took a few steps away when a familiar female voice called Ryo's name.

I whirled around to the entrance, where Sara rushed in with a man who—if I wasn't mistaken—was named Takeru. Sara lifted a single eyebrow as she noticed my presence.

"Bella? Why are you here?" she asked.

Before I could answer, she turned to Ryo, who walked back to where I was standing.

"Sara, Takeru, you guys are here too," he said in English.

She nodded. "Takeru called me, and we decided to come together." Then she took a step forward and threw her arms around Ryo's neck. "I'm sorry. But I believe she'll be okay."

I shifted my eyes, refusing to look at them; just to catch Takeru also looking away. His jaw set. I remembered he'd acted that way when we were at the summer festival. Now I understood why: He loved Sara, but Sara loved Ryo. And Ryo loved me.

Stealing a glance at me, Ryo gently pushed Sara away. "I hope so too." Then he walked to Takeru, who gave him a brief hug and patted his back. Ryo nodded as Takeru said something to him.

He stepped over to me. "They're Akiko's friends too."

"I see." I nodded and looked at him. "Go now. Your parents are waiting for you."

He flashed a sad smile, turned to his friends, and gestured them to follow Kento. Sara gave me a sharp glance before spinning on her heel to follow them. I watched them until they disappeared behind the double swinging doors.

Playing with an empty coffee can, I glanced at the double doors. It had been almost thirty minutes, and no one had come out.

"I hope Akiko is okay," I muttered to myself and put the cup by an empty seat next to me.

Not many people were in the waiting room with me, just a middle-aged man sleeping across three seats and a young husband and wife. The wife was pregnant, her head leaned on her husband's shoulder.

I looked down at my feet when someone approached me. It was Kento. He offered me a small smile when he pointed to the seat next to me.

"Please." I nodded.

He thanked me and sat next to me. His skin looked pale, and dark circles were evident under his eyes.

"Do you need anything to drink?" I asked. "Water or coffee?"

He was startled by the question, then nodded. "Coffee will be fine."

"Be right back." I rose from my seat and went to the vending machine in the narrow corridor for two cans of coffee. I needed another boost to wake me up.

Kento took the can from my hand, lifted the pop-top, and gulped the contents.

"How's Akiko?" I asked.

"Her condition is stable now, but the doctor wants to keep her in ICU for further monitoring," Kento answered in broken English.

I let out a relieved sigh. "I'm glad she is stable now."

"We don't know for how long." Kento clenched the can with his hands.

My head whipped to him. "What do you mean? Didn't you just say her condition is stable?"

"Ryo not tell you everything?"

"Well, he only told me about the heart transplant and the drug effects. And that she is in the hospital because of a breathing problem."

"Akiko is dying." Kento looked down, and a tear dropped on his hand. "And Ryo left the States for good."

"What?" I almost jumped from my seat. My mind was numb as if a bucket of ice was thrown over my head. "H-he won't return to California?"

"Ryo quit his job and returned for Akiko because he loves her so much. Akiko's dream is to live in the States, but she can't, so Ryo fulfills it for her." Kento swallowed hard. "His life in the States wasn't always easy, but he no complain. I bet he's happy to be back here."

I could feel my eyes getting wet and a big lump formed in my throat at the explanation.

Ryo has sacrificed his career and future in the States for Akiko.

Kento must have read my emotions. "He not tell you?"

I shook. "No."

"Please don't feel upset with him because he had trouble telling you that," Kento said.

I couldn't respond because Ryo, Sara, Takeru, and a middle-aged couple—who I assumed were his parents—came out from behind the giant swinging doors and walked toward us.

Kento and I got to our feet as they stopped in front of us.

As our eyes met, Ryo gave a small smile and leaned in to speak to his parents, who looked at me and signaled me to come forward.

My heart started beating triple time because meeting his parents was something that I didn't expect to happen so soon.

"Bella, these are my parents."

His mom's eyebrows furrowed as she looked at her son, who was standing next to me. A small smile appeared on his dad's lips as he extended his hand to me, and I shook it.

"Eiji Yamada, Ryo's dad," he spoke fluently in English. "This is my wife, Kanako Yamada. Nice to meet you, Bell-san."

I bowed slightly to him and his wife. "Hajimemashite, douzo yoroshiku, Yamada-sama."

Ryo's dad chuckled and gave the nod. "Your pronunciation is good."

"Thank you," I said, glancing at Ryo's mom, who didn't say a word. Her face was placid, but her eyes were observing. I was intimidated by her silence.

Then I sensed someone giving me an icy stare. I twisted, and it was Sara. My heart dropped to the floor as I caught her glare before she turned her body, facing the hospital entrance.

"I can drop you off at home, Otousan," said Ryo in English.

His dad waved his hand and pointed at Kento. "He can drop us off. You better drive her back." His eyes shifted to me.

Ryo glanced at his mom, who nodded slowly and spoke to him in Japanese before turning to Sara and Takeru. They nodded.

"I'll have breakfast with you tomorrow morning, and then we can check on Oneechan together." Then he turned to Sara and Takeru. "Thanks for coming."

Takeru put a hand on his shoulder. "Don't mention it."

Sara nodded rigidly.

Ryo and I bid goodbye to them and walked in silence toward the parking lot.

It was half-past eleven when we were sitting in his car. Glancing at Ryo, I heard Kento's voice ringing in my ears.

Ryo quit his job and returned for Akiko because he loves her so much. Akiko's dream is to live in the States, but she can't, so Ryo fulfills it for her. His life in the States wasn't always easy, but he no complain. I bet he's happy to be back here.

I let out a sigh. Maybe too loudly, because Ryo turned to me. "Are you tired? If you are, just close your eyes, and I'll wake you up once we arrive."

"N-no, I'm not tired," I answered quickly and shifted my body to face him. "I'm sorry about your sister, Ryo. I didn't know how bad things were or that you were moving here for Akiko."

"Kento told you?"

I nodded. "I don't have a twin, but I have an older sister. She's good to me, and we did a lot together too. We shared secrets. My parents called us 'cats' because we fought a lot too." I let out a chuckle. "When Adele married and moved to New York, I was despondent and lonely. I didn't lose her; she just moved to the other side of the States to start her new life. But still, it wasn't easy." I took his hand. "My experience can't be compared to yours. You and Akiko are twins, with shared feelings and thoughts. It must be very tough for you."

A tear rolled down his cheek, but he brushed it away brusquely. "Because of me, she's suffered." His voice cracked as he bit his lower trembling lip.

I lifted an eyebrow. "What do you mean?"

He cleared his throat. "When I was young, one of my uncles explained why Akiko was different from me even though we're twins. Back then, it didn't make sense to me. When I grew up and did my own research, everything became clear. When Akiko and I were in our mom's womb, somehow, there was an uneven share of blood and nutrients that favored me the most. That's why I'm healthier and stronger than her." Another tear rolled.

"I'm sorry if I sound callous. But that's not something you could control." I gave a gentle squeeze to his hand. "You shouldn't blame yourself like that."

He brushed my hand from his. His eyes protruded. "But I'm the one who caused her to suffer, Bel. I am!" With the same hand, he punched his chest a few times.

Ryo!

I felt my chest hurt and my mouth dry at seeing his pain. His body shook with anger, sadness, and hopelessness. The tips of his fingers turned white as they clenched the wheel as if he wanted to yank it out and break it.

"You're too emotional to drive. Let's find a parking lot," I said in a low voice.

He brushed his eyes with a hand, sniffing. "I'm okay."

I glanced at him, and a weight settled on my chest as I shifted my eyes out the window. The billboards and neon signs brightening the streets didn't seem appealing anymore. All the way to the apartment, we didn't say a word.

"I'm sorry for being too emotional earlier," he said as we stood in front of our units. "I scared you."

"That's okay, I understand." I gave him a small smile. "Please try to sleep well tonight, okay?"

He nodded.

"Good night, Ryo." I unlocked my door.

"Bella." He put out a hand to stop me.

I looked at him. He looked down, shifting from one foot to the other. "Is it … okay if I sleep in your apartment tonight?"

I blinked; my lips parted.

Under the moonlight and the light on the hallway, his cheeks flushed. He avoided my eyes, rubbing his temple.

"Y-you want t-to …" I couldn't finish the sentence.

He must have realized how it sounded because his head whipped to me. His eyes widened. "No … no … no … I'm not asking you to sleep with me. No, I swear, I'm not that kind of guy," he said quickly, lifting his hands up in a Scout's honor. "Please don't misunderstand me. I just don't want to be alone tonight. Don't worry, I'll bring my pillows and… uh… blankets, and sleep on the floor," he added, pointing to the ground.

A small smile spread on my lips as a bubble of fuzzy feelings rose from my belly to my chest, seeing him with such an innocent and vulnerable expression.

"Yes, of course, don't worry. I didn't think *that*." I flapped a hand, forcing laughter. He let out a breath, which seemed full of relief. "Go, I'll wait inside."

His eyes lit up. "Thanks. I'll be back shortly." Then he unlocked the door and went to his unit.

Ten minutes later, he came to my apartment with his blankets and pillows under his arms. His hair was wet from a quick shower, and he'd changed into his shorts and T-shirt.

"I've already moved the coffee table and cushions to the corner, so you can cover the large rug with your blanket to sleep. The rug is clean, though," I said from the kitchen. "And you can use the cushions too if you want."

"I think I'm good. Thanks, Bella."

"Don't mention it," I entered, bringing in two mugs of warm tea. "Once you're done, let's go outside to the balcony."

"Okay." He smiled.

I gazed skyward when he joined me on the balcony.

"Your tea," I said, pointing with my eyes. "I remember you like drinking something warm before sleeping."

"Thanks." He dragged the empty chair next to me before taking the mug from the table.

For some time, we didn't talk but watched the night sky while sipping our tea.

"Bel," he called.

"Hmm."

"Sorry for snapping at you earlier. I've never shared that guilt with anyone before."

"It must be painful for you to keep that in for so long," I said. "Thanks for trusting me enough to share the story."

He didn't answer but stared at his mug.

"Hey, I think I should go to sleep now because I have to work tomorrow. But if you want to stay here to clear your mind, you're welcome," I added as he stood up from his chair too.

"No, I need to lie down too."

"Okay, then." I took his mug from his hand, and we went inside. As I returned, Ryo was sitting on top of his blanket on the floor.

"Good night, Bel. Thanks for letting me stay in here," he said as I sat on the edge of my bed.

"No worries. Good night, Ryo."

Lying down on my bed, I stared at the ceiling, but my ears focused on Ryo's ragged breathing. Quietly, I propped myself up to see Ryo lying sideways with his back to me. It must have been hard for him to fall asleep in his state.

My heart wanted to comfort him, but I refrained because I didn't want to tangle my emotions deeper than they already were.

Ryo wouldn't be back to the States, and I didn't want a long-distance relationship.

I felt heaviness in my chest as the thought floated in my mind. Heaving a long sigh, I quietly turned my body to the sliding door. The glowing light from outside shone through the crack between the curtains that I'd pulled aside. I let my eyes fixate on it for some time because looking at the light comforted me until my eyelids became heavier and dropped as I entered into slumber.

RYO

The next day, Ryo walked Bella out for work. A pang of guilt crept into his heart when he saw dark circles under Bella's eyes. He shouldn't have asked to stay in her apartment.

"Are you sure you don't want me to take you to the café?" he asked.

She shook. "No, I'm okay."

"Okay, then. See you in two days?" he asked.

She nodded and went on her tiptoes to give him a quick kiss on the cheek. "Enjoy your breakfast with your parents, and thanks for the sandwich." She tapped a hand on her lunch box, indicating the sandwich he'd made her that morning.

Ryo waved and returned to his apartment.

After showering and changing his clothes, he went down to his car and drove to his parent's house. His heart grew heavy because he didn't want to see the pain plastered on his parents' faces. However, he had to be there for them.

It was 9:15 a.m. when he slowed down and parked his car outside his parent's house. A crease appeared on his forehead when he recognized immediately a blue Lexus IS300H that had already parked there as Sara's car.

"What is she doing here?" he muttered, turning off the engine and getting out of the car. "Did Mom invite her for breakfast?"

It wasn't unusual for his mom to invite his childhood friends for meals, especially Sara and Takeru, because their parents were also good friends of her parents.

Ryo didn't open the front door. Instead, he stood on the porch and listened for a moment because the house was silent. It was odd. Usually, when Sara had breakfast with them, he could hear the loud laughter from inside. He licked his lips as his hand was on the doorknob. After taking a few deep breaths, he pushed the door open and padded to the dining room.

"*Ohayou gozazimasu,*" he said as he entered the room.

"Ryo-Kun," his mom gave a small smile. "Come."

Next to her, Sara flashed a smile at him too.

"Sit down, Ryo." His dad pointed with his eyes to the empty seat next to Sara.

"Where's Takeru? He isn't joining us?" He turned to Sara as he sat down.

"He didn't come." She glanced at him and looked down.

Ryo pursed his lips at her response.

"Have you eaten, Ryo-kun?" asked his mom. "Sara-chan made this *tamagoyaki* with smoked salmon. Your favorite." Her eyes beamed at Sara. "After so many years, she still remembers your favorite."

Ryo gazed at the rolled omelet on the table. "Thank you, Sara." He offered a smile. "Itadakimasu."

Ryo put one piece of the rolled omelet on his plate with his chopsticks and then brought it to his mouth. The fluffy omelet melted on his tongue. "It's delicious like always," he said politely.

"Thank you." Sara's eyes glittered.

"Ryo-kun, how were the fireworks last night?" asked his mom, pouring some tea into an empty cup in front of him. "I hope you took videos so your sister can see them."

Putting the chopsticks on their holder, Ryo smiled at her. "Yes, I took some, Okaasan."

Sara whipped her head to him. Her eyes widened. "Y-you watched the fireworks? The ones over Sumida River?"

He nodded. Sara's face crumpled, and regret crept into his chest. He'd forgotten that a week ago Sara had asked him to watch the fireworks with her, and he'd rejected the request.

His mom caught that too and covered her mouth with her hand. Ryo flashed a comforting smile to her.

Sara swallowed, placing her chopsticks on the holder. "By any chance, d-did you go there with Bella?"

"Yes," he answered after quick consideration.

Instantly, a silence fell upon the room. Sitting awkwardly, Ryo caught sadness in Sara's eyes before she lowered her gaze.

"Sara, Ryo." Ryo's dad broke the silence. "If you have something to discuss urgently, go to the next room or wait until we finish our breakfast."

Sara bit her lips, looking at him. "May I?"

He nodded.

Sara stood from her seat and walked into the living room. Ryo sighed and followed her.

"Why did you go there with her?" Sara whirled toward him.

"She hasn't seen them before," he said calmly.

"After you rejected my invitation?" Sara's voice rose as she folded an arm over her stomach.

Sighing, Ryo pressed his hands into his pockets. "Sara, we've been friends for years, and you should know about my feelings for you. I care about you, but you deserve a man who can love and cherish you every moment. Unfortunately, I'm not the right man for you."

He closed his eyes briefly as Sara's hand landed hard on his cheek. It stung, but he didn't care. As he opened his eyes, Sara stood tall with her fingers curled next to her body, shaking in anger. Tears dropped from her eyes.

In one swift motion, Sara marched back to the dining room. He heard her bid farewell to his parents and rush to the front door, clenching her Lady Dior handbag tightly. His nose caught a whiff of head-turning mixed jasmine, cedar, and amber in her wake. At the doorway, Sara turned back and looked at Ryo. "Don't you know that she has to return to the States in less than three weeks?"

Ryo's heart stopped beating for a second. "Sh-she works for Little Bear Japan, right?"

"Have you heard Little Bear *has* an office in Japan?" she mocked. A smug smile flashed on her face. "She's here temporarily, just to train to my employees, and then she has to return. What are you going to do about that? Have you also told her that you won't go back to the States?"

Ryo felt a heavy stone drop in his stomach and stood motionless as Sara walked out of the house without closing the door. He didn't feel it when the humid heat rushed in and brushed his face because his mind was digesting the information.

Bella has to go back to the States soon?

What would happen to their relationship then? Would they be okay in a long-distance relationship?

His throat closed. Dragging his feet, he returned to the dining room. His parents looked at him sympathetically as he sat back in his seat. They'd heard everything.

"I'm sorry for the commotion." He bowed slightly.

"You made Sara-chan upset. Don't you need to follow her?" his mom asked concern all over her face.

"Let her be alone." His dad flapped a hand.

"But ..." his mom protested, but his dad intervened.

"They aren't kids anymore. Let them solve their problems like adults. As parents, it isn't right for us to interfere," he said, sipping his tea slowly. "It's time for Sara-chan to learn to let go of something that isn't for her. It's tough, but ...." His eyes turned to Ryo. "I don't want my son to be trapped by guilt because of our relationship with her parents or how nicely she treats us. Love can't be forced." Then he put his cup gently on the table and continued eating his breakfast as if nothing had happened.

Gazing at his dad, Ryo was speechless because his dad was a quiet and solemn person who didn't like meddling in other people's business. It never crossed Ryo's mind that he'd seen and understood everything over the years and hadn't even been upset with him for falling in love with non-Japanese women most of the time.

"Eat your breakfast, Ryo," called his dad, using the serving chopsticks to pick up steamed broccoli and put it in Ryo's bowl. "And if you have anything that you need to discuss with Bell-san, you have to do it like a man."

Ryo nodded deeply. "I will, Otousan."

His dad pressed his lips together and then continued eating.

BELLA

The morning sun welcomed me with its warmth as I stepped outside the train station. For the first time since I came here, I felt grateful for the kiss of the sunbeam. My heavy heart became lighter, and my mood shifted.

As I stepped onto the café's patio, my mind ran to Sara and wondered if I could meet her without thinking of her cold, sharp glance last night.

"Good morning, Bella-san," Chizuko greeted me cheerfully. "A beautiful day, isn't it?"

"Yes." I smiled. "I'm glad you've kept practicing your English, Chizuko-san." She beamed as I gave her a thumbs-up, and she hummed happily, continuing to sweep.

In the backroom, Nao and her assistants stared at a few sample cups in front of them.

"Good morning," I greeted them.

They looked up. "Good morning, Bella-san," they said in unison.

"Bella-san, come and give us your opinion." Nao signaled me to come.

"Okay." I put my bag in the locker and stood next to her.

"These are the sample cups we are going to use for the soft opening," Nao pointed. "And this is the list of drinks and desserts that we will serve. Most of them are cold drinks because we're in summer." She picked up a paper and handed it to me. "We chose the blended Ghanaian iced mocha, as you said in the training that it's Little Bear's famous cold drink. For the non-caffeine drink, we chose the blended strawberry lemonade. Then lemon mousse and chocolate chip cookies for the dessert."

I read the list. "But we need to introduce other drinks too, right?"

"Yes, we already added them on the next page."

I flipped the pages. "The list looks great. Thanks for your hard work. Do we have enough sample cups?" I returned the list to Nao.

Nao nodded. "We do."

"Great. I suggest using a small clear plastic cup for the lemon mousse. So people can see what's inside."

"That's a great idea. Thanks, Bella-san," Nao chirped.

The door opened abruptly. Chizuko came in, panting as if she'd sprinted.

Disapproval was clear on Nao's face when she spoke to her in a sharp tone.

"Pardon me." She bowed deeply, speaking in English. "Ito-san is here."

"So what if Ito-san is here?" Yukari chimed in. "You need to keep your poise, Chizuko-chan."

Swallowing, Chizuko bowed again. As she straightened her back, she spoke in Japanese at a quick pace, like an auctioneer.

I turned to Nao for help.

"She said Ito-san must have woke up on the wrong side of the bed because she looked unhappy when she came in. She also complained about the floor, the windows, the countertop, everything. And she wants to talk to you, Bella-san."

"Me?" I pointed to my nose. I felt my heartbeat in my throat. *Will she ask about last night?*

Chizuko and Nao nodded at the same time.

"Thanks, Chizuko-san. I'll be right back." I stood up and walked across the room with her on my heels.

As I reached to turn the doorknob, Chizuko whispered in English, "Don't make her more upset, Bella-san," clasping her hands in front of her mouth.

I nodded.

Sara stood near the entrance with her arms crossed as I stepped out of the back room. The rest of the staff was near the counter. Their eyes were following me.

"Good morning, Sara. Do you need me?" I said as calmly as I could.

"Let's talk in my car," she said shortly, and turned toward her car.

Pursing my lips, I followed her quietly.

In her car, we sat in silence—it expanded slowly and became solid as if there were a thick invisible wall between us.

"What are you going to talk to me about that we can't discuss inside, Sara?" I broke the silence.

"What's your relationship with Ryo?" Her glassy eyes glared at me. "Why were you with him in the hospital last night?"

"With all due respect, that's my personal life, Sara. Please, let's stick to talking about business," I said.

"Do you love him, Bella?" Sara forced again. Her fingers curled on her lap.

My lips twitched. Knowing her aggressive personality, it was better if I told her the truth. "It's too early to say 'love,' but I like him *so much*," I answered. I didn't lie. I liked Ryo more than I'd realized. "And from the way he looks at me, I know he likes me too."

A red flush crept up her face. She took a deep breath as her eyes narrowed. "You've just met him when he moved to the apartment, right?"

"Actually, we sat next to each other on the plane on the way to Tokyo and bumped into each other a few times after that."

She arched an eyebrow.

I shrugged.

"Still, it's too soon to fall in love with a man you just met. I think you've toyed with his feelings." Her tone was sharp.

Anger rose from the pit of my stomach. "Excuse me?"

She curled her lips. "Ryo likes you," she said as if she were swallowing bile. "But I doubt that you like him as much as you've said. You're just lonely because you're far from your family and your hometown. Since you know he used to live in California, you found he was a perfect person to share your loneliness with."

"You have no right to accuse me."

She scoffed. "If you care about him as you said, have you told him that you have to go back to the States in less than three weeks?"

"I…" My voice trailed off. I was speechless.

Sara flashed a smug smile. "Ryo's returned here for good. And if something happened to Akiko, do you think he would return to the States to follow you? In our culture, the son has to take care of the parents. Just so you know," she added.

I clenched my fingers, and Sara noticed. She lifted her nose up and looked out the window. "And you don't deserve him."

"Maybe I don't." I managed to make my voice flat. "But he likes *me*, not you."

Her head whipped toward me. Her eyes protruded as she stared at me. Her lips parted, but no words came out of her mouth. Slowly, she looked down at her lap, gathering her thoughts.

"Ryo and I have been friends since we were young," she said after a long pause. "One day, I sprained my ankle at school. He piggybacked me to the nurse's office and wiped my tears while waiting for the nurse. I've been in love with him since then."

Her voice became gentle. "I'm not a shy person because my parents raised me to share my thoughts and feelings. Ryo's known about my feelings because I've shown them to him. But he always brushes it off." She took a deep breath. Her eyes became red and glassy as she turned to me.

"I'm a pretty, sexy, rich, and competent woman. I always got everything I wanted. I was magna cum laude at UC Berkeley. I became one of the youngest successful entrepreneurs in Japan, and now I have a license for the Little Bear franchise. Why can't I have him? Why can't he love me? Why does he fall in love with a woman he just met in such a short time? What did I do wrong?" Tears rolled down her cheeks. She looked away and bit her lower lip hard as a sob escaped from her mouth.

Sara looked pitiful, and my heart ached for her. I swallowed and looked out the window. Contrary to the somberness in the car, outside the sun was shining brightly; the sky was blue, with no clouds at all. A little green bird with white around its eyes perched on the bushes near Sara's car, titling its little head at us. It stared at me for a few seconds before flying away toward Sumida Park.

"Sara." I broke the silence. "You are an admirable woman. You're pretty, intelligent, and successful. At such a young age, you've achieved things that many other women couldn't do. Honestly, I felt jealous when I read your profile because never in a million years would I have achieved what you've achieved.

"Men in the world will fall for you easily. Who doesn't want to date a beautiful, smart, and successful woman? However, your ambition controls you even when it comes to love. You see Ryo as a person that you need to conquer. Once you were able to win his heart, his position in your heart would be the same as your other trophies. Ryo is a smart man, and I bet you a hundred bucks that he must have sensed that too, which might be one reason he doesn't reciprocate your feeling."

I paused, looking at her, and she wiped her tears. "It isn't his fault that he doesn't love you. It isn't your fault either, to have been in love with him for a long time. It isn't my fault I met him, and we have fallen for each other.

"You may hate me after I say this. Sara, your drive to conquer Ryo blinds you and makes you unable to see other men who may have feelings for you. You haven't given other men a chance to prove their love to you."

Sara gawked at me. "I don't want another man. I only love Ryo."

I bit my lips to prevent myself from saying more. It was useless to give your opinion to a strong-willed person; that was what my dad always said.

"Well, I think I'd better go back to work. Nao needs my guidance for the soft opening. Have a good day, Sara." I bowed slightly to her, opened the door, and left her alone in the car.

BELLA

Sumida Park was quiet at seven thirty in the morning: no tourists with selfie sticks, only some locals jogged or walked along the river.

Sitting on the bench, I enjoyed the quietness of the morning. Although I didn't come here in spring when the cherry trees blossomed on both sides of the river, the park was already beautiful. The surroundings felt relaxed and comforting. It was a perfect place to clear my mind.

As the morning breeze caressed my face and hair, I took a few deep breaths and closed my eyes.

You're just lonely because you're far from your family and your hometown. Since you know he used to live in California, you found he was a perfect person to share your loneliness with.

My eyes opened abruptly as Sara's words popped up in my mind.

I let out a sigh. Since I had a conversation with Sara two days ago, I couldn't sleep. I didn't respond to Ryo's texts or calls because

Sara's words had haunted me and made me wonder about my feeling for him.

"Did I fall in love with him because I feel lonely?" I mumbled, looking at the sparkling surface of the river. I did feel lonely. I was homesick. I missed arguing in the mornings with my mom, listening to my dad play his guitar, and gossiping with Adele and Mel.

The homesickness became bearable once I met and became close to Moore sisters, their friends, and Ryo. I wasn't sure exactly when I began to have strong feelings for him. Maybe it was on the rainy day when he gave me his umbrella. Or when he bandaged my ankle. I didn't know. I only knew I missed talking to him or even seeing his face.

So is it love? Or simply a displaced my longing for my family? But what is love anyway?

Sara might be right. Maybe I didn't love Ryo, even though our kiss felt real. I was a selfish person who couldn't control my emotions. If I cared and loved him, I should have told him about my short time here and tried to find a way to keep our love.

The thought loomed large. I covered my mouth as a sob burst from it. My heart was wrenched by invisible hands as the moments I shared with Ryo flashed in my mind. His gentle kisses. His calm eyes. His warm arms. His mischievous smile.

I pinched my arm as hard as I could to contain my sadness. I should stop my feelings for him before I hurt him or myself even more.

In a trance of my own misery, I was startled when my phone rang.

Wiping my tears, I took the phone out of my bag but didn't recognize the number. It kept ringing as I debated whether to pick it up.

Clearing my throat, I pressed the green button. "Hello?" My voice was thick.

"Bella, it's nice to hear your voice again." I heard a familiar male voice from the end of the phone. "Hey, what happened to your voice? Did you get a cold?"

"Is it …?" My voice trailed off. *It can't be.*

"It's me, Tristan. I'm at Narita Airport with Jill."

Groaning inwardly, I covered my eyes. Yes, he'd mentioned that he'd be here on the fifth week. "Hey, sorry I don't recognize your number. Is it new?"

"Yes, because someone stole my phone, and the office replaced it," he answered. "Hey, can we meet tonight? Or tomorrow?"

"Tonight will be great," I answered after giving it some thought. "By the way, shouldn't you guys be coming in a few more days?"

He chuckled in a deep voice that I used to think was sexy. "Are you afraid we'll find the mess you made?"

I let out a dry laugh. "Give me your hotel address, and let's meet tonight."

"Will do shortly, once we arrive at the hotel. See you tonight, Bel." He hung up.

I rubbed my eyes with my palms and gave a quick glance at my watch. It was almost eight. I still had enough time to calm myself before going back to the café.

After work, I picked up Tristan and Jill at their hotel and took them for dinner in a *teppanyaki* place where they served Kobe beef. It was pricey, but the company paid for it. Besides, Tristan was a senior manager, so he was allowed to have an expensive meal.

Later, I brought them to see my apartment.

"Oh my God, it's so small! How do you cook in such a narrow corridor?" Jill exclaimed as her hand ran on the kitchen counter.

"I think you've been in Southern California for too long, Jill," Tristan teased her. "Lots of apartments in New York are small and narrow too."

"That's right, you lived there for a year, right?"

He nodded.

"But still, this apartment is too small." She stood and stretched her arms to touch the walls.

"It is, but I've gotten used to it now," I admitted. "Besides, I'm busy working, so I don't have time to cook, anyway."

"Listen to her." Jill pointed at me with her chin. "You need to enjoy your youth, Bel. Don't only think of work. Haven't you met a nice man here?"

Her comment was like a jab to my stomach. But I managed to smile and nudged Tristan. "Does it mean she approves me going anywhere in Tokyo but the café?"

Jill leaned to my ear. "Only if you want to get a bad performance review."

Tristan and I cackled.

"Is it okay if I check out your bedroom?" Jill asked.

"Go ahead. There isn't much to see."

As I followed her and Tristan, my doorbell rang. I raised my eyebrow because I wasn't expecting anyone.

"Go ahead," I said to Tristan. "I'll check the door."

But Tristan didn't move and waited for me.

I went to the intercom that connected to the camera outside. As I turned it on, my stomach twisted as Ryo's face appeared on the screen: the face that I wanted to forget. He had called and texted me, but I hadn't answered.

Ryo leaned forward and pressed the bell again.

I bit my lip and turned around to see Tristan's eyes on me. "Are you okay?"

"Um …" I pointed at the camera while gazing at him as if I'd never seen him in my life.

"Why are you looking at me like that?" He tilted his head.

"Tristan, could you please help me?"

My voice must have sounded pitiful because Tristan looked into my eyes and nodded. "Okay."

RYO

R yo pressed the doorbell for the third time. Glancing at his watch, 9:45 p.m., he was sure that Bella was already home.

Maybe something happened in the café that made her late, he thought. Since he'd returned from the hospital yesterday, he hadn't been able to reach Bella. She didn't return his calls or texts. Somehow, she'd disappeared.

Then he remembered his heated conversation with Sara in his parent's house two days ago. *Did Sara confront her?* He felt his heart pound at the thought. But it was impossible because Bella was a representative of Little Bear. Although Sara was an ambitious woman, she'd know better than to involve her personal feeling in her business.

That thought calmed him. Letting out a sigh, he couldn't wait to see Bella. There were many things that he wanted to discuss, including her short presence in Tokyo. He also wanted to share his conversation with Akiko yesterday. The conversation flashed in his mind.

"I was told you went to the fireworks last night with your girlfriend," Akiko had said.

"Kento told you?" he'd asked.

Akiko had nodded. "Can I see her picture?"

"Sure." He'd shown the picture of him and Bella holding the fake ice cream and cookies.

"She's beautiful. Like Chibi Chibi Moon," Akiko had smiled. "You should keep her, Ryo-kun."

Ryo had chuckled. Akiko loved *Sailor Moon*, and her favorite character was Chibi Chibi Moon that also had blue eyes and red hair. "Yes, she's beautiful, although I don't think she looks like Chibi Chibi Moon."

"Could you bring her here when you come again?" Akiko had asked.

"Okay, Oneechan."

A gentle smile appeared on her pale lips when Akiko signaled him to come closer. He had obeyed, and held her skinny fingers. "Ryo-kun, I'm happy to see your eyes sparkling again."

"I want you to be happy too, Oneechan," he had whispered.

"I'm happy. I've been loved by Otousan, Okaasan, and you. And Kento. I don't want to ask for more. But you." She had paused, swallowing. "You deserve to live for yourself now. Don't feel guilty anymore, Ryo-kun. If you did, I'd be sad seeing you from above."

Tears rolled down his cheeks. "Oneechan," he'd sobbed. "Please don't say that. Please don't leave me."

"What a crybaby. You're a grown man, Ryo-kun. Stop crying." His sister had tapped his head gently. "Everyone will die, silly. It's just a matter of time."

Ryo had bitten his lips to hold in his sobs.

"You have to survive, okay? Reach your dream, Ryo-kun. *Your* dream, not mine. Promise?"

"Promise."

"And bring the Chibi Chibi Moon here."

Ryo chuckled, remembering his sister's comment, and couldn't wait to bring Bella to meet his sister. Now he looked at her door, wondering if he had to ring the bell again.

"Maybe not." He pinched the skin on his throat. "Well, I'll check again tomorrow morning, then."

As he was about to turn around, the door opened.

"Hi, Bell …" He stopped, widening his eyes at the handsome, tall blond man who opened the door. "Who are you?" The question stuck in his throat.

"Can I help you …?" the man asked, pausing to examine him.

Before Ryo responded, he heard Bella's voice. "Who's that, babe?"

Babe? Did she call this blond man … "babe"?

Ryo gritted his teeth as he began to feel the ground underneath his sneakers shake.

The door opened wider as Bella's head poked out. "Oh, hi, Ryo." Her hand waved as she smiled widely.

"Ryo?" The blond man asked as he put a hand on Bella's shoulder. "Is this your neighbor who used to live in the States and helped you when you rolled your ankle and when your friend Avery was sick?"

Bella smiled and nodded. "Yes, the one and only. He's the most helpful person here." She turned to Ryo. "Ryo, this is Tristan, my boyfriend. He just arrived this afternoon." Her eyes gleamed.

"Nice to meet you, Ryo, and thanks, man, for helping my girlfriend." Tristan extended his hand to Ryo, who accepted it hesitantly.

"Likewise." He tried to say it cheerfully, though his stomach hardened. He wanted to brush Tristan's hand off Bella's shoulder.

How did Bella suddenly have a handsome boyfriend? If she already had a boyfriend, why did she agree to spend time with him—and even kiss him? *What's happening here?*

Then a thought flashed in his mind that made his heart stop beating.

She must have been lonely from being far away from her boyfriend.

He had been fooled before: by the last girlfriend who had big eyes like Anne Hathaway, and now by Bella, with her innocent baby blue eyes. Ryo bit his lower lip as the blood drained from his face.

"So, anything I can help you with, Ryo?" asked Bella.

Clenching his jaw, Ryo looked at her and shook his head. "Ah, nothing. I just wanted to check on you since you haven't returned my texts or calls. But"—he glanced at Tristan—"everything looks okay, even better than I'd thought."

"Thanks again, man. Even though I know that Tokyo is safe, I was afraid to leave her alone. But I was being silly because she has many good friends here now." Tristan squeezed Bella's shoulder and gave her a peck on the cheek.

Ryo swallowed and nodded. "I've got to go. Nice to see you, and enjoy your time in Tokyo, Tristan." Then he looked at Bella. "Bye, Bella."

Rigidly, he turned around toward the elevator. His steps shuffled down the hallway, his limbs heavy, and his chest tightened as he heard the man coo, "I've missed you so much, Bel," before the door closed behind him. His chest hurt as he shut his eyes tightly to push the thoughts of what could happen between them right now.

BELLA

Jill crouched in front of me, where I was sitting on the genkan. Tristan stood next to her, leaning his back on the door.

"Thank you for helping me." I looked at Tristan. "You nailed it." I gave a thumbs-up, but my voice cracked.

Tristan sighed and rubbed his temple. "I feel bad for fooling him like that, because Ryo seems to be a good guy."

"He is." I looked down, biting my lip before lifting my eyes to him. "I'm sorry for asking you to do that." Letting out a heavy sigh, I shifted to Jill, who looked tense and worried. "I'm sorry, now you know how unprofessional I am."

Jill took my hands and clasped them in hers. "Bella dear, falling in love can't be predicted; it can happen everywhere."

Tears dropped on my cheeks as I shook my head hard. "I should have focused on work. Besides, Sara Ito loves him too. She must be upset, and I'm afraid that what happened between us will affect our business relationship." I looked at Jill. "I've worked hard for this project; I really have. I even worked some weekends to ensure the café staff had adequate knowledge. I wouldn't lie to you."

Jill nodded. "I believe you, Bel. The progress on Tokyo's café is way better than the ones in Osaka and Kyoto, considering the trainers there are more senior than you. So I believe that you have worked hard here. About Ito-san, no need to worry. She spoke highly about you, including the role-playing you suggested to her employees. That's a great idea."

"Maybe she'll begin to complain about me now." I groaned.

"Hush!" Jill chided, releasing my hands. "Don't think badly of anyone yet. Sara is a smart woman; I believe she can separate her personal life and business."

I sniffed and wrapped my arms around myself. My heart ached when Ryo's shocked expression flashed in my mind. He stiffened his posture while gazing incredulously at Tristan and me as we fooled him.

"Bella," called Tristan. "Are you sure you don't want to tell Ryo the truth?"

I shook. "No. I let him hate me because if he hates me, he'll forget me faster." Then I turned to Jill. "When I helped the project in Singapore, the trainers didn't need to be present for the grand opening. I've thought if I could do the same."

Her eyebrows curled. "You mean, you want to go back earlier? Are you sure?"

I nodded firmly. "If it's possible."

Tristan exchanged a glance with Jill. "I think it should be okay. You and I will be here until the grand opening anyway."

Jill nodded. "I'll tell HR to change the date of your flight back home."

"Thanks."

Jill kept her promise. My return date was pushed forward to Tuesday next week. My presence in the café was limited too because Jill was the best person to help Nao and the staff for the soft opening while Tristan had meetings with Sara.

My admiration for Sara didn't change. She was a true businesswoman and no longer mixed her personal feelings with her business. In front of others, she praised me as usual but kept our relationship at arm's length. I didn't blame her. However, I was sad because I really wanted to be her friend.

Since Ryo met Tristan in my apartment, I hadn't bumped into him anymore. His unit was quiet, as if he was no longer there. There was no humming sound from his kitchen exhaust or constant background noise from the TV.

Yesterday, I leaned my ear on the wall between his unit and mine, hoping to hear any subtle noise from there: just wanting to know that he was around. But the quietness haunted me.

"Ryo," I whispered, pressing my forehead against the wall. How I wished I could go back to the time when we were happy in Harajuku or when we were watching the fireworks in Sumida Park. Or even when we bumped into each other in front of the convenience store in the rain.

My chest tightened because I successfully hurt his feeling, and at this very moment, he probably hated me. He must have erased me from his memory.

Harper's jaw dropped in shock when I told her about our break-up in her apartment on Sunday morning. "So you have a boyfriend?"

I scoffed. "Of course not. Tristan pretended to be my boyfriend so Ryo would believe I only dated him because I was lonely. I wanted him to forget me quickly."

"That's cruel, you know." Harper propped her chin on the coffee table. "Are you sure he can forget you? How about you? Can you forget him?"

"We just went on one date. Our feelings aren't deep yet, so it should be easy for us to move on." I turned to her. "It's useless to continue our relationship because I don't want to try long distance."

"If that's the case, why did you approach him? You broke his heart, Bel." Harper gave me a sad look. "I can tell he likes you very much. Even Ida didn't make a move once she realized something was going on between you and him."

Pain stabbed my chest as I listened to her. All of a sudden, tears threatened to fall. I looked at the ceiling to air-dry my eyes. "H-Harper." My voice was shaky. "I—I broke my heart too."

"Aw, Bell." Harper scooted closer to me and wrapped her arms around me. I sobbed on her shoulder. She patted my back gently as I told her through my tears why I showed my feelings to Ryo, how important he was for his family, and how Sara had confronted me.

"Thanks for listening." I wiped my tears with a tissue after I calmed down.

"Anytime," she said. "So, when will you move back to the States?"

"Tuesday."

Her eyes widened. "In two more days? That's fast."

I shrugged. "My part in the training is done. Jill will oversee the soft opening on Monday because that's her role here. Tristan will work with Sara for marketing and advertising. As the trainer, I don't need to be around during the openings."

"Wouldn't it be nice if you were there, though?"

I nodded. "Yes, but I can't stay here any longer."

"How about the café staff? Have they known about your last day?" Harper asked.

"Jill announced it yesterday. We've already exchanged phone numbers and promised to keep in touch. I'm going to miss them because they're awesome people."

She sighed. "Well, who knows, you can visit them one day. But, I'll miss you, Bella."

I forced a smile. "I'll miss you, too, Harper."

Harper pressed her lips tight and then stood up to her kitchen. When she returned, she brought four cans of beer, a bowl of roasted green peas, and a bag of dried shredded squid to the table. She opened two cans and gave one to me.

"For our friendship." She clinked my can.

"Yes." I giggled and took a swig of my beer.

Harper was a heavy drinker. As I finished half of my drink, she had already opened the second can.

"What's your plan once you go back home?" she asked, plopping a handful of peas into her mouth.

"Hmm." I tilted my head, chewing a piece of calamari. "I should continue my online school because I promised my mom I would. If I don't do it, she'll be so mad. Then I'll continue working as usual because I have bills to pay. And grouse about the dry California weather and the wildfires. Just a regular boring life." I shrugged. "How about you?"

Swallowing the peas, Harper shrugged. "I might need to move to a one-bedroom apartment because eventually, Avery will move into her boyfriend's apartment. I'm glad Kevin took responsibility for the pregnancy. Something I have to admire about him."

"Don't you want to move in with Mike?" I asked, taking a sip of my beer. "If you do, you'll split the expense, right?"

She shook. "Not now. I've learned from my previous relationship not to move in until both of us are ready. Trust me, I had a horrible experience once I broke up with my last boyfriend. So right now, I'm happy where I am, and Mike is happy where he is.

Once we feel that we need to move our relationship forward, I'll consider it."

"Wise lady." I winked.

"I should be." She laughed. Then she looked at me solemnly. "You should keep in touch once you go back. I'll be so upset if you don't."

"I promise." I tilted my can her way.

She touched my can with hers, and we drained our beers in a long swig.

At ten on Tuesday morning, I was already on the plane. My two seatmates were a lady and her little daughter, who must have been around five. She was cute and kept telling me about her fantastic day in Tokyo Disneyland and Disney Sea. I smiled, listening to her. She stopped when her mom told her to and encouraged her to play with her toys.

I leaned against the window, looking out onto the runway. As my finger touched the button that could control the shade for the window, I couldn't hold in my smile, remembering my first meeting with Ryo. He'd looked so grumpy at the time. Now I knew that he must have been worrying about Akiko's health.

"Ryo," I whispered and caressed his bandanna wrapped on my wrist. I'd thought I returned it, but I was glad when I found it among my clothes yesterday.

I also found the uchiwa fan from the Sailor Moon in Harajuku. Initially, I'd wanted to throw it away, but I'd changed my mind. The fan was a memento of my lovely day with Ryo, which I now recognized was the day I fell in love with him.

Too bad I'd returned the umbrella to him. If not, I would have had three mementos from different times I had with Ryo.

Heat swelled behind my eyes as I unwrapped the bandanna and brought it to my lips. The shock on his face when I announced that Tristan was my boyfriend rushed back into my mind. I was crushed to see him in heart-wrenching pain that night, but I had to do it.

The hollow feeling in my chest became more pronounced as the plane left the ground. I shut my eyes tightly.

Goodbye, Ryo.

RYO

Ryo had just left Takeru's house when Harper texted him. Since the shocking night, he'd stayed with Takeru because he didn't want to see Bella anymore. He'd skipped attending the grand opening of Sara's café yesterday for the same reason. It hurt him so much to think of Bella and her lie.

Can we meet at Ohayo Café after lunch?

Ryo frowned. *Okay, but I already had an early lunch*, he responded.

Not a problem. Dessert would be the best.

Okay, he typed.

When Ryo arrived, there was no one in the café but Harper. Pain stabbed his chest to see her sitting at the table where they'd had breakfast with Bella last time.

She smiled as Ryo approached and took a seat in front of her.

"I took the liberty of ordering German chocolate cake and New York cheesecake for us. My treat. They're tasty and perfect with matcha tea," she said.

Ryo chuckled. "Sure."

The same woman as last time brought their desserts and tea. "Nice to see you again," she said to Ryo. "Enjoy." Then she returned to the kitchen.

Harper took a tiny piece of her cheesecake with a fork and bit it slowly.

"Sorry for not contacting you. I've been busy lately," said Ryo. "You know: my sister, job interviews, and I need time to rest. I don't mean to be rude, but I'm in a hurry. If you could tell me why you asked to meet me now, I'd appreciate it."

Harper nodded and put her fork next to her cake. "I'd heard what happened to you and Bella. That's unfortunate because you two were a good couple."

Ryo sighed because he'd guessed that Harper would make a comment like that. *Don't say her name again. It's over!* He screamed in his head. But he didn't say that out loud. "I don't want to hear her name anymore." He rose to his feet.

"She loves you."

Ryo scoffed. "She never loved me. She only dated me because she was lonely. She . . ." He gritted his teeth and leaned forward. "Don't ever say that she loves me," Ryo snapped, but then he caught the waitress peeking her head out of the kitchen. His voice must have been louder than he'd realized. "Sorry, Harper. I don't mean to snap at you. I'm exhausted, bye." He flapped his hand and walked away.

"Ryo!" Harper called, but Ryo ignored her and reached to open the door.

"She lied about Tristan."

The sentence stopped him. He spun and walked back to Harper. "What did you say?"

"Bella had to make up a story because she knows your parents and Akiko need you. She also knew a long-distance relationship might be too hard. One thing that she misunderstood was about your status here. She thought you came here to visit your family as you'd told her on the plane."

Ryo sat back in his seat and ran a hand over his hair. "That's what she thought?"

"That's why she showed her feelings to you. If not, she wouldn't have done it." Harper looked at him. "And Sara confronted her and questioned her feelings for you too. Which made her wonder if that was true. That night, Tristan and her boss arrived in Tokyo for the Little Bear Café. And she took the opportunity and asked him—"

"To help her lie to me," Ryo interjected.

"Pretty much."

Ryo clenched his fingers. "Harper, where's Bella? I want to see her before she leaves."

Harper looked straight at him. "Bella already left Tokyo ten days ago."

"What? She wasn't even at the café's grand opening?" Ryo almost jumped from his seat. "Why?"

"She said she was done with the training. So she requested to return to the States earlier than she was supposed to."

Ryo covered his eyes with his hands. "She did that because of me. God, what have I done?"

A hand touched his arm. Harper looked at him gently. "I suggest you talk to Tristan, but you need to catch him tonight in Narita. His flight is around ten; try to be there before then," Harper suggested.

"Okay." He stood up and walked across the room to the entrance.

"Hey."

Ryo turned around.

"I like you and Bella. If you really love her, try to win her back and find a way to make your relationship with her work." Harper gazed at him.

Ryo took a deep breath. "I'll try. Thanks for your confidence."

❧❀

At eight in the evening, Ryo was already at the JAL counter. He didn't care to sit on vacant seats near the counter. He was restless, and his eyes were searching for Tristan among travelers. Then he found him with a woman wearing loose yoga pants.

Tristan seemed to remember Ryo because he spoke to the woman after they checked in and gestured to Ryo. The woman looked at Ryo, then nodded to Tristan before walking to the security checkpoint.

"Tristan," Ryo called, walking toward him. "Remember me?"

"Yes, a good neighbor of my girlfriend," Tristan said, and stopped in front of Ryo.

"I know you helped her lie to me," Ryo said quickly. "Can we talk somewhere?"

Tristan was taken aback by the question, but a tiny smile broke out as he nodded. "Sure."

Ryo took him to a ramen restaurant in a quiet corner, a perfect place to talk. They settled on the empty seats outside the restaurant.

"What do you want to know from me?" asked Tristan, tilting his head.

"Be frank with me. Are you Bella's boyfriend?" Ryo asked.

"No, I'm not."

Ryo's eyes narrowed. "What's your relationship with her?" he asked again.

Tristan smiled. "I work at Little Bear as a senior manager of marketing. I came here to helping create the marketing campaign for our franchisee here."

"So, you don't have any feeling for her?"

"Nope. I have a fiancée."

Ryo felt all tensions lifted from his shoulder. "Thanks for your clarification."

"That's it? That's the reason you came here?"

Ryo nodded.

Leaning back in his seat, Tristan looked at him. "By the way, who told you that I'm not Bella's boyfriend?"

"Harper, Bella's good friend here. She lives in the same building as Bella and me," answered Ryo honestly.

"Since you know the truth, will you chase her to the States?" asked Tristan. He looked curious.

Ryo tapped his finger on the table and thought about the question.

"No." He answered after a few beats.

Tristan lifted both hands; a disappointment was evident on his face. "Why? I don't understand. You came here to confront me, and after everything was settled, you said no. You're driving me crazy."

"I wish I could chase her, but there are many things I have to do here. Besides"—Ryo took a deep breath—"eventually she'll forget me. Our relationship hasn't been going on long, anyway. So it won't be hard for us to forget each other. I came to meet you to ease the pain and find out the truth."

"You're a good man, Ryo. I can tell," said Tristan. "I'm sorry about your sister and for lying to you. When Bella asked me, I couldn't say no to her begging face. It's my fault. I should have refused her request. Maybe you could have a chance to get an explanation from her."

"Or maybe not. Maybe she'd be silent forever without anyone knowing the real reason," Ryo disagreed.

"Ah, that's true." Tristan nodded and fished out a business card from his wallet. Then he wrote something on the back before giving it to Ryo. "This is my personal phone number. Call me if you come to the States. My fiancée and I will be happy to have you in our house. And I promise I won't tell Bella if you come. Unless you want to meet her, then I'll try my best to help."

"Thanks, I will," Ryo said. In his mind, he had doubts about being back in the US again.

"Ryo, please don't lose hope," Tristan said as if he could read his mind. "Let's say in a few more months, you don't love her anymore, and that's okay. As you said, Bella may forget about you anyway. However, if you still love her after a few months and I find out that Bella still loves you, I don't mind being your matchmaker. So, keep in touch with me."

"Appreciate it." Ryo smiled.

Tristan glanced at his watch. "Hey, I should leave now." He extended his hand. "Nice to see you, and good luck with everything."

Ryo shook his hand. "Likewise."

Ryo followed Tristan until he joined the people in front of the security checkpoint. His heart felt lighter as he turned around and walked toward the exit. That was what he needed.

BELLA

"Bella, take this and put more steamed veggies on it." My mom handed me an empty plate. "And stop nibbling that pretzel because I haven't seen you eat anything other but pretzels." She shook her head as my finger reached out for the soft pretzel bites with cheddar cheese.

I grinned, plopped two in my mouth, and took the plate from her hand. A minute later, I brought the plate back full of steamed veggies. When I reached for another pretzel, my mom smacked my hand.

"Ouch!" I yelled. "If you don't want me to eat so many today, you should bake more often. Not only for the Fourth of July."

"Don't listen to her, Mrs. B." Mel chimed in and sat on the outdoor chair next to Andrew. "I would eat more because those are too delicious to skip."

"True." I winked, grabbed a plate for my dad's delicious barbecue ribs, and sat next to her. "I think you should get the recipe from Mom and bake it for your future husband. Right, Drew?"

Under the outdoor light, Mel's cheeks turned pink, but she pretended not to hear what I said.

With a mouth full of ribs, Andrew nodded and grinned widely.

A month ago, right after Mel graduated with her master's degree, Andrew proposed to her, and she said yes. My parents and I were happy for her because Andrew was a good, responsible man.

To be honest, I was sad too because the house would become quieter once Mel moved out. It had already been quiet without Adele, and soon Mel would be gone too. However, unlike Adele, who had moved to New York after getting married, Mel would live in a townhouse not far from my parents' house.

"Bel, what's the formal way to say 'good morning' in Japanese again?" asked Andrew, wiping his fingers with wet napkins. A plate with piles of rib bones was on the ground, next to his feet.

I shrugged, rubbing the neck of my base at a sudden itch. "I only said 'ohayo,' and everyone understood."

He nodded and typed something on his phone. Since I'd moved back from Tokyo last year, he'd become obsessed with learning the language.

"I think you should keep honing your Japanese because learning a new language is good for your memory," Terry, Adele's husband, chimed in, holding their three-month-old baby, and sitting next to me. "If you haven't used it, you'll forget it easily."

"Well, I don't think I need it anymore, but thanks, I'll keep it in mind." I forced a smile.

"Why do you say that? You may go to Japan again, right?"

I bit my lips, then rose to my feet and walked back to the house. "Hey, anyone knows when the fireworks start?"

"In an hour," my mom answered.

"Great," I said. From the corner of my eye, Andrew and Terry exchanged a glance and winced when Mel and Adele slapped their shoulders and glared at them while pointing their heads toward me.

They'd known something happened in Tokyo because I didn't talk much about it—other than to say that the training was successful—and I was also more focused on my work and studies.

Yes, I continued my school as I'd promised my mom. It had been tough juggling full-time school and a full-time job, but I did it anyway. To my surprise, school wasn't as bad as I thought. At that speed, I'd get my bachelor's degree in less than a year and then continue to get my master's degree.

My mom was happy with my decision and thought it was because of her influence. Actually, it wasn't. After meeting many people at my work, I'd realized that having a degree meant more chances to advance in my career than not having one. Besides, if I had a higher position, I could empower more people, especially women.

After things happened in Tokyo, my relationship with Tristan became closer. I also became his now-wife's close friend. They were a lovely couple, and I was happy to be part of their family.

At eight sharp, the fireworks began from the youth park a block away from my parents' house. I loved it because we didn't have to go anywhere to watch fireworks.

Sitting on the window seat in my room, I watched the fireworks dancing in the air. The bay windows gave me the best view. The sky was lit by yellow, purple, red, and golden lights, followed by hissing, screeching, and crackling sounds. Once or twice I heard car alarms go off from the loud booms.

"Tsuki ga kirei desune." Ryo's gentle whisper rang in my ear as if he was sitting next to me, like when we watched the fireworks in Sumida Park.

I covered my mouth to muffle my sob because I knew the meaning of it by now. Back then, I thought he praised the half-moon hiding behind the cloud. He even chuckled when I protested that the moon wasn't beautiful enough.

But it wasn't what he meant.

He used that phrase from Japanese novelist Souseki Natsume to say "I love you." Ryo had loved me, and I hurt him.

The sound of my door opening startled me.

Through the blur of tears, I saw Adele enter the room.

"Bel-bel." She called my nickname, striding across the room. Without saying anything, she pulled me into her arms to hug me. She rubbed my back as she had always done whenever I was upset about something.

"He loves me." I sobbed. "And I lied to him so he could forget me and stay there for his sister and family."

"I know … I know," Adele cooed at me in a low voice. "It's painful."

"I want to forget him, but why I can't forget him? It's been a year, and I should have forgotten him."

"That's because he is a good man for you, and you know that. Don't blame yourself too much, Bel," she said, pushing my shoulder gently. Looking at me in concern, she caressed my bangs and tucked a strand of my hair behind my ear. "Whenever you want to dump your feelings, I can be your ear. You know that."

I nodded, sniffing.

"Come, let's watch the fireworks together." She sat cross-legged on the window seat. "And lay your head down here." She tapped her lap a few times. "When you were young, you liked sleeping on my lap whenever you felt upset about something."

Between sniffing, I let out a chuckle. "Adele, I've drunk wine and kissed a man now."

But I surrendered at the look at her eyes. I sat sideways and fit my body to the length of the window seat before laying my head on her lap. Her face slanted skyward, and her fingers caressed my hair. "Now, tell me, how did you meet him?"

My tears were flowing again, but my voice was steady when I began to tell her from the beginning.

It was six thirty in the evening when I left my office. It had been a long, busy day, and I wanted to sleep. I was walking down the front steps of my office when I sensed someone watching me. I stopped midway, and when I looked around, I saw a man standing twenty yards away in the parking lot. My eyes squinted, and I covered my mouth with both hands as I recognized him. Hands in his pockets, Ryo sauntered toward me and stopped at the bottom step, looking up at me.

"Bella Bell-san," he called. His cheekbones looked more pronounced than the last time we met, but his smile was more expansive.

"Ryo?" I whispered, taking a step backward. The yearning look on his face stung my heart. "Am I dreaming?"

"No." He took one step up. "You aren't."

For a few beats, we looked at each other in silence.

"W-why are you here?" I asked, breaking the silence.

"You left without saying goodbye. But ..." He spread his arms to the sides. "Here I am."

The evening midsummer breeze was blowing gently at my back, tossing strands of my hair to my cheeks. My chest hurt as if it held a giant balloon ready to explode.

"Why are you here?" I repeated because that was the only thing I could say.

He sighed and inserted his hands in his pants pockets. "I'm looking for you."

"Not funny."

"I'm not joking."

I swallowed and rubbed the bridge of my nose, racking my brain to find an escape. "How's Akiko?" I finally asked.

Ryo looked down. "She passed away six months ago."

I touched a hand to my lips. "I'm sorry."

"Thank you. She looked peaceful, though." He gave me a small smile and took a few steps up to where I was standing. His hand fished out something from his khakis' pocket. "And she wanted you to have this." His palm opened, revealing the Airou keychain.

I shook my head. "I—I don't think—"

"She insisted I give it to you."

I swallowed and took it from him. His fingers were cold when our fingers touched briefly.

"Thanks." Weighing the keychain in my hand, I looked at him. "Don't you need to take care of your parents there?"

"Why did you lie to me?" he asked, ignoring my question.

"W-what are you talking about?"

"You and Tristan." He looked straight at me. His tone was an absolute challenge.

"What?"

He repeated, his eyes boring into my skull.

"H-how did you know?" I blinked.

"Harper."

"What a traitor." I frowned.

"And Tristan."

I blinked hard. "T-Tristan told you? When?"

"On the same day you were supposed to leave Tokyo," he answered.

My mouth was ajar. "But how did you know when his flight was?"

"Harper."

I closed my eyes briefly. "I shouldn't have shared it with her," I mumbled under my breath, and stepped down.

But Ryo was fast. He held my arm to stop me before letting his hand drop to his side. "Why did you do that?"

"If Tristan and Harper told you, you've known the reason." I exhaled, turning to him. "Go home, Ryo. There's nothing we can talk about."

"There is. I asked you to tell me your reasons." His eyes stared determinedly.

I chewed the inside of my lips. "You sacrificed your career for your sister," I said. "Now Akiko's passed, and you need to take care of your parents. That's your duty as the first son, right?" I asked in a matter-of-fact tone.

He tilted his head. "You've become a Japanese culture expert."

"Don't be sarcastic."

"I'm not." He shrugged. "I wonder how you know that. Hmm, let me guess, Sara?"

I looked away, avoiding his eyes.

"Bella, listen to me." He lowered his voice. "You're right. It's my duty to take care of my parents. But do you know where my parents are now?

"They're in Switzerland," he continued when I didn't say anything, "and in two more weeks, they'll be in France, and then ... uh ... I don't know since I don't remember their one-year itinerary."

"A year ... for vacation?" I cocked my head.

He nodded. "Before Akiko passed away, she wanted my parents and me to have fulfilling lives because she didn't want us to be miserable. She knew that my parents had sacrificed a lot for her and never left her side. So, when she passed, we found a box full of her diaries and a map of the countries she wanted to go to. My parents thought if she couldn't do it, they could fulfill it for her. So, two weeks ago, they left Tokyo and began their first long trip using Akiko's map"—he chuckled—"that's what we called it. That's what they've been doing right now."

His eyes were on me as he paused. "And she gave me a task too."

I lifted an eyebrow at him in silence.

"Don't you want to know?" He pressed.

I shrugged. "It doesn't hurt to hear."

He flashed a smile and looked down, scratching the floor with the tip of his shoes. "She wants me to reclaim my heart that has been stolen. So here I am."

Ryo reached out to touch my shoulder, but I stepped away. Hurt was clear in his eyes as he pressed his hands into his pockets. "Well, I'm glad you moved on. But don't worry, I won't bug you anymore." He cleared his throat. "Goodbye, Bella."

Slowly, he turned around and dragged his feet descending the stairs.

"What will you do if you meet the thief?" I asked as he reached the last step.

"Huh?" He twisted back to me.

"Your story is a cliffhanger." I clenched my bag strap. "You said you came here to reclaim your heart. If you meet the thief, what will you do?"

He lifted his shoulders for a few seconds and dropped them. "I'll humor you." He bit his lip as he looked at me. "If I meet the thief, I want to ask if the thief is still interested in keeping my heart."

I nodded slowly. "And what happens if the thief isn't interested in keeping it anymore?" I asked again.

Ryo set his jaw as sadness clouded his face before answering. "The thief can throw it away." I could hear the pain in his voice.

"Okay. Thanks for the answer," I maintained my voice flat.

His fingers curled. Letting out a long, low sigh, Ryo looked at me for a few moments and began to walk away.

I pursed my lips and scanned heavenward until I found what I was looking for. "Ryo," I called him. But Ryo didn't stop. I called him again louder. "Ryo!"

He stopped and turned around reluctantly.

I pointed at the moon in the sky behind me. "Tsuki ga kirei desune."

His mouth hung open. "W-what did you say?"

I bit my lips and put my hands beside my cheeks like a megaphone. "Tsuki ga kirei desune."

He froze but not for long. In one stride, he took two steps at a time, and so did I. I didn't know who arrived first, but I knew his hands cupped my face, and our lips collided. Gentle shock waves ran throughout my body, and my stomach fluttered at the feel of his warm lips.

"I love you," he whispered, brushing his lips to mine before kissing them again.

"I love you too, and I can't believe you're here," I whispered as I pulled away, wiping the smear of my lipstick off his lips. "And I can't believe that I kissed you in front of my office." I chuckled, then covered my mouth, sniffing.

He pressed his forehead to mine. We shared our breaths.

"Don't ever leave me again," he whispered.

"I won't."

He leaned down to kiss me again before a voice called his name. Startled, we broke away to see Tristan standing with his back against the pillars. "Get a room, guys, get a room," he teased.

My cheeks warmed as I looked away. I didn't know how long he'd been watching us.

Ryo wrapped his arm around my waist. "Thanks, Tristan."

I looked at Tristan and then turned to Ryo, raising my eyebrows. Tristan shrugged and came down to stand on the same step as us.

I pushed Ryo, who was grinning widely. "Now I get how you knew I was still in the office." Then I turned to Tristan and punched his arm.

"Hey, I'll tell your supervisor that you dared to punch me." He snickered.

"Thanks for helping us," I said as Ryo held my hand.

"Happy to help." Flapping his hand, Tristan stepped down until the last step, then he turned around. "Kissing always takes a lot of energy. So, are you guys hungry?" he said. "My treat."

I leaned toward Ryo. "His salary is higher than mine. Why don't we take advantage of it?"

"I hear you, Bel."

I snickered. Holding hands, we followed Tristan.

"Good to see you again, Yamada-san," Tristan said as we walked next to him. "Since I helped you, are we on good terms now?"

Ryo laughed. "I'll punch your face if you try to pull my leg again."

"Wow, Bella, look at him. Behind his calm and handsome face, he's scary." He cackled. "You should be careful."

"Yes, I didn't know you had such aggression in you, Yamada-san," I teased him.

His eyes twinkled as he pulled me closer. "You don't know a thing about me. Should I prove it to you? Maybe tonight?" he whispered loudly, and winked.

"Ooohhhhh," Tristan roared, overhearing us.

"My dad will kill you first." I laughed and slapped his shoulder a couple times.

"Ah, that's right, I should ask permission to date you from Bell-sama— your dad," he teased me.

I grinned widely and wrapped a hand around his waist.

In the sky, the stars twinkled. The moon was round, and its silvery light flooded everywhere. It was beautiful and bright, as if it was smiling to see us.

Wise men say, only fools rush in
But I can't help falling in love with you
(Song by Elvis Presley)

ACKNOWLEDGMENT

Wear gratitude like a cloak, and it will feed
every corner of your life. — Rumi

Tokyo is a fascinating city with many different characters.
It is a city where you can find a beautiful and quiet garden where you can hear birds chirping, just a step away from noisy streets.

It is a city where you can find ancient temples and shrines rubbing shoulders with skyscrapers.

It is a city where tradition and modernity collide.

It is a city whose chaotic beauty I've fallen in love with.

And it is a city where I was inspired to write my novel, *A Warm Rainy Day in Tokyo*, and I had a lot of fun writing this lighthearted story.

However, this book couldn't be done without much support from friends and family.

Special thanks to Yuka and Ikuko. Our meeting was brief, but I was stunned by your kindness when you both agreed to read my whole first draft without hesitation and gave your valuable feedbacks on Japanese cultures and taboos. *Arigato gozaimasu!* You guys are fantastic!

Thanks to my Instagram friend, Ganfujinze, for answering my questions about Tokyo's weather and summer festivals.

Thanks to fellow writers in The Write Practice for your feedback on the first chapters.

Thanks to Tasia for giving your opinion about the cover.

Thanks to my friends (Cayung, Dina, Odi, Joy, Tepi, Olin) for your moral support. Also, to Irma, Dina, Susan, and Fenny for always asking more about my books.

Thanks to my in-laws, brother, and sisters for your love, prayers, and encouragement. Love you guys!

To my furry baby, Gladys. Your death broke my heart, and my tears fall each time I remember you. Thanks for accompanying me for almost eleven years. Please watch over Meeko.

I can't forget to thank my readers. Without you this book is nothing. You guys are rock!

To my better half, Steve. Thanks for being supportive and so patient with me. I love you to the moon and back.

To my mom and dad, who love me unconditionally and also are the source of my strength. Thanks for always believing in me. I'll never be able to repay you for all you've done for me. I love and miss you both.

Last but not least, I lift my thanks to God for accompanying me whenever I felt down and lonely. I was able to finish this book because you strengthen me day by day. Thanks for your grace and love.

EXCERPT
NO-SECRETS-ALLOWED

CHAPTER 1

A crisp, early winter morning greeted me as I left my aunt's house. Vapor rose in the air from my breath. Gazing up, I noticed the color of the sky matched the gray sidewalk, although the Weather Channel had predicted a bright, sunny day in Boston. Well, so much for expecting a warm day today.

As I turned onto the main street, the hustle and bustle of the city surrounded me. The sound of passing cars and the groaning and hissing of the city bus when it halted at the nearby bus stop overwhelmed the chatter and footsteps of people rushing to and fro. Twenty feet from me, a man yelled and waved his fist as a biker swirled past him on the sidewalk. It was against the law to ride a bike on the sidewalk, especially where it was prohibited by signs, but sometimes, people did it anyway. I chuckled and shook my head.

When I moved to this city four months ago, I hadn't liked its hustle and bustle. Too noisy. However, I was used to it now and felt something inside me come alive every time my ears picked up the familiar sounds.

I sped up a bit, speed-walking toward the O`ahu Café for my favorite winter drink, a mint-flavored mocha latte. Another nearby café had the same drink, but the one from the O`ahu was better and not too sweet. The best part was the location of the café near the bus stop, which allowed me to take shelter from the frigid weather while waiting for the bus.

My idea wasn't as brilliant as I'd thought because, looking through the big window, I saw a long line waiting inside the café. My favorite table near the window and facing the street was already occupied. When the café wasn't too crowded, I enjoyed sitting at that particular table while drinking my coffee, watching pedestrians pass by on the sidewalk.

Seven people were waiting in line, but thankfully, my bus wouldn't be coming for a while.

The bell above the café door made a soft ding as I pushed it open. A couple of customers near the door turned to see who had entered, as well as a young man in a beige apron behind the counter, whose brown skin made many people jealous of his natural tan. His long hair was tied up in a bun and hidden beneath his black beanie. I felt a twinge of envy over his long, shiny, black hair.

Standing next to a girl with a pixie haircut, who was currently taking the customers' orders, he waved to acknowledge me, and I waved back at him.

As I approached the counter, he signaled the cashier to change places with him so he could ring up my order.

"Good morning, Aurorette Arrington," he sang. "You look great this morning with your red nose like Rudolph." He tapped at his own nose.

"Good morning, Tyler Sheridan James Kahale," I teased him back. "You look great too, with your long hair that makes me jealous hidden under your beanie."

The wide grin on his face faded. Ty, as he wanted people to call him, had never liked his long name. He always said that he wanted to change his name to "Tyler James," making it short but cool. However, after his dad passed away, he decided to keep it.

"No more free espresso for you, since you called me by *that* name." He pouted, but his eyes twinkled with good humor. He rang up my usual order, a small mint mocha latte.

"I can deal with that." I smiled sweetly, tapping my card on the reader.

Ty scoffed and closed the register. He asked the girl with the pixie haircut to ring up the next order. The girl switched places with him, seemingly used to acting on the whim of the owner's son.

"Where have you been? You haven't come around lately," Ty said, pumping two shots of mint syrup into a cup. "My mom has been asking about you."

His mom, Dot, was my aunt's closest friend in Boston. After her husband had passed away, Dot had begun managing the café with Ty, her daughter, Brie, and three workers. My aunt came and helped out sometimes when the café was extra busy or if one of the workers couldn't come in.

"Busy, busy, busy." I sighed dramatically. "It's almost Christmas, and my office has been super hectic since October. I haven't had a chance to stop by because I've been exhausted by the time I get home. Please tell Dot that I'll stop by after work for her delicious chicken pesto panini tonight."

His mom's panini was one of the café's specialties. Made fresh, people loved the crunchy texture and delicious pesto sauce. Usually, I texted Dot to put aside one or two that I'd pick up later after work.

"Yeah, I'll tell her. By the way," Ty said as he poured an espresso shot into my cup, "I heard from her that your aunt got a new coffee machine for her birthday last month, but she doesn't drink coffee, does she? Now, tell me, why would someone give her a coffee machine? I'll bet the giver isn't a very thoughtful person. Just saying," he added, giving me a meaningful smile.

In return, my smile was sour. The giver was Peter Ryder, my long-distance, British-born boyfriend, who lived in California. He'd known that my aunt loved tea more than coffee and bought an English tea set for her birthday. He also bought a coffee machine for me from the same store. Somehow, the store had messed up the orders and sent the coffee machine in beautiful wrapping paper to my aunt instead of the tea set. My aunt was upset and thought Peter wasn't a thoughtful person. When I told him, Peter freaked out and complained to the store. My aunt felt better after he apologized and explained it to her. Later on, the store called for clarification and sent her another tea set by way of compensation.

"It wasn't his fault. The store messed up the order," I said quickly. "Besides, my aunt now has two beautiful new English tea sets while I got the coffee machine."

"Ha! I knew you'd defend that useless guy," Ty said, pointing at my nose. A proud smile plastered his face. "Aurorette, you should date me, not a guy who lives far away in California. Since I live close to you, I wouldn't make a blunder like that. Three years younger means nothing in this century. Besides, I think I'm more mature than him. And where does he work now?" Leaning toward me, he placed his hand behind his ear.

"Yeah, yeah, yeah. I've heard that before." I waved a hand. "And instead of dating *me*, you should find a girl your age. Besides," I leaned toward him and whispered in his ear, "you're working for your family business too." I gave him a wink.

His mouth opened slightly and then closed again. "But this is only temporary until I finish colle—"

His words were cut off when a large, tall woman, her gray hair wrapped in a hairnet, came from the kitchen. "Ty! I'm busy, and the milk company will be here soon. I need you to receive the delivery." Her dark brown eyes widened as our eyes met. "Oh, hey, Rory. Sorry, I didn't notice you there. Where have you been, dear?"

"It's been crazy at work," I replied. "I'm glad I saw you today, Dot."

Dot smiled and nodded. "Well, enjoy the coffee. I have to get back to the kitchen again. Do you need some panini today? One or two?"

"Two would be great, and I'll pick them up after work. Have a good day, Dot."

"Thank you. I'll save you two panini."

Dot retreated to the kitchen, and Ty handed me my order. "Come again tomorrow. I'll give you a free shot of espresso," he said, his voice lowered so the other customers wouldn't hear.

"Okay, but I can't promise anything," I said.

He pouted.

I grinned widely before taking my drink to the condiment bar to retrieve additional chocolate powder and a lid.

As I turned, a young boy rushed toward the door and bumped my elbow, spilling the hot drink onto my hand. I shrieked and jumped sideways, losing my grip on the cup.

The next events seemed to happen in slow motion.

Mocha splashed onto the man waiting nearby for his order before the cup hit the ground, sending the rest of the hot liquid everywhere.

The man gave a tiny yelp and tried to shake the coffee from his light blue sweater. The brown stain was already spreading down his chest.

"Oh my God!" Ty screamed, grabbing a roll of paper towels from the counter before rushing toward us.

"I'm sorry," Ty and I said almost in unison.

"You should be careful next time, young lady," a voice said from behind me.

I turned and saw a bald guy standing near the condiment bar.

"He could have been scalded by the hot coffee," he continued.

"That's not my…" I glanced at the bald man before turning to my mocha victim. "The kid bumped my elbow and—"

"At the very least, you can take him to the doctor to treat his burns, and pay for his dry cleaning," the bald guy interrupted.

I took a breath. It was clear this guy loved making trouble. "Yes, that's what I'm going to—"

Before I finished, the mocha victim turned to the bald guy. "Hey, man," he said, "thanks for your concern. The coffee wasn't too hot, anyway, and I don't need a doctor. And this young lady"—he pointed to me—"didn't do it on purpose. That means she doesn't need to pay for my dry cleaning."

The bald guy mumbled and moved toward the door with his nose in the air. A few customers murmured and glanced at him as he left the café.

Sighing, the mocha victim turned to Ty. "Please show me where the restroom is, so I can clean my shirt." He pointed to me. "Would you mind watching my luggage while I change my clothes?" He indicated the luggage at his feet.

I nodded. "No problem at all."

"The restroom is this way." Ty ushered him down the narrow hallway. "I can give you our café sweater for free, too," I heard him say.

"Is your hand okay?" asked Dot, who must have heard the commotion from the kitchen.

I picked up a beige jacket from the floor, assuming it belonged to the mocha victim. One sleeve of the coat had a coffee stain on it.

"Yes, I'm fine, Dot," I said, searching for the young boy who had caused the ruckus. When I didn't see him, I assumed he must have run off.

"I've never seen that boy or the bald guy before," said Dot, following my gaze to the front door. "Let me replace your drink, dear."

Before I could decline her offer, she'd already walked behind the counter and apologized to the customers for the commotion.

Shortly after, Ty and the mocha victim came out of the restroom. The man now wore a bright pink sweater with the words "I need my coffee now!" printed above the cartoon picture of a sullen lady in pajamas with rollers in her hair. Ty had drawn the cartoon, and every time I saw it, I smiled.

But not this time.

As our eyes met, I mouthed to Ty, "Pink?"

Ty shrugged.

The mocha victim seemed relieved as I handed him his jacket. He put it on quickly, buttoning it up to conceal the sweater.

"I'm sorry we don't have any other color, sir," said Ty apologetically. "Our new order will be here in two days. If you don't mind waiting, I could go upstairs and lend you one of *my* sweaters."

The man shook his head. "That's okay. I have no time to waste as I have a plane to catch."

"How about me paying for the laundry service?" I offered, using the chance to look at him clearly.

He was a head taller than me, sturdy but slim. Behind his glasses, his eyes were blue with a hint of green. His light brown hair was neatly cut with clean edges, making him look like the classic gentleman. I guessed he couldn't be over the age of thirty-five.

"Don't worry about that. I was here for my business trip, hence I can charge my company for a new, expensive sweater," he said, half joking. "Thanks, but it's unnecessary. Besides, I got a free pink sweater." He grinned after saying the last sentence.

"But—"

"It's okay." He shook his head again. "Accidents can happen anywhere. And this wasn't your fault."

Before I could say more, Dot brought me a new mint mocha latte. After thanking her, I turned to the man, but he was already gone. I exhaled, waving at Ty, who was busy mopping the floor to prevent people from stepping on the spill. I tried to put the event behind me and walked to the bus stop.

All the way to work, I couldn't shake thoughts of what had happened earlier.

The poor guy.

He was here for a business trip, and on the day he had to fly back home, his sweater and coat were ruined by a mint mocha latte.

I'll bet he bought a new sweater at the airport rather than wearing that bright pink one.

I pressed the red stop button as the bus rolled closer to my destination and waited until it came to a halt. Once the door opened, the fresh air rushed in, wrapping its cold fingers around me.

Walking slowly along the sidewalk toward my office, I pulled my beanie down to cover my ears and adjusted the scarf around my neck. The tip of my nose was growing numb from the frigid wind. I missed the mild winter season in Southern California. After living there for more than five years, I'd been spoiled by year-round warm and sunny weather.

Boston was beautiful, but I would have liked it more if the winter wasn't so harsh and the summer wasn't so humid.

No one had forced me to live in Boston. After I graduated from college, my aunt had suggested that I move in with her, but I loved California and was happy when I got a job as an accountant at Myriad Food and Beverage. I'd thought I was ready to settle down there. Many things had happened in August, including the horrible car accident after I resigned from Myriad. My aunt was my only kin, so after the accident, I decided to move and stay with her.

I entered my office building and took the elevator to the tenth floor, where I got off at Veles Capital, a financial holding company possessing a diversified line of community banking and commercial finance. I'd worked there as a senior analyst in the risk department for almost four months. My boss, Sally Kranda, was the nicest boss compared to my bitchy, bully boss at Myriad .

"Good morning, Marsha," I said, passing my coworker's cubicle.

"Hi, Rory. Good morning and happy Friday," Marsha Wilson said cheerfully over her shoulder.

"Happy Friday," I responded.

Sitting on my chair, I fitted my electronic notebook into its docking station and turned the power on.

"Too bad you didn't join our happy hour yesterday," Marsha said, sliding her chair to peek inside my cubicle while I logged into my computer.

"Why? Did something happen?" I glanced at her before turning my attention back to the computer.

Still sitting on her chair, Marsha slid into my cubicle.

I should tell her to stop doing that because she looks silly with her bulging, six-months-pregnant stomach.

"Last night, Kelly was drunk and confessed her love to Ryan," she whispered.

I covered my mouth with my hand. "Really?"

She nodded. "Yup. Crazy, huh? I don't understand her. Did she think it was okay to get drunk during happy hour with her coworkers? If she'd wanted to get drunk, she should've just gone with her regular friends. We don't want to go out with people who can't control themselves. Besides, our happy hour is for relaxing and bonding, not for drinking excessively. That stupid girl doesn't know how to limit herself, and she confessed love to her senior while Leslie joined us for the happy hour." Marsha rolled her eyes when she mentioned Sally's assistant manager. "It's a good thing

Leslie doesn't care what people do outside the office. If she did, Kelly would be doomed."

"What did Ryan say?" I asked.

Marsha shrugged, tossing her bronze, shoulder-length hair behind her. "As you know, Ryan loves joking around. It surprised me how maturely he handled Kelly. Obviously, he isn't interested in her. Kelly knows he prefers you over her that's why she's always bitching about you."

It didn't take a genius to know that Ryan Harris had been crushing on me since I'd joined the company. He'd also been my classmate in university back in California.

I hadn't recognized him right away. Ryan had changed a lot, and the only things that had stayed the same were his sweet smile and his dimples. He was no longer a quiet, pale, lanky boy with long, dark brown hair, who wore black every single day. His lean and muscled body, along with his messy, medium-length hair made him look adorable. He'd also become a pleasant person to talk to, easy-going, and a reliable coworker. No wonder people, especially females, loved talking to him.

Meeting him again after years brought back the sweet memories in me. In college, we'd done everything together, starting from orientation, and some people mistook us for a couple. I didn't know what he'd felt toward me because he never said it. If he'd ever asked, I wouldn't have minded, because I liked him. Unfortunately, we'd grown apart after choosing our majors.

Since meeting again, Ryan had openly showed his attention toward me and looked unhappy upon learning that I had a boyfriend. I felt a familiar light flutter in my belly every time he looked at me, and I wished he had had the courage when we were in college.

I opened my mouth to respond when the general manager's office door opened. Sally emerged, her expression one of grave concern. She walked by us as though in a trance.

We exchanged glances, and Marsha slid her chair back to her cubicle while I focused on my monitor. We almost forgot to greet Ryan as he arrived and sat in his cubicle. When his head popped over the partition, he raised an eyebrow. I shrugged and jerked my head toward Sally's office. Without another word, he sat down and started working.

Twenty minutes passed, and Sally's urgent voice called out, "Rory, Marsha, Ryan, come to my office."

Right away, we all stood and hurried to join her.

"Please take a seat," she said, sitting in her chair.

I sat next to Marsha, and Ryan dragged an empty chair next to me.

Sally let out a heavy sigh before she laced her fingers together and gazed at us.

"Stone Dealership," she said, "our new automotive client in the California office, is in trouble. From their financial statements, I can tell they used the loan for personal expenses, because the million dollars we approved six months ago has quickly dwindled. This dealership is a subsidiary of Stone Transportation Services, one of our biggest clients. We can't share assumptions like that with them. Mr. Stone would be upset if we accused his younger brother of being incompetent." Sally stopped, taking another breath before continuing. "So, this project needs to be handled delicately, or Mr. Stone will move his businesses to another loan company."

My first day on the job, I'd been told that Stone Transportation Services had been one of the biggest clients at Veles Capital since its establishment two decades ago. The mutual relationship between the companies had been solid for years.

"And you know that, recently, Martin lost three of his field auditors and an accountant." She closed her eyes briefly before opening them again.

Martin Travers was the risk manager for the California office and Sally's counterpart. His team was smaller than Sally's, but I'd heard that he was losing some of his staff again this year because of his tough personality.

"I don't want to tell you why they quit simultaneously, but Martin needs our help. Also, the office doesn't have many clients in the automobile industry yet, and they don't have a person familiar with the business. So…" She turned to Ryan. "I want you to help the office."

The dimples in Ryan's cheeks became pronounced. I knew the business trip was a wonderful opportunity for him to expand his skill and experience, both of which would help him work toward a promotion. A willingness to go on business trips definitely improved the career outlook as well.

"And you, Rory," Sally turned to me, "your background in accounting would help Martin's team tremendously. You can give the dealership's employees basic accounting training. Martin also informed me that they've recorded everything incorrectly since the dealer joined us. The risk analysts are having a hard time analyzing Stone's financial report."

My heart leaped. California! I'd been thinking of it that whole morning, and suddenly, I'd been assigned there. What a coincidence. I couldn't wait to tell Peter. He would be dancing around like a crazy person.

I couldn't daydream about it for too long, though, because Sally's voice brought me back to the current conversation.

"And Marsha, I can't let you fly with them because of your condition, but I need your expertise to perform a deep analysis based on Rory and Ryan's findings. Leslie will take care of one of your clients, if necessary."

"How about you?" Marsha asked. "Are you going there too?"

She nodded. "I'll be there in two days, but I don't think you two will fly this week. You should be in California in a week's time. Belinda is already arranging our plane tickets and hotel."

Sally's eyes shifted to the picture on her desk of her husband hugging their daughter and son. Her finger trailed over it. Everybody in the office knew how much she loved her family. She didn't like to go on business trips, but she did what was needed. Her eyes remained on the picture another moment before she turned back to us.

"I know all of you have your own projects to do, but I need you to push them aside and focus on this one," she said solemnly. "And you two," her eyes shifted to Ryan and me, "I'm not your mom, but I do take care of my staff. Please act maturely and professionally, especially you, Ryan."

Ryan chuckled and spread his arms to each side. "Why me? How about her?" He pointed at me. "Her boyfriend is in California."

Sally rolled her eyes. "I was young once too."

"You're still young," Ryan said smoothly. "How old are you? Thirty-five?"

Sally chuckled. At fifty-three, she looked much younger than her age.

"Stop kissing my butt, Ryan," she said in her Boston accent, and laughed, waving her hand toward the door. "Get outta here!"

Grinning, Ryan walked out of the office, followed by Marsha and me.

We all loved Sally. She could be serious, but she could also be an easy-going person who loved to joke around.

When we returned to our cubicles, I checked the distance from the California office, which was located in a city called Irvine, to Peter's apartment and almost yelped. It was only twelve miles. Not far. My heart burst in anticipation of seeing his face in person, and I couldn't wait to tell him about my business trip to California.

CHAPTER 2

"**I**'m coming to California!" I almost shrieked during our video call that evening.

Peter's face broke into a wide smile. "Wow, that's awesome," he said in his British accent. "After that, can you take a week off?"

"I wish," I said, taking my phone to the kitchen so I could grab a glass of water. "This project will keep me busy starting next week until it's completed. I can't take any vacation until next year."

Aunt Amy, who was cutting fruit on the countertop, raised her eyes to me as I entered the kitchen and mouthed, "Peter? Say hi from me."

I nodded. "By the way, Aunt Amy says hi to you." I turned my phone toward her and let them wave before turning it back to me.

Peter rubbed at the back of his neck, and an expression of disappointment showed clearly on his face. "When will you fly here?"

"My boss said we're scheduled to fly next Sunday morning. I

guess I could be there by Sunday midnight and rest before going to the office. Then I should fly back on Friday night," I said, taking a sip of my water.

"Could you fly out on Friday and stay at my house for the whole weekend?" he asked.

"Stay at what?" I asked, nearly choking on my drink.

"My house."

Across from me, Aunt Amy raised her eyebrows.

I shrugged. It was news to me, too.

"Don't you mean your apartment?" I asked.

Peter shook his head. "No, my house. I bought it two weeks ago."
What?

"You hadn't said anything." I glanced at my aunt before walking back to my room.

"Well…" Peter scratched his temple. "I wanted to surprise you, but since you mentioned you were going to fly here, I just blurted it out."

"Ouch, what a bummer," I teased, trying to imagine the kind of house he'd bought.

He grinned. "The house is small," he said as if he could read my mind. "Let me send you the link so you can see what it looks like."

I opened the link on my notebook and immediately thought the term "small" meant something far different for Peter than it meant for me. The 3,200-square-foot, two-story house on a 7,000-square-foot plot of land was huge compared to my aunt's 1,500-square-foot townhouse. My eyes nearly fell from their sockets to see the price of the place, but Peter's family could afford to pay that much.

Located in a beach town, Peter's new house was a combined design of modern and tropical, consisting of two-and-a-half bathrooms, four bedrooms, and a loft space. The backyard led to a sandy, white beach. The master bedroom included an en suite bathroom with a skylight above the bathtub, and its interior featured a palette of white, gray, and beige colors, giving it an elegant and cozy appeal.

"Have you checked the link? Do you like the house?" Peter asked when I'd gone quiet. "The picture doesn't do it justice. You need to come and see it for yourself."

"Yes, I'm looking at it now. It's awesome," I nodded. "I like the kitchen. It looks modern and roomy."

"Yes, I can imagine you sitting in there while I make pancakes for you." His smile broadened. "I *do* hope you can fly earlier on Friday."

I held my breath, imagining the possibility of spending time with him on the weekend. Besides, I was curious to see the house in person.

Chewing my lower lip, I said, "I hope so too. We'll see if my boss approves my flying on Friday morning."

Leaning forward, Peter looked at me. His light brown eyes widened and shone. "It would be fun to have you over for the weekend. I miss you, Rory. It took me a while to get used to living here without you. I miss living with you like we lived in your old apartment."

I smiled, remembering the good times we'd had as roommates.

"Yeah, I miss that time too," I admitted. "By the way, let's say I'm allowed to fly there earlier. I still can't stay at your house for the whole business trip. I may be needed for a late meeting or overtime."

"Yeah, I understand," Peter said. His shoulders drooped as he rubbed his eyebrows.

"At least we could have each other for the weekend. So, keep your hopes high and I'll let you know what happens tomorrow," I said, smiling.

He nodded.

"Hey, tell me about Tom. How's he doing?" I asked, curious about what his half brother had been doing.

Peter met my gaze and nodded, understanding that I didn't want to continue talking about staying in his house. "He's doing fine. But we haven't seen each other in ages because we've both been so busy. Just so you know, I think he still feels guilty about what Phil did to us last time, because he's avoiding me." He sighed. "I know my brother, so I'm giving him some space until he's ready to open up again. I hope he doesn't mind seeing you while you're here."

Phil, Tom's ex-boyfriend, worked as a finance manager for White Water, Incorporated, a prestigious wine distributor for US and Canada, where Peter was working as president of the company.

Born into the Sandridge family, Peter and Tom were part of Britain's old entrepreneurship families called Sandridge Group that had run many businesses in several countries for decades.

Their last name wasn't Sandridge but Ryder. It was from their grandpa's last name, the current chairman, who was born from the youngest daughter of Sandridge. Although their last name was different, Peter and Tom were in line to take over the businesses when the time was right.

Four months ago, when Peter had been assigned to replace his sister as president of White Water, Inc., Phil didn't like it. He didn't think Peter deserved to take the position, considering his wild youth of partying, drinking, causing trouble, and using drugs. Phil sabotaged the selection and spread rumors, fabricating photos of Peter. He hoped the elders of the Sandridge family would revoke the decision and choose Tom instead. However, Phil didn't know that Tom had zero interest in the family business, which was why he lived in California rather than London. Tom found out about the dirty trick his boyfriend had played and broke up with him after asking Peter to fire him immediately.

"Tom shouldn't feel that way," I said, feeling sad for the man. I liked him, and we'd been friends for a while. "This hasn't been easy for you either, has it?"

"No, it hasn't." Peter shook his head. "I already lost Jane, and I don't want to lose my brother too. I love him. He barely talks to me now, and of course I can't talk to Jane. I feel especially lonely when I want to share a burden that relates to our family."

He let out another sigh and stared into the distance, his face reflective.

I didn't have siblings, but I could understand his loneliness. "Let's hope he shakes those feelings of guilt sooner rather than later," I comforted him. "I miss him too."

A slight smile appeared on his lips. "Yes, let's hope so. Don't forget to let me know if you can fly in earlier, because I want to let him know you're coming."

I nodded. "Okay."

Although tired, Peter smiled. Nothing made him happier than seeing his girlfriend's smiling face, and she would be there next week. If he hadn't remembered he was in his office, he would have hollered with joy.

Since that morning, he'd been in back-to-back meetings. He wanted to rest on the couch in his office for at least an hour before teleconferencing with London, but he didn't want to miss a video call with Rory. Since he had another meeting soon, their call had been cut short, but it had been enough to make him happy.

"Rory," Peter whispered, caressing the picture sitting on his desk. She looked lovely in her pale-yellow dress. The light freckles on the bridge of her nose, that she always complained about, made her look adorable. He chuckled as he looked at her photograph, remembering how chaotic their first meeting had been.

He'd never wanted to work in his family's businesses. When Jane had asked him to help her with her project in California, he couldn't refuse. However, a week before Jane flew to the States with him, she'd had emergency surgery that forced her to stay in the hospital. Later, Jane instructed Peter to fly alone and stop at a rental place to cancel her stay, where she'd already signed a six-month lease.

Knowing her eccentric personality, Peter hadn't bothered to ask further. He'd assumed Rory was Jane's ex-boyfriend or male friend. Everyone in the Sandridge family, including his grandpa, let Jane do whatever she wanted because she was a brilliant businesswoman. If Jane didn't want to stay in a hotel, they would rent her a house. If she decided to rent a room in someone's home, they wouldn't argue with her.

When he'd stopped by to tell Jane's roommate about the cancelation, it had surprised him that Rory was a female name. In Britain, it was a male's name.

Jane's new roommate had seemed shocked about the cancelation, and Peter detected that Rory had some financial troubles. Seeing her distress, he'd offered to continue his sister's rental agreement.

To his surprise, she'd accepted.

It had never crossed his mind that living with Rory would change his life forever.

She taught him everything, including valuing money, something he'd never concerned himself with. He also learned to appreciate the money he earned.

Rory also taught him about honesty and acceptance. She wasn't shy to admit that she'd been born out of wedlock and raised by her old-fashioned aunt after her mom passed away. She told him the truth about not knowing her father. He also knew her aunt didn't approve of Rory having a male roommate, afraid Rory would make the same ill-timed decisions her mom had made.

Something had slowly changed inside him. Peter learned to be a good man, different from the spoiled and selfish person he'd been in his youth. He wanted to be better for Rory.

If Jane were alive, she would have been happy to see his transformation.

Thinking of Jane made his heart thud dully in his chest. She'd been gone for more than three months, but he couldn't seem to shake his sadness. Jane had been more than his sister, especially after his mom abandoned him as a child. Peter had attached himself to Jane. She'd been his confidant, his protector, and his "little mom." Whenever he had an issue, he'd always asked for his sister's advice.

Now, she was gone forever, and his brother wasn't talking to him. No one had been around for him through his anxiety over the new position as president of White Water.

Their father, Archibald "Archie" Ryder, had flown from London to California to give him some management training. Peter didn't have a close relationship with him. His presence didn't help because Archie was known for having an iron fist, and he never let Peter slack off. Nights, mornings, weekends, and weekdays, his father forced Peter to work better, harder, and faster. As a result, his body and mind were tired, and he wanted to take a break.

When people in the States were celebrating Thanksgiving, Peter had to fight to take some time off and spend his first American Thanksgiving with Rory and her aunt.

For the first time in a while, Peter felt brighter and happier, knowing Rory would be there soon.

CHAPTER 3

I couldn't contain my smile when Sally allowed me to fly on Friday instead of Sunday morning. She knew my boyfriend lived in California and that I wanted to spend time with him.

Sally was an amazing boss who knew how to deal with the staff. Although harsh at times, she also knew when to loosen up. When someone made a mistake, she would call them in privately and speak calmly with them, making her one of Veles Capital's favorite managers.

Guess who else was excited about my upcoming visit with Peter? Aunt Amy.

Once she knew I was flying to California in a few days, she bought ingredients to bake marble cakes, chocolate chip cookies, and brownies, because Peter loved them so much. When I first met Peter, he didn't like those things. Then, when he visited for Thanksgiving, he found he really liked my aunt's cookies and cakes.

That made her happy, but it made me nervous. I knew my aunt, and I was afraid she would go overboard.

When I came home from work, the countertop was covered with two marble cakes, two nine-inch square pans of brownies, and three dozen chocolate chip cookies sitting on cooling racks. A few plastic containers sat nearby, ready to be filled with all the goodies.

"Wow!" My jaw dropped. "That…those cookies and cakes are enough for twenty people."

"I don't think so," said my aunt, glancing at the sweets.

"Now, how am I going to bring them with me?"

"I already found extra luggage," she said, slapping my hand when I reached out to steal one of the cookies. "That's for Peter," she scolded me.

I snatched one anyway. "I'm your niece. Shouldn't I get priority? You haven't baked me anything, and now, you're feeding him like he's starving. Well, if you want to make him fat, keep feeding him with your sugar and carb-filled snacks."

She chuckled. "Rory, sweetheart, these are healthier than the store-bought ones because I use organic ingredients and not too much sugar." Aunt Amy glanced at me as she cut into a tray of brownies. "And I smell some jealousy from you."

"Nope, not jealous."

"Yes, you are," sang my aunt.

"No, I am not," I sang back, taking a seat on a stool as I watched her. "All right, fine, maybe I am."

My aunt gave a cheery smile.

I didn't like it. "That's because you never bake me anything. Not even for my birthday," I added.

My aunt stopped and stared at me. "I always baked birthday cakes for you."

"Nope." I shook my head. "You always bought those cakes from France Bakery."

She laughed, her shoulders shaking. "My dear Rory, that's because you always complained that you wanted to be the same as your classmates, whose parents always bought a birthday cake from some famous bakery. I...we didn't have money at the time. I had to trick you. On the day before your birthday, I asked my friend who worked at the bakery to give me a box and a ribbon with the store name printed on it. I put my cake in the box and gave it to you, so you'd think I bought the cake from the bakery."

I almost choked on the cookie in my mouth as her eyes twinkled.

"So..." I cleared my throat, and guilt rose into my chest. "You always baked it for me?"

"Yes, sweetheart. I always did on your birthday. Once you were twelve, I stopped baking because you said you wanted to control your weight. I baked a few times for different events at the church or for my friends. Now, I have Peter to spoil with my baking."

"Sorry for being selfish," I said.

She chuckled as she finished packing and looked down with pride at the containers. "That's okay. It was my fault too. I should admit that I wasn't patient enough with you, anyway, and caused you to misunderstand me. If I'd been kinder and more open, we wouldn't have had so many arguments, and maybe you would've been more open with me. I could've given you different advice about many things."

Her words touched my heart. I stood and walked around the counter and threw my arms around her.

"Oh!" she exclaimed.

I heard the smile in her voice as her arms tightened around my shoulders.

"Well, enough of this sentimental stuff." My aunt gently pushed me away, a smile still lingering on her lips. "Now, bring me the blue luggage so I can pack this."

I retrieved the luggage, and she loaded the containers inside.

"So, are you going to stay at Peter's house?" she asked, fastening the zipper on the luggage.

Her question didn't really surprise me, and I'd expected it, anyway. It might have sounded odd for most people that my aunt asked a twenty-four-year-old woman whether she was going to stay at her boyfriend's house.

I'd never known my father. My mom had always been upset whenever I asked about him, so I stopped. I understood, because her pregnancy had brought too much stress to her family and strained her relationship with her parents. My Japanese grandpa, Grandpa Kenji Ishida, couldn't accept the fact that his daughter would have a baby without a husband. His extended family shunned us, but my Grandma Audrey Arrington Ishida, who was German-Australian, was more open-minded about her daughter's pregnancy. As she couldn't hold her upset feeling any longer, my grandma brought my mom to America, a country where she immigrated with her family when she was ten years old.

After my mom passed away, my aunt took me under her wing and vowed to try and prevent me from making the same mistake her sister had made. She watched me like a hawk, only becoming more lenient after I graduated from college. I eventually understood her strictness, especially after seeing a few of my friends and coworkers around the same age who had a tough life because they were raising babies without husbands.

Some regretted their decisions and wished they could turn back the clock. Witnessing their struggles, I felt sorry for them and didn't wish to be part of the group. I didn't want to burden my aunt with my fatherless child, as she'd had enough problems raising me.

I cleared my throat and said, "Well, I'm planning to stay at his house over the weekend, and then move to the hotel on Monday because I want to show Sally that I'm professional and don't take this business trip lightly." I looked at her solemnly. "And I won't break the promise I made to you on the day you allowed me to live alone a few years ago."

Aunt Amy looked at me and tapped me on the shoulder. "You're an adult now, and honestly, I'm more concerned about your professionalism. This is your first business trip for this company, and if you've been chosen for this job, it means your boss trusts your skills. However, I'm relieved that you understand the importance of this project for your career."

I smiled at her.

"Now," she added, glancing at my suitcases, "let's weigh your luggage. I hope it isn't too heavy."

"If I ate some, they wouldn't be overweight," I offered.

My aunt glared at me and shook her head when I gave her an innocent grin.

That night, I tossed and turned in bed. My eyes refused to shut, and my mind was racing. The thought of seeing Peter again thrilled me to bits. The last time we'd been together was on Thanksgiving Day. I wished we could meet more often, maybe once or twice a month. However, our working situation didn't allow us to have such a privilege. Peter was busy with his management training, and I was busy in my new office. We'd acknowledged the issues at the beginning of our relationship and promised to endure the challenges.

However, I dreaded to think about being alone with Peter.

It was nothing to do with the promise I'd made to my aunt. It was my traumatic experience that no one knew about because my lips were sealed tight.

I was sixteen when it happened. Behind my aunt's back, I'd had a boyfriend. My aunt watched me like a hawk, but she couldn't be with me twenty-four hours a day. I'd learned to wiggle free from her watch.

My first boyfriend was a classmate and one of the cutest boys at school. I'd never imagined that he would ask me to go out because I wasn't an attractive girl, and I was too skinny for my age. After that, we went out a few times.

One day, when we kissed, his hand slipped into my shirt and touched my bosom. I cringed and told him to stop. He looked at me as if I were from another planet. "It's normal to show your boyfriend how you care about him," he argued. I knew it wasn't right, but I didn't want to be seen as immature. It wasn't a secret that a few of my female classmates, including my best friend, had had the experience. Everybody was doing it, as they said. Besides, we didn't do anything more than touching above the waist underneath our clothes. After debating with myself, I let him have his way.

The next day at school, he avoided me, and a few of his close friends giggled when they saw me. Feeling confused, I asked him what was going on. His answer surprised me. He said he wasn't interested in me anymore because I was too flat and too rigid. A cold sweat dripped down my back as I felt an invisible hand slap hard across my face, again and again. It wasn't my fault if my body hadn't developed in time.

Feeling dirty and sick to my stomach, I left school that day and sat under the cold, running shower at home for hours, hoping I could forget my foolishness for letting him touch me. When my aunt came back from work, she didn't understand why a girl who was healthy in the morning had come down with a fever in the afternoon in summer.

Then, six months later, we moved to a different state because of my aunt's work. By then, my body had filled out in all the right directions, and I always looked good and sexy in any dress. Still, I became self-conscious and careful about choosing close male friends. My relationships consisted of no more than kissing and hugging.

My final year in college, I met Ben, my ex-roommate, Lizzy's, coworker. We met when Lizzy and I were in a mini-golf amusement park. Somehow, we felt a connection and saw each other often after that.

Everything went smoothly for a while. Ben was six years older than me, mature, and independent. He wasn't a man who would drag his girlfriend into bed after just ten dates. I'd thought Ben was "the one." Even my aunt had the same thought.

When our relationship became serious, Ben said that I was too chubby. Stupidly, I accepted it and forced myself to diet hard until I collapsed and was rushed to the ER, while Ben was cheating on me with some pretty, skinny woman. For almost two years, I avoided having a romantic relationship with a man until I met Peter.

Peter was interesting. He wasn't as sexy and handsome as Chris Hemsworth or Chris Evans, but he was the type of man who could make girls whirl their heads and gawk at him in awe. He stood out with his six-foot height, chiseled face, fine bone structure, and trim body. His nonchalant gaze and aloof smile drove girls crazy. Still, every time we were together in public, Peter kept his eyes on me as if I were the only girl on the planet, and that flattered me. He seemed to enjoy spending time with me, without sending any signal to go further than kisses and hugs. Even when he kissed me, he always did it gently and lightly, as if making sure I was comfortable before his kiss became firmer and more certain.

I wasn't naïve or afraid of going to the next step in a relationship. I dreaded it because it had taken me years to glue the shards of my self-esteem back together, and I couldn't imagine someone breaking it again. If things went the way I thought they were going at Peter's house, this trip would change me forever.

CHAPTER 4

Lights from buildings and moving vehicles sparkled from above, like scattered sparkling pieces of jewelry, as my plane descended toward John Wayne Airport.

When the plane landed, joy at being back in California consumed me. The last time I'd seen this state was at the end of summer, and now, only a few months later, I'd returned. I'd thought I wouldn't be here again for at least a year or two.

While waiting for the seat belt sign to go to "off," I turned on my phone and saw a few text messages from Peter. I grinned as I read his texts.

Miss you, and it is 2 p.m. here.

Miss you at 2:15 p.m. Oh, why does it feel like it's been two hours already?

Are you here yet? Maybe not.

On my way to the airport.

I'm waiting in the arrival area.

Are you here yet?

Please tell me you're here.

Rory...

Rory...

His last message said, *Now I'm turning into your possessive boyfriend.* He followed it with a grinning emoji.

I smiled but refrained from responding because people were getting their luggage out of the overhead compartments. Once I got mine, I waited patiently to get off the plane.

The baggage claim area wasn't very crowded. After waiting ten minutes, I found my luggage, piled them on the airport cart, and pushed it toward the arrival gate. I paused to fish out my phone and send a text to Peter.

My flight got rerouted back to Boston.

My phone rang.

"Hi, Pet—"

"Really? Seriously, your flight got rerouted back to Boston? Are you at the Boston airport now?" Peter asked without saying hello. "But why does the flight status say your plane is on time?"

"Maybe they haven't changed it yet because we turned around halfway into the flight," I said, biting my lip to keep from laughing.

"Are you already at the Boston airport now?" he asked again after some silence. His tone sounded disheartened. "When will you be coming, then?"

"Um, I'm not sure when," I said, pushing my cart toward the waiting area. "Too bad. You can't eat Auntie's cookies and marble cake—"

"I'd prefer you to be here," Peter interrupted me sharply. "Now I'm upset."

"Sorry," I said, scanning the crowd until I spotted a familiar figure in a light orange sweater over his untucked gray shirt. He stood with his back to me, holding a phone against his ear.

"What happened? I don't understand." Sounding upset, Peter scratched his head with his other hand.

He didn't hear me behind him and shrieked when I poked his back. As he spun on his heel, his eyes bulged, and his mouth dropped open.

"Ta-da! Miracles can happen if you believe," I said, grinning widely.

"Oh my God, you…" His voice trailed off.

In one movement, I was in his arms.

"Hi, Peter," I said, my voice muffled against his sweater.

"You…" He didn't finish voicing his thoughts, but he tightened his arms around my shoulders. "That's not funny, you know. That's… not…funny. Don't joke like that. Promise me you won't do it again."

"Sorry, I just wanted to tease you," I said, hugging him. A warm feeling spread through my chest, and I inhaled his familiar scent. I made a note to tell him not to change his cologne because it smelled good. Tightening my arms around his waist, I pressed my forehead against his chest. "If my flight was canceled, of course I would've told you earlier."

"Still not funny," he grumbled. "I'm almost crying."

"I don't believe you," I said, looking up at him and grinning.

Peter rolled his eyes but smiled back at me. "So." He tilted his head. "As much as I love holding you, if we don't leave soon, people will eventually start to suggest that we get a room."

"Ha ha ha. Funny," I said, releasing him.

"Come on." He took my cart, offering his arm. "I parked nearby." He smiled when I looped my hand around his arm.

My heart squeezed in my chest as I noticed his gentle gaze. I'd missed that.

Once we'd loaded everything into the trunk of his Tesla, I slid into the passenger seat.

"Rory," Peter called as I reached for my seat belt.

"Hmm?" I turned toward him, attempting to click the seat belt into place.

Leaning over the center console, Peter cupped my face with his hands and kissed me. His lips were soft against mine. The seat belt recoiled as I shifted closer to kiss him back.

"I'm happy to see you again," he said, brushing my cheek with his thumb.

"Me too," I said.

"Are you hungry?" he asked after pulling back. He put the car in gear and headed toward the exit. "I already bought some food for you, unless you want to stop somewhere else."

I glanced at the clock on the dashboard. It showed 7:30 p.m., which was 10:30 Boston time. I was alert enough to eat, but I wouldn't mind going straight to his house and hitting the sack right away.

"Nah, let's eat at your place," I suggested.

"Okay."

The I-405 North traffic was crowded as we hit the freeway. Cars moved slowly, and one or two vehicles tried to cut off the cars merging onto the interstate. I didn't really care because I was excited to be back with Peter again.

"Auntie baked and forced me to bring your favorite cakes and cookies," I said. "Believe me, those cakes and cookies are more than enough to feed an army. Next time, don't tell her what you like."

Peter chuckled. "I love her food and cakes. Why can't I tell her the snacks I like?"

"Because she'd find a way to feed you until you became fat and couldn't move, lying on the floor like a starfish." I stretched out my arms and feet, pretending to be a starfish.

"Do I detect some jealousy?" Peter looked upward as though searching for something in the sky. He laughed when I reached out and poked his cheek.

"I'm not jealous."

"Yes, you are," he sang in the same tone of voice my aunt had used. He grinned widely as his hand stroked the back of my head.

It was good to be with him. I'd missed even the simple things like his big smile and riding around town with him. Long-distance definitely sucked.

CHAPTER 5

Peter's car slowed at the curb and stopped in front of a house with a white picket fence. "Welcome to my house," he said, his eyes gleaming with pride.

I got out of the car and stood there, gazing wide-eyed at his new home.

The two-story house looked even better than it had in the pictures Peter sent me the week before. Although we arrived at night, the sky was clear, and the moon was visible. Illumination from the garden lights and the streetlight gave me a clear view of the house. I caught the subtle fragrance of roses and jasmine as I stepped onto the stone path leading to the front porch.

"Come in. I'll show you around," Peter said, my luggage in hand. He opened the door and waited.

I nodded and followed him inside. As I stood in the hallway, I instantly fell in love with the house.

The interior was mostly white, and the flooring was a sandy color. The gray furniture gave the spacious room a cozy, contemporary feeling.

Peter took me through the first floor, giving me a tour of the sunroom, living room, and dining room, which had a tall glass window with a beautiful view of the beach. French doors topped by trapezoid-shaped windows led from the sunroom outside to the backyard.

The kitchen, spacious and modern with a beautiful marble countertop and backsplash, was also on the first floor. If Aunt Amy were here, she would have been thrilled to cook and bake in that kitchen.

Like in my aunt's townhome, all the bedrooms and bathrooms were upstairs, and the powder room was on the first floor. As we stepped onto the landing, Peter sat my luggage near the first door.

"My room," he said, as though he could read my mind. "I'll show you the other rooms later. This is the loft." He gestured at the open space above the living room and then took my hand. "I'm going to convert it into a library. I've already ordered books and bookshelves. Also, I'll add a coffee table, chairs, and big pillows to make this room comfortable for reading."

"That's gonna be nice."

"I think so too. Now, let me show you the guest room." He pushed open the door of the first room. It had two nightstands, a dresser, a queen-size bed, and a long closet on the other end, with tall windows opposite the bed. The room had far more space than my bedroom in Boston.

The other two rooms were the same size. Peter used one of them as his home office.

"Now, let's go to my room." He gently pulled my wrist, leading me as he walked back to the room next to the loft.

I held in a gasp when he opened the door. His bedroom was even more spacious than the other three rooms and had the same tall window, but it covered half of the room. A blackout privacy curtain hung to the side. His king-size bed faced the window that overlooked a beautiful view of the beach.

"Wow, look at that!" I moved closer to the window. "This breathtaking view sprawls in front of you every time you wake up or go to bed."

"Yup." He nodded.

"You know what?" I looked at him over my shoulder. "If you moved your bed closer here, Peter, you could stargaze before going to sleep."

"Good idea," he agreed, placing his hand on my shoulder. "And it would be nice if I could enjoy the view with you by my side. Besides," he turned me to face him, "this room and the bed are spacious enough for two."

I felt my breath catch in my throat and noticed his light brown eyes narrowing on me.

Our first night together in his beautiful house would have been an unforgettable, steamy, heart-pounding night, if only I could respond to him by wrapping my arms around his neck, kissing him hard, and pushing him onto the bed.

But I couldn't. I didn't.

My throat tightened as I reached up to brush his brown hair and touch his cheek. With his eyes still on me, he leaned against my palm after giving it a quick kiss.

Then I felt a nervous, squirming sensation in my stomach. Unaware, I chuckled.

Peter looked at me with a question in his eyes.

Taking a deep breath, I looked at him and said quietly, "I love you, Peter, and I'm so excited to finally be alone with you again, but"—I searched into his eyes—"I don't think I'm ready, because it's gonna be a huge leap for me to slee—"

My word stopped midway because Peter leaned in and gave me a quick kiss. The corners of his eyes wrinkled as he straightened his back.

I was stunned. Frowning, I continued. "As I said, it's gonna be—"

Peter stopped me again with a quick kiss.

"You keep stopping me," I said.

His smile widened as he tilted his head. "What was your assumption when I said this room and the bed are spacious enough for two?"

"Uh…" I blinked. "Do you want me to…?" My voice trailed off.

His eyes widened, prompting me to go on, but I clamped my mouth shut.

Peter tsked and put his finger on my chin. "Stop overthinking. Didn't I only say, 'This room and the bed are spacious enough for two'?"

I detected no joke in his eyes. He was sincere.

My lips parted, and then I frowned. Now, I wondered if I wasn't attractive enough for him.

"So?" Peter made his way out of his bedroom. "Which room would you choose?"

"Um, the second one," I answered, following him.

His eyes sparkled as he turned to me. "Are you sure you want to sleep in the room next to mine?" he teased me.

I chuckled and whacked him on the arm.

Peter touched my cheek and said solemnly, "You must be hungry and tired. Go unpack your clothes, and I'll heat up our dinner."

"Let's prepare it together," I offered.

The corners of his lips drooped. "Are you afraid I'll burn the food?"

I snickered. "Okay, but don't forget to take the suitcase with your cakes." I pointed at the other suitcase in front of his bedroom.

"Got it."

After I was done unpacking, I went down to the kitchen as Peter was putting the cakes and cookies in the fridge.

"Aunt Amy really worked hard on these," he said. "I'll call her tomorrow morning to thank her."

"She'll be happy to get your phone call. You're her favorite person, you know."

"Am I your favorite person, too?" he asked, closing the refrigerator door.

I moved toward him and rose on my tiptoes to kiss him on the nose. "You're my special one, how about that?"

"That sounds better."

I smiled.

"Hey, why don't you go check the backyard while I'm preparing dinner? The sky is clear, and you'll get a good view of the oil platforms," he suggested as he reached out to turn on the stove dial to light it.

I looked at him for a few beats before nodding. "Okay." I walked toward the sunroom and opened the French doors leading to the backyard.

A gentle breeze swept my hair to the side as I stepped onto the crushed gravel path. I stopped in the middle of the path and looked up at the sky, where thousands of stars were twinkling against the black background. I had a clear view of the moon too, shining like a spotlight in the air.

Peter was right. I could see the light from the oil platforms on the horizon under the starry sky. They'd been strung with LED lights and turned into a sort of offshore decoration.

"One...two...three...four...five...," I counted. I could see five platforms clearly from where I stood.

Curious, I walked closer to the chest-high fence and turned to watch Peter cooking through the window. It was hard to imagine that he used to be so clumsy in the kitchen. But now, he appeared confident and...so handsome too. I chuckled and took a few minutes just to stare at him.

Continuing to explore, I realized that his house was in a secluded area with only two other houses farther down the beach, one on the right and one on the left. There was a hill near the left house.

It was peaceful and quiet here, which gave me a brilliant idea.

Maybe I would ask Peter to sleep outside tomorrow with sleeping bags. It might be nice to sleep under the stars without neighbors snooping around. I felt giddy at the thought and hoped Peter would agree.

"Rory, the food is ready," Peter called from inside.

"Okay."

On the countertop, he'd set out a few plates with all the foods I liked: a variety of onigiri—Japanese rice balls wrapped with seaweed—a spicy salt pork chop, and a big bowl of Taiwanese beef soup.

My stomach growled instantly at the delicious smell coming from the pork chop.

"Someone is complaining," Peter teased me, pulling out a high barstool for me.

I sat, and Peter sat next to me.

"Thanks for buying the food for me," I said, pouring the soup into a small bowl for myself. I didn't pour any for Peter because I knew he didn't like it.

"Don't mention it. I know you miss the food here." He reached for the onigiri.

"You like it now," I commented, watching as he ate it.

"Yup. Initially, I didn't like it because of the seaweed. It tastes like paper, don't you think? I'm used to it now, though."

"I'm happy you like it," I said.

Peter's eyes sparkled as he gazed at me.

After dinner, he cleared the table and washed the dishes, and I went to the guest room and took a shower. It was wonderful to have a warm shower after my long flight. It helped my tense muscles relax and alleviated the cramps in my right thigh from sitting too long.

Part of me wanted to sleep right away, but I also wanted to see Peter before going to bed. I went to the living room, where he sat watching TV. He'd already taken a shower, and he'd changed into a long-sleeved shirt and sweatpants. Smiling, he patted the empty spot next to him.

"What are you watching?" I asked, sitting next to him and looking at the TV.

"Just a series that I recorded because I don't have much time to watch. Oh, I have something for you. Give me your hand."

As I held my hand out to him, Peter slid something onto my wrist. I took a closer look at it and smiled. A bracelet of gold-filled glass beads on an adjustable black nylon cord was tied around my wrist.

"Aww...so cute! Thank you."

"Could you tie this one for me?" He slid a similar bracelet, but with black beads, onto his wrist.

"Oh, is it a couple's bracelet?" I asked, tying it for him.

"Yup." He nodded and then admired the bracelet he'd bought. His eyes caught mine as I gazed at him.

"Why are you looking at me like that?" he asked.

"Do you know the meaning of these bracelets?"

He nodded.

"It means a commitment, and people would see us as a couple," I said, as if I didn't see him nodding.

He nodded again.

"Are you sure?" I looked directly into his eyes.

Peter's hand brushed against my bangs. "Why not? I want people to know we're a couple. How about you? Are you sure?" he asked back.

I smiled and gave him a peck on the lips.

"That's it? Man, I expected long, hot, sexy kisses," he teased me.

I laughed and punched his arm playfully. Little wrinkles showed on the bridge of his nose when Peter laughed and pulled me closer. I looped my hand under his arm and leaned my head on his shoulder.

"Oh, you should feel the beads' surface," he suggested.

I rubbed my fingers on the beads and felt the dots there. "What is this? Braille?"

He nodded. "On yours, it says 'love,' and mine says 'forever,' with number four before 'ever.' And this part"—he pointed at the charms dangling on our bracelets—"is a magnet. If we hold our hands like this..." He positioned his hand next to mine, and the charms clung together. "The charms attach automatically."

For a moment, we admired the bracelets. His looked good on him too. Then Peter turned his eyes to the TV again, and we sat quietly together. My eyelids grew heavier, and my vision became blurry. I smiled sleepily when I felt Peter drop a soft kiss on the top of my head.

CHAPTER 6

"Rory, if you feel sleepy, let's go upstairs," whispered Peter, reaching for the remote to turn off the TV. His eyebrows rose when he didn't hear a response.

Tilting his head down, he chuckled because Rory was already sleeping on his shoulder. Her breathing was deep and even.

Peter was mesmerized by her face and couldn't take his eyes off her. He'd seen her sleeping once on the patio in her old apartment when they were roommates, but not this close up. She looked beautiful in her sleep.

Almost without realizing it, he lowered his head to study her more closely. Her hair cascaded around her face. He brushed back the long locks, revealing her flawless face that bore no makeup. Her soft, angled eyebrows looked as though someone had painted them on. Her eyelashes were long and thick, but they looked as soft as a feather. He wanted to run his fingers over them, but he didn't dare.

Lowering his eyes, he gazed at her nose before glancing down to her slightly parted, pinkish lips. Peter's heart drummed in his chest, and his eyes fixed on those soft lips. He'd kissed them many times, but his heart beat at an erratic pace every time he looked at them.

His heart wrenched, then leaped as he leaned in closer to steal a kiss from her lips, but he stopped a couple inches away, close enough to feel her breath on his face.

"No." He shook his head. "If I do, she'll wake, and I don't want that. I want her to feel secure around me. Maybe one day, when she's my wife, I'll wake her up with a feverish kiss that will make her beg for more." Grinning sheepishly at the thought, he pulled away.

In his early twenties, he would never have given that thought any consideration. If he'd wanted to give his girlfriend a kiss, he would have done it no matter how sleepy she was.

But with Rory, everything was different. His heart had softened, and what he wanted most was to protect and cherish her. He was worried about her being hurt. Maybe he'd finally become the mature man Jane and his mom had always wanted him to be.

Whatever it was, Peter wanted Rory to feel secure around him no matter what. In silence, he continued looking at her innocent, sleeping face.

(find out more...)

ABOUT THE AUTHOR

Kana Wu's love of writing started as soon she could hold a pencil. She used to work as an accountant before deciding to be a writer in 2018.

Her debut novel, No Romance Allowed, was the winner in the Romance category for the 2020 TCK Publishing Readers' Choice Awards Contest.

She lives in Southern California with her husband, a rescued Jindo dog, books, and some hummingbirds.

Be the first to know when Kana has a special offer or a new book by checking her website or following her on social media.

https://www.facebook.com/kanawuauthor

https://www.instagram.com/kanawuauthor

www.kanawuauthor.com